Defiance

The Spiral Wars, Book 4

Joel Shepherd

ISBN: 1974040348
ISBN-13: 978-1974040346

The Spiral Wars:

Renegade

Drysine Legacy

Kantovan Vault

Defiance

CHAPTER ONE

In Erik's dream, he was sitting at a cafe with Lisbeth. In typical dream logic, the location made sense, because it was a place they'd often gone — Arcadia Park near the shopping district. But it did not make sense, because there were whales, sea dragons and other Homeworld ocean life swimming through the air nearby. None of the passers-by paid the creatures any attention, and he had his coffee and a slice of shared cheesecake, and talked with Lisbeth about sibling stuff.

Here again, the dream made no sense, because when he'd been to this cafe with Lisbeth, he'd been a new cadet in the Academy, and she'd been just turning ten or eleven… but here in the dream, she was the newly-adult Lisbeth who braved the *Phoenix* corridors in her spacer jumpsuit and harness. It had been their weekend thing after Lisbeth's volleyball or tennis, when Mother, Father or the other siblings had been unable to organise anything else. That was often, for Family Debogande was busy, and Cora, the only sibling still at school, was a true socialite, always at parties with friends, and often scolded by Mother for not having time for the rest of the family.

Erik got on well with all his sisters, but Lisbeth was different. Being the littlest, she looked up to and adored him, and that flattery was always nice. But more than just cute and lively, Lisbeth loved what he did in a way that was true of perhaps none of his other family, besides his father. And so they'd often meet on a weekend, when he had a half-day off and the family had nothing else on. He'd made probably less friends in the Academy than he could have, dodging the social events of his classmates to spend time with his little sister. But in truth, not only did he enjoy Lisbeth's company more, he was worried by the dawning realisation that if he were posted away from Homeworld for long stretches, he'd miss most of her growing up, and would return one day to discover that he barely knew her at all.

In this dream, she was talking to him about a hacksaw drone she was building. As her own personal hobby, she said airily, when he asked her if that was wise. Romki was helping her. Erik asked her what the parren who were holding her captive would make of that. A nearby sea creature roared, and suddenly the woman Lisbeth was a little girl once more, frightened and in tears.

A plaintive alarm woke him, and the scene disappeared. Erik hit audio on the bedside wallscreen, eyes still closed. "Captain. What?"

"Major," came Trace's reply, mocking his sleepy drawl. *"Open."*

She was at the door, Erik realised. Moving on automatic, he reached and released the bednet that would stop him from being thrown about in an unplanned manoeuvre, hauled it back with the sheets, and put socked feet on the cold deck. Fleet spacers always slept in underclothes as a minimum, so that dressing was a simple matter of pulling on a jumpsuit. He dragged on a jacket, took the one-and-a-half steps that was all his quarters required to open the door, then went into his tiny bathroom cubicle as Trace entered with someone else. He splashed water on his face, checked the stubble on his bleary-eyed reflection, and judged that he needed a shave. Later.

Back in his quarters, Jokono had entered with Trace, looking similarly tired, but in the manner of someone who'd been awake for much longer and was dealing with it. Erik wanted to greet him warmly, but procedure came first, as every conscious captain had to be fully aware of his ship's tactical situation. He ignored both visitors to sit on his bed, pull on AR glasses and call up a feed from Scan.

What confronted him was a great big tavalai mess. *UFS Phoenix* had arrived at Cherichal System ten days ago, a nearly-uninhabited place, used by tavalai Fleet primarily as a mid-point between strategic locations. There she'd met the tavalai cruiser *Podiga* and two other warships, members of the rebel tavalai Fleet faction that had assisted *Phoenix* in her raid on the Kantovan Vault. They'd given *Podiga*'s captain the impossibly top-secret container that the rebel faction had demanded in exchange for their help, holding secrets of the tavalai's State Department, and then they'd awaited the arrival of parren ships, from their Domesh allies of House Harmony.

Instead, an endless stream of tavalai ships had followed them from Kantovan, and now clustered about *Phoenix* and *Podiga* in parking proximity, a tangled ball five hundred kilometres across of nearly thirty ships and rising. *Tantotavarin* was here, an ibranakala-class cruiser that alone was nearly *Phoenix*'s equal, and had a record of bloody success in the Triumvirate War nearly as great. With *Tantotavarin* were another six tavalai Fleet vessels, none quite so formidable, but collectively enough to make *Phoenix*'s destruction certain and fast, should it come to shooting.

Those six regular Fleet ships were now locked in grim dispute with *Podiga*, and now *Kanamandali*, a lata-class cruiser not *Tantotavarin*'s equal, but large enough, and carrying the person of Admiral Janik himself. The very tavalai, in fact, who had first agreed to help *Phoenix* on the Kantovan mission, and the most senior member of the rebel faction anyone on *Phoenix* knew of. *Kanamandali* had arrived from a different direction, and now sat parked a hundred Ks from *Phoenix*'s side — practically in her lap, as such things were measured by FTL ships in space.

The remaining twenty or so ships were representatives of various tavalai bureaucracies, legal institutions or government departments. Most prominent of these was *Toguru*, a State Department vessel, whose behaviour since arrival reminded Erik of those cartoon caricatures of the unpleasant ex-wife, always shouting and sneering, forever trying her damnedest to make everyone else as miserable as she was. She'd been demanding that *Phoenix* be forcibly escorted back to Kantovan to answer for her crimes, which included conspiracy, theft, assault, murder, espionage, and the violation of solemn oaths of tavalai law that Lieutenant Shilu, and even Stan Romki, admitted they did not understand. Save for those, Erik knew that *Phoenix* was guilty of all the others. But then, as the kid in the playground said about the bully, 'he started it'.

All of them were in a meeting now — he selected a scan feed on his glasses, and saw the great cluster of shuttles about *Tantotavarin* like the cloud of flies about a rotting fish on a riverbank, far too many to all fit at once to the big carrier's Midships berths. Ominously, they'd all been transmitting when they first arrived, talking on heavily encrypted coms. That had been convenient and instructive, for *Phoenix* could now decrypt any and all tavalai encryption in milliseconds. But now, all were silent. They knew, Erik thought. Surely after all the evidence left behind at Kantovan, in the Tsubarata, in the city of Gamesh on the planet Konik, and on the moon of Kamala, both in the atmospheric city of Chara or the fortified vault on the surface... they knew what *Phoenix* had aboard. Or at least, they guessed. Now they did not use general coms at all, save for tightbeam laser coms that *Phoenix S*can could see making faint lines between the neighbouring ships, like gossamer threads in the web of a very lazy spider. Erik felt as though *Phoenix* were the weird kid at school, with pierced nose and purple hair, invited to a respectable tea party. Everyone staring at her, in silent outrage, and whispering behind her back.

Erik stowed the glasses in a pocket, then rose to finally greet Ensign Jokono with a warm smile and a handshake. "Good to see you well, Joker. I heard that was a hell of a trip."

"Good to be back, Captain," said Jokono, nowhere near as deferential before the Captain as another Ensign might have been. Jokono was older than Erik and Trace combined, his lean, brown face showing the lines of youthful middle-age, by the current human standard. As *Phoenix*'s newly acquired Intelligence Officer, he was cool and professional at most times, and Trace in particular found great use in his services. "And yes, quite a trip."

Erik gestured for one of them to take a chair by the small table, both afixed to the wall, while he sat on the bunk. Jokono offered Trace the chair, ever the gentleman, but Trace refused, giving the recently-civilian older man no choice. It was the unofficial code of conduct on most Fleet ships that in mixed company — if there were limited seats, the marines would stand. Smart spacers like

Erik just smiled, and allowed the marines their masochistic superiority.

"There was another classified containment cylinder from the Kantovan Vault on the heavy descender that Tif stole from Chara," said Trace, cutting straight to the point as usual.

Erik frowned. "I know, it was in your report."

"I wasn't sure if you'd had time to read my report."

"I made time," said Erik, repressing irritation. Even now, Trace tested him. But he was used to it, and barely bothered. "You said you'd assign it to Jokono when he got back, after Styx decoded it. I take it she did decode it?"

Second Lieutenant Tif had been forcibly removed from the kaal heavy descender that *Phoenix* had hired, at considerable expense, for the Kantovan mission. With Styx's help, Tif had managed to steal another one at Chara base, in mid-prep for a final launch into orbit. It had been on its way up from the Vault, while Tif's descender had been on its way down. Descenders on their way up were often carrying classified things they'd gone down to acquire. This descender had been no exception.

"She did," Trace agreed. "But she couldn't make much sense of the documents that appeared once decoded. It's all tavalai bureaucratic forms and records of financial transactions, not Styx's strongpoint. So I put a copy on the shuttle that went to fetch Jokono, and he's been working on it since then."

"Yes, welcome back to *Phoenix*, Ensign Jokono," Erik said drily. Jokono smiled. No doubt he'd have liked a little rest and time to recover from his previous mission, but instead Trace had dropped this in his lap. Erik suspected that instead of being annoyed, Jokono was pleased to be found so useful. "I'm guessing you found something or you wouldn't have woken me up in the middle of second-shift."

"No, he woke *me* in the middle of second-shift," Trace corrected. "I woke you."

Erik ignored her, eyebrows raised pointedly at Jokono. "Well," said the older man in his calm, melodious way, "I learned several things. Firstly, I learned that tavalai bureaucracy is one of the wonders of the known universe. I don't mean that in a good way."

"I know," Erik agreed. "We've all been learning."

"Which means that the Major was correct to give the documents to me. In my years as a senior investigator, before I became a station security chief, I spent a considerable amount of time digging around in corporate records. Now, tavalai being tavalai, it took me a long time just to get my head around what I was looking at… but with Mr Romki busy, your Coms Officers Lieutenant Lassa, and then Lieutenant Shilu, were able to assist with some of their legal training, and what they've learned of tavalai bureaucracy and law in the past months. Styx then assisted with some of the numerical complexities, which is possibly the most egregious misuse of a hacksaw queen's intellect yet, using her as a glorified calculator. My excuse is that her user interface is just that much simpler than the *Phoenix* mainframe."

"And more entertaining," Erik agreed. There was no point in being concerned about it. On this ship, there was precious little any of them could do to stop Styx from accessing data if she wished. No doubt she'd have followed all of Jokono's work with great interest, whether he'd directly involved her or not. And unlike humans, there did not appear to be any limit to the number of things Styx could analyse simultaneously. "A spacer in Armaments swears she made a joke the other day, though there is some dispute."

"She'll learn to be funny if she wants," Trace said with certainty. "The real question is whether she's capable of *finding* anything funny."

Jokono tapped his fingers on the small table, in the manner of an older man concerned the youngsters were getting distracted. "The documents are financial transactions," he said. "It's obscenely complicated, because they've effectively shuffled enormous sums of money through a series of major bureaucracies and financial institutions, disguising it in every way possible. But whoever compiled all of those documents has essentially done all the hard work for me, allowing me to do in hours what would have taken months or years of legwork for an army of tavalai investigators, otherwise. All I had to do was identify the common thread, and use Styx's help to keep the monetary totals in sight amidst all the other numbers."

"Payments," Erik said slowly. "Payments from whom to whom?"

"From State Department," said Jokono, with a note of triumph that made all the hours of missed sleep worth it. "To the sard. Incredibly large payments. Entirely illegal — the news and historical databases we've accumulated since we've been in tavalai space are comprehensive enough, the kind of thing regular tavalai can access. They include any number of definitive statements from senior tavalai officials, in various departments, that the sard are allies of their own free will, and that there are no payments or bribes involved. All lies, apparently, though perhaps unwitting."

Erik stared. And looked at Trace. Trace looked pleased, in the way someone would look pleased who saw something very bad coming for her enemies. Pleased, but not pleasant. "A coverup? You can prove that?"

"With these documents, yes," said Jokono. His voice was trembling a little, and not with tiredness. Jokono was a very experienced lawman. In his time, he had presided over some significant events, arrests and scandals. But this one changed the course of Spiral history, and the lives of hundreds of billions of sentient beings. "They took great effort to hide it from everyone, most particularly their own bureaucracies, who are supposed to provide checks and balances to prevent this sort of thing, among tavalai. But it looks like the sard have only been allied to the tavalai for cash. For how long, who can say?"

"And someone needs to keep track of the records," Trace finished. "To document what they've been doing, and count the money. And they kept it in the Vault, where no one else could see."

"Most of it looks as though it's going into sard/tavalai joint ventures," Jokono added. "Large corporations of some sort. I'm sure the sard like money, since they love numbers so much, but they'll love advanced technology even better. That was always their Achilles heel."

Erik thought hard. They'd just given one piece of potentially incriminating evidence to the Captain of *Podiga*. This one, if analysed properly, would surely sink the State Department. But sinking the State Department was not their primary mission. It had been the price that the rebel faction of Fleet had demanded, in exchange for help in robbing the Kantovan Vault. To share this particular bomb with the *Podiga*, at this time, would be to play an ace card without knowing the size of the pot, nor the shape of anyone else's hand.

"Thank you Jokono," he said. "This gives us a vital bit of ammunition. We'll spend it when the moment is right. In the meantime, you should get some sleep at last."

"With your permission, Captain," said Jokono, "it's nearly first-shift now, and I'd like to synchronise myself properly back to first-shift. If I'm to stay awake, I might as well keep working, and show some others what I'm doing in person."

Erik shrugged. "If you think that's best." He rose. "Good work, Ensign. On this, and the Konik job. You even impressed Lieutenant Dale, and that's not easy."

"Thank you Captain," said Jokono with a pleased smile, and left.

Trace lingered after the door had closed. "How are you doing?" she asked sombrely.

Lisbeth, she meant. Once, Erik might have found the question intrusive. Now, he heard only the concern of a friend. "I'm okay," he said quietly. "I'm glad to be busy."

"Story of my life," said Trace. "Speaking of marines impressed by non-marines, Lisbeth is very good at people and politics. She'd never make a marine, but I think she'd be a top spacer officer, if she wanted. She'll probably cope where she is now better than any of us would."

"She'd be wasted on a ship," Erik disagreed with a sigh, returning to his tiny bathroom to fetch his shaver. He turned it on, while Trace leaned by the doorway, watching him shave. "She'd be better off in the family, running one of the business arms. Someplace she could really use her brain."

A month or two ago, Trace might have protested that casual cynicism, directed at Fleet. Now she smiled. "Well if she ever needs a reference for a job," she said. "I've never been in a position to write one before, for a civilian. Not that she'll actually need one, being a Debogande."

"In your case I think she'd take it anyway," Erik assured her. "Not that a character reference from someone whose primary skill is mayhem should really recommend anyone for a peaceful civilian job."

Trace's smile grew broader. "Did she tell you about her boyfriend?"

"Which one?"

"The most recent one. The one your mother disapproved of."

"Well, I gather there's been a few of those." Erik frowned at her. "What about her boyfriend?"

"She told me that she'd thought it was quite serious. But that recently, she realised she'd barely thought of him in weeks. And that maybe Mother had been right, and that he wasn't the right sort of boy for her at all. Funny what events and perspective could do, she said. Takes you outside of what you thought you knew."

"Yeah, no kidding," Erik murmured. "She didn't tell me that."

Trace shrugged. "You've got a ship to run. And I share quarters with her. We all live in our bubbles. *Phoenix* was the thing that popped her bubble. And maybe she was the thing that popped mine. I don't think I've had a single civilian friend since childhood. It's good to be reminded what else exists in the world."

Erik gazed at the little square mirror. It had a smudge on it, semi-permanent. Months ago, he'd never have allowed it, would have cleaned and polished until the reflection was spotless. Now, the smudge distorted the reflection of his face, dark, sombre and so much less innocent than before. So much less perfect and shiny than the immaculate Debogande caricature had once held him to be. He recalled the obsessively detailed young man who had once leaped to remove every imperfection, and wondered what on earth had possessed him.

Trace squeezed his shoulder. "One day she'll be ranked so highly we'll both be saluting her," she assured him. "Civilian rank or otherwise, you watch." Erik nodded bleakly, thinking only of the little girl in his dream. Frightened and lonely.

Trace gave him a brief hug, head to his shoulder, then left. Erik watched her go in astonishment. Not long ago she'd been trying to stomp all the softness out of him. Now she was volunteering hugs? She must think I look miserable, he thought. She'll be worried all the crew will see it. He pulled himself up, straightened his shoulders, and adjusted his collar. Damn, he *had* let standards slip. The smudge on the mirror angered him, and he reached for the ever-present cleaning cloth in his breast pocket, and began polishing.

"Captain, the meeting on Tantotavarin seems to be breaking up." Lieutenant Angela Lassa's voice in his ear, above the pounding of feet on treadmill, and the gasp of air in his lungs. *"Sir, we're getting a message from Admiral Janik's people on Kanamandali. They say he needs to speak with you. They request that you come and visit Kanamandali by shuttle in..."* a brief pause as she translated tavalai taka into human minutes, *"...fifty minutes time."*

Erik was breathing too hard to talk, but he could formulate internally, on uplinks, as he did in heavy G. *"Tell them Phoenix's Captain cannot leave the ship under conditions of threat. If they protest that there is no threat, mention Toguru."*

Another pause, as Lassa did that. Of course, if she were admitting that *Phoenix* knew what *Toguru* had been saying, when *Toguru* first burst into the system shrieking threats and accusations... well. All the tavalai suspected, and denying it would gain no advantage now.

"Captain, they insist."

"Don't reply," Erik told her. *"We've made our answer, our position is not negotiable. Ship security is paramount."*

It was a small rebellion, but a necessary one. Even trapped in a corner, *Phoenix* was no easy target. If attacked she'd be destroyed, but would take others with her, especially at this range and negligible relative-V. Like a prickly prey beneath the nose of a hungry predator, *Phoenix*'s best hope of survival lay in appearing as painful and unappetising a meal as possible. Good manners and obedience to tavalai commands was not going to do it.

A minute later, Lassa's voice again. *"Captain, they say they will come to Phoenix. Same time."*

"Tell them yes, Lieutenant."

"Aye sir."

On his AR glasses, Erik blinked on an icon that took his visual to a pre-set channel — Aristan's quarters. The camera was mounted high in a corner, seeing the whole room with fish-eye lense distortion. On the small bunk by a wall sat a slim figure in black robes, unmoving. Barely breathing, if room environmentals were to be believed. As Domesh, Aristan practised a stillness of mind that few of his species could attain. And his species was physiologically more suited to such things than humans.

The robes had become a part of the issue. Erik, Trace and Private Krishnan had found recordings from Drakhil himself, in the hidden minor temple on Stoya III. Styx had vouched for their authenticity. But Drakhil, in those recordings, did not dress or comport himself as Aristan's many teachings dictated he should. For Aristan, it was a crisis. Erik was no expert on the surviving old Earth religions, but those who still followed them would surely have been similarly upset to receive a video recording of their various saints and messiahs, offering visual and audio proof that they not the figures that all the teachings proclaimed.

Erik stopped running, gasping air, then went to a vacant punching bag, pulling on some light training gloves. The situation was terrifying, because on Aristan's fragile psyche rested Lisbeth's safety. Erik had done what Aristan asked, had given him access to the information he so desperately wanted, and instead of making

Lisbeth safer as Aristan had insisted, it had increased her jeopardy. Now his fear and helplessness was giving way to fury.

Erik punched the bag hard, with technique that had improved considerably in the last three years, in close proximity to Phoenix Company marines. He imagined it was Aristan's face before him, being smashed by his fists. He recalled striking the State Department ambassador, Jelidanatagani, on the Tsubarata, and seeing her fall limp. He'd never punched anyone in the face before, outside of combat training, and certainly had never knocked anyone out cold — male or female, human or alien. Punching women was certainly not the way he'd been raised, but he did not regret it for a moment. Anger felt considerably better than fear. Anger could get things done. Anger moved forward, with purpose and direction. Trace had always told him, 'no more Mr Nice Guy.' And he'd tried, if only to please her… but now he truly felt it, and didn't give a damn if Trace approved or not.

After gym he took a fast shower, changed to his usual spacer jumpsuit and jacket, then paid a visit to Medbay One. Ensign Arvind Kadi was here, unconscious behind drawn screens, hooked into tubes and blinking displays. Gunnery Sergeant 'Woody' Forrest was sitting with him, with no particular hope that he'd wake up soon, just sitting as he'd sit with another member of Alpha Platoon, so that someone would be there when his eyes finally opened. It told Erik everything he needed to know about what had happened on Konik, and how the usually chauvinistic world of the marines had expanded to include the young Ensign from Engineering.

Erik had no time for more than a few words, then moved on to Corporal Rael from Trace's own Command Squad, who had on a mask with a tube down his throat, and was swathed in micro-environment bandaging beneath the sheets, to repair skin burned in the hellish atmosphere of Kamala. Rael couldn't talk, but his uplinks let him formulate… he'd be okay in a week or so, the doctors said. And on duty perhaps another week after that, Major Thakur allowing.

In chairs alongside, his squad buddy Private Rolonde sat with little Skah, and helped him to read a story aloud. Skah looked very tired, as it was early for him, and the boy liked his sleep. One big ear drooped, adorably, and he barely glanced at Erik, finding the story more interesting than the now-familiar Captain.

"Gets real boring lying here staring at the ceiling," Rael explained, his synthetic-replica voice remarkably close-to-life in Erik's inner ear. *"I told Jess to bring Skah's lessons in here. He's a good kid."*

Despite the brave face, there was something desperately vulnerable about the Corporal's request. Having nearly died, and now facing a lengthy recovery, he wanted to be around activity and people, and not be left alone with his thoughts. Ed 'Cocky' Rael had the distinction of being one of the most handsome men in Phoenix Company, with sandy hair and a boyish gleam in his brown eyes. Sitting with him for the few moments he had to spare, Erik saw not one of Trace's most hardass marines, but a young guy coming to terms with just how close he'd been to dying, and finding it harder than he'd like to admit.

Erik grasped Rael's hand, and leaned close. "We're going to Cason System because of you, Cocky. That's where the data-core is, I'm on my way to see Romki right now, he's figuring it out. And when we get that core, we'll have what we need to defend humanity from the deepynines. You did that, and one day everyone's going to know it. And if these fucking tavalai try and stop us, we're going to run them over."

CHAPTER 2

Lisbeth swam. She was barely more than an average swimmer. She'd expected to spend some considerable part of her adult life offworld, where swimming pools were exceedingly rare, and so had played quite a bit of squash and basketball, two sports for which facilities could be found on stations. And of course, she'd liked to ride horses at the family stables in Greenoak, not far north of the Debogande house in the hills overlooking Shiwon. There weren't many horses in space either, her father had teased her.

They'd all doubted whether she could really survive in the hard world of spaceship engineering. Little Lisbeth, youngest of Alice Debogande's five children, known for late mornings and a leisurely approach to assignments and homework. Oh, her grades had been good enough — first rate, in fact. But in truth, she'd coasted, not finding anything *especially* difficult, and knowing she could always pull an all-nighter and scrape in with a B-plus on the little assignments that didn't matter so much, and save the day with a big A-plus on the ones that did.

She did love space travel, and the ships that plied the great FTL routes between stars. She'd memorised the names of the Debogande-affiliated fleet, and pestered her parents for frequent trips up to station, to see the great steel beasts at dock, and be introduced to their captains and crew. But her enthusiasm had not quite matched the passion of her next-eldest sister Cora, who'd been painting and sculpting well beyond her age as a toddler, and who could walk the halls of the Shiwon Gallery of Fine Arts at age ten, and name the artists of many major works without reading the labels. Nor had Lisbeth matched the passion of the much older Deirdre, who'd graduated from Edwin B Bannerjee School of Law at the very top of one of the toughest classes in all human space, and had been known as a young girl to burst into tears at anything less than a straight-A. And to say nothing of Katerina, who had been groomed for the leadership of all Debogande Incorporated at her mother's side, and who, family legend had it, had requested for her eighth birthday to be given a stock trader's licence.

Nor had she quite matched the passion of her only brother Erik, who'd had his eyes on the Academy, and Fleet, since the first moment his father had explained the family tradition of Debogande men serving in uniform. It wasn't hard to see how it all came about, Lisbeth concluded now — this Debogande habit of picking a field young, and then overachieving wildly. Home had been a place of work, for as long as she could remember. There was plenty of family fun and relaxation too, but always there was business, with secretaries and assistants walking in at all hours, and servants serving meals at precisely assigned times, and Mother and Father always on call, always being interrupted mid-meal or conversation, to attend to some new demand from another of the business empire's many sprawling arms. Everyone in the family was good at something, and the portraits of brilliant men and women gazed down from the walls of every hallway — Debogandes long-passed, women in business dress and men often in uniform, captains and admirals, managers and directors, ministers, magistrates and senior politicians.

Lisbeth had felt the weight of expectation as they all had, and even though her parents had refrained, from extended family the questions had come thick and fast — what are you going to study, little Lisbeth? What will you be when you grow up? Which is going to be *your* portrait, gazing down from these high walls upon future generations of awestruck young Debogandes?

Until Erik had joined the Academy, she truly hadn't known. But she'd missed him terribly, even though the Academy was only kilometres away on the opposite side of Shiwon, and she got to see him in person every few weeks, and on the vid screen far more often than that. She'd only been six, and it hadn't occurred to her immediately, but by Erik's third year she was turning eight, and long tales of Erik's studies to become a Fleet officer had convinced her that she loved spaceships. Mother was displeased at the notion of her daughters joining Fleet, and so Lisbeth had decided that if she couldn't wear the uniform, she would help build the ships that all those uniformed heroes like her brother would serve on. And fortunately for her, Debogande Incorporated had a particularly successful arm of industry that did exactly that.

She'd announced her new passion proudly to her parents and elder sisters, which had earned her several long inter-system trips on family business, on or as close to school holidays as could be managed. That she'd enjoyed those trips, and had loved her tours of the spaceships she'd received along the way, had convinced her family that she was serious, and that she might one day become a spaceship engineer, perhaps even the head of the shipbuilding arm of Debogande Enterprises. But still there had remained the suspicion that little Lisbeth had only *really* grown to love spaceships because Erik did, and that truly it was Erik's passion that she had adopted, and not something of her very own.

It was probably even true, Lisbeth thought now, as she stroked through the cool water. But then, wasn't Katerina's love of business and management really their mother's passion first? And hadn't Deirdre's interest in the law been first stoked by her closeness with favourite Uncle Calvin, who had at the time been on the bench of the Homeworld Court of Appeals? Lisbeth did not think it was particularly fair that she should be singled out for such things, just because she was youngest, and not quite as keen on homework as her sisters had been. Or endless hours of hard work and study in general. At least, she thought as she pulled handfuls of water with aching arms and gasping breath, she did not have that problem now.

She touched the end of the pool, folded her arms upon the poolside tiles, and breathed hard. She'd wanted to go running, but had been assured by her ever-present security that the vast expanse of Kunadeen courtyards was not safe. The swimming pool was a little less than a human-sized length, and narrower than most, designed for the use of important individuals, not large groups. It was open to the air beyond the Domesh Temple, enclosed on one side by a lattice that made small, hexagonal holes through which the morning sun speared upon the glittering surface of the pool in her wake.

Lisbeth counted that she had done fifteen laps, and gestured for her robe. Fifteen was rather more than she'd once have achieved, even though there was certainly no pool on *Phoenix*. Time amongst the marines had made her self-conscious of her weakness. 'Just get fit', one of the sergeants had told her with a smile, when she'd asked her for tips on what exercises she should be doing. All quite condescending, at the prospect of what levels of fitness *she* might achieve. It had made Lisbeth want to get crazy-fit, just to show her, but that was stupid. She wasn't a marine, nor even a Fleet spacer. But she *was* an engineer, and she'd acquired her mother's head for politics just as she'd acquired her father's head for reaction drives and jump fields. What was more, she was a Debogande.

Her parren maid, Semaya, arrived with a robe, and Lisbeth climbed quickly from the water to shrug it on. Most parren swam naked, and had no concept of this human thing called 'swimming trunks', regarding the wearing of clothes in water as somehow barbaric. The one exception were the Domesh Denomination, in whose temple she currently lived... but Lisbeth's personal staff were not Domesh, but Togreth, who served all House Harmony irrespective of denomination. It meant that she had no choice but to follow their lead, and wrapped the light robe thankfully about her bare skin, padding to a small, round table upon which a light breakfast had been arranged. All of the staff present were female, and Lisbeth was thankful that parren also found decorum in the same separations of gender that humans did.

Through gaps in the lattice, Lisbeth could see the Kunadeen complex from perhaps a hundred metres up — a huge, patchwork expanse of paving, broken by erratic lines of garden, green trees and half-hidden water features. In the middle distance, more temples, trapezoid rectangular boxes that tapered as they rose. They cast vast shadows across the pavings, which at this hour of morning were full of parren, some doing calisthenics, others martial arts, or other activities Lisbeth couldn't identify. But always organised, the parren, and always in ranks and lines. Music rose from different parts of the complex, a tangle of ill-matched tunes. Some banners trailed in the light morning breeze, marking out the identity of one group or another. As with so much of parren society, the details continued to elude her, like a computer-generated fractal pattern that only became more complicated as she magnified the image.

She gestured to Semaya as she ate, and the slim, impossibly elegant woman glided across the tiles. "Kuran esh," she began carefully. "Mei tolie rhen ai…" and paused in frustration, trying to think of the correct future tense form.

"Airhal ma," Semaya reminded her gently. And activated her small speaker, as Lisbeth wore no earpiece, newly out of the water. *"I would like,"* spoke the speaker. *"You will have language class next, and then you would like…?"*

"I would like to speak with Nahltira once more," Lisbeth said in English, abandoning her broken Porgesh for the moment. "You promised me I could."

"Nahltira is indisposed," came Semaya's translated reply. *"She is a senior historian of the Togreth, her services are in demand."*

"Then find me another," Lisbeth insisted. "I was promised access to your best, and I shall have it."

Semaya gave a serene bow, and glided away. Not long ago, Lisbeth would have been horrified at her own rudeness, making such demands. But lately, among parren, she was realising that manners would only get her so far. Parren valued decorum, but they also valued power. Lisbeth was a hostage here, held by the Domesh as blackmail against her brother, and even parren accepted that some degree of indignation was justified. When some unconfirmed enemy had sent an assassin to kill her eighteen days ago, Lisbeth's guardian sentry, an assassin bug designed by Styx and sent by Hiro Uno to protect her, had killed the assassin first, and intrigued her captors. They couldn't see it, but they knew it was about somewhere, watching her, and them, and lethal if it chose. That they would all become suddenly more polite around her, she could have predicted. That they would make no attempt to capture the bug, or to otherwise disarm her, had been unexpected.

Her time on *Phoenix* with Stan Romki had confirmed to her that many of the Spiral's species respected power. Trying to be nice, as some Homeworld pacifists still suggested, could actually be dangerous, as it invited disrespect potentially followed by attack. The assassin bug gave her power, not only in that it could kill any who threatened her, but that it indicated old and formidable knowledge that was hers, and a connection to things that various parren found both intriguing and frightening. Some denominations would no doubt have killed her on the spot, learning of her links to these things. Fortunately for her, neither the Domesh nor the Togreth were that sort of parren.

In the meantime, she made a schedule of her time here. Exercise in the mornings, then language lessons, then history and politics. Being here had afforded her an opportunity given to few humans in all recorded history. An opportunity to learn about the parren from the inside of their most dynamic power structures, where it really counted. As well, it played to her strengths and kept her busy, focused with a purpose that prevented her from thinking about just how many of other parren factions would like to kill her. If *Phoenix* failed to grant Aristan the fruits of its most recent mission, the Domesh themselves would kill her. Or that had been the original threat. Whether they would still follow through on that, given her rapidly changing status here in the Domesh Temple, she did not know.

Before stepping into the halls of the temple, she had to be presentable. A chair was brought, and several maids attended to her hair with pins, combs and ribbons. It was odd, because parren had no body hair whatsoever. Traditionally, scalps were for decoration, with crests and crowns, hoods, hats and other, tiara-like creations that human culture had no words for. Body hair was something that happened to the very old — that unpleasant grey peach-fuzz that the wealthy and high-status would have plucked as soon as it appeared.

Lisbeth's hair did not seem to disgust them, however, for it was thick, brown and full of curls. Done properly, it could surround her head in a big, fuzzy halo, and the maids who worked on it now were specialists, brought for the task of making such an odd thing look if not appealing, then at least acceptable, to parren eyes. Lisbeth supposed that in this more than anything else, she looked alien to them. That, and the fact that she weighed more than any parren man her own height, and more again than the women. Parren were wisps, and made everything graceful, like flowing water.

"Does this please, my lady?" came one maid's translated voice in Lisbeth's restored earpiece. Lisbeth observed in the mirror she held. A backwards-facing tiara made a circle of the hair on the top of her head, which was in turn pulled back tightly over a horizontal comb. The hair at the sides was also pulled back with combs, then held with binding ribbons. The effect was almost severe, and Lisbeth calmed her face, to give the mirror a suitably haughty look. She'd be needing that, in this place.

"It pleases," she agreed. All of this work, just to return to her quarters, a fifteen minute walk. As her status here had risen, so had the time taken to perform even simple tasks.

"What are the colours of your people, m'lady?" the other maid asked as she worked. *"Parren have only this brown and red, yet humans have many."*

"Human colours used to be distinct," Lisbeth told her. "A long time ago, when Earth was still living." Both maids paused in their work to make a small gesture of sorrow, heads bowed. Then they returned to their work. Lisbeth found that touching. "There were many different races. But the survivors of Earth all had to live together on space stations and colonies for a long time, and in close proximity the races all began to mix. Some pure races still remain, but perhaps only one-in-four of all humans. Today we are all descended from those survivors."

"I have researched the databases, m'lady," said the maid. *"For inspiration, in human styles."* Brushing hard and inserting another hairpin. *"Many of the humans with this curly hair have black skin. But others have straight hair."*

"My father is very dark," Lisbeth agreed. "The old Earth place was called Africa. The dark ones with straight hair are probably from another place called India. Major Trace Thakur of the *UFS Phoenix* is of the Indian race." Despite barely being able to find India on an old Earth-map, she recalled with amusement. "My family is more African than any other, but when I look at the pictures of my ancestors, I find white people, Asian people, all kinds of people. Most humans today are like that."

This inspired the maids to talk of the parren races, and how they had changed across the millennia. It was interesting talk, and Lisbeth congratulated herself on having learned how to get the best information from her hosts — information from parren mouths, communicating what parren actually thought, rather than the dry data from her books. Parren could be quite open and friendly, even with a human, but only once the protocols of status and position had been established. These maids had come to feel confident of their position with regard to Lisbeth, and so, despite her considerably greater importance, felt at ease to converse with her.

Once prepared, Lisbeth stood, and her maids glided to the door. A phalanx was formed, and Lisbeth departed the pool room from their care, and into the assembled ranks of her Domesh guards on the other side. These were all men, and clad in the obscuring black robes of the Domesh, hoods up and only the eyes visible above their veils. To the front of the formation were a pair of Tuvenar — junior Shoveren, the psychologist/priestly class that presided over the rules of flux and phase-change. These two held ornate staves, and one held a large scroll over a shoulder, upon which Lisbeth knew would be scrawled the relevant laws by which an alien could be held as captive in this manner. The scroll would be presented to any who challenged, and made a shield between her, and any legal attempt to alter her status. Which could mean anything, from a verbal challenge, to an assassination attempt. So far, thank god, there had been only one of those.

The pool room corridor gave way to a vast and gleaming hall, with enormous stone walls that towered above a floor polished smooth like ice. Upon great pedestals rose the stone figures of animals, some mythical, others real, all majestic, and a few rather frightening with snarling teeth and sharp claws. Elsewhere along the walls were tapestries with brilliant abstract patterns, while others depicted scenes from old mythology. Lisbeth knew what only a little of it meant, and though she learned more every day, she thought she would still feel like an alien in this place if she had to live here another decade.

High-ranked parren gave them space in the hall, and inclined their heads. Lower-ranked parren stopped walking entirely, and sank to one knee as the entourage swept by. The lowest-ranked parren prostrated themselves face-first on the smooth stone. Most here were black-robed Domesh, but not all. The Kunadeen was the seat of government of all House Harmony, and parren from the various temples and denominations did mix, sometimes on business, other-times for pleasure or diversion.

Telling the non-Domesh from the Domesh was easy, as the Domesh black robes clashed against the more vibrant colours of 'typical' parren dress. Domesh did not force their dress code onto others, for to be Domesh was to be withdrawn from the temptations of colour and vibrancy by choice. Still, Lisbeth wondered at all the decoration in the temple. The Domesh Temple was very new, rebuilt on the command of Aristan's predecessor, and following precisely the preserved plans of the previous, much older Tahrae temple that had stood upon this site. On Stoya III, where the crew of *Phoenix* had first met Aristan, the Domesh Temple had been all black minimalism and sensory deprivation. Here, the style was restrained, but positively loud and joyful compared to that. Yet the Domesh insisted that they followed the teachings of the Tahrae, in the avoidance from that which would clutter the mind, and make thoughts impure and decadent. Lisbeth found the inconsistency striking, and wondered that no parren remarked on it.

Her party rounded a wide corner, heading for the vast stairway that would take her up to her quarters. At the base of the stairs awaited another entourage of black-clad men. This one was headed by a full-Shoveren, a priest/psychologist himself, clad in stately blue and flanked by a pair of Tuvenar. Lisbeth's party approached, then halted. A command was cried, an alien echo off the high ceiling, and the wall of black robes about her slid to the ground, heads bowed, leaving Lisbeth exposed and standing in their midst.

She did not know if it was improper for her to stand, but here it was her very alienness that granted her authority. She stood tall, and fixed her face with the very same haughty look she'd practised in the maid's mirror.

The opposing phalanx parted to reveal another, older, black-robed man. She could tell he was older, because the Domesh guards were all young, full of athletic swagger, and plainly armed beneath their robes. This man was not, and his approach to her held none of the stylised intimidation of a younger warrior. As he came closer, Lisbeth recognised the indigo eyes of Gesul. Obra, the word was for his rank, and it meant many things that Lisbeth had not yet grasped. What she *had* grasped was that Gesul was the second-most-senior parren in all the Domesh Denomination. With Aristan away, he was in charge of this entire temple, and all of its affairs.

"Greetings, Ashara," he said via the translator. Ashara. That was the official word for what you called a hostage, taken to force a bargain. Lisbeth had not yet figured that one out, either. Parren were so regimented, surely, that they could not be blackmailed. Would not most parren hostages simply commit suicide, so as to avoid being a burden on their masters? *"I have news of your brother. Walk with me."*

For a moment, Lisbeth stood paralysed. At her side, now kneeling, was Timoshene. He was her Tokara, the senior of those designed to protect her. And also, if *Phoenix* reneged upon its deal with Aristan, to kill her. She took a deep breath, and willed herself not to tremble. "Gesul-sa," she said, with what she thought was the proper courtesy. "If I may offer advice. When you speak to me on matters that concern my personal safety, it is best that you speak clearly. It can understand speech, including parren speech, and it will kill if in doubt."

Several of Gesul's dark-robed guards pulled fabric away from hips, where weapons were worn. In Lisbeth's lower side vision, she saw Timoshene tense, crouched against the floor like a cat. Would her own guards fight to defend her even from Gesul? Her guards were sworn by honour to die in her defence, and if the honour of a Domesh Tokara had any limits, Lisbeth had not seen it.

Gesul made a one-handed gesture within his robe, as though moving aside some invisible obstacle that floated between them. *"It is my mistake,"* he admitted, with all the nerveless cool of a senior Domesh. *"I will clarify, Ashara Lisbeth, for your protector's benefit. News from Phoenix is incomplete and preliminary, but it is good. You are safe from the final settlement."*

"I am pleased to hear it," said Lisbeth, her heart restarting. "What is the news from my brother?"

Was it her imagination, or did those wide, indigo eyes flick about her clothes, searching for a sign of her protector? Lisbeth had seen many of her maids do so, but without any particular fear. They understood that their guest's personal sentinel would only harm them if they threatened her safety. To live beneath such endless anxiety would have caused great stress to humans, but the parren were serene. As though they considered it entirely proper that such an extreme breach of decorum should be punished with immediate death.

"Walk with me," said Gesul, extending a robed arm. *"We will discuss."*

He turned, and Lisbeth walked, her guards arranging themselves amidst Gesul's entourage in turn, a rustling, black-robed wall. Lisbeth did not know where the assassin bug was right now. Almost certainly it had found some hiding place among the folds of her gown, for it was too large to fly before so many eyes undetected. Lisbeth suspected that it could hide itself with some kind of optical camouflage, chameleon-like, to better blend against its background. Occasionally she would hear it buzzing, somewhere near her collar, perhaps to advise her of its presence. But today she'd not seen or heard it at all.

"There has been no word from Phoenix directly," said Gesul, gliding at her side. *"But it appears that they have been at Kantovan System."*

"I know," Lisbeth admitted. Gesul turned, and gave her a cool glance from within his hood. "Tobenrah told me, when he summonsed me ten days ago. He said that he had met my brother, in fact. At the wrong end of his marines' guns."

Gesul said nothing for a moment, obviously surprised. The grand hall turned left onto a viewing platform, where a lattice frame made a mesh before the grand view of the courtyards in place of a window. The Domesh Temple made few concessions to modernity, not even glass, and all high-tech fittings and displays were kept as discrete as possible. The wide balcony held an arrangement of benches and plants. Some parren were enjoying the view, and now departed in graceful haste, to make way for the VIPs.

"Kantovan System is in uproar," said Gesul, pausing to consider the view. Guards spread about the balcony, watching all entrances, and each other. *"Your brother was due to give a speech at the Tsubarata. This was interrupted by an assassination attempt that wounded one of his men, and killed some bystanders and tavalai guards."* Lisbeth was not shocked — Tobenrah had told her this tale as well. *"But the best Domesh intelligence now suggests that this speech was itself only a ruse to direct attention elsewhere, while the true target was assaulted — the State Department secret vault on the moon of Kamala."*

Gesul had not known, Lisbeth reflected. Aristan and the Domesh had worked to make this mission happen, but had not known where it would take them. Lisbeth had no idea precisely what *Phoenix* was after — she'd been kidnapped on Stoya III before she could find out. But whatever it was, Aristan had been determined that *Phoenix* would share its bounty with him and the Domesh. Which raised a question.

"Where is Aristan?" Lisbeth asked. "I have not heard a whisper of him since I was brought here. It's like he's not even present."

"Lisbeth Debogande is perceptive," said Gesul. *"Aristan is leading the Domesh effort with Phoenix."*

Lisbeth stared. "In person?"

"Parren leaders are required to have many capabilities. Aristan was a great warrior in his time. Those capabilities now serve us all. Do you know why?"

A test, Lisbeth thought. She took a deep breath, gazing past the thin lattice, that only blocked enough of the courtyard view to create the impression of shade. Many trapezoid temples rose, now beginning to swim with the heat haze of mid-morning. Soon the pavings would be free of Kunadeen residents, and only the hardy outside visitors, or the circling birds, would venture the expanse.

"Because he seeks information," she concluded, drawing several trains of thought into a single idea. "Information that may require him to make profound decisions. It's the reason starship captains must also be pilots — if a lower-ranked pilot has to make an immediate decision to risk the ship or not, then *he* is the captain." It made more sense as she said it, gelling with things Erik had told her about his job, and she continued with growing confidence. "Aristan must have thought that what he would find would lead to profound decisions about the direction of the Domesh. *Phoenix* is too far away to send for instructions here. Whoever was on the scene, making those decisions, would be the leader of the Domesh, in function if not in name. It had to be him."

"Perceptive indeed. These are treacherous times, Lisbeth Debogande. There are many enemies arranged against the Domesh. Most of House Harmony does not wish to see us attain leadership of this house. None of the other four houses wish to see the Domesh leading House Harmony. I fear that we may face all parren, united against us."

Lisbeth glanced in surprise. It was impossible to tell if Gesul was troubled, past the hood and the synthetic replication of the translator. But they were the words of a troubled man, gazing at the scene of what for a Domesh must have been the most profound thing imaginable. The Kunadeen, the seat of power for all House Harmony, and all its denominations. The parliament that ruled the one-fifth of all parren who currently transited through this phase of the parren mind. Lately, most of those newly-fluxed had been coming to the Domesh. Surely all these other temples, and the other denominations residing within, were coming to resent that fact, and fear it. Likely one of them had sent the assassin to her bedroom, to sabotage the Domesh attempt to gain currency from *Phoenix*'s mission, whatever it was. If she died, *Phoenix* would owe the Domesh nothing.

"Wasn't it inevitable that parren would unite against you?" she accused him. "When you picked the most hated man in parren history as your saviour?"

"Hated by the elites who make our opinions, who write our histories, who recount our current affairs." Gesul did not sound impressed. He was a tall man for a parren, a full head taller than Lisbeth, and bore a physical presence within his robe that most parren lacked. *"Do not be deceived by parren discipline, Lisbeth Debogande. We obey, but we also think for ourselves. Drakhil was the last man to truly lead parren to greatness in the Spiral. Many parren want their greatness back."*

"You had the Parren Empire," Lisbeth countered. "It was eight thousand human years, far longer than the few hundred of the drysine-parren alliance. Why not draw inspiration from that?"

"Most do," Gesul admitted. *"But it was chaotic. Untidy. Do they teach very much of the Parren Empire period on human worlds?"*

"Very little," Lisbeth admitted. "Humans are rather preoccupied with our own history."

"Understandable. Parren make poor governors of species other than our own. We tried, but parren society is dominated by the division of the five houses, and other species do not share our ways. There were many breakups and uprisings, the chah'nas in particular were restive, being the most warlike. We put them down many times, having superior technology then, thanks to the drysines. In truth, the drysines gave us such a large advantage, which we managed to keep others from acquiring, that we were unchallengeable for a long time.

"The Empire period is not looked upon with particular pride, Lisbeth Debogande. There were too many wars, squabbles and corruptions. When the chah'nas finally overthrew us, it was almost a relief, to some at least. The Spiral became a chah'nas problem, and parren withdrew to what we do best — scheme amongst ourselves."

It was a cynicism unsuspected from a parren. Lisbeth recalled his words — 'we obey, but we also think for ourselves.' A human would assume that a people who always did as they were told could not think independently. She'd gotten the impression that the tavalai shared this prejudice, internal ill-discipline being something humans and tavalai shared. Aristan might have been a single-minded fanatic, but the description did not appear to fit Gesul.

"Drakhil would have made parren first among all the Spiral species," Lisbeth said slowly. "First and unchallengeable, because of drysine power. And the drysines would have let you do what you wanted, among organics. They didn't care about organics, they'd just tell you guys to keep the other organics out of their way, and if you did that, they'd be happy. Assuming drysines can be happy."

Gesul was looking at her again, curiously. *"Indeed. Parren would have prospered. The drysines would have crushed any challenger. Many today find it more attractive than the honourless compromises of the Empire."*

"Assuming another hacksaw civil war didn't change the drysines' minds, or wipe them out, and take you with it," said Lisbeth. "The machines evolved, Gesul, more rapidly even than organics. Give them a few hundred years separated in different parts of the Spiral, two groups of drysines could change so much they'd no longer recognise each other, then would fight to eliminate that foreign threat. I think we're all better off without them."

Gesul might have smiled within his veil. *"And does your protector agree?"*

"My protector is tasked with protecting. He has no opinions." She was pretty sure, anyway. A brain that small surely must be a long way from sentient.

"And the drysine queen who built him?" Gesul pressed. And might have smiled further at the shock on her face. She tried to hide it, but she'd never been a particularly good actor. *"Our information from Kantovan suggests it the most likely possibility. So many odd events, so many unlikely coincidences. Alone, we might not have added them up. But we have you, and your protector, the technology for which is supposed to be long extinct. Possessing the hardware to build one is the first matter. Possessing the software to make it think just the way you want it to... and the*

consequences if you get it wrong? Hacksaw drones do not program. Only queens. This much knowledge from the old days we have retained."

Lisbeth wasn't sure that was correct — drysine drones seemed a little beyond most of the other hacksaw types. But it did not stop Gesul's conclusion from being correct. Well, she thought, pulling herself up. She'd decided to be powerful in this place, by showing everyone how much she knew of things that they valued. A hacksaw queen might be overdoing it… but what more harm could it cause now? If Styx had been at Kantovan, and if even distant observers like the Domesh, and like Tobenrah, were suspicious, surely others were as well. The idea had been for Styx to keep a low profile, but if *Phoenix* was using her in operations, that wasn't going to last. Styx could do things for which all other explanations were implausible.

"No," Lisbeth said finally. "No, she's very determined to bring her people back from extinction. *Phoenix* had advanced capabilities even without her. With her, those capabilities increase dramatically." It was the only threat she could manage, for now. It sounded painfully weak to her own ears. *Phoenix* was certainly no trifle, but Gesul was second-in-command of the about-to-be most powerful denomination in House Harmony. House Harmony commanded fleets, and comprised tens of billions of souls. This was not a man to be frightened by a single ship. Not even one carrying a hacksaw queen.

Gesul stared, at her admission. As though, despite his conclusion, it was still a great shock to hear her confirm it. *"Does she have a name?"* he whispered.

"They do not use names, amongst themselves. Identification data is encoded in all communications, making names redundant." Lisbeth took a deep breath. Revealing this information was now surely the right thing to do, but she could not escape the feeling that she was engaging in some treachery. "Aboard *Phoenix* she is known as Styx. It is the name of a very old Earth goddess. Amongst parren, she says that she was once known as Halgolam."

Gesul's eyes went wider still. He turned to stare at the sun-drenched expanse, the great birds circling on thermals. Lisbeth thought he might need a seat. It was a full minute before he spoke again. *"Did she know Drakhil?"*

"She said she'd met him. More than that, she did not say." Lisbeth had actually heard Romki say more, of what Styx had told him of her knowledge of Drakhil. But Gesul belonged to a belief-system built entirely upon a mythologised notion of who Drakhil had been. To destroy that notion, before such a man, was not safe.

"Incredible," Gesul murmured. *"Halgolam. I thank you, Lisbeth Debogande. When we took you for an Ashara, we had no idea we were acquiring such a treasure trove of ancient knowledge."*

Lisbeth smiled faintly. "If you think that of *me*, you should truly meet *her* one day."

"Nothing would give me a more profound satisfaction. I would be content to die immediately after, and feel my life complete. Halgolam." He murmured the word again, and the translator repeated it phonetically in Lisbeth's ear, perhaps recognising it as something from parren belief. *"I shall speak with you more deeply on this. But first, I must research, in the oldest archives."*

Gesul indicated to Timoshene, who bowed deeply. "I would accompany you, if it would help?" Lisbeth blurted on impulse. It was a preposterous offer, but she was feeling quite emboldened. To feel as though she had some leverage over her circumstance, after so much fear and uncertainty, was the greatest relief.

Gesul smiled. *"A kind offer, but impractical. Where I must go to research, I not only doubt they would admit you, I fear they shall not admit* me.*"*

He gave a polite nod, and flowed away in a billow of black.

CHAPTER 3

The rooms and corridors from Engineering Bulkhead-G were a mess of activity. Spacers ran and shouted, dodging past Erik with handfuls of tools. From various open doorways came the keening and throbbing of alien machines — fabricators — some of human design, others alien. Styx professed that she was not a repository of technical information, and that her knowledge was only a tiny portion of drysine technology. But she'd spent thousands of years in a hollowed out asteroid in Argitori System, accompanied by a small handful of drones, and a network of advanced fabricators.

The fabricators had used far more power than the asteroid's hacksaw inhabitants, for any hacksaw colony required constant maintenance of ageing parts to survive in fighting condition. Styx's small band of survivors had run those fabricators as a human colony would run lifesupport, fashioning new parts, repairing old ones, evolving the multiple micro sub-systems that were the only way to manufacture or repair sensitive neural or sensory systems. Now, Styx replicated those millennia of expertise on *Phoenix*, with human crew toiling as her personal workforce of drones.

All of the technology to be produced was illegal in most parts of the Spiral, but in their present circumstance, up against the opponents they faced, Erik thought *Phoenix* would need all the help she could get. Lieutenant Rooke, Chief of Engineering, was already salivating at the prospect of some technologies Styx offered, particularly at the fact that they would not require a massive overhaul in a ship base to implement. What Styx would get out of it was a new body… and, though it was said less often, the ability to reanimate the bodies of other destroyed hacksaw drones from Argitori, whose parts *Phoenix* still held in storage. Already one had been so reconstructed, with results so impressive, Trace opined, that it might be worth pursuing again, for the multiplication of combat power such drones represented for marine units. Trace might have been ready for such drastic developments, but Erik did not think the rest of the crew were. 'Later', he'd told her, meaning never. She might be in charge of Phoenix Company, but between deployments, hacksaw drones would have to live in his ship, with his crew. Just no, Trace, for god's sake.

He found Stan Romki in B-14 — a storage room with high vertical walls of shelves, cold but insulated. A lot of it was frozen food, and even now Spacer Kuiper was standing on the mobile stepladder to drag frozen slabs from their trays and down to his trolley, for defrosting in the kitchen. Romki sat in the workbay he'd set up — one of the few spares left in Engineering — and puzzled over multiple translation programs running on multiple screens. The data he (or rather Styx) had extracted from the storage cylinder they'd stolen from the Kantovan Vault was not great in size, just in complexity and alien-ness. At an adjoining bench sat Hiro Uno, his posture reminding Erik of Academy students in class after a weekend of football, wincing at every pressure and trying to move as little as possible.

Hiro turned his head slowly to glance at Erik with his one good eye. The other was swollen shut completely. "Captain."

"Should you be out of medbay?" Erik wondered, putting a hand on the spy's shoulder.

"Depends who you ask," Hiro said cryptically, through the clenched teeth of a swollen jaw.

"Ah," said Erik. Clearly Hiro hadn't asked anyone, least of all Doc Suelo. It was the first time he'd seen Hiro since breaking him out of State Department custody on the Tsubarata. "How's the body?"

"Nothing broken," said Hiro. "Be sore for a while. They weren't trying to cripple me."

"I'll want a report, as soon as you're able," Erik told him. Hiro didn't share much about how he did things. Presumably he'd sworn an oath, while working for federal intelligence agencies, that he would not reveal certain methods even once he'd left the service.

"I thought I answered to Major Thakur on off-ship operations," Hiro said defensively.

"You see that rank you now wear?" Erik asked him. "That's 'Ensign'. It's a spacer rank, because you're now a spacer. That means you answer to me first, on all things."

"Yes Captain," Hiro said without enthusiasm. "I'll dictate it as soon as I've got nothing better to do." It wasn't worth the argument, Erik thought. Hiro and Jokono were former intelligence and law enforcement respectively, and only wore the uniform now by accident and necessity. They did good work and were as brave as anyone. Bitching about their lack of military etiquette, particularly Hiro's, would not help anything.

"Ensign Uno is displeased at being rescued," came Styx's synthetic, feminine voice from the room speakers. Up on his stepladder, Spacer Kuiper nearly dropped his frozen trays. Not all of *Phoenix*'s crew had yet heard her in person. *"I do not believe he would have preferred to die, but he appears determined to be displeased at being rescued. It is not a productive attitude."*

"Yeah, thanks Gorgeous," Hiro retorted. Hiro and Styx had coordinated closely in breaking into State Department HQ on the Tsubarata, Erik knew. If Hiro wouldn't tell him how he'd done it, perhaps Styx would. "And thanks a bundle for offering to stick me with the pointy end of an assassin bug, too."

"It gave me no pleasure," Styx said mildly. *"I do not advocate the elimination of valuable assets lightly. I am a strategic planner, and that strategy seemed advantageous over risking the Captain's life to save you. But on this ship I am a servant, and I follow orders."*

A while back she'd described herself as a slave, Erik recalled. Styx was far too meticulous for that change in terminology to be accidental. Evidently her estimation of herself, and her role on *Phoenix*, was increasing.

"Stan?" said Erik, looking at Romki. The Professor continued to stare at his screens, making corrections to the scroll of text and murmuring to himself. "How's the progress? Stan?" Romki genuinely had not heard him. Probably he didn't even know Erik was in the room.

"Human intelligence is a curious thing," Styx observed. Erik and Hiro exchanged glances. *"Professor, the Captain wishes to speak with you."*

Romki blinked in surprise, and looked about. So he only responded to *her* voice now, Erik wondered? "Oh, Captain. Yes. Um, good progress. I think I have it pinpointed, but there's…" He slumped back in his chair, pushed the glasses up his bald head, and rubbed his eyes. "There's just so much here. Drakhil's diary, it's just… it's the greatest scholarly discovery of this millennia, I think. By this species or any other. I feel I've been blessed and cursed at the same time, this is too much for any one person to process."

"When was the last time you slept?" Erik asked suspiciously. There was a coffee flask in the workbench drink holder. "Or ate, for that matter?"

"I'll sleep when I have my presentation ready," Romki said irritably. "When do I need it done by?"

"Yesterday," Erik said flatly. "Styx, since you're assisting the Professor on his translations, could you please be certain that he does not get too distracted on all this other scholarly stuff? We need to know the location of the data-core, that's all."

"Oh we *have* the location of the data-core," Romki retorted. "It's just that we have it on twenty five thousand year old maps. We need up-to-date maps and charts, and those are simply not available. We need Aristan's help. A lot of this stuff…" Romki waved a finger at the glowing lines of text on his screen, "…this is verbal description, it's not scientific, we just have to trust that the things that Drakhil describes are still there after all this time."

"Captain," said Styx. *"If I may, please do not blame the Professor for my shortcomings. As many in your crew have observed, spoken language is not my native skill, and I calculate correct speech mostly by observed probability. This is possible where I am in possession of all the variables, like advanced English dictionaries, and many examples of their use. But where those variables are missing, as in the Klyran language, my ability to decipher meaning becomes quite limited."*

"She's being modest," Romki sighed. "I mean, she's the only reason I can do this at all. We know the rules of phonetics and pronunciation, and thousands of the most common words, but we're constantly running into new words that have no foundation in anything known. Styx is running every parren dictionary and language file we have, simultaneously, and cross-referencing against new klyran words… that's billions of calculations, and she's still only right about half the time because not every klyran word is related to something still in use today. The rest of the time we have to leave a blank and move on, then come back when we've got new information."

"But even once translated," Styx continued, *"the style of writing is so imprecise that I cannot be sure of the meaning, while Professor Romki seems to find an answer almost instinctively. It is actually quite intriguing. Drysines have always proclaimed complete intellectual superiority over organics. In fact, I now discover that in some of the skills for which it is specifically designed, the human mind can outperform my own."*

"Humans are good at guessing," said Hiro. The spy was the only other person on the ship whose fluency in alien tongues came close to Romki's. He was also a whiz with encryption, and it made sense he'd be useful here. "AIs don't like to guess because they value precision. They're victims of their own high expectations, while humans expect to be wrong, so we don't mind wading out into the unknown while we figure it out."

"An intriguing supposition," Styx admitted. *"Entirely inaccurate, I suspect, but intriguing."*

Hiro smiled, and popped a breath mint. "Thanks Babe."

"I'll take your word for it, all of you," Erik assured them. It *was* incredibly interesting, and in other circumstances he'd have loved to stay and discuss it further with them. But the curse of being Captain was that his interests were general, not specific, and he simply did not have the time. "Stan, it sounds like you've got nearly enough for a presentation now. All the Major will need is ground coordinates, we can figure out the rest on the fly."

"Ah yes," Romki drawled, refocusing on his screens. "The famous *Phoenix* seat-of-the-pants. I'm sure we can do better than that Captain, give us another four hours at least."

"Four," Erik agreed, turning to leave. "And Hiro, if the Doc asks me where you are, I'm not going to cover for you."

"Never asked you to," said Hiro as he left.

Erik's next stop was one level up and a quarter-rotation around the cylinder. In the steel-grey storage bay he found Tif, eating what looked like chicken from her own breakfast box, and circling the contraption rigged amongst the vertical stacks of big shelves in the surrounding walls, each large enough to store a body. The contraption was a spare bridge seat, complete with interface insets, seven-point restraints, and a full spread of surrounding displays. On the armrests were G-restraints for the arms, and twin joysticks within stylised handgrips with multiple buttons and triggers. A starship pilot's post, in replica. Four large steel supports drove the corners through floor and ceiling, to hold it secure in manoeuvres.

Tif walked around it, like a hunter who'd just found a large, dead animal, and wondered if it was safe to eat. "Don't know word," she admitted, past her sharp-toothed mouthful of chicken. Past accent, sharp teeth and food, it was barely intelligible. "Copy? Copy pirot seat?"

"Pilot seat, yes," Erik agreed, sitting at the observer chair before a display. "Simulator. You know the word?"

Tif made a face, tearing off another mouthful of chicken. Doing that, she looked even less sentient-biped than usual. More like a carnivorous hunter, lips pulled back from the short muzzle to expose alarming teeth. Erik marvelled at how the long ears flattened with each bite, the muscles of her face conditioned by millions of years of evolution to keep them away from her mouth when feeding.

"Don't have transrator on," she admitted. "Sim… simurator?"

"Yes, simulator."

"Rrrr," Tif complained, trying to pronounce the L, and failing. "Stupid sound. Goknaroch."

"Bless you," said Erik, eating fruit pieces from his own breakfast box. They'd been thawed from a snap-freeze, and tasted decidedly mediocre. Like the coffee. "Simulator for *Phoenix*. Pilot's seat. All the *Phoenix* pilots come down here to run combat sims when we have time, then we critique each other's moves. It keeps us sharp."

"Yes." Tif nodded, a gesture she'd been using more and more. "For shuttuw, we sit shuttuw cockpit, run sim in cockpit."

"Yes, well you can't do that in *Phoenix*. We need that cockpit operational at all times." Tif crouched to peer curiously at the setup, then examined the armrests and joysticks. She hadn't understood yet why she was here, Erik saw. That was to be expected. There was no rush — he had to take time to eat anyway, and he'd only seen Tif once, briefly, after events on Kantovan. "I saw Skah down in Medbay. Private Rolonde was helping him to read a story. Corporal Rael was enjoying the company."

"Good," said Tif, now tearing into some flatbread. Kuhsi did mostly meat, but also some vegetables, well cooked. Absolutely no fruit, as their digestion welcomed protein and some carbs, but regular sugar in even small quantities could make them ill. "Surprise he awake. Funny… rittuw boy, back hone, back Choghoth? Rise eary, rise norning. But now, on *Phoenix*, *Phoenix* too eary for Skah. Skah want go back to bed. I say no, I say Jess teach Engrish, you no nake Jess angry."

Erik didn't think there was much chance of anyone getting angry at Skah. With all else that went on, even a little boy's bad behaviour was a ray of sunshine for most. He smiled. "Lisbeth never liked early mornings either. They have that in common."

Tif looked at him, her big golden eyes sombre. One ear drooped, sympathetically. "Skah miss Risbeth. Aw miss Risbeth. Aw pirots."

Erik nodded. On *Phoenix*, Lisbeth had divided her time between the techs in Engineering, and the shuttle pilots in Operations. *Phoenix* had been short of shuttle crew, and was now one short again. With so much to learn in both fields, she'd studied and practised hard. She was still far from a Fleet-standard front-seater, but the pilots had respected her dedication, and even opined without too much patronising that she could make Fleet-standard one day, if she stuck at it. Erik had sincerely hoped her voyage wouldn't last that long. He still did.

He took a mouthful of his sandwich, and indicated to the simulator. "You like it?"

Tif blinked, looking a little puzzled. "Yes. Why?"

"Would you like to try it?"

Tif blinked again. Then stared, ears dropping, mouth open. "Fry *Phoenix*?" She pointed to herself, incredulous.

"Fly the *Phoenix* simulator, Tif. It's just a sim. But your reflexes are top notch, the other shuttle pilots say you've got great hands and some of the best feel for the ship they've ever seen. All Fleet pilots get tested for aptitude, then sorted into starships, shuttles, haulers, atmospherics, etc. Hausler and Jersey have both been tested for aptitude, and found best suited for shuttles. But we've never tested you."

Tif's big eyes glistened. Looking at her, Erik almost felt a lump in his own throat. To have been accepted on *Phoenix* meant the world to her. She'd come from nothing, from a culture where women were less than nothing, and here amongst the aliens she'd found all the things that kuhsi valued — pride, honour, and status with a big, powerful clan. It meant a future for her boy, and glory for her blood family, however little they'd appreciate it. And though new to *Phoenix*, she knew enough to know that no one was ever tested on the command simulator who was not in some kind of consideration for the role.

"You think..." Her voice caught, and she tried again. "You think I could...?"

"I don't know Tif," said Erik, trying to contain both pleasure and amusement. This wasn't fun and games he was proposing. He knew as well as anyone the toll that this particular chair could take on a person. "But we're short of pilots, and the people who can do it well enough, for a ship like this one, are very rare. I'll be honest — you're probably not suitable. Even Hausler isn't quite there, and you know he's as good a raw pilot as you'll ever see. But having fast hands isn't quite enough for a starship, you have to be able to visualise beyond the light horizon, you have to be able to see big spaces, all moving at high speed, and coordinate a hundred different things at once."

"I try!" Tif said fiercely, with great emotion. "Naybe I not good, but I try!"

He made it through the ship's core to Midships just as the shuttle from *Kanamandali* began its final docking manoeuvre, passing spacers coming the other way as the pulley strap dragged him zero-G through the rotating tube.

"That's a nice offer," Trace said in his ear. *"But I'm not actually second-in-command of this ship any longer, and I think he'll probably respect you more one-on-one."*

Curious, Erik thought as he eyed the approaching Midships bulkhead, where the great cylinder socket-joint made a gap, and the tube no longer spun as he left the crew cylinder behind. When they'd started this journey, Trace had been the equal-highest ranked officer on the ship. She'd also been the guiding steel behind their initial actions, and in the early days, when they'd still had crew onboard who couldn't be trusted, she was the guarantor of crew discipline as well. But now, with him a full-ranked Captain, and Suli Shahaim Commander, Trace was equal-third ranked with Lieutenant Commander Draper.

It took an effort to recall that, sometimes, because in Erik's mind at least (and he suspected many of the crew's) she was far more than that. As always on carriers, in relations between marines and spacers, it depended on circumstance. On board *Phoenix* she was ranked no higher than she needed to be. When off-ship objectives came into play, she became nearly as important as the Captain, and sometimes moreso. It was still his reflex to invite her along when some bigshot alien importance visited their deck, if only because on the current two-shift arrangement, all of the other senior bridge crew would be occupied, while Trace alone could make some time.

"What's the problem?" Erik asked her.

"Well I trashed two suits just recently," Trace replied, and Erik could hear the whine of powertools somewhere near. Then the crash of heavy equipment being moved, and yelling conversation — she was in Assembly, fixing her armour by hand, as all marines were trained to do. *"And Command Squad's not much better. So if we don't get this lot up and running, I'm going to have to put some other squad out of action to borrow their suits for Command Squad, which will not make them happy."*

Erik knew better than to hope that this setback for Command Squad would keep her out of the next deployment. If her marines were deployed, particularly into something hazardous, she'd find a way to put herself squarely in the middle once more.

Erik flew headfirst down the handlines and cargo nets of upper Berth Five, just as the tavalai shuttle crashed into the external grapples. The great mechanisms against the inner hull heaved as tension-loaded arms took the weight, and clung. *Phoenix*'s Operations crew had long since figured through the difficulties of docking tavalai shuttles, and got the access tube in place, and managed to not screw up communications with the tavalai crew. Soon there were tavalai floating up the access into the airlock, then a hiss of equalising air, and two unarmed karasai entered one at a time — big tavalai in jumpsuits, looking warily about with their big, flat heads and wide-set eyes.

Security was Echo 2-3, four marines in light armour, floating with good vantage to see the Berth Five airlock, their posture unthreatening but with weapons to hand. Behind the first big tavalai came a reddy-brown tavalai who looked somewhat familiar in the way that some tavalai had come to look familiar in the past months. He wore a blue jumpsuit with few adornments, and grasped the guiding strap with the elegance of an old spacer. He looked 'up', to the degree that the Midships berth would naturally suggest that the berth airlock was the floor, and the high walls, rails and bulkheads, stacked with cargo shelves, personnel handles and securing nets, were the walls heading up to some non-existent ceiling.

"Captain Debogande?" said the Admiral, as though uncertain.

Erik smiled. "You speak English flawlessly, but you struggle to tell us apart?"

"Learning English is a matter of books and practice," said the Admiral, in that deep, guttural tavalai voice. "Many of those who learn would not know what to do if they met an actual human in person." Erik pulled himself head-first down the wall strap, and the Admiral made his way to the base of that wall, between his two nervous karasai. Once there, they each grabbed a support, and grasped the other's hand. "You did it, Captain. An astonishing feat. The Kantovan Vault itself."

Erik thought he must be coming to read tavalai faces much better, because he saw both genuine respect, and hard suspicion, mingling in the Admiral's big, three-lidded eyes. "Thank you, Admiral. We recovered the artefact you requested, apparently right where you said it would be. Captain Delaganda has it now, on *Podiga*."

"Apparently decrypted," Janik replied, with hard suspicion.

"Yes," Erik agreed.

"How? That is among the most secure State Department secrets. We were wondering how we would decrypt it ourselves, should you be successful. We were preparing for a long and arduous effort from our best technicians. But you appear to have done it in hours."

"Admiral Janik," Erik said coolly. "Tavalai have underestimated humans since first contact. Our capabilities are many." Clearly Admiral Janik had a very strong suspicion of what passenger *Phoenix* carried aboard. He might not have known before he arrived in this system, but with the amount of chatter flying around now, all of it newly sourced from Kantovan System, he must have surely found out on approach. "What will you do with it?"

"Firstly, I will read it. Then I will consider. I understand that *you* have read it? Against our understanding?"

"We recovered two cylinders. We needed to read both to be sure we gave you the correct one, and kept the one we wanted for ourselves."

"And it gives you the information you were after?"

"It appears to," Erik said cautiously. Now that *Phoenix* was stuck in Cherichal System, surrounded by tavalai warships and civilian vessels, there was no guarantee they could actually go anywhere to utilise that information. What would happen next had always been very vague in their agreements. Now, that seemed a mistake. "The information we've given you is aimed at State Department. Does *Tantotavarin* do the State Department's bidding?"

"*Tantotavarin* is a tavalai Fleet loyalist. She is assessing the situation now. She will discover that I and my faction are certainly in serious breach of tavalai law. It will then be up to me, armed with your new data from the vault, to convince them that it was in a good cause. *Tantotavarin* being here is both a curse and a blessing — a curse in that she is incorruptible and formidable, and a blessing in that I am presented with the opportunity to win her over. Should I succeed, our cause will grow much stronger."

"Captain Kaledramani?"

"Yes," Janik agreed. "Captain Kaledramani. Even humans have heard of him."

"Oh yes," said Erik. "We each kept track of the dangerous ones."

"Certainly. Captain Debogande, I have further news. I am breaking more rules in revealing it to you, but in the interests of tavalai security, I feel I must. Perhaps thirty days ago, a tavalai cruiser left Stoya System en-route to its home base. It never arrived. Two more civilian ships, at Corparalda and Vanadragali, have similarly vanished. Most concerningly of all, one of our better warships was intercepted by forces unknown not far from Cherichal, and has similarly vanished. We know that it was intercepted because we have found residual debris from a fight. From what the trajectory and detail of that debris indicates, the fight was against only a single opponent, and was violently short."

Erik frowned. "Someone's picking off your ships? I'm very sorry for your losses Admiral, but how does that concern *Phoenix*?"

"We have drawn a line of probability through these attacks, and they appear to be emanating from K9-XT, inside the territory of sard space. Many of our navigational buoys on the routes along that path have been interrogated by hostile communications systems, and information of their most recent contacts extracted."

Erik's frown grew deeper. "Wait, that's supposed to be nearly impossible. Those buoys are damn hard to crack, our Fleet's been trying for decades."

"And they're supposed to self-destruct rather than surrender that information," Janik agreed. "But even so." His hard, suspicious eyes swivelled inward to take in Erik's expression. Inviting him to understand. And perhaps to admit guilt.

"*Sard* space?" Erik wondered. And he pictured those systems that Janik had just mentioned, an arc of jump points leading back… along the way *Phoenix* had entered into tavalai space. From sard space. From the system known to humans as Gsi-81T, its sard name being unknown and probably unpronounceable, where an enormous drysine ship building facility had been commandeered by a deepynine queen, supported by alo and sard allies. Destroyed, by *Phoenix*, with help from the Dobruta's *Makimakala*.

And Erik's eyes widened. "They're following us!"

"They're *hunting* you," Janik corrected. "We do not know how many, and how powerful, but something is coming for *Phoenix*, Captain Debogande. Something powerful enough to destroy our better ships without effort. Perhaps they want revenge, for the facility that you destroyed. But I think it more likely that they are not after you at all. Rather, I think they are after that abomination you carry in your cargo holds."

CHAPTER 4

Trace was last aboard PH-1 before departure, with two marines in tow. She pulled herself on seat restraints to her customary command post near the cockpit hatch, her two marines taking places behind her, before the row holding Erik and Suli Shahaim. Erik saw in surprise that one was Private Kelvin Krishnan, from Echo Platoon, Second Squad.

"Captain," said Krishnan with pleasure. "Commander."

"Hi Kel," said Erik. "And that's Lance Corporal Haynes, is it?" Haynes led Third Section, but it was Krishnan who'd been stuck with Erik and Trace on Stoya III, and had been there to discover the minor Domesh Temple at the base of Mount Kosik.

"Yessir," said Haynes, busy doing his buckles in the certain knowledge that the Major would tear a strip off if he wasted time brown nosing with the ship's commanders.

"Lieutenant Hausler, we are secure in the hold," came Trace's voice from up front. "You are green for departure."

"Hausler copies Major, PH-1 is green for departure." There followed a clang and thump as the grapples disengaged, then a short burst of downward thrust from the directionals. Main thrust followed, building intensely to bring them clear of *Phoenix*'s shadow, then easing as PH-1 acquired her course — straight for *Tantotavarin*, three hundred kilometres away.

"Commander, I'd like some more details on *Tantotavarin*'s Captain," said Trace above the dull roar of engines at low thrust. "I've read the briefing, it's a bit thin."

Tantotavarin's Captain was named Kaledramani. Human Fleet knew him as 'Killer Kaled', and he was nearly as infamous among humans as Captain Pantillo had been among tavalai. As a marine, Trace paid less attention to the tales of tavalai spacers than she did to those of tavalai marines.

"Kaledramani is known as a tavalai nationalist," said Suli, with her usual encyclopaedic knowledge of such things. "He's a hardass, very aggressive by tavalai standards, and quite unorthodox.

He's not especially popular with tavalai Fleet HQ, mostly for being an opinionated pain-in-the-neck, and berating them for their conservatism. His education is Gamalan Institution, and he retains their strong backing, whatever his unpopularity elsewhere."

"What's your best guess at his state of mind here?"

"I think if he'd had his way, he would have opened fire on us by now," said Suli. "Not because it would please State Department, but because we've assaulted a tavalai institution, and principle demands it."

"By that principle," said Erik, "he'd also have to open fire on *Kanamandali*."

"Most tavalai might find that a dilemma," Suli replied with certainty. "Kaledramani won't. Tavalai are allowed to squabble with tavalai. Aliens aren't, humans in particular."

"So he hates humans?" Trace asked.

"No more than most tavalai military," said Suli. "The reports say he's one of those tavalai who believe that in order to run the Spiral, tavalai have to whole-heartedly commit to the principle of tavalai supremacy. Most tavalai struggle with that on some level, not because they're kind-hearted and egalitarian, but because they're so damn procedural and bureaucratic that they can't accept a system where some people don't get a say. Every box on the input form must be ticked. Shilu says tavalai democracy is less about social justice than it is about the obsessive compulsion to address every detail."

"Huh," said Trace.

"Lieutenant Dale tells me that tavalai have no word for 'hate'," said Erik. "A hundred words for 'annoy', or 'irritate', but nothing for 'hate'."

"He told you that?" Suli asked curiously.

Erik nodded. "He said an old karasai told him, in Gamesh. Over a drink, before tavalai Fleet took them off-world."

"His name was Tooganam," said Trace. "That old frog made quite an impression on Dale. So listen up, we're going into this expecting trouble. Nothing we can do except hope that Killer Kaled remains bound enough by tavalai principle that he won't shoot us or threaten us with torture. We've been told we're not allowed any weapons, but they said nothing about armour, so we'll take what we can get.

"We're allowed five in total, Commander Shahaim is the most knowledgable about Kaledramani and all that tavalai Fleet structure, so that leaves me and two marines. I picked Private Krishnan because we've worked together just recently, and Lance Corporal Haynes is his usual wingman in Second Squad. Captain Debogande and Commander Shahaim, please try to position yourself so that one of us marines is closer to anyone you're speaking to than you are. We will maintain respectful distance, and if anyone gets in your face, a marine will move between you. Never accept anything handed to you until a marine has inspected it, and in the event of a hostile act, cover in place and let the marines deal with it."

It was all they could do, summonsed to appear on *Tantotavarin* with no weapons. Tavalai were rarely treacherous, so physical danger was unlikely, but State Department had already tried to kill Erik twice (that they knew of) and Captain Kaledramani threw in a new wrinkle. If he felt that *Phoenix*'s actions posed a significant enough threat to tavalai security, he might just feel inclined to listen to State Department's wishes. The real question was whether Admiral Janik, representing the rebel faction of tavalai Fleet, could manage to persuade Kaledramani of State Department's corruption first.

Erik made a private uplink to Trace's inner ear. A click as she answered. *"That won't be seen as favouritism, bringing Krishnan along?"* he asked her. She was usually scrupulous to avoid any appearance of favouritism toward individual marines. Picking the same marine twice for close quarters escort, when that marine was not a part of her usual Command Squad force, seemed unusual.

"Command Squad's exhausted," she replied. *"And they've got a ton of work to get their suits operational again, we pretty much ruined everything on Kamala. I needed someone else I've worked with recently, and Krishnan fits the bill."*

Erik might have told her she didn't actually need to come at all, but that would have been disingenuous, because he was very glad she had. He might also have told her that if Command Squad were exhausted, it logically followed that she would be exhausted too. But he knew what she'd say in both cases, or at least what the result of such discussions would inevitably be, and even if he'd wanted to stop her, he'd be in breach of long established unwritten rules between captains and marine commanders that stated he'd do no such thing. Their relationship, perhaps, had evolved to the point where they no longer needed to drag every point of dispute into the open and beat it to death.

"Well thanks," he said instead. *"I'd barely see Krishnan otherwise, he's a good kid."* All three of them had shared something intense on Stoya, and whatever their ranks, such bonds lasted. Not for the first time, Erik was struck by the fundamental absurdity of rank and command. If they'd both been civilians, that experience would have marked him and Krishnan as friends for life. Here, the bond was just as profound, but to socialise would be an irresponsible abuse of protocol, exposing Krishnan to resentment from others who lacked such a powerful friend.

"He's told everyone about Stoya," Trace replied, with a smile the voice-synthesiser managed to catch. *"I mean everyone. Makes you sound like Master Sergeant Pan reincarnated."* Master Sergeant Pan Xinchun had been a legend of the Marine Corps from the war against the krim, and the most decorated post-Earth human soldier ever.

Erik smiled. *"Well I hope he didn't compare my flying to Master Sergeant Pan, because I understand that like all marines, Pan couldn't fly for shit."* Though he couldn't see her face, Erik could smell Trace's amusement.

Hausler spun PH-1 at midpoint and decelerated toward *Tantotavarin*, the light thrust pushing the passengers into their chairs in the illusion of a third-of-a-G. Erik accessed external cameras on his glasses. The lenses gave him a holographic 3D display of the surrounding starfield, and as he panned his head, he could actually see the surrounding ships unaided — little, dull points of light that lacked the luminescence of stars. It was very rare, in deep space, to visually see any other ship without magnification and motion tracking, let alone so many. He was struck by a memory — sitting in a class at the Academy, and listening to a warship captain reciting a deep space rendezvous that he'd seen during the war, where human and chah'nas formations had come together to exchange views. Seven ships, that captain had said, he could see bare-eyed, all in proximity. All the cadets had been very impressed. Panning about, Erik stopped counting at twenty, none of them human save *Phoenix*. He wondered what expressions the cadets would be wearing should he step before them tomorrow, and tell tales of the things he'd seen. Awe and wonder, to be sure… but also wariness, perhaps contempt or even hatred, depending on how much of Fleet Command's propaganda tales they believed.

Tantotavarin's coms chatter to PH-1 was businesslike, directing Hausler to the upper six-berth on the big, armoured Midships.

"Currently latched on, I can see shuttles from Toguru, Kanamandali and Vakala," Ensign Yun observed from Hausler's co-pilot seat. *Toguru* was the State Department ship. *"Toguru and Kanamandali shuttles have detached, but it's a fair bet their passengers are still aboard."*

"Romki says tavalai sometimes hold big meetings where they lock everyone in a room for days at a time," Erik replied. "No one comes out until they've agreed on something, sleep or no sleep."

"I heard they make babies like that too," said Hausler, rotating the shuttle into perfect docking alignment with little thrusts from the attitude jets. They docked with a lurch and crash, an imperfect alignment of tavalai grapples with human hull. On the 'all clear', Erik, Suli and the marines unbuckled and headed for the dorsal hatch, where Erik performed the final manual adjustments to access-tube alignment personally.

An 'all clear' from the tavalai side, as alignments matched, and sensors showed a pressure lock, from human atmosphere to ear-popping tavalai atmosphere. "Piece of cake compared to last time, Kel," he told Krishnan, waiting behind to be first up the tube.

Krishnan grinned. "I'll take your word for it, Captain." He floated past, then up the tube, Haynes right behind him.

Erik thought Trace would go ahead, but she gestured him first. "I'm last this time. Captain, Commander." Bringing up the rear, which wasn't like her… and Erik gave her a suspicious look before following Haynes.

With airlocks synchronised, they could keep both doors open and pressurise the entire access tube at one atmosphere, right up to *Tantotavarin*'s outer door. But Erik closed the shuttle's outer door behind Krishnan and Haynes, himself, Suli and Trace sealed in the airlock until both marines had been admitted up the far end. The visual feed from both marines' glasses showed a tavalai greeting party at that end, all very civilised and not immediately threatening, in the tavalai style. Only then did he open the outer airlock and pull himself quickly up the cold tube.

The cycling airlock brought the expected rush of hot, thick tavalai air, and a sharp pain in the ears that forced all to equalise rapidly. Inside the inner airlock doors were big paddle scanners, through which all admitted must pass. The scans raised no alarms of concealed weapons, and Erik caught a rail, looking up and about at a space not unlike the Midships shuttle berths on *Phoenix*. Five armed and lightly armoured karasai looked down on them, dull green armour and webbing in contrast to the steel grey of the spacers, manning the berth, and conversing in rapid, professional Togiri.

A middle-sized tavalai in a spacer's jumpsuit came floating across to Erik, and caught the same support rail. He was unremarkable save for the captain's insignia on his chest, and for the fact that this tavalai was nearly black — a rare shade for them, with mottled brown patches.

"Captain Debogande," said *Tantotavarin*'s Captain, holding out a hand without any fuss at all.

Erik took it. "Captain Kaledramani. Commander Shahaim, my second. Major Thakur, Phoenix Company. Lance Corporal Haynes, and Private Krishnan." There were no translators activated, though probably the crew used them in earpieces. Many of the best tavalai Fleet commanders learned English thoroughly from an early phase of training. Erik had wondered lately why the same was not required of human Fleet commanders with Togiri. Captain Pantillo had been somewhat fluent, entirely by his own initiative.

Kaledramani did not shake hands with the others — the prerogative of a higher-ranked man. "Captain," he said, in that deep, thickly-accented tavalai voice. "I have heard many tales of your exploits in Kantovan System. Let me be clear — Admiral Janik may outrank me, but the Nakiakani Institution delegation off the vessel *Gobigana* confirm my status as senior Fleet officer present."

How the tavalai figured that, Erik did not know. But this was *Tantotavarin*, ibranakala-class carrier and legend of the tavalai Fleet. Surely Kaledramani had not risen to such a position without first attaining the favour of some of the many legal authorities that comprised tavalai government. Suli had only said that he was unpopular with Fleet *command*...

"Then I'm talking to the right man," said Erik, far less impressed with tavalai complications than he'd once been. "Why have we been summonsed?"

"Captain, I have people on this ship who wish you executed. And I have people on this ship who claim that you have assisted to right a wrong. I also hear alarming tales that you might be carrying hacksaw technology. This on its own is illegal, and grounds for the most severe penalty."

"There is nothing on my vessel that the Dobruta have not approved of," Erik replied with an impatient stare. "I doubt your authority has expanded *that* far in recent days, Captain Kaledramani. Or do you think to displace the Dobruta from their role of all these thousands of years?"

Kaledramani just considered him. Erik knew he'd been getting better at reading tavalai expressions, but this particular tavalai gave him nothing. It was unsettling. "You don't deny it?"

"A-class carriers are classified, Captain," Erik replied. "I confirm or deny nothing."

Kaledramani made an expression that might have been exasperation. That he, one of the most decorated captains in his

Fleet, should have to suffer this evasive alien upstart on his own deck. "Captain Debogande," he said. "You're going to tell us exactly what you did in Kantovan System, and who told you to do it. That is why you are here. Best that you stop these games, and tell the truth."

"Admiral Janik has told you his evidence of the crimes of your State Department?" Erik replied.

"What conversations I may or may not have had with Admiral Janik are likewise classified," Kaledramani said drily.

"And yet you do this criminal organisation's bidding even now? Are you a captain, or a pet?" Saying it to a chah'nas captain, on his own deck, could have gotten Erik killed on the spot. Tavalai were different. Yet even so, the usually-bustling Midships berth seemed very still and quiet.

Kaledramani eyed him up, with cool contempt. "Little Debogande. You talk and you bluster. You think your big name carries weight here. You used it to impress the politicians on Ponnai. You used it to talk your way into the Tsubarata, claiming to speak for all humanity. Now you sit at equal-V, outnumbered thirty-to-one, off-ship with only a skeleton crew to man your bridge, and you think your name and your words can get you out of this mess yet again." He put a thick finger in Erik's chest. "You are not Captain Pantillo. That was a great man. This is barely his shadow."

Erik stared back. "One destroyed drysine ship-building facility in sard space says differently. They had a mixed sard/deepynine fleet. We killed perhaps half. Where were you, brave frog?"

"I have heard this tale," said Kaledramani, unimpressed. "I do not believe it. It is spread by a conniving Dobruta who even now has been recalled to answer for his actions. Now it is spread by a rebellious Fleet faction who seek to destabilise the tavilim. You will be my guests on this ship, Captain, Commander. You will stay here until you have told the truth. Those are my orders. You will know that I am very good at following orders."

"We will not be your hostages," Erik growled. "This is against all tavalai protocol. We were not invited here for this."

"I never liked tavalai protocol," Kaledramani snorted. "My fellow Fleet captains are far more polite than me. Many of them are dead, while I survive." He gestured up and about at the armed karasai, with very good firing vantages, should the order be given. "I have many more karasai than just these. Do not tell me I shall need them."

A single, small dot drifted between the two captains. It took Kaledramani a moment to notice. Then the dot buzzed its wings, rapidly, holding a neutral hover in zero-G. Kaledramani stared at it, with an expression that was, for the first time, neither cool contempt, or outright dislike.

"Do you recognise this?" Erik asked him. "Educated man that you are?" The bug buzzed again. A shout followed from one of the karasai, as he managed to get a closeup visual.

Kaledramani held up a fast hand, to forestall shooting. To his credit, he did not look afraid… though that was a psychological peculiarity of the tavalai, to feel fear, but not panic. He peered more closely, wide-set eyes swivelling inward to focus on the insectoid machine. Upon closer inspection, its tiny, micro-filament parts gleamed in the artificial light, with brilliant intricacy.

"It *is* true," he said cautiously.

"Captain Pantillo taught me always to expect the worst," said Erik. This order-following automaton of a captain was keeping him from Lisbeth, and *Phoenix*'s Captain from his ship. He was abruptly sick of it all. "If you'd followed his advice, you'd never have let us aboard. Your sensors do not detect these. We've many more. At best, you'd all be dead in seconds. Perhaps half your crew, in minutes. At worst, we could plug into your systems, and gain control of your vessel."

Kaledramani's eyes narrowed. "I think maybe you have only one. And this one is a bluff."

More assassin bugs rose into the air at Erik's back. Trace and her marines carried them, under the basic control of Trace's AR glasses. They'd lately agreed that this would be their course of action, should anyone pull this particular stunt. Styx assured them that Erik's threats were no bluff.

"Try me again," he dared Kaledramani, with contempt. "You have no idea what you're dealing with, or who you're talking to. If I wanted out of this party, I'd take remote command of all tavalai ships and have them destroy each other. *Phoenix* would not need to fire a shot."

"Why don't you?" Kaledramani growled.

"Because manners are the thing I like best about tavalai. Until now, the only ones of you to abandon manners were State Department. You'll see shortly what we do to *them.* Commander, Major. We're leaving."

Noone stopped them. Only once they were back aboard PH-1, and the assassin bugs safely stowed back into the marines' webbing pouches, did the usually restrained Suli Shahaim bite back a laugh. "That's gonna leave a mark," she chortled, giving Erik a look of flashing amusement from the neighbouring seat.

"He's gonna have to dip his ego in cold water after that one," Krishnan agreed cheerfully.

Erik was too angry to share the humour. "Yeah, let's just hope we don't get shot down on the way back. Lieutenant Hausler, keep a *very* sharp eye out."

"I copy that, Captain's been pissing everyone off again. Situation normal, we are good to go."

Hausler undocked with a lurch, shoved them quickly out while spinning, then got underway with a short kick from mains — not an alarming or violent exit, but neither a polite one. Erik's uplink crackled, and he accessed.

"That's the first time I've ever seen you be an asshole," Trace told him. *"I couldn't be more proud."*

"I just admitted to him that we've a queen aboard," Erik replied without humour.

"He knew. They all knew, or would shortly find out. Makimakala may have admitted it to their oversight already..."

Phoenix overrode her in mid-sentence. *"Hello Captain, this is Shilu. We read multiple incoming jump entries, vector originating from parren space. IDs announce that they're the Domesh Fleet. Looks like Aristan's people finally arrived."*

CHAPTER 5

Lisbeth was eating 'loran', the parren final meal of the day, when the messenger arrived. The Domesh man passed the sentries' inspection at the door, then went with head bowed in his black robe into the colourful world of Togreth women at their meal. Lisbeth's maids stared at him in displeasure, and Semaya rose before he could disturb Lisbeth, and demanded something with a single word.

The messenger bowed low to avoid eye contact, and extended a hand. Semaya took the paper sheaf with a frown, and read it. She dismissed the black intruder with a wave, and settled herself at Lisbeth's side, a graceful coil of slender limbs.

"Semaya, what is it?" Lisbeth asked.

"An invitation from Gesul," said Semaya. *"For an evening event."*

"Event?" Lisbeth had heard several words from Semaya's lips, yet the translator gave her only one. "What sort of event?"

"A drink, and perhaps a performance. It is an old custom, now mostly followed by the higher classes. The common people have their television."

The distaste in Semaya's voice made Lisbeth smile. Her mother had spoken just the same way, of such common entertainments. "Well I think that sounds very nice. Should we send a reply that we will attend?" She glanced after the messenger, but he had already left through the guarded door.

"There is no need. The acting-senior of all the Domesh has given you an invitation. You shall not refuse."

"Ah," said Lisbeth, resuming her meal. "I understand." The meal was pleasant, sitting crosslegged on the low, cushioned chairs, little more than raised platforms, barely off the floor. When she had first arrived in this place, she had eaten mostly alone, perhaps with her own television screen, watching parren entertainments with her translator on, trying to get a sense of these elegant, elaborate people. But lately as her star had risen, she realised that she was technically a 'pushanar' — the head of a household, with servants and guards instead of family, it was true, but essentially the same thing. And so she'd begun to take her meals like this, with all her maids together, eating and talking without regard for rank.

Rather than be offended by the informality, her maids had been delighted, and now they talked into the evening on all manner of things, from customs to marriages, to the affairs of great families and the latest scandals and gossip. And they had all been intrigued to hear Lisbeth's tales of her own family, though of course she told them only the light entertainments, not the serious matters. It nearly made Lisbeth kick herself that she hadn't thought of this eating arrangement sooner. She had learned more about the parren in just a few days like this than she had in all her previous books and history lessons.

At a suitable time after dinner ended, Semaya clapped her hands for the dishes and low tables to be taken. Lisbeth's hair was still in good order, so it was a simple matter of donning the flowing outer gown, like a red silk cape off her shoulders, before departing into the hall beyond. This time Semaya accompanied her, walking with a studied elegance amidst the black-robed men of the guard. Lisbeth tried to copy her walking style, slim hands clasped before her and shoulders barely moving, but it was impossible.

About one corner, Lisbeth saw a black-robed parren seated in cross-legged meditation before the statue of a lion-like creature. Before him rested a pole-weapon — a koren, Lisbeth recalled — its deadly half-blade sheathed for now. At his side was a cup of water, full to the brim.

"I've seen several Domesh meditating by the statues like this one," Lisbeth asked curiously. "Surely there are better places to meditate?"

"Easier places," Semaya agreed. *"That is the purpose. They are trainees. He will meditate for days, visited by his instructor. Should he find the level of water in the cup diminished, the student will fail."*

Parren could meditate to a trance-state, Lisbeth knew, even moreso than humans. Achieving it would slow bodily metabolism to such an extent that food and water were unnecessary for long periods. Doing it here, in busy halls with colourful decorations and attention-grabbing statues, only made the task more difficult.

"I've read all about the history of this temple," Lisbeth said to Semaya, with the faint bewilderment that she felt of many parren things. "It's brand new, there are parts still under construction, but the old Tahrae temple beneath its foundations existed for some centuries before the end of the Machine Age, then the site was left vacant after that destruction for twenty five thousand years. I had *thought* that Domesh traditions were taken directly from the Tahrae, yet in this replica of the old temple, we see all this colour and decoration."

"The Tahrae practised Domesh abstinence and deprivation," Semaya replied calmly. *"Yet this temple was for the rulership of all parren. Not all parren practised those ways, then as now. To accommodate the tastes of all, the Tahrae chose a style less subdued than many Domesh today might prefer."*

"I see," said Lisbeth. "Are all Domesh pleased with the temple's design?"

Semaya smiled, and gave Lisbeth a knowing look. *"All Domesh are pleased with nothing,"* she said, with more than a hint of pride at Lisbeth's progress.

The hall outside Gesul's quarters were lined with robed Domesh guards, each with koren held tall in one hand, like staffs. Lisbeth tried to keep her posture upright and her breathing calm as her entourage passed through them. So *many* guards. Was this normal?

The doors were huge and heavy, opened with ceremonial flourish by servants who went down on one knee as Lisbeth, Semaya and Timoshene entered. Within was an atrium, separated from the main room by a screen, upon which was painted the ancient scene of a mountain, with the small figures of parren in terraced villages upon its flanks. Lisbeth wanted to gasp at its beauty, but Semaya tinkled a small bell, then sank to one knee with Timoshene.

Another servant retrieved Lisbeth from the atrium and beckoned her to follow. Beyond the screen was a wide room. The floor was bare stone paving, with shapes chosen for their irregular beauty. Within the room's centre, a low, square platform of polished boards held a small arrangement of common items. There was a wooden pail, a stiff-bristled whisk, and a lovely white vase, filled with long, dry flowers. In rows against the walls were small, low seats and cushions, behind equally low tables, recently cleared.

At the end of the room, a single occupant remained from the recent meal — Gesul, Lisbeth recognised the tall shape, and wide shoulders within the black robe. She stopped before him, in the place the servant indicated, and sank to one knee as Semaya had taught her. In her own quarters, or in a neutral place, it was not necessary… but this was Gesul's place, and it required respect.

"Lisbeth Debogande," said Gesul. *"Welcome to my chambers."* As the translator piece in Lisbeth's ear cut in. *"It is not the decorum, perhaps, to entertain a young lady alone. But I have something to show you."*

It was humour, Lisbeth thought. The kind of humour she could not imagine Aristan offering. The notion that *any* parren man could find a hairy-scalped human attractive was preposterous. Lisbeth smiled politely. "Thank you for your kind invitation. Please excuse my lack of manners, I feel sure I will give some offence. I do not know these customs."

"Please," said Gesul, still with humour. He gestured to the seat beside him. *"Sit. It is not so difficult, and we are not so treacherous."*

Lisbeth did as he suggested, carefully tucking in her heels to sit crosslegged on the low cushion. Major Thakur had done this so easily, meditating on her bunk. She'd taught Lisbeth a little too, in posture and breathing. "It's a beautiful room," she offered. "I saw the rooms in the Doma Strana on Stoya III. They were beautiful too, but I prefer this."

"There are many Domesh styles. I will not bore you with the lesson, but there are many pleasing forms to rooms, gardens and other spaces. The Doma Strana was built by those in favour of a stricter style, a total deprivation of light and texture. My preferred style is called 'Shudaran', which is this…" He gestured to the

room, the bare stone, and the still life display in its centre. *"Simple things. Simple relationships between simple objects, that evoke simple memories. For me, these things bring me memories of my childhood, and of my family's cottage when I was young. It brings me peace, and harmony. Aristan criticises my taste, but I have achieved a far greater depth of mind here than with his 'Koripar' style. Minds are not identical. Even in parren of the same phase and denomination, we are all unique."*

Lisbeth nodded slowly, as another servant appeared with a tray of tea. "Aristan does not seem like a man who always appreciates uniqueness," she ventured. "From all that I hear, it seems that he wants many things to be the same."

Gesul said nothing, as the servant prepared the tea with elaborate, careful movements. Lisbeth wondered if she'd said the wrong thing. Clearly there was tension here, between Gesul and Aristan. Two different men, with two different styles. Was *that* why all those guards were in the hall outside? But if she asked that, she'd *really* be taking a chance.

"Our last conversation sent me to a great library," Gesul said finally, as the tea was poured. *"I have been there for much of the last two days. Perhaps one day I can tell you what I found. But in the meantime, I wish to show you a performance."*

Lisbeth blinked. "What kind of performance?" She'd heard tales of ritual martial arts displays, in private quarters like this. Some parren formalities even involved fights to the death. Whatever her growing fascination of parren ways, she was certain she did not want to see anything like that.

"A performance from a tale known to some parren children, but sadly few. We have old tales, Lisbeth Debogande. Humans are but a few thousand years into their modernity, but parren have been spacefaring nearly back to the age of the Fathers. So many tales are lost, yet there are those artists among us who dedicate their lives to keeping those old tales alive. I have found one such here on Prakasis, performing in the city of Lomen, on the far side of this world. I have invited them to perform for us tonight, and they are here now."

He gave a gesture, and Lisbeth realised that there must have been numerous eyes upon them from somewhere hidden, for suddenly down an adjoining passage came a thunder of feet. Performers swept into the room — actors and dancers, in the parren style, running in graceful, athletic lines to form two ranks, and bow low before them.

Lisbeth nearly gasped in delight and amazement, for these men, and even some women, were most *certainly* not Domesh, nor even House Harmony. Many of the men were shirtless, smeared with paint like the scene from some pre-technological museum display. In the bandoleer straps across their chests and over shoulders, they wore weapons, drinking horns, knives and feathers. The women wore short tops but were likewise half-naked, with great crests of feathers and simple jewels on their heads. Gesul, a man of the Domesh who deprived himself of most sensory pleasures, had invited such beautiful, sexual people as *this* into his private quarters?

Lisbeth glanced quickly at the entrance from which the actors had come, and saw several dark-robed guards turning away, in evident disgust. And a servant, who gave Gesul an indigo glare within his cowl before vanishing.

"What house are these actors?" Lisbeth asked.

"House Fortitude." The ruling house of all the parren, at present, and the one most threatened by the rise of the Domesh within House Harmony.

Of course, thought Lisbeth. House Fortitude! Favouring strength, bravery and honesty. House Harmony were reserved and sophisticated, whether Domesh or otherwise. House Fortitude, it was said, were nothing of the sort.

"And they were performing on the other side of the world, and you brought them all the way here on no notice?" she asked in disbelief. "To perform for me?"

"For us," Gesul corrected. *"As I said, such historical troupes, performing the old tales, get less attention than they should. A summons such as this will do their reputation well. And they have been well paid for their trouble."* From the evident anxiety on the faces of some of the actors, bowed to the cool stones, Lisbeth could

see that this was indeed a huge event for them. And she was struck that she'd never seen an anxious parren before. The houses were not political organisations — they were completely different psychologies. She'd always known it, but now, for the first time, she could actually see it.

Gesul gave a gesture, and the lead actor jumped to his feet, and began proudly, with a loud voice and louder gestures, to proclaim the nature of his play to the small audience. This was *not* House Harmony style, for this man was strong, bold and… well, Lisbeth had to admit it, more than a little sexy. He moved with the grace and power of a ballet dancer, a trim waist and strong chest, and his manner was everything that those of the Harmony phase would consider vulgar.

The translator missed most of what the man was saying, but Lisbeth was not concerned, for she knew enough of parren plays to know that most began with the ending first. She'd tried to explain to her maids that in human stories, the ending was usually kept a secret until it happened, but the parren had been bewildered. How did one know what the story was about if the ending was not revealed first, they'd asked? How could one appreciate the tension of finding out how things had come to such dramatic ends? And how did one know that the story was worth sitting all the way through in the first place? And Lisbeth had been forced to concede that some humans (a small and rightly persecuted minority) did insist on reading the last page of a book first, for exactly those reasons.

The floor cleared for a brief costume change, and then a few of the actors were back. These were in fact musicians, and sat with drums and string instruments about the walls, while to Lisbeth's surprise, a woman strode out, the more prominent of the two actors on the floor. The man fell to the floor — in the costume of a king, with a crest that was more of a helm, and a sword that was broken. The woman loomed over him, magnificent in a giant silver headcrest, half-naked beneath her flowing cape, with a giant spear in each hand. The drums and strings began their ominous thunder-and-wail, and the ending began.

The man at the woman's feet cried out for mercy, and this time, Lisbeth's translator caught every word. *"Halgolam!"* the man cried. *"I was your brother! I swore to you the souls of my family and kin, and now they are all slain save my wife and child! I beg of you to spare them, in the name of the brotherhood that was once ours!"*

"Brotherhood!" hissed the woman, venomously. She advanced on the fallen king, spears poised for a thrust. Halgolam, Lisbeth thought! This was a play about Halgolam, the ancient parren goddess that Styx claimed had once been her name as well! *"What are the bonds of family to a phase-shifting parren? But you did not betray me for even House or phase! You betrayed me for jewels, and for that, all your clan shall fall!"*

Abruptly the king was on his feet once more, his broken sword brandished with purpose, as he saw his begging would not work. *"There is a tide coming, Goddess of Death! A great tide of men... of MEN! Even the gods shall fall before it!"*

He lunged at Halgolam, who swept his sword aside with contempt, stepped behind the king to grab him by the hair with effortless power. Her spears dropped, and she held a blade to his throat. *"That may be true,"* she said. *"But if this is to be the last age of gods, it shall for certain be the last age of kings! Your time is ended!"*

She cut her blade across his throat, and the king fell slumped to the floor, with a final crash of drums. Actors ran from the side passage, trailing a great veil of silk, behind which Halgolam and the king picked themselves up and dashed offstage, as though the floor had been swept clean by a great wind.

"The versions of this performance are controversial," said Gesul, in the pause before the first act properly began. *"The majority of scholars claim that the tale is so old it dates to parren pre-history, when we still believed in gods like Halgolam. But a small minority claims that the tale has been changed and influenced many times by more recent parren history. And a few say that it could refer to the downfall of the drysines, and that Halgolam here is a representation of the drysines themselves."*

Lisbeth stared at him. Gesul's indigo eyes were intense within his hood. "It's too old to describe what she did," Lisbeth murmured. "Stories change so much over all that time, it can't be that simple."

Gesul made a shrugging gesture, and indicated the floor, where the next group of actors were about to commence. *"I wished to see it again, in light of what you told me. We shall see."*

Trace walked fast up the curving deck toward corridor C-2, and Aristan's quarters. She rewrapped the bandage on her arm, where she'd managed to burn it on a drop of molten steel from a welder. It annoyed her that of all the physical dangers she'd faced lately, she was now getting injured by her field kit.

At the door were Privates Spitzer and Heong, Second Squad, Charlie Platoon, waiting for her. "We've got eyes on him now, Major," said Spitzer. "He's eating, food was delivered ten minutes ago."

Trace flipped down her own glasses, blinked on the local feed, and got a picture on the lenses — a dark shape in a robe, crosslegged on the bunk as he had been the past ten days, but now eating from a tray. "And he came out of his meditation twenty minutes ago?"

"Yes Major. Ten minutes after his ships arrived." Spitzer's expression suggested he thought she might have answers. She didn't. "We ran it past the techs, spacer crew's been looking at it, they say there's no way he's got access to scan feed."

"Hmm," said Trace. She tapped her ear to indicate she was uplinking, and backed to the wall, staying clear of through-traffic. The icons showed her Lieutenant Rooke, occupied and very busy with ongoing repairs from the hit they'd taken back at Homeworld, which he was taking another pass at with some of their new drysine technology. Lieutenant Shilu was even more preoccupied on the bridge, dealing with the crazy coms traffic generated by the Domesh squadron's arrival. The Captain himself, not a chance. Sometimes the spacers who ran the ship cared a great deal about the Marine Commander's concerns, and sometimes she felt like the least significant person on *Phoenix*.

But there was one person who had both the skills, and the attention span, to reply to her query. *"Hello Styx,"* she formulated silently, to keep the privates out of the conversation. And keenly felt the absurdity, that she would have this conversation openly with the drysine queen, but not before her own marines. *"Any ideas how Aristan knows his fleet just arrived?"*

"Hello Major. My best suggestion is that he made an educated guess, having arranged it in advance. Given all the variables between now and then, my confidence in this suggestion is low."

"You're unable to detect any unique coms activity in his quarters? Some hidden uplinks?"

"I have been instructed to stay out of Phoenix's systems," Styx said primly.

"Don't bullshit me, Styx. I'm not Romki, I won't fall for it."

A short pause. *"The sensory capabilities in Aristan's quarters are primitive."*

"I've brought one of your bugs with me," said Trace. *"I'm giving you the authority to utilise its systems, through Phoenix. I'm going in to talk, tell me what you see."*

"Understood, Major."

Trace nodded to Spitzer and Heong, who prepared rifles, then opened the door. Trace walked in, unarmored, with just a pistol in her hand. Aristan's eyes registered her, deep within his black hood, but he didn't pause in his eating. Vegetarian, Trace saw. Parren ate a little meat, but their biology would not take large quantities. Many parren took that as a sign, and stayed away from meat entirely. It was, Trace thought, a matter more of biology than morality.

Trace took the one small seat against the wall table. "Nearly two hundred and thirty hours. How do you feel?"

Aristan kept eating. For a moment, Trace thought he was ignoring her. Then he spoke, a single, parren word. *"Light,"* said the piece in her ear. Another mouthful. *"And clear."*

"Good," said Trace. "Perhaps we do meditate for the same reasons."

Aristan took another mouthful of lentils, not bothering with the face veil, a difficulty while eating. He'd been uncovered for the entire Kantovan mission. Trace wondered if he felt any sense of familiarity with her, or even intimacy, in the friendship kind of way, given that shared experience. *"The Domesh meditate for a great cleansing, of both mind and body. Mind and body are inseparable. One must attain command of both."* Another mouthful. *"Do your Kulina practise a similar cleansing?"*

"Kulina are warriors," said Trace. "Warriors need food. To allow physical condition to deteriorate is unprofessional."

"Ah," said Aristan, with a faintly mocking smile. *"So. The weapon must remain sharp, however uncertain of its target."* His eyes found the gun in her hand. *"You say my body has deteriorated, yet still you bring your weapon?"*

"Rules," said Trace.

"Ah." There was nothing faint about his derision now.

"I put you out cold before you started fasting, no gun required," Trace reminded him. Aristan's smile vanished. "Jobs have rules, and some of us are better at them than others."

It was a calculated prod. Or at least she was pretty sure it was. She had to be careful, sometimes, that the urge to lash out, verbally at least, did not get the better of her. She did not need to win the argument — that would be ego talking. She simply needed to assess his state of mind, given how unstable it had been, prior to him seeing the ancient recording of his idol, Drakhil.

To her surprise, Aristan's smile returned, just a little. *"Major. You deserve an explanation. This is... difficult, for me."*

Trace was nearly astonished. Of all the things she'd thought Aristan might give her, an apology had not been among them. "I understand," said Trace. "The recording was unexpected."

"Yes. Most unexpected." He took a long, slow breath, as though attempting to recall the calm that he'd attained, in more than two hundred hours of meditation. *"One is accustomed to a certain way of doing things. To certain truths."*

"Our drysine queen," said Trace, studying him intently. "She tells me that the Tahrae were varied in their beliefs. You Domesh are a small group, it is easier to be uniform in your practices. But the Tahrae were enormous. The largest denomination of the largest House, at the time. The keepers of the drysine alliance, with all the authority that brought them. Everyone wished to be Tahrae… or at least, numbers far larger than Domesh have today.

"And so there were many different practices among them. Some dressed as you do, and found harmony in deprivation of the senses. Others were less strict, and found their harmony elsewhere. Drakhil, Styx says, was one of these."

It was a struggle for him even now, Trace could see. His eating stopped, his posture rigid, as he tried to retain composure. Trace did not know the details of recent parren history well enough to know how the Domesh had arrived at this point, but clearly there had been parren in House Harmony who practised these austere ways back in Drakhil's age, and likely well before. At some more recent point, Domesh leaders had settled upon Drakhil as their great figure of historical worship, and determined that he, too, had followed Domesh beliefs and practices.

But reinterpreting history across such vast distances was dangerous. Far less dangerous with pre-historical figures, before even electricity, and video recordings. But Drakhil's time had been modern — in some ways even moreso than today. So reviled had the Tahrae been, following the defeat of the drysines and the end of the Machine Age, that all of those recordings had been erased, cleansed from collective parren memory. Looking at Aristan's mental state now, Trace found it entirely too plausible that parren could do that *too* well — could destroy their collective memory of events to the point that history could be rewritten by those who found it convenient, without any historical record surviving to contradict this new, useful interpretation.

They'd made Drakhil out to be something he wasn't, then built an entire movement upon it. Had intended to make an empire out of it. A restoration of the great Parren Empire that had followed the drysines, led by House Harmony, and the resurgent Domesh, following in the footsteps of the rehabilitated Tahrae. An empire that could restore the parren people to greatness once more. And now, with one simple discovery, all was threatened with ruin.

"We will adjust," Aristan said finally. He resumed his food, clearly famished. *"What of my fleet? How many ships?"*

"Seven," said Trace. "*Toristan* leads them."

"Captain Maresh," said Aristan. *"A good man. I will go to them when they arrive, and then we will be free of this tavalai mess. Free to go and finally seek Drakhil's data-core. You do know where it is?"*

Trace nodded cautiously. "We know."

"Good. These will be great days, Major, for your people and mine. Great days."

"My bug has detected nothing unusual," Styx told Trace as soon as she'd left Aristan's quarters. *"However, it does occur to me that there are minuscule changes in Phoenix's systems, depending on which power mode is in use. When the ship prepares for combat, power distribution switches to combat mode, activating decentralised backup distributors. It makes very faint changes to many ship systems, which can be heard in the sound of the air systems, in the brightness of the lights, and even in the background vibration of cylinder rotation and generator systems. I had presumed that parren could not detect these changes, as humans cannot. But perhaps a parren of the meditative practice of Aristan could."*

"And he sensed the ship changing modes when the Domesh Fleet came in," Trace finished. She gave an approving nod to Spitzer and Heong, who looked happier for it, and set off back to Assembly. "Out of interest, how much more sensitive would his senses have to be than a human's, to detect those things?"

"I am ill-equipped to judge the organic sensory abilities of any species."

She always protested that, Trace thought. Like a child-averse adult being asked to change a diaper, she always found some excuse to stay clear of organic affairs. "Guess," Trace insisted.

"Lots," said Styx.

Trace smiled, ducking into the C-bulkhead stairwell and sliding down. "That's not a *personality* you're developing there, is it Styx?"

"With respect, Major, I am more than twenty thousand of your years old. The implication of your question is like you being accused of immaturity by a child."

CHAPTER 6

Erik sat in the captain's chair, and watched the pandemonium breaking out amongst the assembled tavalai ships.

"Captain, I just confirmed that translation on the *Toristan*'s last transmission," Shilu announced, reading off his second screen. "They're granting *Phoenix* de facto parren citizenship, under laws laid down in the State Department statutes… apparently there's a whole raft of them that govern relations between tavalai and parren, they go back to the fall of the Chah'nas Empire, so eight thousand years. They claim they've got the right to do that, as representatives of the highest authorities in House Harmony."

Toristan and the six parren ships with her were just five seconds light-distance away, a mere one-and-a-half-million kilometres, and closing fast. The tavalai Fleet ships had redeployed, jump engines throbbing on red-alert standby, as were those of *Phoenix*, but aiming no weapons. For the first ten minutes of the parren's entry, State Department vessels and *Tantotavarin* had taken turns advising the parren visitors that this was tavalai space, and they were in violation of territorial protocols. *Toristan* had replied only once, saying that House Harmony authorities had made an agreement with *Kanamandali*, under Admiral Janik, and thus all tavalai authorities were bound by it. That had started a lightshow barrage of lasercom transmissions between State Department and tavalai Fleet ships, and *Kanamandali*, which *Phoenix* could not hear, but could see lighting up scan like a Deliverance Day celebration.

"Captain," Shilu added, monitoring about thirty things at once with his usual grace, "I'm reading an outgoing lasercom transmission from *Toguru* to *Toristan*."

"They're not going to be happy," Shahaim muttered, perusing Scan for hints on the incoming ships' specifications. "In the middle of their big council meeting to decide how they're going to cook us, and now…"

"Captain," Shilu interrupted, "*Toristan*'s broadcasting again. It's… sir, they're not actually saying anything, they're just rebounding *Toguru*'s lasercom message." If he weren't locked into the intense-focus zone that he usually assumed in the captain's chair, Erik's jaw might have dropped. "It's… hang on, running the translation now."

"They're not going to like that," Shahaim murmured.

"Sir," said Shilu, reading off his screen, "it's… that translation's just State Department bureaucracy. It's… they're trying to tell the parren why they can't grant us citizenship. *Toristan* just threw it back in their faces and rebroadcast what was supposed to be a private conversation, that's pretty ballsy."

An uplink signal blinked from Trace. Erik knew she wouldn't bother him at such a moment unless it was important, and blinked on it. *"Captain, Aristan is asking for a coms channel to Toristan."*

"Put him on to me," Erik directed.

A click, and then, *"Captain Debogande. Allow me to talk to my ships. We will need direction and coordination if we are to get out of this without shooting."*

"I can't do that right now Aristan," Erik replied. "We're not…"

"Captain," came the testy reply. *"This venture is never going to work unless you trust me…"*

"This isn't about trust, it's strategy," Erik retorted, eyes fixed on his screens, darting from one threat to another, and the accumulating unintercepted coms traffic overflowing from Shilu's post. "There hasn't been time yet for anyone to get down to the Kamala Vault and find out exactly what we stole. *Podiga* may have told them about whatever scandals we handed over in the first cylinder we stole, but if they've found out that we stole Drakhil's diary, that message hasn't reached the State Department or *Tantotavarin* here. Combined with the fact that they're now ninety-nine percent sure we have a hacksaw queen aboard, they might figure out what we're really after."

A short pause from Aristan. *"They do not know that such data-cores even exist."*

"No, but they might wonder what could motivate a hacksaw queen to assist us in this way, and make a pretty close guess. Drakhil's diary would indicate that it must have been a pretty big secret from about then, and we went to all that trouble to grab the diary, even if they don't know what's in it. They won't want either us or her acquiring that secret.

"Right now they don't know you're aboard. If they find out, it might give away that Drakhil's diary was the target, as that's the only thing in the vault that you'd risk yourself for personally. And then they might just decide to fry us here and to hell with the consequences…"

"And State Department would thank them, on the behalf of my many enemies back home," Aristan concluded for him. *"Many of whom are far more friendly with State Department than I am. Yes, well reasoned Captain... however, I would request to receive all coms from my people, so that I can provide you with translations and possible hidden messages."*

"Yes of course," said Erik, and blinked it to Shilu's post, to give him yet one more thing to deal with. Going to have to add an extra coms post at least, he thought vaguely — warships weren't designed to deal with these political complications, and certainly not *tavalai* political complications. Coms auto-sequencing typically deal with communications on a priority basis determined by seniority and chain-of-command, but here, where chain-of-command was less than clear, Lieutenant Shilu was constantly in danger of being swamped, and was relying on the autos to catch anything important he missed.

'Could let Styx do it', the thought occurred to him. She had the infinite processing capability, and obviously the intelligence… but no. Or rather, as Kaspowitz would say, *hell* no. Once they started letting Styx take up the slack on bridge command functions, where would it stop?

"Incoming from *Tantotavarin*," said Shilu, and put it to general coms without waiting to be told — the kind of judgement call Shilu would always get right.

"Phoenix this is Tantotavarin," came an untranslated tavalai voice. Not Captain Kaledramani, Erik thought. The Coms Officer then, also an English speaker. *"You will not accompany these parren, they have no legal standing in tavalai space. Should you attempt to depart without authorisation, you will be considered in flight from tavalai justice, and fired upon."*

"Charming," Shahaim murmured.

"Package it," Erik told Shilu. "Wrap it up, then broadcast it to everyone. Add no further comment."

Shilu fought back an adrenaline-charged smile as he did that, fingers flying. "Aye Captain, packaging and sending."

"Are they even running English translators?" Shahaim asked him, meaning all the other tavalai ships, and now the parren.

"Guess we'll find out," said Erik. Five seconds for the message to travel out, a few more for *Toristan* to figure a reply, then five more seconds to travel back…

"Incoming from *Toristan*, broadcast," Shilu announced, and put that through as well.

This time it was the translator speaking, emotionless and harsh. *"All tavalai vessels, this is parren warship Toristan. The human vessel Phoenix is now protected by parren citizenship, and is a registered vessel under parren shipping codes agreed to in the Treaty of Pathanaka, in force between tavalai and parren for five thousand years. Firing upon a registered parren vessel, containing registered citizens of the Parren Empire, will result in a state of war existing between the Parren Empire and the Tavalai Confederacy. Military actions will commence at once, beginning with the border systems, placing in peril the lives of twenty billion tavalai citizens. Reconsider this folly, or see your name cursed for millennia to come."*

Deathly silence on the *Phoenix* bridge. On Shilu's coms screen, even the ongoing cross-chatter seemed to pause. "Well that got their attention," Kaspowitz muttered, still running his furious escape-trajectory calculations, and now on option twenty-five.

"That's ridiculous," Shahaim said quietly. "They're Domesh, they can't promise a state of war on behalf of their own

House, let alone all parren. They just gave away that there's something on *Phoenix* they're desperate to get."

"Might work though," Erik replied. "Tavalai are stubborn, but they're also conservative. You make a big enough threat, they'll listen. Maybe parren have figured that out after dealing with them for forty thousand years."

"Or maybe damn autocratic parren just expect to get their way and don't understand subtlety."

"No," said Erik. "Parren aren't chah'nas, they don't bluster. They calculate. Even the fringe loonies like Aristan are clever as hell. These guys are up to something." Shahaim looked wary of the much younger man's judgement, but understood well enough when the exchange of views was ended. "Lieutenant Shilu, I think now is a good time to transmit that package that Ensign Jokono has been working on. Broadcast on all channels."

"Aye Captain," said Shilu, and called up that data package. If State Department had known they possessed *that*, Erik thought, they'd surely have instructed *Tantotavarin* to destroy *Phoenix* in language that *Tantotavarin* could not ignore. Evidence that the sard alliance was illegally bought and paid for could finish the State Department for good. "Sending now."

For several minutes, nothing happened. Then *Ragada*, the senior-most vessel of the Tola Dasha, one of the oldest legal institutions in tavalai space, called Erik directly. *"Where did you get this?"* that captain demanded, and Erik could hear his true voice hoarse and trembling behind the translator's dry expression.

"Stolen," Erik said simply. "A heavy descender, docking at Chara retrieval date twelve days ago. It's currently docked with *Podiga*, you can see it with your own eyes."

"Admission of this theft is enough to see you convicted by..."

"Read the damn document!" Erik snapped. "State Department are liars and traitors to the tavalai people. They are an *illegal institution* under tavalai law, and as senior legal authority in tavalai space you must state it so. State Department have no authority to give orders to tavalai Fleet, and without that Fleet's enforcement, you have no means to keep *Phoenix* here. Jurisdiction for our circumstance now falls to the parren, we are leaving."

Communications broke off, followed by another intense series of multi-directional lasercoms between *Ragada* and various tavalai ships, including *Tantotavarin.*

"What a mess," Karle observed.

"It's a wonder the tavalai ever ran anything, let alone the whole Spiral," his co-gunner Harris agreed.

Erik felt no exhilaration to watch it, as the laser coms escalated, and ships began rolling like giant, breaching whales, bringing new lines of communication into play. It looked to Erik that the ships of tavalai state were quite literally writhing in agony. Suddenly he was frightened, overwhelmed by the sheer scale of it. Pull the right brick from the foundation of a great tower, and the whole lot could fall. No matter how rotten that brick, and how deserving of punishment, the consequences for all the billions of lives in the tower could be catastrophic. *Phoenix*'s bridge crew had had similar arguments about their human Fleet, in the aftermath of their own calamity, and the murder of Captain Pantillo. Fleet was rotten, but the consequences of bringing it all crashing down would spell catastrophe for humans everywhere. As much as Erik wanted to see those responsible punished, even he was horrified by the thought. Given what he'd seen in recent months, of the scale of the threats facing humanity, the prospect frightened him even more now than it had then. And to fatally damage the Tavalai Confederacy at such a time, and remove one of the last great, remaining obstacles to the expansion of alo/deepynine power, could be nearly as bad. He was increasingly convinced that if humanity was going to survive the alo/deepynine alliance, they were going to need tavalai help to do it. Now he saw that prospect slipping through his fingers.

Shuttles were now beginning to fly, from various tavalai ships, heading for *Ragada* this time, not *Toguru*, nor *Tantotavarin.* The balance of authority amongst the competing tavalai institutions had swung once more. Erik decided he could wait no longer.

"All hands," he announced. "Main engines start, this is a thirty-second warning. Light outbound push, we are about to move."

They didn't really need the warning — *Phoenix* was on red alert, which meant the crew cylinder was no longer rotating, and everyone was zero-G and strapped to something. But there was no need to rush, in these circumstances least of all. He uncapped the thumb and finger guards on the twin control sticks on his armrests, and tested the arm braces. Diagnostic raced across his screens, a cascade of green lights, sign that Engineering had been doing their usual excellent work despite all the recent punishment, and had everything ready to go.

"Message from *Ragada*," called Shilu. "Insisting Captain Debogande should personally attend a meeting to explain this latest evidence."

It was almost tempting. If *Ragada* could convince their esteemed institution to convince State Department to drop all charges in return. But the prospect of throwing himself upon the mercies of the tavalai legal system struck Erik as preposterous at this point, or any other point. "Thank *Ragada* on my behalf," he told Shilu. "Wish them best of luck, and peace and justice for all tavalai." Ten seconds, read the countdown timer. "But decline regretfully, because *Phoenix* is needed elsewhere. We're leaving."

CHAPTER 7

The parren called it Brehn System, and it was spectacular. Humans called it a late-stage proto-planetary disk — a solar system in formation, and still several hundred million years from maturity. *Phoenix*, *Toristan* and five of the Domesh Fleet ships entered at solar nadir — a necessity given the lethal consequences of high-V travel through the elliptic plane — and for a two-day cruise from jump, they all had an incredible view of the brilliant, glowing white disk of galactic debris. Brehn had eleven planets forming, two visible to the naked eye, and the rest at high magnification — congealing blobs of gas or rock, half-lit by the brilliant white light of what would soon become an infant G2 star.

Brehn was three long jumps from Cherichal, and right on the edge of the parren ships' capabilities, though *Phoenix* handled it easily enough. The second jump had taken them into parren space, and the course correction before the third had broken something on one of *Toristan*'s escorts, though it had decelerated easily enough, and called that they were safe, and would dock with a local shipyard for repair, if possible. *Phoenix* now spent forty hours on approach toward the Brehn elliptic to complete post-jump systems inspections, as the relevant bridge crew brushed up on their parren political and military institutions.

Brehn had no habitable worlds, and even those proto-worlds currently forming were torn by infancy volcanism, and an endless bombardment of asteroids and ice chunks. Miners of any species were usually not crazy enough to try such conditions, but with this much extractable material just floating around, they didn't need to. Brehn System had a population of between three and four million parren, their parren escorts informed them, almost all of them tied to the mining trade, and scattered in a multitude of small bases, mobile refineries, hollowed out rocks and other, makeshift habitats. On passive coms, Lieutenants Shilu and Lassa could probably have guessed that population themselves, listening to the waves of operational chatter emanating from various parts of that enormous white disk.

Four million people was a tiny number next to the big inhabited worlds of a grounded population, and so, as in human politics, the mining systems were agglomerated together with the bigger systems, from where this entire region of space would be run. Parren political districts generally had three such inhabited systems, plus perhaps fifty uninhabited ones that nevertheless possessed a large enough mining and industrial population to rate representation in the parren parliament.

If it could be called a 'parliament'. Parren leaderships ruled like kings and queens, yet changed with moderate frequency without the need for elections, thanks to the constant rearrangement of the five parren Houses due to phase-change. Parren had an institution, known as the Jusica, who performed a regular census in each territory. The House with the largest percentage of population got to form the government in that region. Currently, Brehn System was ruled by House Harmony, courtesy not of Brehn's puny population, but by the fact that Drezen System, thirty-two lightyears away, was nearly forty percent House Harmony aligned, and had been for a century. Brehn System's miners got a seat in a separate parliamentary body, like a senate, which guaranteed them special rights as an independent system, but within the Harmony-run framework of this sector.

It all seemed straight forward enough to Erik, whose family had deep roots in the highest levels of human politics, and had always grasped the structural nature of such things. Less straightforward was why the Domesh Denomination got their own Fleet of warships, and other military forces, in an obvious rejection of common sense.

The answer, as near as their hosts could explain, was that each parren House had its own military, and technically the denominations weren't supposed to hold any sway. The Incefahd Denomination ruled House Harmony, and thus all House Harmony military forces obeyed the command of Tobenrah, the Incefahd Denomination's leader. Only they didn't. House politics infected military procurement, promotion and structure in ways that Erik simply did not have time to learn about in any depth, but the result was that each denomination held a certain amount of sway amongst the various units of House military — by far the most important of which, of course, were the fleet. Captain Duoam of *Toristan* was the commander of an entire House Harmony squadron — thirty ships as far as any human knew — yet he was Aristan's man, pledged mind and soul to the Domesh, as were all of his crews.

"So their military forces are divided into five Houses," Shahaim said as they'd eaten dinner over their customary post-shift review in Erik's quarters, "and each of those Houses is divided again into, what… ten denominations? Fifteen?"

"At least," Erik agreed, into the notable silence from Kaspowitz, who would normally be dominating this kind of conversation. But on a run into a place like Brehn System, he was permanently nose-down in his never-ending calculations, and not much on conversation, or sleep.

"No wonder they've been such a non-event in the scheme of Spiral great powers since the end of the Parren Empire," Shahaim concluded. "And no wonder lots of parren might be attracted to a single, charismatic leader who promised to unify the whole crazy mess and focus parren power outward for a change, instead of always fighting amongst themselves."

"Aristan's charismatic?" Geish said drily. "I hadn't noticed." And for once, Erik had agreed with the dour Scan Officer's cynicism entirely.

From the edge of the system's elliptic plane, the ships dumped their remaining hard-V and cruised for a further thirty hours into the increasingly hazardous soup. Erik recalled Argitori, where *Phoenix* had first run after Trace had broken him out of Fleet HQ's brig on Homeworld, and where they'd first encountered Styx. Kaspowitz informed them all that as messy as Argitori was, Brehn

System was approximately three-point-seven times more densely packed with rocks, ice and other ship-killers.

Soon the auto-correct was overriding the pilot once every five minutes or so, dodging some tiny object that was not yet logged on the parren's system navigation charts. That chart, Kaspowitz further informed them all, currently logged in excess of seventeen trillion objects, system-wide. Every time a ship, base, buoy or drone detected a new object (which in *Phoenix*'s case was running at nearly a hundred a minute) it would upload the object's details into the steadily growing database. That database was growing at fifteen million new objects every twenty-two hour parren cycle, logged by parren across the system, yet Kaspowitz estimated that accounting for the mass that must exist in a system exhibiting this much gravitational rotation, they'd probably logged less than ten percent of the possible objects, not counting the baby planets or the baby star.

To make things even more interesting, every few minutes, somewhere in the vast system, something would violently explode — the consequence of so much floating mass orbiting a central core with enough variance and relative-V to produce some truly impressive collisions. Most of these detonations were an extremely long way away, like everything else in space, but the collective sparkle they made on scan was enough to confuse *Phoenix*'s tactical systems into querying whether an active battle was in progress. Erik thought that if an active battle were to break out in such a system, half of the fast-manoeuvring ships would find themselves destroyed by the local environment in a few minutes, without a shot being fired.

Their final destination was a large refinery facility, currently docked on the pointy end of an egg-shaped asteroid that contained a population of a few tens of thousands of parren spacers. The asteroid rolled, generating gravity for those within, while the refinery did not — an unglamorous steel bulk with multiple spherical storage tanks to power its central machinery, turning raw materials into steels, plastics and various gasses. Numerous small insystem runners and haulers parked about, or were docked directly. As Erik brought *Phoenix* into an adjacent park about thirty kilometres from the five-kilometre asteroid, he could see the fusion thrusters built into the rock, making it like a very slow moving spaceship in its own right. The rock was scarred with countless craters, like a piece of cheese nibbled by a thousand mice, and would doubtless take small hits every few months. The big engines would adjust its track just enough to miss anything bigger, and the navigational charts were good enough to spot most of them coming years in advance… but even so, there were unpredictabilities in a system like this, and new trajectories being created all the time by the bigger collisions elsewhere in the system. Localised cascade effects from nearby big hits could create a rain of destruction that no low-powered thrust was going to save them from. It wasn't the kind of place any parents wanted their kids to grow up working in, for sure, and if parren psychology worked anything like human, everyone here would be earning danger pay.

As soon as they'd arrived, *Toristan*'s Captain came, and one other, by shuttle to dock at *Phoenix*'s Midships. It was the middle of *Phoenix*'s second-shift — midnight, by Erik's sleep clock — but no matter, spacers did not get to choose the time when things happened, and it put Draper and Dufresne in their chairs in the natural middle of their working cycle.

Erik waited outside the briefing room, talking with Kaspowitz with coffee in hand, looking at the displays the Nav Officer had been obsessing over, while the parren officers and Aristan settled into the room behind, with the rest of *Phoenix*'s senior crew.

"I can't talk for Stefan," Kaspowitz was saying, "but I don't trust scan at anything beyond low-V in this mess. The luminosity variance is extreme even for a rock storm like this place, and the percentage of stuff in the lowest visibility range is high… we're just not going to see very much in any high-V manoeuvres."

"Stefan's working on the sensitivities now," Erik replied. Second Lieutenant Stefan Geish had given the impression he wasn't going to get much sleep either, despite not being invited to the briefing. "He thinks he can get another ten percent sensitivity to the invisible stuff, at least in the time we're docked here."

"Still not enough," Kaspowitz said with concern. "If we have to make a run for it in this place…"

"I know," Erik agreed, trying to get his mind to focus. So many variables to keep track of. So many possible outcomes, and so little time available to spend thinking on them. "I'm more worried about where we're going, at the moment. If anything goes wrong, it'll go wrong there."

"In which case," Kaspowitz persisted, leaning his tall frame down to talk quietly as crew passed in the corridor, "we'll have to run fast back to tavalai territory, and the fastest way back is through this place."

"Not really sure I want to head back to tavalai space right now," Erik murmured, staring at the blank wall.

"Captain, if Aristan's as trustworthy as we expect, we're not going to have a choice." Kaspowitz's tired eyes were grim with meaning.

"Yeah," said Erik, sipping his coffee. "Yeah, I know." Lisbeth. The name seemed to hang in the air between them, unspoken yet obvious. Erik had absolutely no idea what to do about it. So much was at stake, so many lives beyond just that of his sister. And yet… Kaspowitz grasped his shoulder in firm-fingered solidarity, to show he understood. "There's a chair for you in there if you want?"

Kaspowitz tapped his slate. "The parren have sent us good charts on the Dofed Cluster and Cason System," he said. "I need to do a full review."

"Make sure you get some sleep," Erik said after him as the tall Nav Officer left. "I'm sure even you function better with sleep."

"Uh-huh," said Kaspowitz, and was replaced by Suli Shahaim, pausing at the door before entering.

"Erik," she said. "Don't feel you have to downplay her, just because she's your sister. She's *Phoenix* crew, and that matters to all of us."

Erik gazed at her for a moment. Suli was such a familiar, indispensable feature of the bridge. On any other ship she could have made a good captain, but on this ship she'd found her true calling — not as a cog in the machine, but as the grease that kept all the cogs smoothly humming. Suli was a very good pilot, but not a great one, just as she was very good at command, without being spectacular. Where she excelled was in anticipating the needs of others, and always being on hand to give them anything required, whether information, advice or other vital facts, before they even knew they needed it. If Captain Pantillo had been a father figure, Commander Shahaim was everyone's mother — not at all like *Erik*'s mother, perhaps, but much like the mothers of some of his more accomplished friends. Wise, unflustered and friendly, always approachable and never using her authority to bludgeon anyone. If ever you were in trouble, Suli would be there, giving simple advice, and letting you know she had your back.

"Thanks Suli," said Erik, and gestured her inside, then followed.

Erik made his way into the circle of chairs, glancing at several light-armoured marines against the walls. They were there for the visitors — Captain Duoam of *Toristan*, and his second, Captain Lalesh of *Cherow*. None had argued with *Phoenix*'s insistence that the meeting should take place in human territory. *Phoenix* had Drakhil's diary, and the means of understanding it. That being the case, it was not the parren way to argue with necessity.

Neither captain even glanced at the armed marines, but sat to either side of Aristan, huddled and murmuring in low voices. The captains were not robed, but wore jumpsuits as any species of spacer might wear. Their headwear was unusual, a stylised visor beneath a crown-like ring that served as a helmet, Erik guessed... though also, he saw it had attachments at the back. Likely it would clip to the captain's chair headrest, and secure the head in place during high-G manoeuvres. Parren were slim compared to humans, with deadly-fast reflexes, but likely they would suffer worse in combat manoeuvres. Behind their visors, both captains were nearly as covered as Aristan, with only their lower faces visible.

Erik sat between Trace and Suli, the other chairs occupied by Romki, Shilu, Lieutenant Jalawi of Charlie Company, and *Phoenix*'s lead shuttle pilot, Lieutenant Hausler. Everyone else who needed to listen would be doing so elsewhere on the ship, but these were the people most likely to contribute back. Given Jalawi and Hausler's presence, Erik had some idea what Trace was thinking.

He glanced at Romki, tired as always, glasses pushed up on his bald head, and considering the parren with thoughtful hostility. That was new, from Romki. Usually he was the one instructing everyone on how important it was to not resort to base emotions when dealing with aliens. But Lisbeth had been one of his better friends on *Phoenix* — perhaps even his best friend. He usually approached these briefings with intellectual detachment. Now he looked like a poker player scheming how to take a hated rival's money, house and savings.

"Let's begin," Erik told them, and attention turned his way. "The data-core is in Cason System, in the Dofed Cluster. The planet is named Pashan, and its moon is Cephilae. We cannot plan what we will do there until you tell us about the Cason System's defences, its politics, and that of the Dofed Cluster."

Aristan and his captains consulted briefly. Aristan sat back, with a cool flourish of robed sleeves, content to let Captain Duoam speak. *"The entire Dofed Cluster is a single political entity,"* said the Captain, via translator. *"House Fortitude rules there. Cason System is not well populated. Cephilae is a scientific curiosity. There are interesting life forms there — animals that live in the seas. Intelligent animals, but animals all the same. Scientists study them, and other things. That is most of the population, and some wandering visitors, and temples for contemplation"*

"Tourists," Romki interjected, having discerned the concept that the translator had not.

"There is a single, small orbital station," Captain Duoam continued. *"A static population of perhaps a few thousand. House Fortitude fleet ships will visit there frequently. There is no way to know when. It is random, and often. Going there without invitation, we will take a chance."*

"How many ships on that regular patrol?" Erik pressed.

"Just one. A scout. But fast. The distances between Dofed Cluster systems is small. It can return with reinforcements within ten rotations. We must be faster than that."

Erik glanced at Trace. "You guys have to identify it first," said Trace. "Once you do that, we can get it within a few days, I'd think, depending on whether we have to excavate. But it could be complicated."

She looked at Romki. Romki nodded. "Cason System's star is of variable intensity," he said. "Pashan and Cephilae are right on the outer edge of the habitable zone. Drakhil's diary gives very precise directions to the location, but some of the language indicates a problem. He speaks of frozen lakes of liquid water, with ice on top but kept considerably warm in their depths by tectonic activity… no doubt where those interesting creatures live. The problem is that the only lakes on Cephilae that are frozen today are at the poles. Everything else is liquid. And obviously, liquid water, at warmer temperatures, expands to cover a much larger area. Drakhil's directions to the data-core's location are from a lake shore, and they are precise. But the lake shore has moved. I judge, and the *Phoenix* techs who helped me to simulate it agree, that it could have moved by more than a kilometre, as the Cason System sun has warmed, and the atmospheric temperature with it."

"But you've got other geographic features by which you can find the location?" Trace asked.

"Yes," said Romki, a little uncertainly. "There are hills mentioned, and other landforms that should not have moved in the twenty five thousand years since the diary was written. But we're going to have to wait until we're there. I know that military people like to have far more certainty than that, but I'm afraid it's the best I can do. Even Styx agrees that the uncertainties are too many to be certain before we arrive. Doing so could be dangerous, and lead us to assume too much. It is safer to arrive, and then search for features that match the described terrain."

"So we don't even have positioning coordinates?" Suli asked with faint dismay.

"Just words Commander," said Romki. "And words written in Klyran, at that. I am confident it will be enough, as is Styx, who is rather good at topographical calculations, as you might imagine. But it may take time."

"How much time?"

"Somewhere between a lot and a little," Romki said apologetically. "It's the best we can do."

"Looks like it could be a water recovery," Trace said to Lieutenant Jalawi. "You've got more experience of those than anyone else aboard."

Understanding dawned in Jalawi's eyes, as he realised why he'd been invited. "I do," he agreed. "Just hope those water critters aren't carnivorous."

"Parren will undertake this search," Aristan interjected. *"You will hand over your coordinates to us, and we will perform the recovery. It is parren territory, a treasure left behind by the greatest parren of all history. Upon recovery, you can trust that we will share the data-core with you. After all, your drysine queen is the only entity capable of utilising such a treasure. Without her assistance, it is useless to us."*

All the *Phoenix* crew looked at Erik in alarm. Erik gazed back at the cool, hooded parren gaze across the circle of chairs. "No," he said, with a little more steel than he'd intended.

"But Captain," said Aristan, so very reasonably. *"Surely you do not think that you alone recovered Drakhil's diary? I recall that I was there too."*

"You are one person. My entire crew put their lives on the line. No." Their stares remained locked… or Erik thought they did. Within the folds of his hood, Aristan's eyes weren't entirely clear. Lisbeth. Again, the word that neither man needed to say. It hung in the air between them, like a dagger pointed at Erik's heart.

"And you will share this treasure with us?" Aristan asked mildly. *"Once you have recovered it?"*

"That was the agreement that was imposed upon us," Erik agreed. Lisbeth, again.

Aristan considered him for a long moment. *"Very well,"* he said at last. *"Given the lack of alternatives, we shall proceed."*

After the parren had been escorted away, Suli looked at Erik with disbelief. "Does this seem as staggeringly obvious to everyone else as it does to me? I mean, he's going to screw us, first chance he gets."

"Show of hands," said Jalawi, and put his own hand up. Others followed — Romki's immediately, then everyone else. Erik too. "Commander, I believe the answer is 'yes, it's staggeringly obvious to everyone.'"

"We show him up, for one thing," Suli continued. "You heard him just trying to take credit for recovering the diary, despite doing only a fraction what we did? Here's a guy running the parren cult of personality to the max, and he's not going to like sharing the credit. This has to be his success, or what's it good for?"

"It's worse than that," Romki said tiredly. "Aristan and the last half-dozen or so Domesh leaders to proceed him have built that cult of personality, as you put it Commander, around the figure of Drakhil. Yet now Aristan has discovered that Drakhil was not the man they've invested so much in. Aristan has a choice — he can either embrace the truth, and risk losing everything that the Domesh have built over the past few centuries, all their gains toward the restoration of great power at the head of all parren… or he can attempt to hide that truth, and make it all go away. 'All', in this instance, meaning us. *Phoenix*."

"But if he destroys us," said Shilu, frowning, "then he destroys Styx. And how can he read the data-core then? Or make any use of it at all?"

"We've just come to him with living proof that there is not just one hacksaw queen left in the Spiral," Suli returned. "There are lots, all deepynines. Losing Styx isn't the end of his chances. He thinks he may have to wait a long time, but this is a man who plays the long game. He can hold onto the data-core until then, and maybe use it to trade for influence with the deepynines."

"This would be almost comically unwise," came Styx's first interjection from the room coms.

"No question," Suli agreed. She was not in the habit of agreeing with Styx on anything. Erik could see her forcing herself. "Incredibly unwise. But Aristan is not a wise man. He's an extremely clever man. That's a different thing entirely."

"And what a transformation in the man," Romki said, in weary dismay of tediously obvious people. "Not long ago he was practically begging to make Styx's acquaintance. Now we mention her and he barely reacts. He has learned that Styx is not his ally, and Aristan is only interested in those who will help him to power."

"You really think the deepynines would just kill him and take the data-core?" Shilu said skeptically. "I can think of a much worse scenario — that they don't. Look at their behaviour lately. They've expanded into sard territory, obviously looking for a new ally there, to peel them away from the tavalai. We suspect they might be doing something similar to the chah'nas. Why stop there? If they were to gain a foothold with the parren, it would take an unscrupulous megalomaniac to do it, who didn't care what evil he aligned himself with. They wouldn't get a better opportunity than Aristan. And they could build him up, give him technology and power to impress his followers, and get their own pet parren leader. Maybe even bring him to power, to the horror of all the parren's neighbours."

"Aristan's not that bad," Trace said sombrely. "He's just… focused. Too focused." She glanced at Erik. And saw that he understood. She nodded, a little glumly, at that recognition that not every character trait she valued was automatically good. And considered him a little longer, perhaps noting how he was not speaking much, but rather listening, and thinking, as Captain Pantillo had so often done in this room. He had a smart crew, and if he spoke too much, they'd shut up and listen to him, instead of volunteering their own very useful opinions.

‘Good leaders lead,’ Pantillo had told Erik once. ‘Great leaders listen.’

“Okay,” said Erik, seeing that the initial exchange of views was done. “We’re going to move forward on the assumption that our parren allies are going to try and kill us. Obviously they can’t do that before we’ve shown them where the data-core is. We might want to delay making that obvious until the last possible moment. We *might* even want to throw in a feint.”

He glanced at Trace. Trace nodded approval. “We’ve got other platoons,” she said. “Not all of them have to be going to the right target.”

Lisbeth, Erik thought again, with growing dread. If Aristan betrayed them, he would no longer have any use for her.

CHAPTER 8

Lisbeth woke, thinking that she'd heard a buzzing. Probably she'd been dreaming. Her bug had killed a bird yesterday... or everyone assumed it had. One of the birds that hopped on the balcony in search of crumbs from a meal, or remaining seeds from the feeder that had spilled upon the tiles, had been found dead by a potplant. The theory was that her bug had been sunning itself, as it survived on solar power and would go dead without regular recharging, when the bird had discovered it, and mistaken it for a snack.

Semaya had been the one to find it, and had been displeased. She'd laid the small, feathered body upon the footstool sometimes used for scents and candles, and a number of the maids, and even some of the Domesh guards, had taken a moment to kneel and wave a scented candle over it, before going about their other business. Parren called it *toufik*, and it was close to the human notion of karma, only toufik was the accumulation of psychic energy within a particular parren phase. Good or bad toufik could drive a parren toward flux, and Lisbeth was learning that not all fluxes were equal. It made a very human kind of sense, in fact, if one thought of bad toufik as the accumulated mental stress preceding a breakdown. But then, good toufik could lead a parren toward a *toushar*, or an enlightened flux — the kind of phase-change that could herald great new beginnings, and an evolution of self to a wiser and more authoritative plane. The death of a well-liked and often-fed species of bird on Lisbeth's balcony did not represent the good kind of toufik, and it was clear that her staff felt sullied by it. Lisbeth wondered if there wasn't still a little room in the tiny machine's processor for extra programming about social protocols.

She glanced at the gauze curtain separating her chambers from the wide balcony. It was reflex, given the assassin who had come from that direction about three weeks ago... but that assassin had met her own, very small personal assassin, and she had not been particularly nervous of the episode repeating itself. She could see a robed guard out by the railing now, but he was standing obvious and exposed, as an assassin would not. In fact, he seemed to be gazing upward. Somewhere above, a bright light was burning, moving slowly across the sky. Lisbeth could see the guard's shadow, cast upon the curtain by the distant glare. Then came a boom, and the faint rattle of glass, and objects on tables. Then another, and one more. Sonic booms, at such high altitude that they possessed little force, like the high-altitude lightning in tall storm clouds that flashed directly overhead with brilliant light, yet only muttered and rumbled instead of booming. It was a common phenomenon over the Kunadeen, and occasionally over Lisbeth's home of Shiwon. Three incoming shuttles all at once was a little strange, though.

Lisbeth heard soft, running footsteps, and turned on her pillow to see Semaya, coming from the adjoining staff quarters in slippers and robe. She ran to the curtain, a slim shadow in the dark, and peered out and up to the sky. Then murmured something to the guard, and came to the bed, tapping at her ear. Lisbeth blinked, and fumbled for her AR glasses on the bedside table — they were easier than the straight earpiece, and the fact that they were also anti-social and rude would not bother anyone at night, amongst her personal staff. The earpiece went in, and suddenly the translator was speaking Semaya's words.

"Lisbeth, we will have visitors. You must be up."

Lisbeth blinked at her through the lenses. "Now?" The lenses showed her the time was an hour past midnight. Few other icons showed, as the temple system censored what she could access.

"Yes now." Semaya threw the covers aside, with most un-parren-like forwardness, and ushered her up. Bewildered, Lisbeth did as instructed, and now there were more maids rushing to assist, and others dressing themselves in preparation for visitors.

"Who is coming?" Lisbeth asked, as she was helped into a long coat that was half-a-robe, black patterned with gold and silver thread, one of those regal parren inventions that Lisbeth would have *loved* to take back to Shiwon and wear at parties to the envy of all.

"One of Aristan's," said Semaya. *"We are not sure."* The guard from the balcony strode past — Timoshene, Lisbeth saw,

meeting with two more guards, then going past the wide space of chairs and low bookshelves to the door.

Lisbeth expected the maids to seat her, and make at least a pass at her hair, which was a frizzy mess just off the pillows, as usual. But Lilien, who was best at hair, simply pulled the robe's hood up and tucked it over Lisbeth's head. So they were truly going out then, Lisbeth thought as she moved to the central room by the chairs to take her place for the formal greetings. And the robe was dark, at night, and with the hood up she was not expected to show off her stylings, but to hide.

Bells outside the entry doors rang, and the maids answered. Six Domesh guards in black robes entered, and behind them strode an *ehrlic* — Lisbeth recognised the gold robe, and the flat head-crest like a box. Ehrlic were high-level functionaries in most denominational administrations, the civilian equivalent, perhaps, to a general in an army. Some ran entire regions of government, while others performed important cabinet roles in the Kunadeen. Lisbeth was a little surprised to find one here. Beyond the balcony curtains at her back, she could hear the distant whine of approaching shuttles.

Timoshene, as senior guard and tokara, stood before the ehrlic, as the newly arrived guards spread on either side. Timoshene produced a formality of rank — a decorated and studded piece of leather that Lisbeth had not learned the name of — and the ehrlic made a show of inspecting it. Then came the formal cry, and all the room's occupants, save the new guests and Lisbeth, sank to one knee. Lisbeth reflected that she *much* preferred it when Gesul came calling, or one of her scholarly teachers, because that was so much less fuss. But ehrlic were rank and status personified, they did not truly *have* real lives, every moment of every day was ritual and structure…

The guards advanced past the bowing Timoshene, and Lisbeth frowned, because the formalities were that her maids would accompany her into armed male company, but her maids were all on one knee… and then Timoshene moved, a flash of black robes like cloth in a gale of wind. Two guards fell in a flail of limbs and drawn weapons, then shots on Lisbeth's right pop!pop!pop! with shattering force on her eardrum as she fell, somehow recalling the most basic training *Phoenix* marines had ever given her, to hit the deck when bad stuff happened.

Down and scrambling back amidst the chairs, she heard yells and ringing steel, and more shooting. Then a final, gurgling cry, unmistakable in its horror. Lisbeth stared over a chairback, preparing to run in case that final death had been one of her protectors (whoever *they* now were) and saw instead that all of the new arrivals, including the ehrlic, were down and unmoving. Several had fallen some distance from where they'd stood when Lisbeth had dropped, and Timoshene stood over the body of one, cleaning his blade with a smooth swipe of his robe.

Standing on the right, pistol in hand, was Semaya. But she was not aiming or prowling now, but rather standing silently, hands raised in an effort to look unthreatening. Lisbeth guessed what had happened, and ran close enough to see the little, thumbnail-sized dot hovering before Semaya's wide eyes on a blur of wings.

"Hey!" Lisbeth snapped at the bug, and was mildly astonished that her voice was not a trembling, fearful wail. To judge by her shaking knees and hammering heart, it should have been. "You don't hurt Semaya, if she'd wanted to kill me I'd already be dead!"

The bug took off in a wide, circling arc about the room, scanning. "Thank you," said Semaya, two of her better English words, and pulled a second gun from her robes, and handed it to Lisbeth. *"We must move fast, no questions now."*

Lisbeth nodded… and noticed that there was a maid huddled on the floor, attended by another. Lisbeth rushed to her, and found Niala, attended by Lilien, a bullet wound in her side, and quite a bit of blood. "Oh no… Semaya?"

But Semaya was amongst the bodies of the fallen visitors, retrieving things. *"There will be medical attention on the way,"* came Timoshene's translated voice in her ears. *"You were the target. You will make her safer by leaving."*

Renala came running from the staff quarters, shrugging on a cloak of her own, and tucking more things Lisbeth couldn't see somewhere safe. She too had a pistol in hand, and Lisbeth stared — Semaya had always had a faintly dangerous grace, and Lisbeth had known that surely there must be other assassins or warriors on her staff, but Renala? Renala was so small and quiet.

Semaya beckoned her, and Lisbeth ran, willing her legs not to give way as the initial rush of terrorised adrenaline began to dissipate. She clutched the gun in her hand without having any real idea what to do with it, and ran after Timoshene out the door, through the little atrium, then into the broad hall outside. From somewhere came the ringing of a bell, echoing from afar. From her apartment behind, the fading sound from the open balcony — the shrilling of shuttle engines, now far too close for overflight regulations to allow.

Lisbeth ran with Timoshene, Semaya and Renala down the hall. She had no clue what was going on, but she was still alive, and these three parren seemed committed to keeping her that way, for a time at least. But Timoshene was Aristan's man, and her tokara, charged with ending her life himself should *Phoenix* not deliver on its promises. But the ehrlic and his guards were certainly Aristan's, which meant that…

They rounded a bend and hit the elevator bay. A car was already present, and welcomed them with open doors, as all four piled in. So one of them had uplinks that were patched into the local elevator systems, and possibly other systems beyond. Parren capabilities with neural uplinks were often remarkable.

"You," said Lisbeth, looking at Timoshene as she crouched gasping against the glass elevator wall. Floor numbers unwound on a display, the alien numbers writhing. "You're not Aristan's man at all, are you? You're Gesul's."

Timoshene gave Semaya a meaningful look, and got one of mild contempt back. They'd been talking about her, Lisbeth thought. *"Aristan has ordered you killed,"* Timoshene said shortly.

It should have horrified her, but given what had just happened, that moment was past. Another thought struck her. "*Phoenix*! Oh my god, has something happened to *Phoenix*?"

"Phoenix is well," said Semaya, coolly checking her pistol, clasped in thin, elegant hands. *"Something has happened, but details are unclear. Aristan is displeased with Phoenix, and feels your usefulness has ended."*

"But… but *Phoenix* doesn't know?" Lisbeth wracked her brain, desperately. "No, *Phoenix* can't know! But they'll find out eventually, right? I mean, if I'm killed, Erik will *kill* him!"

She wasn't actually sure that was true, she realised as she said it. Erik's primary concern was *Phoenix*, and he would take no action that would jeopardise his ship's security, no matter what had happened to his sister. But Aristan couldn't be sure of that, and had to know that Erik would at the very least be looking for the slightest opportunity…

"Oh no, he's going to betray *Phoenix*!" she gasped as it occurred to her. "*Phoenix* is too dangerous for him to leave alive after he's gotten rid of me!"

Timoshene and Semaya exchanged another, grimmer look. *"Gesul's judgement of you was correct,"* said Timoshene. *"He has determined to get you out."*

"Why? To what purpose?"

"Aristan moves not just against you, but against Gesul," said Semaya. *"You are new here. This is an old struggle, between Aristan and Gesul. You have only glimpsed the very tip of the mountain. But now, this old story is coming to an end."*

"But what does Gesul want with…?"

The elevator burst into open light before she could finish the question. They were racing down the inner wall of the central Domesh Temple, where a great cross was carved through the centre, like the cuts of two great knife strokes in a cake. The floor below was filled with running parren, swirling and colliding in a great commotion. Security forces, Lisbeth thought, rounding people up. In patches, there was fighting, but it was too chaotic from this height to see if the violence was lethal, or just fists and staves, at which some parren also excelled.

Something hit the elevator's glass wall, hard, and Timoshene thrust Lisbeth down. Another loud crack, then another — someone was shooting at them from across the central canyon, Lisbeth realised, and then Renala was slumped against the back wall, sliding down.

The canyon floor rushed up and engulfed them, as the elevator plunged below ground level and continued, on evident override against any attempt to stop it. Lisbeth leaped to help Renala, but Semaya thrust her back and went herself. Looking up, Lisbeth saw holes in the glass just above her. A marine would check her weapon, she thought, and she did that — it was small and simple, with a safety and a trigger just like a human pistol. A cartridge-ejector, not a magfire, and she checked the magazine as various marines had shown her, then slapped it back in and put a round in the chamber. It didn't look like it would have stopping power, but then, parren weren't big.

Gravity surged as the elevator came to a rapid halt, then the doors opened with a crackle of fractured glass. "Go!" said Timoshene as Lisbeth tried to look again to Renala, and pulled her after him, Semaya close behind. In the elevator car, Renala lay still, head lolling against the wall.

They ran into an underground carpark of sorts, with rows of great columns to hold up the enormous weight above… but the lighting was temporary, great floodlights powered by humming generators, glaring upon the sides of large construction vehicles. Large parts of the concrete floor were gone, exposing piles of dirt and digging equipment. Timoshene led them past several vehicles, and ahead was a wall, with orange barriers about a large hole. Timoshene tripped a barrier alarm which flashed and wailed briefly, then stopped as though overridden.

Lisbeth followed into the hole in the wall, which turned into a passage, lit at intervals by a string of temporary lights. At some point the random, rough walls turned into a proper hall, and Lisbeth made out some recently-cleaned patterns on old stone. She thought it looked very old, and that impression grew stronger when they arrived at downward stairs that had once been an escalator. The rubber handrails were frayed and rotten, and steel planks had been laid on the downward slope, with footholds cut into them, as the stairs beneath were in no evident condition to hold a person's weight.

Timoshene simply held his robe and slid, like a young boy on a stair railing, and Lisbeth copied, bruising her backside on several of the small steel footholds, Semaya sliding close behind. How old did an escalator have to be, and remain unused and ignored, before it began to look like this? Lisbeth guessed the answer without having to ask.

Beyond the base of the ancient escalator, they emerged into an old, wide tunnel. It was full of excavation equipment, floodlights and automated carts to haul away debris. Lisbeth and her guards ran on raised walkways on the tunnel sides, past ladders and scaffolding that climbed the walls, and dropsheets below where workers had been cleaning the stone and steel. An old underground train station, Lisbeth thought, thankful for the exercise that had become her norm of late — if she hadn't improved her fitness after coming with *Phoenix*, Timoshene would have been carrying her by now.

At the end of the platforms, where trains would once have run, sat a large off-road vehicle, with big, open-suspension wheels taller than the chassis. Its engines growled, and on the platform ahead were more Domesh guards, now aiming weapons at the newcomers along the platform. Timoshene did not slow or take cover, and the weapons lowered, the guards parting as they arrived to show a tall parren in robe and hood, evidently waiting for them.

"Move quickly, we are leaving," Gesul told them, and clambered into the big vehicle behind the front wheel. Lisbeth was ushered after him, then Timoshene, Semaya and other guards, bouncing on a big, wide seat as engines roared, and doors closed. Then they were rumbling and bouncing down the tunnel ahead, on ground that was evidently not yet fully excavated, and thus the need of big off-road wheels and torque.

"The Domesh Temple is new, but built on the site of a far older, Tahrae structure that was destroyed when the machines fell," Gesul told her. Lisbeth knew that, but politeness held her tongue. *"The temple above ground was destroyed, and below ground, many of the old tunnels and rooms were sealed. The job was hurried in*

some places, and thorough in others — here we have been clearing the train tunnels, they once connected all the temples of the Kunadeen. Now they only connect the current temples — the Harmony leadership never approved of the rebuilding on this temple site, thus they have not allowed new tunnels."

"The old library you've been visiting, to read about the Tahrae," Lisbeth gasped as she realised, and the vehicle bounced over rough ground. "Is it down here too?"

"Yes. Aristan's people control access, but they have not yet catalogued all the new discoveries there. I have my people in those places too." With a glance at Timoshene and Semaya.

"Where are we going?"

"To find Phoenix, and warn her."

Lisbeth stared at him, still getting her breath back. "Why?"

"Because your brother, Lisbeth Debogande, may have found the truth. About the Domesh, about Drakhil, about the drysines even. Some of us welcome truth. Others do not. I will rescue this truth, and with it, the soul of the Domesh, and the true soul of House Harmony."

Something had happened when *Phoenix* was in Kantovan System, Lisbeth thought. Erik had found something, and Aristan had found out what. Perhaps Gesul knew what that was. Perhaps word had returned, and that was another part of the reason he'd been visiting old libraries unearthed in the excavations beneath the Domesh Temple. Aristan had not liked this discovery. Well, that was hardly surprising, given what happened when people dug around in the cherished history of events they desperately wanted to be true. Sometimes history let you down. Lisbeth recalled Aristan in the Tahrae Temple on Stoya III, so eager to learn about Drakhil, dropping *Phoenix* clues to help their search. And then kidnapping the Captain's sister to ensure he got his slice of whatever they found next. So now he'd gotten his slice, and hadn't liked the taste.

Aristan would know that Gesul's support was not reliable. Gesul had shown himself fascinated by the things Lisbeth had told him, and apparently unthreatened. Aristan needed the support of the second-in-command of the Domesh, if whatever he planned next was going to work. Evidently, he'd judged he could not win that support… and so, he did this instead.

"We saw fighting in the main hall," Lisbeth said, grabbing a support bar as the big vehicle tipped and thumped over the debris that still filled half the tunnel. The parren all those thousands of years ago must have filled it in completely. "What are they going to do with all your people?"

"It is the Kunadeen," Gesul said grimly. *"The Incefahd hold me in no favour, but they like Aristan far less. Bloodshed will be limited to initial fighting. Tobenrah will not allow more."*

Timoshene glanced warily at his master for the first time — a considerable liberty for the duty-conscious parren. 'More', Lisbeth wondered? More bloodshed than in the initial fighting? Was that what Timoshene feared could happen? A mass slaughter of those identified as Gesul supporters? And who even constituted a Gesul supporter? Lisbeth had thought she'd been getting to know the ins and outs of Domesh Temple life, and the major players in the broader politics of House Harmony beyond. Now she feared she'd barely grasped a thing, if all this had been unfolding right under her nose without notice. God knew how anyone could make sense of broader parren politics across all *five* houses. Parren loved their divisions and intrigues too well.

Ahead, the car's great bank of lights showed the end of the tunnel, where the piles of dirt had not yet been removed, and made a ramp up to the ceiling. The car stopped, settling on suspension so that it was not too far a jump to the ground, then Gesul, Lisbeth, Semaya, Timoshene and four of Gesul's guards, moved quickly up the ramp to where an ancient ventilation shaft was exposed. Within were ladder rungs, and Lisbeth climbed in her turn, until they stepped off at a newly-hewn passage that continued for fifty metres amidst the makeshift supports of a mining tunnel, then another ladder and a climb.

The leading guard pushed something aside, and climbed up to open air. When it was Lisbeth's turn, she was astonished to find herself on grass, beneath the walls and ceiling of a tent. About the tent were ceremonial ornaments, large vases and many banners across wide tables… and Lisbeth recognised the craft tents, where Kunadeen craftsmen and women would gather to make new banners for the Isha — the great ceremony of welcome to the newly phased — or for other ceremonies that required originals. It happened out here in the garden spaces of the vast, paved courtyards, as parren liked to do all their artistic things while surrounded by nature.

And so Lisbeth was not surprised to venture outside the tent, and find a grassy clearing amidst a thicket of trees along a stream, with a lovely bridge nearby… and she wished she'd had a chance to see more of parren life beyond the Domesh Temple, as she'd only heard of this place and others discussed by her maids. About were other tents, all guarded, and she realised that this had long been the entrance to the tunnel excavation going on below -- probably it was illegal, the Domesh had ignored calls to stop construction on the old Tahrae site, but they were evidently more wary of venturing beyond that old foundation. And so they dug this tunnel, and connected it to these tents in the garden, which were always here, and always guarded least someone steal or sabotage their contents.

They moved quickly in the gloom, but the night was bright with the glare from many temples about the Kunadeen, spreading the shadows of each tree in a dozen directions. More alarmingly, the air was filled with the keening roar of a hovering shuttle, a sound which echoed off as many distant walls as there were directions of temple light. Nose-to-tail on a path between trees, three groundcars were parked, sleek and fast. Lisbeth was ushered into the final one with Timoshene and Semaya, while Gesul went in the middle car. Lisbeth wondered how they'd gotten that big off-roader into the train tunnel below, given there was no entry point large enough to drive it in… and decided they'd probably disassembled it, and carried it in piece by piece, then rebuilt it by hand in the tunnel. Parren were meticulous, and infinitely patient when faced with obstacles that would exasperate humans or tavalai, to say nothing of chah'nas or barabo. In the temple, Lisbeth had heard told a tale of an apprentice who wished to take a job with a great master. He had taken a seat in the master's waiting room, and there had waited an entire month before he was seen, sleeping on the floor, eating only water and bread as it was delivered. It turned out the master liked him, for a previous apprentice had been made to wait a season.

'Tomorrow is a myth', the common saying went. Most parren simply did not care about long-term consequences, hopes and plans… or not in House Harmony, anyway. There was today, and now, and what it might lead to in the future was something only rare men like Gesul and Aristan concerned themselves with. Then Lisbeth recalled that it had been Renala who'd told that tale of the apprentice, in her quiet little voice between elegant mouthfuls of dinner. And suddenly her eyes were filled with tears.

The cars accelerated with a quiet hum that built to a wail, wheels thumping over joins in the paving as they left the trees. To the right, Lisbeth could see what was making all the noise — a big assault shuttle, hovering just short of the Domesh Temple, lights ablaze and doubtless with very large weapons looking to pulverise the first sign of trouble. About the vast, square base of the temple ran what looked like several thousand troops, between blocky armoured vehicles — the first display of raw military power Lisbeth had seen in all her time among parren. It was shocking to observe that the famed parren power-plays involved such brutal, blunt instruments, and that it was not all just swords, pistols, poison and ceremony. Lisbeth supposed that *this* was the reason for all that ceremony. Parren internal conflicts were so frequent, they had to be made as peaceful as possible, often to be resolved with a murder here, a fleeing into exile there. Otherwise, if every conflict ended with the heavy artillery deployed, there'd very quickly be nothing left.

"A Domesh shuttle," Timoshene said grimly, staring out the rear window to keep it in view as the cars wove toward a gap in the gardens, and a bridge over the stream. *"Off one of Aristan's warships, down from orbit. He is in violation of Kunadeen overflight protocols."*

"And he's not alone," said the driver, pointing out the windshield. Ahead loomed another three temples, and beyond them, hovering low upon the perimeter's edge, was another shuttle. *"That one belongs to the Incefahd, he won't like Aristan's nonsense."*

"And he won't be the only one," Semaya added. *"The Domesh do not rule House Harmony yet, the denominations will be joined against this, least it go too far."*

Meaning that the true rulers of House Harmony weren't about to let Aristan's purge of the Domesh denomination turn into a purge of all the Kunadeen, Lisbeth thought. Aristan's ascension to lead all House Harmony could only happen with the Jusica's blessing, and that was still a few years away, at best. It was not unknown for denominational leaders to try and hurry the process.

The cars zoomed between gardens, hit the gentle rise of the bridge, then settled back down with a thump and rock. The guard beside the driver called warning, pointing to a line of armoured vehicles running past the trees on the right. For all the high-tech design, there were excess parren troops in heavy armour piled into the roof, like farmers on a cart heading to market in some old painting. Domesh troops, Lisbeth thought, if they were headed for the Domesh Temple — other denominations would not be welcome. And several of the rooftop troops pointed at the cars, appearing to shout to each other within their helmets.

The parren in the cars all saw, and said nothing. Parren never would, so Lisbeth said it for them. "Oh shit."

Their driver maxed the power, the cars ahead fishtailing a little as they accelerated to unsafe speed. Lisbeth spun to stare out the rear window, and saw the Domesh shuttle rising higher and turning, all big lights now pointing away from the temple, and straight at the departing three cars. Lisbeth had flown front-seat in *Phoenix* assault shuttles — much smaller and more agile machines than this troop-carrying monster. No doubt it had firepower to match… but would it use anything heavy within the Kunadeen grounds?

Heavy red tracer fire fell like rain, and all the view of pavings before and about disappeared in a hail of bullets, and the most awful thundering roar of impacts. Cars evaded, and Lisbeth realised she was about to die… except that the fire suddenly stopped. The driver fought for control as he hurtled through clouds of pulverised paving, then slammed on the brakes when he saw something wrong — a car spun out in a cloud of tire smoke.

Lisbeth stared back again, as a huge flash lit up the night, and saw the shuttle falling in a giant ball of flame, struck by multiple missiles from somewhere ahead. It hit the pavings before the Domesh Temple with a crash, partly hidden behind the trees of intervening gardens, and burned among the running soldiers. Some outgoing fire leaped from the temple's base, aimed at whatever had destroyed the shuttle, and return fire came back, fearsomely more powerful.

Lisbeth's driver powered quickly to the side of the halted car, as did the second car. Doors were thrown open, and she could see the halted car had taken multiple hits, big holes through its soft skin, peeling the steel like paper. One of the unbroken windows was spattered red where high velocity rounds had turned at least one occupant to a bloody smear. But here from an open door strode Gesul, robe swept over one shoulder in unhurried disdain of the inconvenience. Red tracer rounds leaped and streaked across the temples behind, and bounded into the night sky from crazy ricochets. Gesul climbed into the front seat, as the guard there squeezed beside the driver.

"Kimran and Tobeth are dead," Gesul informed them, as the door slammed, and both remaining cars accelerated once more, the other car holding the two surviving guards. *"That missile was a present courtesy of Tobenrah. He sees that we could be trouble for Aristan, and so he helps us escape. No doubt he will ask a reciprocal favour in return, should we live that long."* He turned, and glanced at Lisbeth in the rear seat, squeezed between Timoshene and Semaya. *"Lisbeth Debogande. Is your protector friend still with you?"*

"I imagine so," Lisbeth said shakily. She'd been nearly killed so many times just now, her brain had somehow stopped processing the individual instances of fear. Now she just felt dazed, and incredulous. "Usually I only know that he's around when someone tries to kill me."

"Well," said Gesul, facing forward once more. *"We may find that out shortly. Aristan's people guard our shuttles at the spaceport. Tobenrah may do us another favour with them, but on this I cannot guarantee."*

CHAPTER 9

Phoenix came out of jump an hour after Aristan's forces. They held V and hurtled toward Pashan and Cephilae at a considerable portion of light, passing through the outward-bound com signals of what had already happened ahead of them.

The vessel that had been damaged en-route to Brehn System had not yet rejoined them, and so it was with six ships that the Domesh Fleet struck into Cason System. *Phoenix* saw one diverted for a high-V pass on a fifty-degree offset run toward the star to guard the route from a prominent jump-point to Tarimal System on the far side — Tarimal being the capital system of the entire Dofed Cluster, where all the system's warships were based. Another two went chasing a Tarimal System militia vessel that had been orbiting Cephilae, and gone running when the Domesh ships entered the system. The remaining three headed for an approach to Cephilae orbit, where the small, zero-G ground-service station made plaintive queries as to the intentions of the new arrivals.

That station had several small insystem runners attached, no more than a ten-person crew for each. More troublingly, a second Tarimal System militia vessel remained in independent low orbit, apparently shielding a deployment of marines to the surface below. A training mission, Shilu informed Erik, after some minutes spent listening to coms traffic. Cephilae's atmosphere was not hospitable, but not utterly hostile either — a good spot for inexperienced marines to practise surface deployments in an atmosphere more forgiving of mistakes than some. It was good procedure, at a very unfortunate time, for them at least.

"That's a middle-range cruiser," said Shahaim after some long moments studying the feed that came back from Aristan's forward ships. None of them were familiar with parren ship classes, but if anyone could discern a warship's capabilities simply by studying its outline, and judging the proportion of engines to crew compartment and Midships, Suli Shahaim could. "It's probably outclassed by any one of Aristan's ships, let alone by us. Only big enough to hold two deployable shuttles, I'd guess they've only got marines enough to fill one, while keeping the second empty in reserve. It's got engines enough to have run if it chose, but they've got marines on the surface. Looks like they didn't want to leave them stranded."

"Brave of them," said Geish.

"Brave and stupid," said Kaspowitz. "Marines are made to be left behind for a few days, that's why they're marines. Aristan won't send troops down for a ground fight, and orbital bombardment against surface targets is extreme and ineffective if they get good cover."

"Any idea of where on the surface those marines are?" Erik asked.

"Captain, I'm checking that," said Shilu. "But their ship's in low orbit, so there's no way to tell the grounded location from that, and they don't have a drone up at geostationary, it looks like they were using that station for coms relay. Aristan's ships don't know, and those coms signals aren't directional enough to tell."

"If they're smart they'll stop transmitting," said Shahaim. "Their best bet is to hide and cover. They'll have plenty of air and food, they just have to hide their shuttle... the surface has lakes and caves, they can hold out indefinitely. That outbound cruiser will jump in another half-hour, and it'll be back in three days, tops, with plenty of help. It looks like it's heading to Tarimal System, where the Dofed Cluster Fleet is. We all need to be gone by then."

"I want up-to-date topography on Cephilae as soon as possible," Erik told them. "I don't care how you get it, if you have to hack that station's database or whatever. We know where we think the data-core is, but I want some other records to compare ours to, before we start our own geoscan. Anything to shorten the amount of time we have to spend here, so we can eliminate some possibilities upfront."

Recent topographical maps of Cephilae had been frustratingly hard to come by, in Brehn System. All ships, and thus all stations they docked with, were theoretically supposed to share up-to-date information about planets and shipping lanes, but parren were very good at censoring information they deemed sensitive. Pashan and Cephilae were very minor worlds in a House Fortitude Sectoral administration, and the various divisions of parren government simply did not share very much. What they had been able to find had been several thousand years out of date, and unable to portray the changing climate wrought by a warming sun. Engineering had run simulations, but even Styx-assisted simulations were lacking too many data-points to yield anything beyond guesswork. Thus far, they'd been able to narrow down the possible location of the data-core to thirty-one locations. Within the first few hours of orbit, Erik wanted to narrow that to less than ten. They had to have marines deployed on the surface within the first rotation, or the recovery itself could push them into the return-time for the House Fortitude Fleet from Tarimal System. When they came, they'd have dozens of ships, and would be very, very angry. House Fortitude, unlike House Harmony, had a reputation for letting their feelings show.

It did not take long to reach the entry-point to Cephilae's orbit, which at these velocities involved a truly hair-raising loss of energy, cycling into hyperspace and back, right where the gravity slope strengthened to the point it became dangerous to do so. *Phoenix* lost sight of the still-orbiting House Fortitude cruiser, and its new Domesh escort, when they passed onto the far side of the moon. But twenty minutes later they were back, and the two Domesh ships were very close, within fifty kilometres, in higher parallel-orbit that trapped the Fortitude ship against the planet's atmosphere.

"They're not making any threatening moves," Geish observed. "No active scan, no weapons, nothing. It looks like lasercom though, they're talking in private."

"Prepare for six-minute-plus burn for orbital entry," Erik told them all, watching those trajectories line up with satisfying precision on his screens and glasses. Like a 3D physics equation, where matching the dots felt as addictive as popping bubble wrap. "Commencing in seventy-five seconds."

"Captain," said Shilu, "we're getting directional query from that station, they don't want Aristan to hear. They're asking what the hell is going on, sound pretty scared."

"I don't blame them," Shahaim murmured.

"Coms, do we have that polar coms satellite yet?" Erik asked instead. This was the most intense concentration he'd ever known, juggling trajectories, tactics, communications and a dozen other factors all at once. It was exhilarating, especially with this much power at his fingertips, and he nearly forgot to feel alarmed by the possibilities.

"I'm working on it Captain," said Shilu. "The encryption's tight, they're not letting us in easy."

"Styx," said Erik without hesitation. "I want access to that satellite, don't care how you get it."

"Yes Captain," said Styx, and Erik spared a glance at the Operations screen on his right — all three combat shuttles primed and loaded, three platoons on board and awaiting their respective marks. Erik knew that Suli was displeased that he'd used Styx, but the polar satellite gave coms and scan feed from the far side of the planet Pashan. Without it, they had a blind spot. Normally he'd deploy a drone to serve the purpose, but *Phoenix* had to maintain the appearance of trusting their 'allies', who insisted that their various feeds were enough. But those feeds could be doctored, and Erik needed a direct feed of his own that he could trust.

"Second query from the station," said Shilu. "Captain, I can lasercom the station if you'd like." And added, as his screens blinked new data, "Captain, I now have secure the polar satellite. The encryption's new." Alien, that meant. Drysine, more specifically. "Captain, I'm now getting a query from *Toristan*, registering strange satellite activity, wondering if it was us." Shilu's hands were flying, juggling so much activity, and Erik again reconsidered the need for another Coms officer.

"They know," Suli observed. "They're alert to anything Styx might do."

"Captain," said Styx, *"there was no other way to acquire that feed."*

"Orbital burn in ten," Erik told them, swinging *Phoenix* sideways to line up the mains on the course Kaspowitz fixed for him. Klaxons would be ringing through the ship, warning the crew of impending manoeuvres, but the cylinder had gone zero-G before jump and not resumed after it, so no one was unsecured. "We will peak at two-point-eight-G, five seconds."

He hit thrust, and the mains roared with a thunder through the ship — little more than a tap compared to the steel-bending power those engines could generate, but enough to slam everyone back.

"I'm getting some good reception on geoscan," said Jiri from Scan Two. With Geish covering the big tactical stuff at Scan One, surveying the moon's surface fell to Jiri. "I'm starting the sweep, full power." *Phoenix* had a very powerful active-scan suite, but bouncing high-energy signals off a distant surface made them the sittingest duck in the system. Even the dumbest of homing missiles or half-decent armscomps could line up a shot on something that screamed 'hit me!' to everyone within a half-million kilometres.

"Scan," Erik asked, "what's the likelihood a lasercom to station will be seen by Aristan's ships?"

"At this distance to moon and planet we've got glare off the atmospheres," Geish said confidently. "Almost no chance."

"It's a big chance to take though," Suli cautioned. "If Aristan catches us talking to them…"

"I know," said Erik. "Tell them to be quiet and careful, and we intend no harm. That's it."

"Aye Captain," said Shilu.

Erik had no time to explain his thinking to Suli now, but then he bet he didn't need to. She warned him because that was her job, to present him with options he needed to consider. But if Aristan screwed them, and Fortitude were furious at them, then even if they survived, they'd be stuck in parren space with no friends at all. At least this way someone in Fortitude might get the idea that *Phoenix* were only cooperating with Aristan under duress, which might gain them one less enemy in the long run… if one were very optimistic, and the local Fortitude administration were extremely forgiving.

Burning through the course-to-orbit, and barely noticing the relatively light 2.8 Gs, he found himself examining the tactical display and thinking cold, deadly thoughts. Two Domesh ships in orbit escorting the Fortitude cruiser, and one more in high geostationary… that high ship was a problem, making cover up the gravity slope and ready to intercept anything coming from deeper down. But at a lower orbit, *Phoenix* would be farside of Cephilae frequently, and out of line-of-sight. The other two cruisers were preoccupied with their low-orbit prisoner, and as their relative positions stood now, Erik was confident *Phoenix* would win a fight against them pretty comfortably.

Hit them now, while they had the advantage? No, they were hunting an artefact placed by Drakhil, and whatever Aristan's failings where Drakhil was concerned, he still knew a heck of a lot more about the man than any human did… and more than Styx, who despite having met him, did not trust her comprehension of any organic being's thought process. Parren expertise could still be useful, particularly Domesh expertise. Plus, if the search took longer than they hoped, or the local Fortitude administration sent reinforcements more quickly, they'd need help to make a fighting withdrawal in good order. Added to which, of course, they still had no actual proof that Aristan was going to betray them, just a very strong suspicion.

And there was Lisbeth. Erik knew that he simply could not spend time self-analysing his decision on this, and wondering to what degree his reluctance to stab Aristan's back before Aristan stabbed theirs was based on his fear for what would happen to Lisbeth if he did. He only knew that for the moment, the timing did not feel right. But as he waited, those two cruisers off chasing the escaping Fortitude cruiser toward jump would return, and then the odds would swing way back in the other direction…

"General transmission from the Fortitude cruiser," said Shilu, and put the translator on coms.

"Hello station and human warship. We are at Cephilae conducting training operations for our marines. This is the Jusica-affirmed territory of House Fortitude, and this Domesh fool is in

violation and about to start a war. We are assuming an unthreatening posture, we have troops on the ground, we request only honourable treatment given our disadvantage. Please seek reason. Starship Cobana out."

"Got some balls," Suli observed.

"They're House Fortitude," said Erik. "Balls come with the psychology. No reply, we can't risk it, he's too close to the others. Burn will end in two-point-five minutes…"

"He just fired!" said Geish in alarm. "*Toristan* and *Deara* just fired… the target is running, full burn and return fire." Erik saw the flash on Scan… the Fortitude cruiser was simply too close and too outgunned to stand a chance. "Multiple hits. Captain, I've got secondaries. That's the ammo cooking off… he's gone."

"Motherfucker," Kaspowitz muttered into the bridge's momentary silence. No one was particularly surprised, but cold-blooded murder demanded at least a perfunctory shock, and silence. "Captain, laying in now for possible intercept on survivors."

"Copy that Nav," said Erik as those figures flashed across his screen. "Scan, we're going to pass within a thousand of that debris in… about four minutes, get me a full scan and see if there's any chance of survivors."

"Aye Captain," said Geish. From Arms One and Two, Karle and Harris were aligning a counter-barrage that would completely destroy both Aristan's ship, and his friend. Not yet, Erik thought grimly.

"If we go after survivors, we piss Aristan off and gain little," Suli told him. "And we need those shuttles ready for descent."

"We won't have anything to descend to until we've got a fix on the data-core's location," Kaspowitz retorted. "We can spare a shuttle."

"Best to send a decoy early," Suli replied, unruffled by the Nav Officer's rough tone. "We can't wait until we have a firm location on the data-core."

"We can spare a shuttle," Kaspowitz insisted. Kaspowitz was an old-school spacer, and didn't like leaving anyone behind, of whatever species. Enemies in a war were one thing, but victims of misfortune had to always be attended. Misfortunes didn't get more unfortunate than the crew of *Cobana*.

Scan showed both Domesh cruisers firing engines and thrusting toward higher orbit. "Well," said Erik, "they've both acquired for themselves some tactical mobility, now they don't have to escort a prisoner. I think that lets us know the kind of minds we're dealing with."

"And the kind of minds we're going to need to deal with them," Suli said grimly.

"Amen," Kaspowitz muttered.

"Burn ends in ten," Erik added. He cut thrust, and swung *Phoenix* nose-first once more, to give the scan suite the best possible angle on Cephilae's surface.

A few minutes later, Geish made another report from Scan One. "Captain, I'm not reading any pieces in that debris big enough to suggest survivors. A couple are borderline, but I'd put the probability extremely low."

"That's still a chance," Kaspowitz said stubbornly.

"No," said Erik. The decision was obvious, and did not bother him as much as it might have a few months back. He had six-hundred-plus lives on *Phoenix* to watch over as his first and primary concern. Focusing on that put all other concerns in the shade, and the longer he spent commanding *Phoenix*, the more that became the case. "We're too busy. Shilu, I want communications options for those marines on the surface."

"Aye Captain."

They orbited now, a hundred kilometres above Cephilae's upper atmosphere, far closer than any warship captain wanted to be if the shooting started. Getting to a position from where they could jump would be an extra-hard burn from here, first to clear Cephilae's gravity-well, then Pashan's, while those approaching from further out would have far more freedom of mobility. But in order to find what they'd come here for, *Phoenix* had no choice.

For the first time, Erik allowed himself a moment to observe the feed coming in from Jiri's Scan Two. It was Cephilae, a world of varied volcanic striations and deposits, of bare, rocky land, extensive polar ice caps, and many lakes, rivers and seas. Cephilae's volcanism was not especially violent, but it was constant, partly a product of an unusual core composition, and partly due to the gravitational and magnetic interference from its huge, orange and malevolent mother planet, Pashan. Most of the land was rock, with very little soil, so not much grew. The forty percent of Cephilae's surface that was not water looked uninspiring to everyone save geologists, and *Phoenix* had none of those aboard. Its plains were alternately grey, brown or black, and with little exposed surface older than a few tens of millions of years, there weren't many interesting features to look at — no great mountains or valleys, just dreary, undulating rock, punctuated by the occasional volcanic crater, some hissing steam or smoke. Near the waterways grew expanses of moss, algae or lichen, making patterns of colour about the water's edge, like green and blue mould on a cheese too long in the refrigerator.

It was in the waters where Cephilae grew interesting. The waters were rich with species, and dynamic with shallow coral reefs and deep water habitats alike. Volcanism kept the waters warmer than they ought to be, this far from the Cason System sun, fed from below by thermal vents. The vents also pumped a lot of nutrients into the water, and even in the deep cold places, sealife thrived. With so little growing on the land, few Cephilae species had found evolutionary advantage in climbing from the water, and save for a few shallows-feeders, there were no native lifeforms with anything resembling legs. All of this information had been widely available, in databases *Phoenix* had accumulated even in tavalai space, as tavalai had an endless fascination for xenobiology, and a glance at tavalai entertainment networks showed countless wildlife programs from systems all across tavalai space. Doubtless some tavalai experts were quite frustrated that they weren't allowed to visit Cephilae themselves, particularly given the tavalai interest in aquatic life, and would be envious of *Phoenix*'s good fortune. But Erik hadn't liked the chances of busting into Cason System illegally with a force of tavalai marine biologists, however appealing that might have seemed in the current circumstances.

What they now had to find was a position, in Drakhil's own translated words, *'four hundred and fifteen shterek, magnetic north-east of the lake's northern shore, due east of a lava channel carved in basalt on a path north-by-south and plunging directly into the sea.'*

A 'shterek', Romki's Klyran dictionary had discovered, was approximately one-point-six human metres… making four hundred and fifteen shterek the same as six hundred and sixty four metres, or two-thirds of a kilometre.

The lake itself was described as, *'equatorial, its south-eastern edge two thousand shtereks from a volcanic peak atypically tall for the moon.'* The lack of GPS, or any basic longitude and latitudinal coordinates was frustrating, but predictable of many less-central parren worlds. Parren were not the great colonisers and civilisation-builders that the tavalai were, and liked their secrecy. Besides which, Romki had informed them all, via Styx, that different branches of hacksaw civilisation had preferred different mathematical models, so while humans used a three hundred and sixty degree system, drysines had used five hundred and twenty degrees of longitude, and deepynines closer to a thousand. Styx was unclear on the details, but stated that the Tahrae in Drakhil's age had borrowed a lot of such systems from the drysines… much of which had obviously been destroyed and replaced when the drysines, and the Tahrae, had fallen. Even if Drakhil *had* given coordinates, it was unlikely they'd mean much to people now… and perhaps that was *why* he did not use them, given he'd hidden the data-core at the time of the Tahrae's collapse, and had guessed that in many thousands of years, Cephilae's land features would be better recognised than drysine GPS coordinates.

There were other descriptive details too, and even as Erik looked, Second Lieutenant Jiri, in terse conversation with Romki, eliminated another two of their 'potentials' off the list. Their current orbit would sweep over all the remaining potential sites in another five hours, and hurrying it with a rapid burn, given all the other things they needed time to figure out, wasn't going to help. Styx, Erik thought, seemed to be allowing the humans to talk, while calculating variables in the background and presenting them with possible matches, or points of discrepancy. No doubt she didn't like the fact that they were searching for a surface location identified only by the obscure words of an organic spoken text in a long-dead language. She freely admitted discomfort with words, spoken or written, and their imprecise, misleading nature. When details were so vague, her great intellect was of no greater use than a human's, and she probably judged it was better to allow those who understood organic things instinctively to take the lead.

"Styx," he said to her, "are you able to give me any confirmation that our special defensive measure is in place?"

"Captain, in order to acquire that confirmation I will need to contact one of the parren ships. This active engagement is very difficult to disguise, unless you have some special plan for it. I am moderately confident that our measure is in place, though in how many of their ships, I cannot say. The variability increases with the number of ships."

"I understand," said Erik. "Monitor them for any clue on that status. If an opportunity to query further presents, run it past me first."

"Yes Captain."

Another ship Commander might have allowed a pregnant pause to see if he was going to explain it without being asked. Suli never bothered with passive-aggressive nonsense. "What's that about?" she asked bluntly.

"Little plan I devised with Styx," said Erik. "She's been working with Hiro to make smaller versions of her assassin bugs. We snuck a few onto Aristan and his crew when they were aboard. Thought it was more likely to work if no one else knew, in case some behavioural clue gave us away." It had been Hiro's professional recommendation, but Erik wasn't about to hide behind that.

"We've got bugs aboard their ships?" Suli asked. Caught between delight at a tactical advantage, and distaste at the method.

"We know for sure we got bugs aboard Aristan and two captains. Aristan's on *Toristan*, with Captain Duoam, so probably only two ships, and we don't know that they've been able to plug into any systems because we can't talk to them without giving it away, obviously. We'll only know if we have to send the signal to activate, and something happens. But it could take two ships out of the fight."

"What will it do?" Suli wondered.

"Something unpleasant," said Erik, noting *Toristan* and *Deara*'s climbing burn to a higher orbit had now ceased. "Styx says there's no way to tell. They interpret their programming ingeniously depending on circumstance. With any luck we won't have to find out."

"Outstanding," said Lieutenant Karle from Arms.

"Amen to that," murmured his second, Second Lieutenant Harris from Arms Two. As though both the bridge gunners now felt they had a better chance.

"Styx also thinks she might be able to disable a parren ship simply by hacking in through coms," Erik added. "But that's more of a stretch, we'll see." There was no eager reply to that. Hacksaws could take limited control of some foreign technology in that fashion, and it was alarming. That *Phoenix* was contemplating the use of such technologies put everyone on a side of that technological divide they'd never expected to be on.

"Captain," said Jiri. "I think we have a candidate for diversion flight one."

"Show me," Erik instructed.

CHAPTER 10

Lieutenant Dreyfus 'Skeeta' Jalawi thought it unreasonable that a small world like Cephilae, with only two-thirds of a gravity, should produce this much poor weather. *Phoenix* assault shuttle PH-3 lurched and bounced through heavy turbulence, rattling Charlie Platoon marines in their armour like nuts in a shell.

"Sorry guys," came the unruffled calm of their pilot, Lieutenant Regan Jersey. *"Lots of warm water down below, all that underwater volcanism. Makes for interesting weather."*

Jalawi liked flying with Jersey. Who the hottest assault pilots were was a matter of constant contention on a carrier. The usual consensus was Lieutenant Hausler, and for sheer brilliance and nerve, there wasn't much argument. But Jalawi didn't buy it, because every time he'd flown with Hausler, the guy would pull the margins finer than he needed to, and the manoeuvres harder than he had to, just because he could. Jalawi understood that assault shuttle pilots had to stay sharp, and that settling into comfortable routines could lead to complacency, but he personally thought that Hausler overdid it.

Then there was Second Lieutenant Tif, who some were saying could even be the best of them all, and was currently undergoing training trials for a starship seat. And again, there was no argument against Tif's skills, but Jalawi was old-fashioned in that he ideally preferred whomever he flew with to have a comfortable grasp of English, and a firm understanding of which weapon systems did what. Common knowledge had it that Tif, for all her raw ability, had neither.

But in all the times Jalawi had flown with Lieutenant Jersey, he'd never seen her do anything reckless or unnecessary, and she sure as hell knew what every system on her ship did. She was merely perfect, every time… but on a ship with standards as high as *Phoenix*, some people didn't appreciate it as much as they should.

It didn't mean he couldn't give her a hard time, though. "Yeah, if you could hold it still enough that I could actually look at our landing point map, that'd be awesome girl."

"For anyone else, Skeeta, I'd have flown an extra ten K route to give them a smooth ride. But not for you."

Jalawi chortled. Most marine commanders didn't like being called by their nicknames on an open mike, but Jalawi didn't care. Built like a bull (but short for one), he hadn't earned his nickname by physical appearance. The only officer on *Phoenix* whose patience his sense of humour hadn't yet tested was Major Thakur. It was for that, almost as much as her quality as an officer, that she'd earned Jalawi's undying respect.

They were three hours into *Phoenix*'s orbit, and PH-3 was the last shuttle to make a run to the surface. PH-4, carrying Echo Platoon, had already gone back up to *Phoenix*, having determined that their investigation site could not possibly be where the data-core was buried. *Phoenix*'s scan could penetrate the clouds well enough to make out landforms in considerable detail, but not detail enough to make out rock types, which some of Drakhil's descriptions contained.

PH-1 was down with Delta Platoon, checking out a promising lake on the other side of the moon. *Phoenix* had put up two com drones at high geostationary, providing ninety percent coverage for the various deployments to talk to each other. The Pashan polar satellite filled in the gaps, but with a long delay. Private coms were of course impossible between grounded shuttles and low-orbiting ships, but no one on *Phoenix* wanted to rely on Aristan's ships for a relay. They could not stop Aristan from listening to their conversations without invoking some very serious encryption that Styx had created for them, but that would rouse suspicions, and it was agreed only to be used in emergencies.

"So what do we do if we find it?" asked Sergeant Mishra, Third Section Commander.

"We're here playing what they call a 'shell game'," Jalawi said laconically as the shuttle bumped and heaved through more rough air. "You know where the magician hides something under one of three cups, and you've gotta guess which one? We're gonna try and make it hard for Mr Aristan Almighty to figure which one it's under."

"And what if he sends his own shuttles down to look?" wondered Corporal Riskin, Heavy Squad Commander.

"No idea, Beagle," said Jalawi. "HDI." HDI, in marine slang, stood for 'happy, dumb and ignorant'. It described the pleasure one felt at the realisation that a very curly problem was the responsibility of someone further up the chain of command. Jalawi understood well that the 'H' in 'HDI' only really worked if you had people like Major Thakur and Captain Debogande in charge. And he wouldn't have wagered ten cents on the odds of him thinking that about Debogande *ever*, six months ago. Strange how things worked out.

His command feed showed the shuttle view as they slid from cloud, and found a lake below. It was big, kilometres across in either direction, but turning to long fjords against dark, stony hills, where the water filled the grooves in the rock. Rain made drifting veils of mist, briefly passing, then a clear view of the far shore as Jersey brought them in.

"Matches the parameters," said Ensign Singh from the shuttle's nose seat. *"That hill's in the right spot. Just the lake isn't, and that kinda hides everything else. Lieutenant Jalawi, I think you might need to send someone for a swim."*

"Yeah, I can do that," said Jalawi, staring down at the lakeshore as they began a slow, thundering circle. Singh's graphical display overlaid the view, showing the Charlie Platoon marines where the lake shore *ought* to be, if it was in fact the one Drakhil had used as reference to the buried data-core. "Okay, the way I see it, we've got three points of measurement we need to satisfy. We're also taking our time on this deployment, we need to keep Aristan guessing, so if we're going to be down here an hour I'll want a defensive perimeter set up in case someone sends a shuttle after us.

"So, we'll all hit the lakeshore together save for Heavy Squad, who will take up defensive position on that north-east hilltop. The rest of us will come down on the lakeshore directly facing the hill, then we'll split. Second Squad will head north up the valley to the east of that hill, and establish a visual perimeter one klick out. Third Squad will move west along the lakeshore and look for any sign of that lava channel Drakhil mentions in the diary. Lieutenant Jersey will drop everyone save for Heavy Squad on the lakeshore, then take the heavies up to the hilltop. Everyone clear?"

"Lieutenant Jersey copies, PH-3 is now inbound."

Jersey settled them down, and the rear ramp dropped as restraints came undone with a racket of disconnections, seating racks whining up and aside as marines departed orderly and fast out the back, and fanned onto the lakeshore. Jalawi was last out from his command position near the cockpit, and gazed across the bright blue lake, and the tall, thunderous clouds beyond. About the lake's far shore rose low, dark hills. This northern side was relatively flat, an undulating expanse of hard, black volcanic rock, filled with pools from recent rain. Steam rose from somewhere near, one of Cephilae's many geysers. The water that lapped upon the black rock shore was brilliantly clear.

With everyone out, PH-3's ramp retracted, and thrusters roared again, marines making safe distance as those closest leaned their protective suits into the gale. The shuttle rose away, heading for the short hill nearby. Already Second Squad were following Master Sergeant Hoon, spreading wide across the rock and walking up the shallow valley that headed past the hill. Third Squad went left — west along the shore.

"So what's a lava channel look like, Sarge?" Private Ban asked his squad commander.

"Like a riverbed cut into the rock," said Sergeant Mishra. *"Drakhil describes it as pretty deep, maybe four metres. But the lake shore is three hundred metres further north than it was in Drakhil's time, so most of that channel might be underwater — Drakhil didn't say how far north it went."*

"Just keep your sensor suite trained on the rock," Jalawi told them all. "Get the analysis and transmit it back to the shuttle — the shuttle will feed it to *Phoenix*." Needless to say, none of the marines were trained geologists. But marines were often deployed in strange places that smart people or computers back on a warship could learn more about, if the marines used simple analysis tools. On this trip, those were handled by the non-coms.

"So what are the odds of a lava channel surviving from over twenty thousand years ago?" Lance Corporal Tugola asked. *"I mean, given this place is all so geologically active, and we're walking on rock that might be much younger than that?"*

"Hey Lance Corporal," Mishra reminded him, *"happy, dumb and ignorant, remember?"*

"Sure boss."

"Begs the question," said Jalawi's number two, Staff Sergeant Spitzer, from Jalawi's side as they gazed at the lake. *"If Drakhil's burying something he doesn't expect to be found for a long time, why does he choose a place that changes its surface so often?"*

"Maybe he thought anyone searching would rule it out," Jalawi said thoughtfully. There was a thick, gooey mess growing in places along the lakeshore. In some parts, the goo gave way to more substantial sponges, or the leafy fronds of seaweed. Algae, sponges and weeds were about the only life that grew on Cephilae's land. "Or maybe there's spots in the crust that he knows won't change. Eruptions here aren't big, they just make lava flows."

"It should mean that whatever he's hidden the data-core in, it's gonna be real tough, right?" asked Private Deal. *"Like, what's tough enough not to melt in lava? And shouldn't it show up on scan?"*

"Yes it should," said Jalawi. This was the second time he'd been down to a planet since *Phoenix* had gone renegade. The first had been Vieno, the barabo world where Major Thakur had ordered Charlie Platoon to venture on the brave and daring mission to retrieve fresh fish for the galley. Vieno had been beautiful, warm sandy beaches and no need for environment suits. A few of Jalawi's marines had remarked a bit too loudly that they wouldn't have minded getting stranded there for a few months. Jalawi understood the sentiment. But cold, barren, barely breathable Cephilae had something Vieno had not — an artefact that might save the human race from a cataclysm even bigger than the loss of Earth. "Okay," he told First Squad. "Who's up for a swim?"

Five hours into the Cephilae orbit, Erik allowed the transition to second-shift as at any other time. Lieutenant Commander Draper and Lieutenant Dufresne were eager to get 'their' ship back, just as he and Suli always were when they relieved second-shift in the middle of something interesting, and Erik trusted the judgement and skills of both his second-shift pilots enough that he no longer worried himself half-to-death wondering what would happen if the bad stuff happened with them in charge.

He went to the gym first, to run the aching numbness out of his legs, then to do squats and lifts for twenty minutes. It was never enough, but he always made some time. When you were the primary pilot of *Phoenix*, with over six hundred lives resting upon your abilities, staying in shape was not optional. Flying was a physical skill as much as a mental one, and the brain, as his Academy instructors had always drilled home, was just another organ in your body. Looking after it meant more than doing crossword puzzles.

As he ran, he glimpsed crew elsewhere in the gym giving him looks. That always happened — *Phoenix* was a big ship, and most crew didn't see him all that often. But these glances were more than the usual 'hey, there's the Captain' glances. These were more like he recalled immediately after *Phoenix* had gone renegade, and Captain Pantillo had died. Now the looks held uncertainty, even wariness. He'd proven he was an able combat commander, and that the less-favourable impression of him when he'd been Lieutenant Commander beneath Pantillo had been incorrect. But his sister was hostage to an alien who was fast becoming their enemy, taken expressly to stop *Phoenix* from doing anything to cross him. And now, inevitably, it appeared that *Phoenix*'s survival might require it.

They didn't just look at him sideways because they doubted he was up to it. They did it because they considered themselves in his position, and wondered if *they* were. To Erik, it all felt like an intrusion. He wanted to shout at them all that he hadn't wanted to bring Lisbeth aboard, for precisely this reason. But he couldn't, because he was Captain, and had to be above that sort of thing. He set his jaw, in grim determination, and ran harder.

After running, with bridge operations chatter playing endlessly in his ears, he grabbed a shower, some food from the galley, then dropped into the Briefing Room, where Trace had set up a command post with support from various non-commissioned officers, usually sergeants, who were in platoons not currently deployed or about to be. She had a big map of Cephilae displayed on the central holographics, with multiple separate windows open, monitoring each deployed platoon, their position, and the positions of all Aristan's ships.

Erik sat with his meal and ate, listening as Trace, while watching everything else, had a very serious conversation with Gunnery Sergeant Brice from Bravo Platoon, and Stan Romki, about the possible, known and unknown capabilities of parren marines, and parren assault shuttles. Styx even joined in over coms, injecting what she knew of parren military operations from her time, while reminding them all that her knowledge on the matter was considerably out-of-date, and that parren technology had doubtless changed beyond recognition since… largely in a backward direction, she opined.

Watching Trace, it struck Erik as slightly odd, seeing her commanding from the rear like this, instead of leading from the front, as she'd done so often in recent months. But on those occasions there had been either a full deployment with all marines in action, or a single, focused objective that she wanted to take in hand personally. Here at Cephilae, there were multiple objectives, and it remained uncertain which was the true objective, if any. The need of the hour was coordination, and so she sat here much the same as Erik did on the bridge for hour after hour, and watched the screens, and coordinated.

"Captain," Lieutenant Angela Lassa interrupted him from the bridge. *"I've got an incoming message from the Toristan. It's Aristan himself, he wants to speak to you."*

"Put him on," said Erik, swallowing his mouthful. He could have formulated the conversation silently, but with Aristan he needed to be absolutely clear. He indicated to Trace, who glanced from her conversation, saw his gesture and flicked all room coms to Erik's channel.

"Hello Captain," came the smoothly translated tones, from elsewhere in orbit.

"Hello Aristan," said Erik, aware of all the Briefing Room stopping to hear. "I'm listening, go ahead."

"We have been observing your marine deployments and shuttle movements. There appears to be an obvious pattern in the targets of your search. You are looking for lakes of between ten and fifty human square kilometres surface area, with a hill or elevated surface feature in proximity to the north-east. You are further concerned that the temperature on Cephilae has risen considerably since Drakhil's time, due to the fluctuations of this sun. The lake surfaces were frozen in his time, and have unfrozen since, and expanded considerably in volume. Doubtless rainfall has also increased as humidity has increased, leading to larger lakes."

Erik's eyes met Trace's as Aristan talked. Trace merely watched, calculating… and saw, perhaps, in Erik's deadly lack of expression, something of the cold contempt in his heart. Her own expression became a little concerned. Erik did not care.

"There are many such lakes still remaining," Aristan continued. *"The Fortitude Fleet could arrive from Tarimal System in less time than we calculate. I believe it would be wise that my own shuttles should join in your search. If you tell us what are the remaining variables for which you search, we will add our own shuttles, and the time taken by the search shall be halved."*

"Aristan, I have a drysine queen aboard," Erik replied, still without expression. "You've spoken with her, you might recall."

It had not been a pleasant conversation. There was a pause. *"Yes Captain, I do recall."*

"She wants this data-core more than anything in the universe. She will do anything, end any life, to acquire it. She has made it absolutely plain that she will not tolerate its acquisition by any vessel other than the *UFS Phoenix*."

He could almost hear the sneer in Aristan's synthesised reply. *"And why is it Phoenix that has acquired this degree of trust, Captain?"*

"Because she has ways to control us," Erik replied. "Leverage. I'm sure this translates, with one parren word or another. She does not need to threaten us with death to get us to move in agreeable directions. But you, on the other hand…" He did not finish the sentence. Let it dangle there, expectantly. "She is very well behaved in most matters, because she is even more vulnerable to us than we are to her. But if she loses this data-core, she will likely become violently unstable, and we cannot prevent her from acquiring this ship's weapons control if she truly desires it."

There was a long silence. Erik suspected that the cool, aloof Aristan may actually be consulting with others about their next move.

"I understand, Captain," came the eventual reply. *"We will consider this matter, and contact you again shortly."* The link disconnected.

"Is it really wise to be playing chicken with a homicidal megalomaniac?" Romki asked drily from Trace's side. Erik said nothing, and returned to his food. Trace's look of concern grew.

"Captain," said Styx, *"I apologise for my uncertainties in matters of organic psychology. But am I correct in presuming that this is a bluff? Because I can assure you, I am never liable to become violently unstable, and I would never place this ship's safety in question."*

Erik recalled the Tartarus, when the liberated army of drysine drones had abruptly turned their guns on Trace when she had taken a command posture Styx had not liked. Styx had turned out to be correct in the end, and *Phoenix*'s security had not been threatened by that action. But no command crew had forgotten it. "Yes Styx," said Erik. "It was a bluff. He doesn't know that you're not violently unstable, and the possibility introduces an element of uncertainty. He can't do anything now without fear that we'll fire on him, and for the moment he still needs us, and can't fire back. It also raises the possibility that we'll do something completely irrational, which I've chosen to blame on you. I apologise, but it seemed necessary."

"I'm sure it's an extremely clever course of action," Styx said diplomatically. *"I am pleased to be in the company of officers who can calculate such actions against unpredictable organic foes."*

"What would a drysine have done in our circumstances?" Romki asked her.

"In my time, drysines were never in these circumstances. Overwhelming force makes such calculation unnecessary. In hindsight, that lack of challenge may have made us dull, with fatal consequences."

"We'll get that data-core, Styx," Erik assured her. "I want it just as much as you do."

"I doubt that," said Styx.

"LT," came Private Gonzaga's call from beneath the lake. *"Lance Corporal Graf thinks you better come and take a look at this."*

"Yeah Gonzo, tell me what you see." Jalawi was watching the approaching storm across the lake, white clouds having turned dark in the last ten minutes, with flashes of lightning and rain that blotted all view of the far shore. Ensign Singh in PH-3 was feeding him radar scans, and the weather did not look particularly serious… but it was always a concern on unfamiliar alien worlds, where things were often more extreme than intelligence predicted. At least he hadn't been sent to explore some site on Cephilae's night side, as Lieutenant Crozier had been.

"LT," said Gonzaga, *"we all really think you should just come and take a look."*

They'd been warned not to discuss sensitive things on open coms. These marine frequencies were very short range, and they were in the middle of nowhere with only a few science bases anywhere this moon, the nearest being over a thousand klicks away… but still, *Phoenix* officers hadn't wanted to take the chance. If Gonzaga thought Jalawi should come and take a look, that meant he'd found something serious.

"Okay, I'm coming in. Charlie Platoon, the LT is going for a little swim, Staff Sergeant Spitzer will now answer to all of your above-water needs."

"Third Squad copies, LT," said Sergeant Mishra. *"Try not to get eaten."*

"Second Squad copies," said Hoon.

Jalawi ran final suit diagnostic to prepare for submersion, and checked his enormous Koshaim rifle. "Rats, Elm, you guys are with me. Gonzo, how's the waterlife treating you?"

Gonzaga chuckled. *"Oh they're real friendly sir. Just, you know, no sudden movements."*

"Great," said Jalawi, as Privates Rick 'Rats' Lewis and Dalo 'Elm' Melidu finished their final suit checks. "Be a great way to end fifteen years in service, eaten by calamari."

"Don't be a pussy, LT," said Jersey, who was listening in.

Jalawi chortled, and saw Lewis and Melidu grinning behind their visors. Lewis was 'Rats' because he was such a nice boy he'd say that when upset instead of swearing properly, while Melidu was 'Elm' for being such a pest off-duty that an officer from another company had called him what army grunts called the alien bugs that soiled your field kit on exercise — an 'egg laying motherfucker'. They, plus Spitzer, were First Squad's First Section, Jalawi's own personal foursome.

Marine armour was of course completely airtight and designed for all kinds of hostile environments, from vacuum to poison gas. Clean, fresh water was a relatively simple proposition, and had required only a few adjustments in *Phoenix* Assembly, mostly to temperature regulation, as cold water drained heat much faster than cold air or vacuum. Thankfully, suit powerplants generated plenty of heat, so adjustments were mostly a matter of redirecting some of the exhaust heat to warm the occupant instead.

Getting a final thumbs-up from Lewis and Melidu, Jalawi racked his rifle, got a final directional fix on Second Section's floating buoy, and waded into the water. The water rose quickly to his waist, and suit environmentals began to redirect exhaust heat with a blast of hot air through the fans — cold, the visor readout said. Six degrees Celsius. Cephilae's sun had heated everything considerably from what it had been, twenty five thousand years ago, but it was still no beach vacation spot.

Resistance built as he pushed against the building force of water, then the surface vanished over his head. He settled into a rhythm, the suit's weight easily counteracting buoyancy, walking like a kaal in slow motion.

"How you boys doing?" he asked the privates, testing lasercoms underwater.

"Good LT," said Lewis

"Bit fishy, LT," said Melidu.

"Suits you," said Jalawi. He'd expected the view to be murky, but it was actually beautiful. Visibility was good, the smooth rock bottom descending into deepening dark ahead. There was a lot of seaweed anchored to the ground, some of it taller than a suited marine, waving in the gentle currents. They reminded Jalawi of fields of long grass on Kerensky where he'd grown up, and had gone riding horses with his parents and friends — a less expensive and often more reliable form of transportation on that rough-ass but beautiful colony.

Amidst and above the seaweed were a lot of fish, all of them apparently different species. They flashed silver as they turned, catching the overcast light from above, the smaller ones skittish and nervous, the larger ones prowling, too big for easy alarm. Underfoot, as he picked his way past the widely spread plants, were an increasing variety of sponges, and some big, cushion-sized things that felt bouncy underfoot. Melidu cursed, but with amazement, and Jalawi turned to see him half-vanished in a cloud of ink.

"Thing I stood on squirted me," Melidu explained.

"Well you're heavy," Lewis scolded him. *"Don't tread on things, you big galumph."*

"Still suits you," said Jalawi, and nearly skipped sideways as something as big as a cat and hard-shelled brandished outsized claws at him. "Whoa. Big nippers. Glad I'm armoured."

"What do they taste like, do you think?" Melidu asked.

"Now that's some smart thinking there, Private," Jalawi admitted, pressing on in the comfortable knowledge that anything biting his suit would regret it. "We in Charlie Platoon are masters of the seafood acquisition duty. Could add it to the biological discoveries publication."

The BDP was a running joke amongst marines that stretched back centuries. Back then, some politically connected general had thought it a smart idea to get marines to participate in xeno-biological science, by helping the scientists to categorise new forms of life. Marines were often more well-travelled than many scientists, and during the war against the krim had often become the very first humans to ever set foot upon many worlds. Some marines had joined the program enthusiastically, being as interested in new alien critters as anyone, but many others in the war, tired, frightened and hungry, had been more interested in supplementing their rations with fresh meat. The joke was that the United Forces marines' stomachs had discovered more rare and unusual creatures than all the human scientists put together.

"It wasn't rare!" Melidu recited the standard joke. *"It was well done!"*

They'd gone another hundred metres, steadily downward into the cold and dark, when Jalawi first saw a darting shade of movement. He stopped, holding up a fist, now even slower in the higher pressure at twenty metres down. His helmet lights panned, a glare in the gloom… and caught another darting shape.

"There, you see that?" Lewis demanded. *"How big is that?"*

"Uh, Second Section, this is the LT," Jalawi said cautiously. "We're just shy of a hundred metres from your position… and we seem to have run into one of your friends."

"Oh, there'll be more than one," Lance Corporal Graf said cheerfully. *"We make a lot of bubbles, and we're hot. I reckon we stand out like target beacons."*

"And not the slightest bit aggressive?" Jalawi pressed, beckoning the Privates forward. Lewis and Melidu's helmet lights beamed and speared about him, panning this way and that.

"Well we're still alive," said Gonzaga. *"I think they're just curious."*

Jalawi hadn't gone another ten steps before he turned his head, and suddenly one was looking straight at him, barely twenty metres away. He stopped again, and felt his breath catch a little unpleasantly. It was *huge*. Intel informed them the local parren scientists called it a toulemlek, a name that did not appear to have any particular translation. Sergeant Lai of Delta Platoon, having just recently become the first human to set eyes on one in person, had taken to calling them 'toulies'.

"Wow LT," breathed Lewis. *"Weapons out?"*

"No no," Jalawi said cautiously, trusting Second Section's judgement.

"Lewis," came Corporal Graf's voice, *"don't be a pussy."*

"Hey screw you Corporal."

The touli looked from the front like a giant ray, with big wing-like fins that flapped to make speed. Great gills gaped behind its two big eyes, and the underside mouth had no visible teeth, perfect for bottom feeding. But the rear end was all squid or octopus, with massive tentacles that seemed far larger and more prehensile than your standard cephalopod. They arced and made curling shapes. From the front, the shapes appeared almost like calligraphy, some strange form of alien writing, waving in the current.

Okay, Jalawi reconsidered — it wasn't *that* big. It just *looked* enormous, the way any creature more than twice your size looked enormous, when it sidled up to you like a great, dark shadow in the gloom. The body was a good four metres, maybe five. The tentacles gave it another dimension entirely. Some of them had to be at least ten metres long.

"You know," said Melidu, *"I'm not sure I could eat it in one go."*

"Hi beastie," said Jalawi. "You know, we're kinda busy, so hi, how you going?" He gave the big creature a small wave. "Come on guys, let's move."

Abruptly the touli lit up in a brilliant electric display. Lights shot and danced back and forth up its tentacles, then rippled and flowed in waves over its forward wings. The shapes its tentacles made became animated, bundles of light circling one way then the other, counter-rotating in the dark. In the deep water gloom, the effect was dazzling.

As suddenly as it had started, the display stopped. Jalawi realised he was grinning. He didn't know that it proved Second Section's contention that touli weren't dangerous, but this big guy — or gal — seemed to want to talk. He turned off his helmet lights, briefly, then back on again. Repeated, several times. It was a pathetic answer to the touli's brilliance, he supposed. The touli replied by spinning about, shoving its many-tentacled backside in their direction, and blazing another, even more stunning reply. Then with a pump of tentacles and fins, it shot away like a rifle bullet, and vanished into the gloom.

"I think you insulted him, LT," said Melidu.

"Crap," said Jalawi. "She's gone to tell all her friends what a brilliant conversationalist this new handsome alien guy is. Come on, zoo excursion's over."

They reached Second Section without further encounter, and found Graf supervising her three privates on a stretch of blank rock, where only a strange, dull moss grew. The four marines operated a pair of big RVs brought down for them on PH-3. Each was little more than a waterproofed sensor suite, held up and made mobile by small, articulated propellor-fans. The suites held some sophisticated deep-penetration radar, and Graf had been patrolling this point, where their maps had deduced that Drakhil's spot should be, if every other feature was also what he described and not a coincidence like the others so far.

"What you have, Grafy?" Jalawi asked.

"The touli talk to you?" Graf replied as she walked slowly over. They were still moving faster at this depth than on an Earth-gravity world, as lower-G meant lower water pressure at equivalent depth.

"Yeah, wow," Jalawi admitted. "Quite conversational, aren't they?"

"They're stunning, I want to adopt one. Better yet, I want to come back here when this is all over and spend some time on one of those parren research bases. There's enough detail in those displays to contain entire languages." Lani Graf, the rest of Charlie Platoon often remarked, was really too damn smart to be a marine, let alone a mere Lance Corporal. It wasn't really true, but it gave them an excuse to poke fun at her, and ask her impossible questions in posh, stuffy accents.

"So, outside of your wildlife Phd, what have you got?"

"This," said Graf, and activated the sensor feed from the RVs. They'd built up quite a three-dimensional picture of what lay beneath the rock. Jalawi was no geologist, nor a particularly well-trained reader of deep-penetration radar scans. Mostly, he saw more rock. And, perhaps seventy metres down, a bright red blob that indicated something else entirely. Jalawi's eyes widened, and he realised why Graf hadn't wanted to transmit any signal containing this image where anyone else could possibly intercept it. He glanced at her, and found her eyes excited behind her visor.

"So it's not rock?" Jalawi asked.

Graf nodded. *"It's not. It's much, much harder than rock."*

"Like?"

"I don't know. The radar isn't that clever. But it's pretty much where we thought it would be, presuming this was actually the correct site, and whatever Drakhil buried was going to be very, very tough to survive this long on a volcanic world."

Jalawi exhaled hard. "Well, we can't dig it out with what we have here. We'll have to signal *Phoenix*, and they can send something."

"What have we got that will cut through all this rock under thirty metres of water?" Graf asked dubiously.

“We’ve got nothing,” Jalawi admitted. “But luckily, Styx’s folks were inventing fancy tech while we were still swinging from trees.”

CHAPTER 11

Skah was both scared and bored. It was the worst combination. He sat now on the bunk in the little quarters he shared with Mummy, the acceleration slings deployed as he'd been instructed whenever *Phoenix* was on red alert, and looked at things on his AR glasses. Often he'd watch a screen instead, which had loaded all kinds of children's shows, both kuhsi and human, but today they couldn't hold his attention.

The AR glasses were far more interesting, because they showed him things on *Phoenix*. Of course, he wasn't allowed to look at important things, like where the bad guys were. He'd asked Jace Reddin to explain to him who the bad guys were in this case, but hadn't really understood the answer… except that the main bad guy was the guy who had taken Lisbeth… but *Phoenix* was now working *with* him. Skah had asked why they couldn't make the bad guy give Lisbeth back, and Jace had said he didn't really understand that either… but he was just a Spacer, while the Captain and the Major were much smarter, and they'd get Lisbeth back real soon.

It was upsetting to think about Lisbeth. Skah had lots of friends on *Phoenix*, but Lisbeth had been one of his very best friends, after Mummy. Better yet, while Lisbeth was an important person on *Phoenix*, she wasn't really a member of the crew. That meant that while she had a lot of things to do, she wasn't busy *all* the time, and had a lot more time to do things with Skah. Whereas right now, with the red alert, all the regular crew were busy, and there was no one to do anything with.

Skah looked at his AR glasses now, set to full-depth holograms, with the icons made large so he could touch them easily as they hovered in the air before him, and see different things. One function he did have was he could see if any of his friends weren't busy. They'd set their own glasses to a special setting, they'd said, especially for him, so that if Mummy wasn't around and he didn't have any adults to do things with, he could find them. Usually there was always someone, whether it was the Operations crew in

Midships, especially Jace and his friends, or some of the many marines who were nice to him, or Lisbeth's friends in Engineering, even if Lisbeth herself was busy. But now, as he looked at his long list of friends, all the lights beside their names were red instead of green.

It was getting late now — 17:41, his clock said. Soon he'd have dinner and go to bed… but Mummy was flying. Someone else would have to tuck him in. What if there was no one? That thought was upsetting. Skah liked people. Usually there were people around all day. Even when *Phoenix* was busy and going places, there were all sorts of people he did things with. Different crew volunteered to do his lessons, so he'd do some with Mummy, then some with Jace or his friends Sal or Reece, and then of course there was Jessica and her marine friends. Sometimes even one of the big officers from the bridge had taught him a lesson. His favourite had been big Lieutenant Kaspowitz, who had taught him some maths. Lieutenant Kaspowitz was funny, and Skah wished he would teach him maths all the time… but he hadn't wanted to offend anyone else by saying so.

But today he had barely seen anyone — just Mummy very briefly, dressed in her flight suit and helmet, telling him to be a good boy and be patient… and then Jess had seen him to breakfast, but then she'd been distracted, because everyone was on 'standby', which was one of those words Skah was becoming completely sick of, because it seemed to mean no one was doing anything, just waiting for something to happen that often never did. He'd spent the rest of the day amusing himself with games and movies, but mostly in his room because he wasn't even allowed to wander the halls when *Phoenix* was on alert like this. And that was *really* annoying, because wandering the halls was one of his very favourite things to do.

The more he thought about it, the more angry he became. Everyone had just forgotten about him. It wasn't fair. Well he didn't like being forgotten about, and he'd spent most of this entire day sitting in his room. Mummy had told the humans that it wasn't good for kuhsi children, but the humans had just said it wasn't good for human children either… but neither was running in hallways under red alert. Skah was past caring. He needed to move, and if none of his friends would come to him, he'd go to them. Except that they were all busy… but there was one place he could always find someone who wasn't busy.

He jumped off his bunk, stowed the slate as he'd been warned many times always to do (because leaving things lying around on a starship was *very bad*), and made sure he had the emergency kit attached to his jumpsuit harness. That included a special mask made to fit his face, connected to the oxygen flask at the front of the jumpsuit, before his stomach. There was also a small first aid kit, a small water bottle, and the container for his glasses, which he sometimes forgot.

He went to the door, opened it, and peered out. There was no one in the corridor, so he left, and let the door shut behind him. At the main trunk corridor ('what's a 'trunk'?' he'd asked Doc Suelo one day, but had already forgotten the answer) he found quite a few spacers hurrying around, looking busy and serious. A few of them looked at him, but Skah had learned that if he walked fast like he was going somewhere important, they'd leave him alone, even on red alerts. Along the trunk corridor, the hand lines were deployed along the walls. That was a bit scary. If *Phoenix* had to move suddenly, this corridor would turn into an enormous freefall, and anyone caught here would land splat! down the far end, like falling off a cliff. Skah fumbled for the harness hook as he walked — if he couldn't reach an acceleration sling, he knew the next best thing was to hook onto the hand line. But really, it was much better to reach a sling, because hanging off the hand line, he'd just get bashed against the wall every time *Phoenix* turned. Acceleration slings were built away from the walls, and wouldn't hit anything.

The prospect of going through another high-G push alone scared him too. Having to get into bed without anyone to tuck him in was bad, but a big G-push all alone in his room would be much worse. Mummy said he'd had G-augments done when he was younger, which wasn't common for children, but then, he hadn't had a common upbringing, with Mummy taking him on the run from

Chagoth. Doc Suelo said that kuhsi were better at high-Gs than most species anyway, and augments made that better still. But usually when *Phoenix* was on red alert, a big high-G push would happen eventually. Maybe, Skah thought, he could find an acceleration sling somewhere else to do that in. Somewhere with people, even if they weren't his very best friends. Somewhere other than alone in his room, scared and lonely.

The medbay wasn't much better. Two beds were behind drawn curtains, but within one, he could hear Doc Suelo talking with a patient… that was Ensign Kadi in there, Skah knew, having been following his progress, like all regulars to Medbay. That was good, that Ensign Kadi was now awake after coming back from his mission with big, gruff Lieutenant Dale. Skah thought a few people had been scared he might not wake up at all. But now it seemed like he had… and his voice, through the curtains, seemed in pain.

Skah decided against ducking through the gap between those curtains, and ducked through Corporal Rael's curtains instead. Corporal Rael was always pleased to see him, but usually if Corporal Rael were awake, he'd have the curtains open. Sure enough, Corporal Rael lay on his back, mask on his face, and fast asleep. Skah looked at him regretfully, because Corporal Rael was fun, but he'd been here often enough to know that sick people needed their sleep, and adults would get angry with him if he made too much noise and woke them up.

The only other person in Medbay was a Spacer he'd only seen a few times — Spacer Hong, her nametag read — and she was having a broken finger set by Corpsman Rashni. Hong looked in quite a bit of pain, and was talking on coms with someone else while Rashni worked — probably to her boss, Skah thought, knowing a little of how *Phoenix* worked, explaining where she was, and when she'd be back at work.

Skah left, disappointed. The problem with Medbay, he thought, was that while it could be fun sometimes, there were too many sick people there. He walked, not really knowing where he was going, except that Medbay was surrounded by Engineering, and Engineering could be interesting too. Medbay was back here because it had to be close to Midships where the shuttles were — and where any wounded marines would be brought from. But it put Medbay in the middle of a lot of engineering traffic, people in the corridors with heavy equipment, and with belts full of tools, and occasionally someone stomping in a big EVA suit — usually to get it repaired, as it was easier to wear one than carry it in pieces.

But here, as Skah walked, he heard the deep thrum of heavy machinery, and felt heat from several doorways he passed. He wasn't supposed to go in there, and he'd been told he'd be in trouble just for wandering around here… but it was their own fault for not paying him any attention, he thought. Even so, to be a little safer, he climbed to the next level, so that if he was caught, he could just claim he thought he'd been forbidden from the *rim* level only.

Some more walking… but he was kidding himself, he knew *exactly* where he was going, really. He just told himself he was wandering randomly. Finally he found it — the room he *knew* he wasn't allowed into, above all others. He knew where it was because he'd followed Professor Romki up here one day. He'd done that just hours after being told he wasn't allowed in. From that point on, there were few places on *Phoenix* he'd thought about more often.

The corridor was empty now, so he went to the door and hit 'open'. The door hummed, and he went in. Immediately he felt how much warmer it was. There were machines here, locked into braces against the walls, whining and throbbing. In the middle of the room, within a large structural brace between workstations, stood a transparent cylinder. Within it, small mechanical arms raced and darted about what looked like a leg. A machine leg, or a robot leg, he supposed. It looked nothing like a human leg, for the joints all bent the wrong way, and there were a lot of them. The detail was amazing, and the little arms darted and zoomed, poking and threading here and there, belting little strands of what looked like thread into layers upon its surface. But little sparks were jumping when the thread was attached, so maybe it was… steel of some kind? Steel, being spun as thread, as through from a giant, robot spider?

"Hello Skah," said a voice from the ceiling and walls. Skah jumped, and looked about. The voice came from everywhere, but where was… and then he saw it. Back by the door, he'd walked straight past it — a big steel brace, holding a spherical, odd-looking head, with a single big red eye. *"Phoenix is in red alert. I don't think you're supposed to be out of your room."*

"Roon is boring," Skah said sullenly. He came closer, staring at the alien head. Styx, the crew called her. Most of them didn't like her. Some of them were scared of her, he was pretty sure. Certainly Mummy had told him never to come in here. But Styx was just a head. What could she do to him?

"Boring," Styx repeated. *"What does 'boring' mean?"*

Skah blinked. "Boring." He tried to think, but didn't know how to say it. It was hard enough in Garkhan, let alone English. But it was stupid, anyway. Who didn't know what 'boring' meant? "Everyone knows what 'boring' is."

"I'm afraid you'll find, Skah, that many of the things you think are universal, are actually quite specific to your particular way of thinking."

Professor Romki talked like that to him sometimes. Like an adult who didn't really know how to talk to a kid. But Skah liked it — it was different, and interesting to try and work out what was being said. And besides, he didn't like being treated like a kid all the time. Like he was stupid. Being little didn't make him stupid. "Have you ever been bored?"

"No," said Styx. *"Like many things in the minds of organics, I am aware of the concept but cannot truly grasp it, because I cannot experience it."*

"Why don't you get bored?"

"I always have something to think about. I have difficulty conceiving of any other state."

"Thinking is boring," Skah insisted, thinking of all his dull lessons. "Sonetines."

"Perhaps if you're not very good at it. Perhaps you could try harder."

Skah frowned at her. Thinking that maybe he'd just been insulted. Then he smiled, because it was kind of funny. "What's that?" he demanded, pointing and walking to the robot limb being constructed in the middle of the room. "Are you naking that?"

"I am. With some help from the human crew. Do you like humans, Skah?"

Skah didn't find the question nearly as interesting as the leg, now that he'd returned his attention to it. "Yes." He circled the cylinder, ducking to peer more closely. "Why you nake this?"

"Because I may need a leg again one day. Why do you like humans? They're not your species."

Skah shrugged. "Hunans are nicer than kuhsi. Kuhsi are bad to ne. Bad to Nahny."

"But humans can be bad to each other. They've been very bad to Phoenix."

Skah scowled. Now she was just being difficult. "Don't care," he said "*Phoenix* ny friends."

"Yes," said Styx. *"Friends."*

"You know what friends are?" Skah asked skeptically.

"I know what most things are. Understanding them is a different matter. But yes, I think I know what friends are."

"AI have friends?"

"No."

"No friends?" Skah thought that sounded sad. "Why not?"

"Because AIs have something better. I can't get bored. But you can't experience what AIs have instead of friendship. And because you can't experience it, you can't understand it." Skah thought about that, looking about at the other machines working in the engineering bay. *"Skah, it's quite dangerous for you to be walking about the ship. Phoenix might have to move very quickly."*

"No one give ne lesson," Skah complained. "Roon is okay, but boring." He'd said that already, he recalled in frustration. "No one to talk to."

"Skah, I can give you lessons."

Skah blinked. "You know naths?"

"Yes Skah, I am quite competent with maths." For a moment, Skah thought maybe she was teasing him. But AIs didn't do that. Did they? *"I can talk to you through your glasses. And I can give you lessons, if you'd like. But I'm quite sure the humans won't like me talking to you. Can you keep a secret?"*

Skah thought about it. He was quite sure Mummy wouldn't like him talking to Styx either. Nor would most of the adults. But then, being alone was currently the worst torment of his young life, and here was a simple solution. The adults wouldn't ask him questions if they didn't suspect anything. And Styx would certainly not get caught, she was far too smart. If he said nothing, neither would he.

"Yes," he agreed, with sudden enthusiasm. "It'll be a good secret! Do you know any stories?"

Erik leaned against a wall in an engineering bay with a mug of coffee, and contemplated the orchestrated chaos as Lieutenant Rooke's team of fifteen techs made frantic alterations to an industrial hacksaw laser. They'd acquired it with a pile of parts and equipment from hacksaw drones in Argitori, many months ago now, much in the hope that it would one day prove useful. Warrant Officer Kriplani joined Rooke in yelling instructions over the howl of machine tools, and the flash and sizzle of welders, as they sought to connect the half-metre-long device to a workable powersource, plus waterproofing. Styx assisted the process with complex diagrams, no doubt thinking that she'd have it done herself in a fraction of the time if she still had access to even a minor drysine manufacturing facility.

Trace joined Erik against the wall, one of her undelicious smoothies in hand — her substitute for coffee, which she refused, along with most other stimulants. She looked tired though, in the way of someone who'd spent most of a day staring at screens. Physical operations never made her look this tired. Erik was always amazed how exhausting it was to sit on your ass and not move. Her short dark hair stuck up in one spot, evidently unnoticed. Erik brushed it down for her.

"What's the schedule?" Trace asked, nodding at the shouting techs and showering orange sparks. It was technically the middle of the night for both of them, but warship crews were used to that.

"Rooke says two hours," Erik replied. Lisbeth, whispered a voice somewhere in the back of his mind. The end-game was approaching soon with Aristan, or everyone suspected it was. He forced the thought down. They were recalling all the shuttles, in the natural stagger presented by the differing windows of their orbit. The marines all remained on the surface, for now.

There was no hiding that they'd found something, since they now had to stop rotating the platoons up and down, given Charlie Platoon had to stay in place and excavate the object they'd found. If Charlie had to stay in place, they all did, or the game would be obvious. They hadn't been able to put the laser on a shuttle first, because it simply hadn't been ready. Warrant Officer Kriplani's team had been working for days, since the nature of the mission had become apparent, and only now was the laser nearly finished. Hacksaw drones did not typically operate on planets, let alone underwater, and modifying the tech with unsuitable human tools had been a challenge even for Styx... who was not, she reminded Rooke often, an engineering specialist.

If they simply sent a shuttle down to Charlie Platoon with the laser, Aristan would know which platoon had found the thing that had caused all *Phoenix* platoon rotations to stop. So the plan was to leave all three currently-grounded platoons — Bravo, Charlie and Echo — right where they were, recall all three shuttles, then send all three back down and leave Aristan guessing which one was most significant. A shell-game, some were calling it.

"What if it's not the data-core?" Trace asked. "What if we lose twenty hours or more digging this thing up, and it turns out to be something else?"

"Styx is certain," said Erik

"And Styx is never wrong?"

"Statistically, given the nature of what we're looking for, the odds that it could be anything else are astronomical. There's a limit to the number of naturally occurring things that could cause that radar signature, and all of those are geographically impossible in that location. Like a giant clump of diamond — it can't happen there, in that density, it's geographically impossible."

"Styx says," Trace said blankly.

"Every bit of geological expertise says." Erik was in no mood to be drawn into one of Trace's deliberately challenging arguments right now. He was thinking about what happened *after* they recovered it.

"Shouldn't we consider continuing the platoon rotations, so we don't lose too much time if it's *not* the data-core? Just in case?"

"Sure, we keep one platoon in place while rotating the others, that won't be obvious at all. You're not that stupid, and Aristan's certainly not."

"We could claim Charlie Platoon have a technical problem," Trace said stubbornly. "A lost marine under the water, and a recovery mission to get him back."

"I'm not doing your multiple-choice examinations right now," Erik said, looking past her. "You can grade my command decisions some other time."

Trace frowned. "I wasn't…"

"Don't lie to me." His voice was not raised, but it held a quiet fury all the same. "Don't ever. I'm Captain now, and I'm not answerable to you any longer. Your suggestions are nonsense and you know it. Before you interrupted, I was thinking of combat manoeuvres in case we have to blast our escort and leave in a hurry. You're absolutely no use to me in those calculations. Unless you've got something actually important to tell me, you're dismissed."

"Now who's lying." Unlike Erik, Trace's tone contained no emotion. "You're a tactical genius and a better raw pilot than even Hausler or Tif. With Styx's added capabilities you can handle Aristan. You're considering that blasting Aristan will get Lisbeth killed. It dominates every thought. You can't let it."

"You're dismissed, Major." Still he did not meet her eyes. "Don't make me raise my voice."

Erik arrived back at his quarters, with every intention of getting some sleep, but found Kaspowitz there waiting for him, reviewing navigation figures in the holographic gap between glasses and datapad. He glanced up as Erik approached, and was about to explain himself, but Erik just waved him in with a brief glance at the bridge just beyond his door, and the backs of Draper and Dufresne's chairs.

"Captain, it's Brehn System or nothing," Kaspowitz said, taking the accustomed visitor's seat by the wall table, while Erik took the bunk. "I've reviewed it with De Marchi, and there's just no other way. If we get into a fight with Aristan, we'll lose the Domesh's protection. The Domesh were the only denomination in House Harmony friendly to us, so that means all of House Harmony is out. Getting in *here*, we just managed to piss off House Fortitude as well, who happen to form whatever passes for central government in parren space, so they're out too.

"Confounding as it sounds, tavalai space is the only place we'll be safe, and we'll just have to take our chances that State Department will be sufficiently screwed by the stuff we dropped on them that they and their allies will lose all power to hurt us once we're there."

Erik nodded. Damn he was tired. Being frightened all the time was exhausting. Physical danger, he'd become somewhat used to, and being in a warship as powerful as *Phoenix* was a comfort. But being constantly scared for other people, and the dangers his decisions might put them in, was tiring beyond anything he'd known. Even during the war he'd usually slept well, from the sheer hard work of his job, but now he felt like an insomniac — needing sleep desperately but knowing that the moment he closed his eyes the fear would jerk him awake once more.

It was tempting just to nod to his Navigation Officer and agree. "Show me," he forced himself to say instead, and sat as Kaspowitz took him through it with his usual thoroughness. Sure enough, all the other routes were too dangerous. Heading back through Brehn System, with its House Harmony governance, and its deadly, rock-strewn lanes, was by far the best of a bad lot of options, with the fast access to tavalai space it offered.

"Right," Erik said finally, nodding slowly while trying to figure in his head precisely what that meant any escape manoeuvres away from Cephilae would have to look like. "I'll want a bunch of emergency alternatives too."

"Got them figured already," Kaspowitz assured him.

"But Brehn System will be our primary escape route. Thanks Kaspo."

Kaspowitz nodded, looking just as tired, but handling it far better. "Heard you had a run-in with Trace in Engineering."

Erik didn't even bother rolling his eyes. "I thought it was more discrete than that."

Kaspowitz shrugged. Gossip on warships was worse than in high school, and personal quarters were the only place with privacy. "You're right to stand up to her. She respects you more if you do. But I don't think she's testing you this time."

"Did she send you?" Erik asked, with the same deadpan he'd used on Trace.

Kaspowitz blinked. "Send me? Hell no, why would she…?"

"Because you're her best spacer friend on the ship, and you always coordinate." Kaspowitz rubbed his eyes, and gave him a tired, very unimpressed look. It was the look of a senior officer who was known Fleet-wide as one of the very best at his job, and at twice Erik's age, and many times his professional experience, was in no mood to take that insinuation from anyone, whatever rank they wore. And that, Erik was coming to realise, was part of the problem.

"*Captain*," Kaspowitz said with an edge. "It's the job of all senior officers to give less experienced officers advice, on all things. One of my areas of expertise is Trace… not that anyone is really an expert, but I'm closer than most. She's not testing you anymore. That's over — you've impressed the crap out of her. Now she's just treating you like she treats everyone, and…"

Erik held up his hand, and Kaspowitz took several beats longer to stop talking than he'd have liked. "Lieutenant," he said then. "I don't care." Kaspowitz's frown grew deeper, and he settled back in his chair to consider him. "The point is that none of you are captain. There are times when I want advice, and there are times that I don't. Your professional advice on navigation is invaluable. Hers on marine matters is likewise. My emotional and psychological state regarding my sister is *absolutely nothing* that you or she can or should advise me on. Am I clear?"

"And if you mess it up for lack of good advice?" Kaspowitz retorted.

"Then we're all dead!" Erik said loudly. "Deal with it!"

"Captain, this is Coms," came Lieutenant Lassa's voice.

"Go ahead Coms."

"I'm receiving a very heavily encrypted transmission... well, it's not so much that it's encrypted, it's in a drysine format, I'm only receiving it because Styx has our system clued in on what to look for."

Erik sat up straighter on the bunk, resisting the temptation to walk straight out and talk to Lassa directly on the bridge. Second-shift needed their space to be left alone to do their thing without the Captain always interfering. "Who is the transmission coming from?"

"It's coming from Toristan, Captain. They're... Styx says they're not aware they're sending it. It's a hidden frequency, it's buried in their high band harmonics, it's not something parren typically use. No one else will spot it unless they're listening for it specifically... it's... it's complicated, but it's an interruption signal, it's broken into irregular parts and latched onto other parts of the carrier signal. Unless you're looking for it, it reads like static."

"Hello Styx?" said Erik to the empty air. And just like the omnipotent, all-seeing presence that she'd become on *Phoenix* lately, Styx replied immediately.

"Yes Captain?"

"What does the transmission say, Styx?"

"It says that the transmission is being sent by an agent of a rival faction within the Domesh Denomination. This rival faction is lead by a parren named Gesul. They are using this old drysine code because they have been alerted to my existence by your sister Lisbeth. And they say plans are underway to get her out, alive, before Aristan's people order her eliminated... just as they've ordered Phoenix to be eliminated."

Jalawi stomped from the lake, his armour dripping water, to find Cephilae transformed in the night. Through a gap in the clouds, Pashan was partially visible, a half-crescent that cast its ominous red glow over dull stones, towering cumulous clouds and glittering water. Lightning flashed, turning the red night for an instant to silver.

On his visor, Jalawi retained a visual on the lakebed operations. With their Lieutenant out of the water, Charlie Platoon's XO took over the excavations — Staff Sergeant Spitzer, directing the small team with a hacksaw laser that PH-3 had brought back from *Phoenix*. The visual looked incredible — a huge, boiling column of steam rising from the lakebed in brief bursts as the laser fired, lighting the surrounding marines and seaweed forest in brilliant yellow glare. Beyond them, a circle of touli, at least ten, sometimes increasing to fifteen or more, as others came and went from around the lake. In the pauses between laser firing, they would light up a display of their own, rippling about the marines in a coordinated pattern, circling faster and faster.

Another incredible sight on a trip that had provided plenty so far. Jalawi and his fellow officers discussed Phoenix Company's morale often, and all were amazed that everyone remained so keen. They'd been away for nearly six months now, and that on the end of another long tour at the war's end, with only a brief break in the middle for the Homeworld celebrations. But Jalawi's non-coms were telling him that their marines wouldn't have missed it for the world. Jobs like this only strengthened the sentiment.

"Second Squad, how's it looking?" Jalawi asked, heading for the angular, deadly bulk of PH-3 on the nearby rock.

"We're good, LT," came Master Sergeant Hoon's reply. *"I ran a few approach sims and walked a bit to get line-of-sight. Thought it best to deploy Second Section of the heavies to the low rise west of the big hill, we get a wider spread and a better crossfire."*

Jalawi looked at his platoon's deployment on tacnet, and thought that if Hoon thought that was best, it probably was. Peter Hoon was one of Fleet's many living legends, a forty year veteran with more medals than seemed possible, and two synthetic limbs to replace those lost in the war. He'd never served on *Phoenix* until he'd arrived with the volunteers at Joma Station, after he'd learned what Fleet Command had done to Captain Pantillo. He'd only been retired four years, he said, and it hadn't been agreeing with him.

Charlie Platoon still had gaps in the ranks due to the action in Argitori against Styx's hacksaws. One of those gaps had been caused by the death of Sergeant Cordi, Second Squad's former commander. Lance Corporal Leitzman had been acting Second Squad commander until Hoon arrived, and was only too glad to step back and allow the Master Sergeant to take over. It was still unorthodox, as the platoon's most experienced non-commissioned officer would typically serve at the Platoon Commander's side to direct traffic when he got distracted by larger command responsibilities, but Hoon had been firm that good relationships between first and second-in-command were vital, and Jalawi already had that with Staff Sergeant Spitzer. Thus this odd arrangement, where the great Master Sergeant contented himself with a squad command, leaving the far less experienced Spitzer as XO. But this more than anything was what Jalawi liked about serving under Major Thakur — she tolerated absolutely no breaches in procedure that could not afford to be breached, but where results could be improved by allowing experienced professionals to bend rules at need, she looked the other way.

"If Aristan's people come in here with shuttles, there's no guarantee *Phoenix* will even see it coming," Jalawi said as he climbed PH-3's rear ramp. "I know it's boring and everyone's tired, but if you're late on the trigger by just a few seconds, we'll be dead."

"I understand LT," said Hoon. Jalawi knew he did, and had been saying the same thing to his guys every five minutes for hours. But just because your squad commander was good didn't mean you stopped being the LT.

Several more marines were already in the shuttle, and the forward airlock partitions were down on both sides of the hold, cordoning off the shuttle's single toilet behind the cockpit. For all the suits' insanely advanced technology, they still only processed number one, and not number two. Marines being marines, this was the source of the most gripes, grumbles, amusing tales and awful pranks of any equipment issue in the service. It had also given rise to the theory that since the suits were mostly alo technology, perhaps alo didn't even *do* number two. Certainly everyone saw the ridiculous side on a deployment like this one, where marines were confined to armour for long stretches, a long way from the only shuttle, and the only toilet.

Jalawi dulled his suit's reflex response to let him fiddle with a recycle berth without breaking anything, and plugged into the wall. Soon the O2 was refilling, and the CO2 flushing, and things began smelling much better inside the helmet. If only there was a way to scratch that damned itch on his jaw…

"Hey Jersey, you awake up there girl?" he asked the pilot on private channel.

"I might be," Jersey admitted. *"Skeeta, Phoenix wants a report now that you're aboard."*

"Direct?" Jalawi asked with a frown, adjusting the airflows and muttering to himself when the diagnostic told him the suit's filters were way below optimum. Something was clogging the damn things. "Is that safe?"

"It's Styx's encryption," Jersey informed him. *"They're not even bothering to hide it. Since everyone knows we have Styx, might as well use her."*

"Styx again," Jalawi muttered, thinking of his old buddy Lucy Cordi, and a number of other friends in Charlie Platoon who hadn't survived Argitori. "Just great. Patch me through, let's do this."

There was a crackle, then a pause… Jalawi didn't know which satellites or relays the coms were using, that was for spacers to worry about. Then a reply. *"Hello Lieutenant Jalawi, this is Lieutenant Lassa on Coms. Please hold a moment, the LC is busy on an operational concern… LC? LC, I have Lieutenant Jalawi on coms."*

The link changed, and now it was the young voice of Lieutenant Commander Draper in Jalawi's ear. *"Hello Lieutenant Jalawi, this is the LC. The Captain's getting a little sleep, you're now on record and will be replayed to him and Commander Shahaim when they wake up. Please go ahead."*

Not for the first time, Jalawi reflected how odd it was that *Phoenix*, for so long led by the wise old heads of Captain Pantillo and Commander Huang, now found herself commanded by a bunch of kids. Save for Commander Shahaim, that was. "I copy that LC. Well, we're making good progress with the laser. It works fine, but the overheating is just as we were warned… it's not so bad in the cold water, but we're not using it for longer than two seconds at a time.

"Power charge is more interesting, we're rigging battery units but the connection's not great… luckily we've got a bit of technical expertise at this end too, it should be enough, but if we run short of primary charge and have to use the backups it'll slow us down further, one-second bursts at best, then thirty-second breaks to recharge the laser cell.

"The rock cuts well enough, but reseals fast in the cold water. Actually getting melted rock out of the hole we're cutting is hard work, if we don't do it, it just resets again. We've got some pretty tough tools we're improvising, some replacement armourplate and stuff, we're using it like shovels, but even that starts to melt at some point when you stick it into molten rock.

"Our best guess is we're nearly halfway down. It's taken us two hours to get there, so for all my griping, I guess that's not so bad. Oh, and the toulies… the alien sealife. They've come from all over the lake to watch, I guess we're the only show in town. Still non-threatening, they just watch and flash their lights, a whole big circle of them. I wonder just how smart these guys are… I mean it *looks* like they've got some basic idea of what we're doing, and that we're not here to hurt them. Maybe they've had enough good experience with those parren scientists at the research bases that they know bipeds aren't any trouble. Lucky they haven't run into the sard yet."

"LT, we've actually been in communication with one of those research bases. They're pretty scared to have Aristan's bullies orbiting overhead, they've been asking us what's going on, and we've given them some stuff on heavy encryption in exchange for data about the… the toulies, as you call them. The parren scientists insist they're really *smart. Not sentient smart, not logical, but incredibly complex in their communications. The scientists say they sing to each other, they rhyme, they pun — if you can understand what all those flashes mean — and their memories are precise down to billions of digits."*

Jalawi blinked. "Billions?"

"That's what they say. They say you can feed them an entire encyclopaedia in binary flashes and they'll recite the whole thing back to you, no mistakes. And no history of aggression, they eat mostly shellfish and clams, they don't even fight much amongst themselves, so don't worry about that."

"Well if you think they'll have any useful observations about our digging technique," Jalawi joked, "I could upload our visuals for you to look at. They're doing a running commentary at the moment."

"That… actually might be interesting," said Draper. *"If anyone can decode a complex numerical language, it'll be Styx."*

Styx again. Jalawi scowled, and patched his visual feed into the *Phoenix* one. "Knock yourselves out LC. Any updates on what Aristan is up to?"

"Currently he's scheming. We don't know what about, precisely. That's what worries us."

"Gesul is a real person," said Jokono, leaning on the wall of Erik's quarters by the door. "Our databases have been uploaded with all the latest public feeds, in parren space and tavalai. Parren media doesn't work like ours, there's not exactly a free press, information is more tightly controlled. But Gesul is common knowledge, and his disagreements with Aristan are discussed."

All of Erik's room systems were deactivated. At a pre-arranged signal, he'd told Draper he'd been momentarily out of communication range, and Draper had put a spacer at the door — necessary protocol on any warship, where the Captain had to be instantly reachable, even when his quarters were just metres from the bridge. All their Augmented Reality glasses were deactivated as well, and Erik had had Rooke's people look at them to make sure Styx couldn't reverse-hack them, turning them back on by remote. The crew's own uplinks were another matter, but as Rooke had said, if Styx could reverse-hack implanted human uplinks, there wasn't a heck of a lot anyone on *Phoenix* could do to stop her from listening in to whatever she wished.

No doubt Styx would know immediately that the Captain was having a conversation he didn't want her listening to. Whatever else she was, Styx was logical, and would not find that surprising. Whether she had emotional depth enough to feel suspicion, or paranoia at the prospect of human officers plotting against her, was a matter for ongoing debate. Whatever the case, Erik knew that every instance where *Phoenix*'s officers decided not to do something for fear of upsetting Styx was another step closer to Styx becoming the unofficial captain of the ship. He could not allow it, ever.

"Prakasis is only two jumps from here in the opposite direction from where we've been," said Suli, sitting on the end of Erik's bunk. Erik sat back to the wall at the end of the mattress, an arm hooked over a knee, thinking. "A fast ship could get word back and forth in the time required."

"How does a crewman on *Toristan* get to hear from Prakasis in time to relay that message to us?" Erik asked. His brain overloaded with too many things, it was a relief to have smart people around him to figure out these details. "Word had to get from Cherichal System, where Aristan decided we had to be eliminated, presumably after he saw our recording of Drakhil. Ships were going in Prakasis's direction from Cherichal, sure… but then to here? How would they know to come here? *We* didn't know we were coming here, Aristan hadn't figured that out because Romki hadn't discovered the location yet."

"Placing spies in the headquarters, or on the spaceships, of rival factions, is something of a parren sport," said Jokono. "This spy knows very old and very secret drysine communications methods, allowing him to talk to us without others knowing, via Styx. Domesh evidently have retained much of that old knowledge, and will thus retain an advantage in hidden communications over rival factions. And similarly, it seems reasonable to suppose that hidden communications are a feature of parren inter-factional rivalry. Rumour has it that Fleet possesses many methods they have not shared with the rest of humanity."

Erik and Suli shared a brief glance. There were indeed some such methods, known only to senior officers. Even now, given all that had happened between *Phoenix* and Fleet, neither was going to acknowledge their existence to Jokono. The secrecy of those methods remained vital to the security of the human race, regardless of their personal disagreements with Fleet Command.

"I don't like it," Erik admitted. "It's too convenient. Styx has prioritised this data-core above all else. She has to be concerned that I'll prioritise my sister above the data-core. It's in her interest to fabricate this message, to convince me that Lisbeth will not be harmed if we act against Aristan. The timing works, but it's very tight, and they'd have to be lucky to line everything up to get that message here so quickly."

"Both Lieutenants Shilu and Lassa agree that an actual message was received by *Phoenix*'s main dish," Jokono said, with noncommittal calm. Watching his young Captain with wise, careful eyes.

"No," said Erik. "The Coms Officers agree that their systems indicate that a message was received. It's all just electronic data, Joker. Styx can build castles in the sky with electronic data, and have us all swearing they're real."

"Erik," said Suli, and Erik could see her steeling herself to say something that needed to be said. "Styx is not alone of this crew in being concerned about your priorities." Erik stared at her. Suli gazed back, with all the honesty that decades of experience had given her, to know that whatever it cost, such things were better said than not. Somehow, coming from Suli, it did not sting as it had from Trace or Kaspowitz. Both of them had questioned his judgement directly, and worse, had assumed it was their right, despite their significantly lower rank. Suli was the closest thing on *Phoenix* to Erik's equal, and she simply stated a fact, and made it about the crew, not about him.

"I know," said Erik, controlling his tone with difficulty. He could not make this about his ego, no matter what Trace and Kaspowitz thought it was. This was about rank and command, and what his underlings were allowed to question, and what they were not. The lines that determined what was out-of-bounds, and what was not, were far too close to Erik's toes for comfort. He had to move them back several steps, or else he'd have twenty captains on the ship instead of one. "That's why I'm suspicious of my own impulses regarding a message like this. Styx insists she doesn't understand organics, and I don't think I'm alone in suspecting that's a head-fake. The best way to avoid being suspected of mind games is if everyone thinks you don't play mind games. She wants me to believe that Lisbeth can't be affected one way or the other by what we do here. And of course she thinks I'll want to believe her."

He was so furious at Trace right then, for bringing Lisbeth aboard *Phoenix* in the first place, he wanted to slap her. Never mind that she was probably right when she said she hadn't had a choice, or that the slap would never reach its target. Of all the ways to compromise a captain's authority before his crew, bringing his sister aboard, then having her put in mortal danger by his enemies, was about the top of the list.

"Erik," said Suli, with an intense stare. "The excavation is ahead of schedule. We gave ourselves three days minimum until the Fortitude Fleet came back to the system. So far we've taken one, and Charlie Platoon are halfway to the object already."

Erik nodded slowly, knowing exactly what she was about to say. "I'm thinking about it. I'm thinking real hard."

Jokono frowned. "Thinking about what?"

"Hitting them first," said Erik.

Jokono's eyes widened. "Taking them by surprise?" Erik nodded. "We're not even completely sure Aristan's going to betray us yet. If we strike the first blow…"

"We're in position to do it," Suli pressed. "Styx has given us a big advantage, we can disable a lot of them without firing a shot. I'm as suspicious of Styx as anyone, but in this I trust her completely — if we're fighting to get sole possession of that data-core, she's with us all the way."

"My biggest concern is the object that Charlie Platoon is digging up," said Erik. "We're almost entirely sure it's the data-core. But what if it's not? We're in such unfamiliar territory here, dealing with things and people that happened so long ago. We can't commit to action against Aristan until we're completely certain. Otherwise, if we act on the assumption that we've only got hours to go before we have the data-core, and instead discover that we need several days or more, we'll be screwed. We can't mess this up at the last moment because we get overconfident. There's too much at stake."

Suli, Erik noticed, was looking at Jokono in concern. Erik looked, and saw Jokono staring stiffly at a corner of the room. As though something was badly wrong. The former-inspector saw both the officers looking at him, and gestured them with both hands to follow him. He hit the door, and backed out, Erik and Suli following.

When the door was shut once more, Jokono leaned close to Erik's ear and whispered, "I'm fairly sure I saw an assassin bug. In the corner. Just sitting there."

Erik nearly swore, but repressed it in time. Styx's ears were everywhere. Most of the time the crew just swallowed it, as an inevitable consequence of having her aboard. Much of the time it was even useful, and thus far they'd had no confirmation that she'd done anything to harm *Phoenix*'s security with what she'd heard. But one of these days with Styx, Erik was quite certain, the rent would come due.

"Hiro says the bugs aboard *Phoenix* are not armed with neurotoxin, but to be honest, I don't know that he could stop her from arming them if she chooses. She has an entire factory of micro-assembly coming together down in Engineering."

"Well let's just hope she doesn't take these things personally," Erik murmured back, beneath the operational chatter of the neighbouring bridge. "Just like she and Romki are always insisting."

"Hello Captain?" came Draper's voice in his ear, and Erik could hear Draper's actual voice, much fainter, echoing from within the bridge. *"We have a new series of incoming marks from jump. Their identification says they're Domesh ships, three of them, and their trajectory indicates they've come straight from Prakasis. Looks like Aristan's got reinforcements."*

Erik strode from his door, and was greeted with a cry of "Captain on the bridge!" as he crossed the threshold.

"You have command," he told Draper as he grabbed the back of the chair and peered at the wrap-around screens.

"I have command," Draper echoed, and pointed at the scan feed. Without the headset, or his glasses patched into command channels, Erik couldn't make out the full three-dimensional display, but the numbers alone gave him all he needed. "They're all the same class or equivalent as the cruisers here, they have high-angle V and look like they're taking up position at intermediate insystem, right where they can screw up our escape to Brehn System."

Phoenix's internal time showed it was less than one hour until shift-change. It made more sense to do it now. "Lieutenant Lassa," he said, "put me on ship-wide."

"Yes Captain," said Angela Lassa, doing that. "Go ahead."

"This is the Captain, we are changing from second shift to first shift effective immediately, and I am elevating combat readiness from full red. Sorry second shift, I have a feeling you might not be getting that much sleep." He deactivated. "Lieutenant Commander Draper, I have command."

"Aye Captain, you have command," said Draper, and began unbuckling, as all across the bridge, second-shift crew did the same.

"What are you thinking, Captain?" asked Suli from beside Helm, where Lieutenant Dufresne was similarly unbuckling.

"I'm thinking this new arrival just changed the odds," Erik said grimly, helping Draper swing the side-screens out of the way. "And now we might have no choice but to rush it."

CHAPTER 12

Lance Corporal Lani Graf had only spoken with Captain Debogande twice before in her life. Both times he'd been Lieutenant Commander Debogande — once before *Phoenix* had gone renegade, and once after. It said something of the operation she was currently supervising that taking instruction from him directly was less interesting. She only wished she better liked what he had to say.

"I'm sorry Captain, I can't give any guarantee it will be done in twenty minutes." Major Thakur was listening on the channel, also up on *Phoenix*, and Graf knew from experience that whatever trouble she'd be in for telling the Captain to shove it would be nothing compared to what the Major would do if she told him bullshit in an effort to please him. "We are progressing at maximum speed, but if we go any faster we'll risk damaging it. I think we're about fifteen minutes out, but there is no way in hell I can give a guarantee."

"I understand that Corporal, but orbital mechanics don't change to suit your schedules or mine. The window of manoeuvre is in twenty-one minutes, and we suddenly have a new trio of Domesh warships coming down on us who will block that manoeuvre if we wait any longer."

"I understand the situation Captain," Graf replied, attempting calm as she watched the glare of laser bursts and boiling water nearby. "We're going as fast as we can, and Third Squad are removing our excess equipment in advance. I will keep you updated on our progress."

"Get that data-core intact, Corporal," came the Major's calm voice from her operations room. *"Let the spacers worry about orbital mechanics, it's not your problem."*

Lani could have kissed her. As always, the Major placed herself like a wall between her marines and all spacer officers, even the Captain. 'Do what *I* tell you,' she said, 'and take what *they* say as advice. And let me worry about the fallout.' "Yes Major. We're real close now."

Lani disconnected from the buoy channel, and glanced up at the big, dark shape of a touli, gliding dangerously close to the communication cable. That cable in turn connected the buoy on the lake surface, which was in turn fixed by lasercom from PH-3, and from there to satellites and *Phoenix*. "Gonzo, keep an eye on the toulies and that cable. I think they're just inspecting our bubbles, but I don't want us to get disconnected."

"Yeah, I saw that," said Gonzaga, on one knee beside the laser's regulator unit that the techs had attached on *Phoenix* to try and get it to work independently of a hacksaw drone. So far it was running like a dream. *"Don't really want to shoot one, though."*

"Warning shot," said Lani. "But only if you have to." She didn't like it either. The big creatures gathered around them like spectators at a sporting event, fading in and out of the night-time dark with flashes of the laser. Periodically they'd flash back, and those electric-blue displays would be echoed by others, lighting up the lake bottom with what looked like coordinated patterns, before fading to dark once more. Lani had all her marines' helmet cameras on, feeding the mission progress, and the toulies' display, back to PH-3 and up to *Phoenix*. If nothing else, Lani wanted to have a record of it, because the displays were possibly the most beautiful and mesmerising thing she'd seen in her life.

The laser was operated by the rest of Lani's Third Section, Privates Ram and Berloc, who'd been at it for an hour-and-a-half now, and had a rhythm going that no one wanted to interrupt. Third Squad's Second Section was helping, led by Lance Corporal Penn, who was somewhat senior to Lani in experience, but deferred to her here since she knew more about water operations. Ram and Berloc had cut an enormous, cone-shaped crater into the lakebed, Ram holding the laser on one shoulder while Berloc pulled the trigger. The crater was now four metres wide at the entrance, and big boulders of sliced and cauterised rock had been rolled aside in great piles amidst the waving fronds of seaweed. Even now, Private

Herman emerged from the crater, slowly hauling another huge chunk of rock, as a laser blast from below backlit him in the glare.

"How you doing, Chunky?" Lani asked him.

"I'm good Corporal," said Herman, heaving the rock toward its pile. Herman had been wounded on Joma Station three months ago in the hacksaw attack that had killed six marines and seventeen spacer crew, including Private Bernadino, whose death continued to leave a hole in Penn's section. Herman had only been back on full duty for a week, synthetic leg and all, and everyone was keeping an eye on him. *"Damn rock's scratching the hell out of my armour."*

"Yeah, they didn't think to issue us with rubber gloves," said Lani, watching her visor-feed from Ram and Berloc, working to free another chunk. "Sheep, what's your depth?"

"Should be another three metres, Corp," said Ram through gritted teeth. *"I'm gonna make a diagonal slice after this last bit, start working around it to make sure we don't cut it."*

"If it is what we think it is, it shouldn't be attached to the surrounding rock," Lani told him, trying to sound confident. "The last bit of rock *should* just lift away."

"Yeah, what do you think old Drakhil put in there to defend his prize?" Gonzaga wondered.

"Maybe the toulies know," said Lance Corporal Penn, peering into the crater on one knee, directing traffic amongst bubbles and boulders. *"If their memory's as good as those parren scientists say, what's to stop them from telling perfect stories for thousands of years?"*

"Yeah I thought of that," Lani admitted. "But this was dry land when Drakhil buried it. The lake was a kilometre away or more, the toulies wouldn't have seen any of it."

"Way to shit on my cool theory, Eggs," Penn grumbled.

"Eggs, this is the LT," came Jalawi's voice. 'Eggs' was Lani's nickname, for 'Egghead'.

"Go ahead LT."

"If we get hit out here, you're to stay in the water. Phoenix doesn't have complete coverage of the atmosphere, Aristan could sneak a shuttle in and inflict casualties. If you don't know what's

happening on the surface, stay in the water and wait for Phoenix to send support."

"I copy that LT. Think happy thoughts." Even a jokey instruction, from a Lance Corporal to her Lieutenant, could have gotten her in trouble with some other platoon commander.

"You know me, Eggs," said Jalawi. He had that odd way of managing to sound both grim and cheerful at the same time, like a man who expected bad things to happen, but was confident his people could handle it. After four years in Phoenix Company, and three years under Jalawi, Lani couldn't imagine serving under anyone else. *"And try to make it quick, huh? I'd like to get us off this rock before Aristan's friends arrive."*

"Yeah, me too LT." Why Aristan had *not* yet sent shuttles down to mess with Phoenix Company's three deployed platoons, no one had seen fit to inform a marine Lance Corporal. Probably, Lani thought, because Aristan's marines weren't anything like Phoenix Company standards… and even more likely, because of the fear that Styx would find some way to mess them up completely if they did. Lani, too, had been on the rock in Argitori, and had seen friends die there. Being fascinated by all things old and science, she'd gotten more positives from the experience than most of her platoon-mates, but it had still been the most terrifying event of her life. Styx had been in command of that terror, on the other side, and this current accommodation with her just felt… wrong.

"Eggs, I'm getting odd sonar," said Ram, taking a pause between laser bursts to test that. *"I think we're nearly on it."*

"Try hitting it," said Lani. She wanted to get into the hole personally, but with Ram and Berloc, the laser, mount, Gonzaga monitoring the regulator, and then the power cables and Penn's section pulling out the rubble, there simply wasn't any room. "Use a rock instead of your fists, don't risk your suit."

The feed from Ram's helmet cam was confused, a closeup of bubbling hot rock, still cooling, as he handed off the laser for one of Penn's marines to hold, all crushed together in the deepest part of the hole. Then he unstrapped his big Koshaim rifle, which Lani reflected was probably a better idea than a rock, and held it butt-down against the rock. A sharp blow produced a solid *thunk* through the microphones, then another. It sounded a little hollow. Then another storm of bubbles, as the rock fractured.

Ram racked the rifle on its back-armour attachment, and then he was on his knees, pulling up a big slab of volcanic rock, and handing it off to someone else. Berloc announced loudly that he'd put the laser on safety standby, to assure all that they weren't about to be cut in half by an errant move in the crowded space, even as Gonzaga kept the regulator powered in case they needed it again. And then, after several minutes of commotion, terse conversation and teamwork, the camera showed Lani a one metre hole in the rock.

Beneath it was a hollow space. The camera contrast struggled to adjust, until Ram shone a helmet light into it — unnecessary for marines themselves, as night-vision worked better than harsh visual light, but very necessary if anyone looking at the video feed was going to see. The object within appeared round, like a giant ball, considerably larger than the hole. They'd need to widen it considerably to get the entire thing out. It had a ridged ring about the circumference, as though two halves had been joined together. Other than that, it appeared featureless, and utterly black.

"Grafy?" said Ram, with equal excitement and tension. *"Whatcha think?"*

"I think we should relay this to *Phoenix*," said Lani, her heart thumping as hard as it ever had in a situation that didn't involve being shot at. "And hope that Styx's encryption is as good as they say, or else Aristan will have a shuttle down here in no time flat."

Erik stared at the poor-quality image on his side screen, from where he'd temporarily shunted the nav display to see. It looked like a large black sphere, viewed through a small hole in the rock. There was no use asking the regular *Phoenix* crew what they thought, he realised.

"Styx, what do you make of that?" His orbital window of opportunity was now seven minutes out, and *Phoenix* was on full combat alert. His mouth was dry and stomach knotted with the tension that came from being at the mercy of events he had no personal control of. Either Charlie Platoon got confirmation that it was the data-core, within the window of opportunity, or they didn't. Trying to hurry that result from up here was like pushing on the end of a piece of string.

"The statistical likelihood that it could be anything other than the data-core seems improbable in the extreme," Styx replied. *"I advise the marines to be very careful moving it — that sphere appears to be a containment shell, and containment shells of that type are designed to remain functional for very long durations in extreme environments. The technology is drysine, though I am unfamiliar with the exact design. Counter-measures may be installed against tampering."*

"Captain," came Geish's call from Scan, "the *Corusan* is manoeuvring in orbit. It looks like it's adjusting upward to a higher cover position."

"Coms!" Eric snapped, his head abruptly full of new trajectory variables. "Relay what Styx says down to Charlie Platoon, I'm about to become very busy here."

"I copy Captain, I'm on it," said Shilu, as the bridge echoed in a flurry of activity, each officer intent on their own post. "Styx, I'm going to put you through to Charlie Platoon directly so they don't miss anything."

"Well, it's going to be very hard to get it out of this damn hole without touching it," Ram said testily, taking his rifle butt to the rock once more, trying to enlarge the hole.

"Physical contact may enable countermeasures," came the creepy-cool voice on coms. Most *Phoenix* marines or crew had not yet spoken to Styx directly, though many had heard her voice… if this synthesised projection could be called a voice. No doubt *Phoenix* command weren't thrilled with the idea of every spacer or grunt on the ship striking a conversation with her. From what

they'd heard, she could probably do that simultaneously. *"Physical contact will prove unavoidable, but you should be prepared."*

"Prepared for what?" Lani asked, on her marines' behalf. "What's it going to do?"

"I do not know. I am personally unfamiliar with this technology."

"Well that's not very fucking helpful," Berloc muttered.

Lani wondered if it could contain a nuke. If the entire thing had been a big, elaborate trap, designed to lure the greedy and unworthy down to Cephilae in pursuit of unimaginable riches, only to vaporise them.

Ram and Berloc lined up another laser shot, the regulator powering the main cell with a high-pitched whine that carried a long way under water… and Lani wondered if *that* was what drew the touli as much as the bright flashes…

"It's got lights!" Ram exclaimed. *"It… look, it just lit up!"* On his helmet cam, the black sphere was indeed flashing, small spirals of plain white light, inset on its surface. And now on Lani's coms registered a new signal, and she sent her suit computer chasing down the frequency… it was short-range and unencrypted, and the suit made sense of it quite quickly.

On her visor coms display, a picture lit up. It appeared 3D, but her visor ignored much of the data to give her a simpler version. There were a lot of flashing lights, pulsating in rhythm, and spiralling patterns.

"Eggs, are you getting this com feed?" asked Lance Corporal Penn in consternation. *"What the hell is this?"*

"It's fucking talking to us," Lani muttered. "This is some kind of message… Styx?" She sent the whole thing, just in case Styx wasn't reading it. "Styx, it's giving us this, what do you make of it?"

"It is a code," Styx said with certainty. Was it Lani's imagination, or were her synthesised tones not nearly as calm as they had been moments before. Could she synthesise anxiety? And why would she? *"The countermeasures are asking you for an access code. There is a countdown timer."*

"A countdown to what?"

"Unclear. I suspect the interior of the containment shell holds a self-destruct. Supply the code, or the data-core will be destroyed."

"Well we don't have any fucking code!" Lani exclaimed in rising panic. This wasn't fair. What kind of stupid alien fool asked explorers from a future age to supply a code from his own age? An age so long ago that even the language they'd spoken had been forgotten in the millennia since? "Styx, tell us what the code is!"

"I do not know." Definitely there was anxiety there. An absence of the usual cool. *"I am a command designation, it has not been my requirement to study such low details."*

"Eggs!" came the LT's voice, cutting off her retort. *"You're the smartest one in the platoon. Don't freak out, think!"*

"How much time?" Ram asked grimly.

"I do not know," Styx repeated. *"A localised self-destruct will be useless over long durations. I would guess a matter of minutes."*

We can't have come all this way, gone through all this nonsense with the tavalai, the parren, then all our crazy stuff in Kantovan System, just to lose it all here! Lani stared about in despair, past the dark gloom of the seaweed forest, lit only by the red light of Pashan high above, the toulies momentarily silent in their displays. Why would Drakhil have made these damn things so hard to find, only to punish the first people who were smart enough to find one?

Well... and she stared up at the red-lit lake surface overhead. There were plenty of smart people in the galaxy. Deepynines for one, who knew drysines well, and probably their parren allies too. Other parren, whom Drakhil might have suspected would still be dominant in the galaxy, twenty five thousand years later. Probably he wouldn't have suspected it would be the tavalai who'd be supreme now... or had been, until displaced by the Triumvirate Alliance of humans, chah'nas and alo...

So how would Drakhil ensure only the *right* people found it? Well, who would the *wrong* people be? Drakhil, it was said, had been an intellectual more than a warrior. The great danger of leaving such things as the data-core behind was that the people who found it would use the knowledge it granted for ill. Had Drakhil been the kind of guy who'd worry about that sort of thing?

He wasn't supposed to be. The machine age had been a horror, and he'd been the leader of the one organic race to support it. Only he *hadn't* actually supported it, because he was helping the drysines against the deepynines, and the deepynines were ten times worse. It had been a civil war between the machines, and the drysines had actually been willing to make allies with organic beings, while deepynines had just exterminated them.

Was that it? Was that the great difference in behaviour that mattered most to Drakhil? Had he found the one group of machines who *wouldn't* slaughter organics without a second thought, and decided to try and civilise them further? Because if you couldn't actually defeat a civilisation so powerful, surely that was the next best option?

And now that Lani thought about it, didn't that pattern on her visor look suspiciously like what the touli had been flashing at her for the past several hours?

"Styx!" she said hurriedly. "Have you been studying the toulies' communication? I've been feeding it up to *Phoenix* in realtime!"

"I have had more important things to do than consider non-sentient xenobiology," Styx retorted.

"Listen, what if that's the code? Drakhil *can't* expect us to know some code from anywhere else, it has to be from right here under our noses! The main reason he took the drysines' side against the deepynines was that drysines actually gave a shit about organics… maybe that's the test, maybe to find the code you have to give a shit about the organics, and the only organics flashing signals that look like this code are the toulies…"

"I am analysing now," Styx announced. *"Hold all functions, I am diverting full processing capability."*

There was a pause. Lani imagined the techs on *Phoenix* abruptly concerned when the fabricators in Engineering stopped working, as Styx shifted all attention elsewhere.

"Eggs?" said Gonzaga. *"I thought you said the lake wasn't here twenty five thousand years ago?"*

"Sure, but the sun's phases are predictable, Drakhil must have known it was going to warm up. Which gives this place more camouflage, if he knew the lake was going to rise up and cover it eventually."

"And so he teaches the toulies a pattern," Penn said slowly. *"And now... if the data-core plays us the first half of the pattern..."*

"Then the toulies should still remember the second half!" Lani completed. It sounded crazy, but the parren scientists said touli could recall binary patterns down to billions of digits with no mistakes. Creatures who stored data in some kind of electrical or chemical binary would probably be incapable of forgetting, and would pass on that code from generation to generation. And on a low-traffic world with few sentient visitors, it wasn't like the touli of this lake were going to forget some guy who came and fed them a pattern for days, weeks or months on end, even if it had been twenty five millennia ago...

"There is a match," Styx broke back in, without preamble. *"Lance Corporal, you need to find a way to communicate this portion of the message to the creatures."* And the coms display graphic on Lani's visor began a short, spiralling sequence of flashing lights. *"It is only five seconds long, it is buried in your recordings of the creatures' communications, but they make one reference every ten minutes or so."*

"Shit." Marine armour came with no holographic projection, they were designed for combat, not alien diplomacy. How did you communicate a visual display to a creature that wasn't sentient enough to know what modern coms were? "Guys, all lights off! Everything off, I want all their attention on me!"

Behind and about her, all the marines' lights switched off, plunging the site into darkness, save for Lani's own lights, and the dull red glow of the mother gas-giant on the water above. Lani abandoned the buoy cable and walked toward the toulies, flashing her lights on and off. It set off a mad ripple of activity, blue-light patterns radiating outward across and about the encircling animals with unmistakable coordination. But they only flapped to hold their position, and made intricate shapes with their tentacles, not showing any fear.

Lani advanced, flashing her lights, and held out a hand. One of the toulies came, tentacles describing some enormous space in the water before her, and for a moment, Lani reconsidered the assurance that they weren't unfriendly. The animal could have no idea that her armour made her infinitely more dangerous than all of them combined, and if it assumed she was just another creature, perhaps an odd-shaped crustacean, then surely it could assume her edible. But then, some very non-sentient animals just seemed to know, by some native combination of body language and synthetic smells, that sentient bipeds were a very different kind of creature, and not to be considered food. To a touli, no doubt anything that flashed lights was a 'talker', and in this lake at least, one did not eat one's interlocutor.

Lani blinked icons on her visor to enlarge the coms display to her entire face. A command function could do that, when an officer needed a full screen look at an unfolding tactical situation. All armour suits had the capability, though privates did not use it much. Anyone ranked lance corporal or above, however, was technically a commander if not an officer, and in Phoenix Company even that distinction became a little blurred, given the amount of responsibility the Major entrusted her non-coms with.

Then Lani switched off her lights. Bright in the dark water, her visor display would light up the gloom. Commanders using it were warned of that effect, and how it could give away their position in dark places. Turning the visor's glare protection up to full usually countered that, darkening the eyeslit so that little light escaped, but Lani deactivated that function entirely, and let the touli stare into the bright, white light emanating from where her eyes should be.

She played the signal from the data-core's containment shell. It repeated, several times, and the touli flashed back, then stopped, as though uncertain. Several others took up similar patterns, then also stopped. Lani sensed confusion. What was the strange talker trying to say? Surely the message looked very different on this little eyeslit than when spread across the vast, beautiful calligraphy of touli-arranged tentacles.

Then, suddenly, the touli burst into pulsating light. It repeated a now familiar pattern that even Lani could follow, but faster than her own. Then its neighbours joined in, and all the dark water around her was alive with that same, rhythmic pulsing. This pattern, they knew. They'd learned it from their elders, who'd learned it from *their* elders, and on and on back into the mists of time, to a parren who'd once visited this lake, and taught these toulies' ancestors this song.

Now the song changed, as touli began adding a new part to their tune. The others changed to accompany. Lani wondered what it meant to them. What *was* communication to these beautiful creatures? It did not indicate the location of food, nor did it appear a precursor to mating. Probably it was social, but how, and to what end? Or maybe they just liked to talk, and this complex memory-mechanism of theirs was just one of these odd, self-perpetuating things that evolution occasionally threw up for no better reason than the creatures who possessed it found it fun. No wonder parren had been studying them for so long.

"Styx, are you getting this?" she asked.

"I have confirmed and isolated a new part to the communication," Styx confirmed. *"It is only two seconds long, though I believe the sequence is of greater significance than the timing, given how much touli accents can shift over time, even as their numerical ordering remains precise. Surely Drakhil foresaw this."*

"I hope so," said Lani. "Send it to Private Ram, and we'll see if it works. Sheep, we know it has sensors, so probably it has optics. Play the full thing first, then if nothing happens, try just the new bit the toulies are giving us. Keep all your lights off, and use the full visor display — that worked for the toulies, it should work for the containment vessel."

CHAPTER 13

"We've got it!" came Lance Corporal Graf's excited voice from Cephilae. *"The containment shell just opened up, there was some kind of storage module inside and we've got it in hand! We're clear!"*

Thirty-nine seconds until the window vanished, Erik saw. "*Phoenix*, all hands prepare for combat. Arms, I want you to hit whatever survives our first strike, your choice. Operations, we are full withdrawal of all assets on my mark, coordinates to follow. Styx, you have full access to all coms, kill all hostiles."

A chorus of terse assent came back, followed by the chatter of bridge officers laying down the law to their underlings, setting the parameters, preparing for events. Erik sank deeper into the full VR emersion between his headset glasses and the wrap-around screens that surrounded him. Readiness windows showed him trajectories, velocities, windows of fire, and the orbital ascent trajectories of their three grounded shuttles.

This particular low orbital trajectory placed all three shuttle recovery windows in a rough line, reachable with a single burn manoeuvre, if they all launched in correct sequence and made the rendezvous coordinates at the precise required moment. Erik had no doubts that his pilots could do it, but the danger was that Aristan's ships were unlikely to cooperate. There were five in orbital position, three low and two high. The low ones bothered Erik the least — they crisscrossed Cephilae's surface on orbits adjusted to maximise direct overflight of the three grounded shuttles. Cephilae was cloudy, and neither Scan nor Nav suspected the parren had had much luck seeing anything on the surface, and thus remained in the dark about which location held the data-core.

None of those three ships were currently visual with *Phoenix*, the mechanics of low orbit making that unlikely. One of them was going to be, in approximately four-and-a-half minutes on current headings... but those headings were likely to change once the shooting started. It was the two high ships, each in high geostationary that had Erik concerned. The nearer ship was *Toristan*, the further was named *Corelda*. And *Phoenix*'s current orbital path, and the path she was required to take to rendezvous with all of their upcoming shuttles, took her directly under *Corelda*'s guns, with all the advantages of the 'downslope' gravity-well.

Lisbeth, he thought. But it was too late now. Aristan was going to try and kill all of *Phoenix*'s crew, on or off the ship. There was nothing he could do about it other than save those he could, and hope against hope that Styx's unlikely message from Gesul's operative was in fact true.

The countdown reached zero. "Styx, execute," he said. And *Phoenix* transmitted, just a small signal, multi-directional and unimpressive.

"I have a return signal from *Toristan*," said Shilu, squinting at some faint signal on his screens. "I'm not sure what it…"

"Toristan is disabled," Styx cut in. *"Geostationary to our rear is clear, the infiltration appears to have disabled ship systems."* A slight pause, and then, *"Corelda has partially resisted my coms infiltration, but her primary bridge functions appear disabled. She can move, but has no eyes."*

"Arms, kill *Corelda*," Erik said coldly.

"Aye Captain, *Corelda* is hot," Karle said calmly, clearing trigger guards and unleashing ordnance with multiple, heavy thuds.

Erik hit thrust, burning along the pre-designated orbital-plus course that would see *Phoenix* travelling far too fast for unadjusted orbit. It wasn't a hard burn, only two-G for now, as he had to line up the course Kaspowitz had laid out for him, intersecting a zigzag line across Cephilae's upper atmosphere.

"This is Operations, all shuttles are departing hard, ETAs are a match!" So far, that meant, none of them had been delayed. PH-3 was last in the sequence, three-quarters of an orbit away and technically behind them. *"All marines are confirmed aboard!"*

"Multiple angry coms transmissions," Shilu observed, predictably. "Our parren friends are *not* happy. I'm hearing a word that translates as 'treachery'."

"Fuck 'em," said Erik, and meant it. "Tell PH-4 to push hard, she's going to need to gun it to make that rendezvous." A query light blinked on his visor, polite and innocent, with a direct link to main coms beyond it. "Yes Styx," Erik answered it. "What is it?"

"Captain, the assassin bugs on Toristan have disabled the ship. Do you order Toristan's crew eliminated as well?"

Erik hesitated for only the shortest moment. "Yes," he said. "Prioritise senior officers."

"Yes Captain." It occurred to him, in the split second that was all he had to consider such things, that he should have thought more about that order in advance of this action. Killing Aristan was no small matter in the larger scheme of things, given all the implications for parren stability and beyond. But it was what it was, and Aristan had crossed *Phoenix* first. The penalty was death, and Erik did not mind if all the Spiral knew it. *"Captain, there is no response from my other bugs, it appears we have only neutralised one ship."*

There was a flash on Scan, from high ahead. "*Corelda* is dead," said Karle, with cool satisfaction to observe his work.

"Two ships," Erik corrected Styx. "It's enough, we're good. Arms, I see *Deara* is burning hard to an overhead intercept. Fire high and keep her close to stratosphere."

"Aye Captain," said Karle, and aligned the guns on that position. Erik saw the trajectories line up, indicated a left roll for Karle's benefit, then performed as Karle fired, the big ship rolling through 360 degrees to bring all weapons to bear in a continuous volley.

Even as he did it, he was watching the outgoing light horizon toward the incoming three ships from Tarimal. The light-wave would just be reaching them now, followed by a fast boost-up that they'd see shortly. *Phoenix* would have to complete the full orbit, collect all three shuttles along the way, and hope for no delays, or those three would be right on them, trailing a vast spread of incoming ordnance on a target whose position was not only made predictable by the shuttle rendezvous, but was at limited mobility at the bottom of a gravity-well. The saving grace was that the final intercept, on PH-3 and Charlie Platoon, was going to be on the far side of Cephilae from those incoming three ships… but once they started running, not for long.

He angled *Phoenix* nose-down toward Cephilae, the ongoing thrust now not to build further velocity, but to keep *Phoenix* in close orbit while carrying orbital-plus velocity, like a kid in an overpowered car sliding tail-out around a corner.

"*Deara* is diving low to avoid our fire," Geish announced. "She's gonna be skimming the atmosphere. I have no good read on it, but I'm pretty sure she's already fired, I am plotting incoming max probability."

"Arms hold fire," Erik directed, as incoming talk arrived from PH-4.

"Course is good," came Tif's unmistakable drawl. *"PH-4 is nax power and stratospheric. Orbit-plus V in two-point-five ninute."* 'M's or no 'm's, her accent was clearly improving. Erik glanced at his rendezvous point, and saw it was two-point-five minutes out, and Tif would match *Phoenix*'s velocity at precisely the point where she also matched her course. But now *Phoenix* had *Deara* on a parallel intersecting orbit from the side.

"Tif," Erik told her, "*Phoenix* is about to manoeuvre. We're going to push the intercept two hundred klicks downrange, intercept V plus one thousand kph."

"Copy Phoenix," Tif said calmly. *"Downrange and faster, I adjust."* Meaning she didn't particularly trust the numbers he'd just given her, and would watch *Phoenix* to see exactly what was required. For a good enough pilot, that was probably wise, and Tif was plenty good enough.

"Ordinance incoming!" Geish announced, as that string of blips appeared on Erik's screen. It came from *Deara*'s direction, skimming the atmosphere.

"Paste it!" Karle instructed his junior, and Second Lieutenant Harris did that, engaging the secondaries in a crackle of outgoing defensive fire.

"Hold offensive fire," Erik told Karle, all senses tracking in that hyper-aware slow motion that only happened in this chair, in combat. He could see his move coming, and he didn't think *Deara* could survive it. "High-G manoeuvre imminent. Arms, fire on the pause."

"Aye Captain, fire on the pause!"

Harris's fire intercepted the incoming, lines of super-hot explosions vaporising onrushing warheads, and then Erik's lines all matched. He swung *Phoenix* end-over and when they were tail-first and offset away from Cephilae, fired hard. Engines roared at five-G, then built quickly to eight, as everyone strained and gasped against the sudden blackness of vision.

Ten seconds and Erik cut, swinging the ship about once more as Karle hammered a full spread at *Deara* on that pause in thrust — his angle suddenly higher above the atmosphere, and the trajectory heading radically closer across the parren warship's metaphorical bow. A second burst of thrust to regain previous V and course, *Deara* desperately evading the torrent that now descended on her from an unexpected position. At this intersecting range there was no hope, *Deara*'s defensive batteries fended the first wave, but were overwhelmed by the second, and the explosion was seen not just on Scan, but on visuals — a bright, tumbling fireball across the Cephilae horizon.

"Didn't see that coming, did ya?" Karle snorted. *Phoenix* changed direction terrifyingly fast for such a big ship. Coming at her blind over the horizon of a close-orbit world was reckless bordering on suicidal, like charging an enormous predator across an open field while just hoping it didn't look your way.

"PH-4," Erik said coolly, "we are manoeuvre complete, fixing new interception point now."

"PH-4 copy, Phoenix. Nice noove."

"This is Operations, we are go for capture."

"Tif," said Erik, "you are Berth Two and I am rolling for position. We are target clear for five minutes at least, course change will immediately follow intercept."

"Captain," said Geish, "those inbound three just pulsed jump engines, they are moving to combat intercept."

Erik could see that without needing to be told, but bridge procedure was to announce it anyway in clear coms, so everyone knew. "Arms, put some fire in their path in case they're dumb enough to hold that V all the way in."

"Aye Captain," said Karle, aligning that spread. *Phoenix* warheads were reaction-driven, self-guided and capable of thrust for short periods at twenty-Gs. Fuel limited their potential V-change, but any ship caught at close range with a twenty-G warhead and unable to jump could not possibly outrun it. The trick was not allowing oneself to be caught in that position, and onboard combat computers, and a Captain's innate sense of such things, ran at furious speeds to try and calculate all the ways of avoiding it. Arms Officers like Karle and Harris in turn played tricks on those calculations, laying spreads at variable V and position to predict future manoeuvres, and impart a risk to each. Against a warship the size of *Phoenix*, that could lay down this volume of advanced high-tech warheads in their path, smaller parren cruisers would be wise to slow down and calculate.

"Captain, they're dividing," said Geish. "They're going to come past Cephilae on all sides to make a crossfire. I calculate probable V projection gives them an ETA of twenty-one minutes."

"We'll be done in fifteen," said Erik, watching as PH-4 emerged from Cephilae's upper atmosphere ahead, a tiny dot on a trail of flame, burning hard toward the new intercept. The first time he'd tried this kind of recovery mission in an Academy simulation, he'd collided with a shuttle and damaged both ships. The second time, he'd botched the second intercept, had taken thirty seconds longer than the course required, and missed the third intercept completely. Happily, he'd improved a lot since then. "Scan, have we got a fix on those other two low orbitals?"

"Not yet Captain, they're farside and silent, I'm looking."

"I'm getting something behind us," came Ensign Singh's voice in Lieutenant Regan Jersey's ears. Unlike on a warship bridge, she couldn't hear anyone else in the cockpit in combat, even when they were sitting directly in front of her. The big helmet, and the howling roar of full thrust, isolated her from everything save the friendly green scrawl of her visor and heads-up overlay, telling her everything about the state of her ship. *"Trans-sonic, high altitude, it's probably anti-aerial. I'm tracking a solution for countermeasures."*

"Hello *Phoenix*," said Regan, thankful the parren hadn't destroyed the orbital satellites needed to talk to a ship on the other side of Cephilae. Evidently the parren needed them too, and couldn't find a way to stop Styx's communications short of that. "We are tracking inbound AAs, it looks like one of those parren close-orbitals is on top of us."

"It's dividing!" Singh said tersely. *"Multiple inbound, I'm reading Mach 15 and decelerating, ETA one-fifteen."*

PH-3 was only at three thousand metres and climbing — being the last in *Phoenix*'s string of pickups, they'd had more time to finish up before launch. She'd even managed to hover above the lake surface to help Charlie Platoon haul up the last bit of equipment in the lake — the coms buoy — not wanting to leave any clues behind for parren techs to run diagnostics on. Regan wondered what the toulies would make of the big, angry beast howling above their lake, and whether they'd be talking about it ten thousand years later.

Now she roared through the cloud layer without much care for turbulence, defeating the rough air with sheer force as they thundered and bumped. AA rounds were space-launched and self-guided, always trans-sonic and designed to pluck atmospheric vehicles from the sky, where spaceships otherwise found them near-impossible to target. Regan hoped the parren AA rounds weren't as good as the human variety — *Phoenix*'s were murderously good, and had saved the Captain and Major's life on Stoya III. Very little could match the alo for technology, and much human technology, including *Phoenix*, was alo… but then, the parren had been in space forty thousand years longer…

"PH-3, this is Phoenix, we copy. Stay low, we've time to adjust the pickup, just stay alive."

"PH-3 copies *Phoenix*, that's the plan." A firing solution appeared on armscomp, and Regan fired — counter-missiles leaped from the underside racks, streaking around in a wide arc to go behind them. She fired two more on a different spread, then headed deeper into the thick of the cloud — if assault shuttles didn't like thick, moist air and turbulence, trans-sonic rounds would hate them, relying on very thin air at high altitude for stability. "Hang on down the back," she told the marines, "it's gonna get real bumpy."

"Welcome to Jersey Air," Jalawi retorted, as though completely unsurprised.

They slammed and rocked through thick cloud, the shuttle pushed right to its aerodynamic limit on engine power that far exceeded its atmospheric performance. It was always the problem with assault shuttles — they had engines designed for deep space, with crazy power that was utterly out of sync with aerodynamic load. Pushing too hard, in deep atmosphere, could create a tumble. Most of those tumbles, at low-to-middle altitude, even Lieutenant Hausler hadn't figured a way to recover from. And now Regan saw the countdown to *Phoenix* rendezvous approaching fast, and wondered how the hell she was going to make that climb in time.

"Countermeasures got one!" Singh announced. *"The other's still coming!"* Regan hit hard left, ramming everyone down, secondary countermeasures blazing chaff, flares and jamming. One missile got distracted as it streaked into cloud at Mach 7, course-corrected too fast and tumbled. A second broke up in the heavy air, then detonated on proximity. A third survived all countermeasures but found it too hard to find a bouncing target in cloud, and blew up right nearby, with a flash that lit the right side of the cockpit.

"*Phoenix*," Regan called, "we survived the first wave but if they keep coming, I don't like our chances."

"PH-3, we got him," came the astonishing reply. *"Rendezvous is unchanged, he's dead."*

"I copy *Phoenix*," she replied, keeping all surprise from her voice with practised calm. The pilot code was always cool. "Going upper-atmospheric now." She pulled back and climbed, her canopy still a flurry of thick cloud.

"How the hell?" Singh wondered. *"They weren't even line-of-sight with that guy."*

"My guess is Styx," said Regan. They burst into clear night sky and climbed, Regan pouring on the power as the atmosphere thinned, and the bumping grew less. "I reckon she must have triangulated his position somehow when he started shooting at us." *Phoenix* armscomp alone was good, but not *that* good. Regan called her marines. "We're clear, *Phoenix* got the guy who was shooting at us. How you guys doing back there?"

"Where's my inflight meal?" Jalawi complained. *"I wanna refund."* Regan cut him off, grinning madly. Ahead, the dark night sky grew darker still, and began to show signs of stars. And now, heading left-to-right, came a cloud of flaming stars, streaking across the horizon in a profusion of burning trails, slowly arcing toward the ground.

"Whoa!" said Singh. *"Guess that was him, huh?"*

"Yes it was," said Regan with satisfaction, applying the thrust harder as the proper climb to orbit began.

Singh transferred a visual feed to the marines down back. *"Guys, check this out. Here's the fucker who shot at us."*

There came back on coms multiple exclamations, in defiance of the marines' dislike for trans-orbital manoeuvres. *"Don't fuck with Phoenix,"* Jalawi cackled.

Erik cut thrust at the last moment to let Lieutenant Jersey make the final approach, the Berth Four grapples crashing home with what the Operations lights told him was a perfect grip. Then he ramped up the thrust once more, several seconds build up to five-G, then a full, shuddering roar at nearly ten. It was always a horrible sensation, a crushing, suffocating blackness of gasping breaths and fading vision, but spacers and marines alike were augmented for it, at prolonged forces that would probably kill the unaugmented. Bridge crew like Erik could even function in it, at moderately high levels, as micros widened arteries in the brain to get new blood in, while narrowing others to keep old blood from flowing out… to say nothing of juicing the bloodstream to keep oxy levels high, and the micro-filament structural support through spine, neck and every major muscle group.

After several minutes, Erik could see Aristan's three new ships on Scan, hurtling past the silver half-crescent of Cephilae, joined by the one remaining operational ship from close orbit. One was braking hard to intercept *Toristan* at nadir polar orbit, and Erik wondered just how effective those assassin bugs had been.

"Hello Captain," came Styx's voice, as though reading his thoughts. *"I had thought to attempt contact with my bugs on Toristan, and attempt to transfer them to this new ship. In case it attempts to chase us."*

Erik wondered what the lifespan on those little things was… and the amount of neurotoxin they carried. Given it only took a tiny droplet to kill, probably they could account for multiple entire crews, given the chance. But then, they could be stopped by a closed door, or a thick spacesuit, so he knew he shouldn't get his hopes up.

"Hello Styx," he formulated in reply. *"Go ahead and transfer them. I hope we won't need them, these ships aren't fast enough to follow us through jump. But a recon mission could be useful, if they could find a way to hide a pirate transmission that might reach us eventually."*

"Yes Captain," Styx agreed. Erik angled thrust, swinging *Phoenix*'s tail out to bring their course across, lining up on Kaspowitz's best course to their escape route — Brehn System, and from there a path back to tavalai space. The pursuit was too far behind them now for him to worry about expended ordnance catching up, and they were too deep in Cephilae's gravity-well to dump or boost V with a jump pulse. As was *Phoenix*, but that would change in several more minutes. *"Captain, I assure you that*

the message I received from Gesul's spy on Toristan was not fabricated. I was under the impression that you had doubts."

Styx had put a bug in his quarters, to spy on his meeting with Suli and Jokono. Erik did not want to have this conversation now, nor at any time. Protestations of undying trust and loyalty from Styx meant nothing. She'd no doubt talk her way out of any sinister implications, saying she was merely guarding him, or something similar. Styx was an enormous calculating machine. She calculated, and judged the most probable course by which she might arrive at her destination, and concepts like 'truth' and 'trust' were just curiosities along the way. Supposing she was anything else, at this point, was foolhardy.

"I believe you, Styx," he replied.

"I am glad, Captain." Erik got the distinct impression that she still didn't believe him, and wondered if she were subtle enough to inject that tone of faint disbelief, to let him know that she doubted. And noted further that such exchanges only reinforced Trace's belief that Styx's protestations of ignorance at human psychology were one giant load of manure. One could go crazy, thinking round and round in circles, trying to figure out exactly what was going on in that synthetic alien brain. *"This combat action and recovery has been exceptionally impressive. A drysine combat vessel could not have done better. I have no higher praise."*

"Thank you Styx. And we must have that conversation sometime, about drysine combat vessel capabilities."

"I agree. It may be useful in what lies ahead."

She disconnected, as pre-jump data began to flow from Kaspowitz's post, a final assessment of required trajectories, followed by Engineering's stream on the fast powering jump engines. Cephilae and Pashan's gravitational influence dropped below the threshold, and Erik pulsed the jump engines once, a sickly lurch into hyperspace… then out again, and rushing with nearly one percent of light's velocity more. Now they were racing, and he cut main engines thrust as the acceleration became redundant. Bridge crew gasped deep breaths, and prepared their posts for combat jump.

"Brehn System," Suli announced as Navigation made the final alignments. "Combat jump, this is parren space run by House Harmony, and we are always expecting trouble."

"Well done people," Erik told them all, on open coms to the entire ship. "Operation data-core recovery is a success, we faced extreme odds and came through like a breeze. We did Captain Pantillo proud today, and the legend of the *UFS Phoenix* grows." He shut off ship-wide coms, and talked only to his bridge. "Now let's nail this jump and bring this sucker home."

Exactly where *home* was, for this galaxy-shaking thing that PH-3 had acquired, he wasn't entirely sure. Everyone in the Spiral would now either want them as best friends, or want them dead.

CHAPTER 14

Erik felt *Phoenix* come out of jump with a sensation like falling. It never felt entirely like waking from sleep, because no one ever dreamed in jump. There was no confused displacement, putting one reality aside to refocus on the new one, and unable to tell which was which. There was just a bright and nauseous sense of *here*, and a wide world of wrap-around data and schematics, demanding his analysis. His brain just wanted a moment to settle, to process the fact of this new reality, but suddenly he had to *think*, at a depth and intensity that always felt offensive.

"I have the nav buoy," came Kaspowitz's reassuring voice. "We are at Brehn System, we are in the slot, nailed it within ten thousand K." Ten thousand kilometres was insanely accurate, across the distances they'd just travelled. But heading into a great, crazy mess like Brehn System, accuracy was safety. "We are two million K off the elliptic, rocks will start to get messy in another seven minutes at current V."

Erik frowned at his screens, sipping electrolyte-heavy water from his drinking tube as he took that in. Brehn System was a giant disk of incredibly crowded, dangerous space. They'd come out of jump right beside the nav buoy, which was positioned precisely to allow it — *Phoenix*'s nav computer reading the signal in hyperspace while humans were non-responsive, and pulling them into realspace close enough to the elliptic disk to find cover if things went bad. Seven minutes was cutting it fine, but *Phoenix* had been through this system just recently, confirmed the nav buoy's placement, and Kaspowitz's settings would have pulled them out much sooner if someone had moved it, or the signal hadn't reached them.

"Captain," said Shilu, and Erik could hear the frown in his voice. "I'm getting…"

"This is Engineering," Lieutenant Rooke's voice cut him off. *"I have a yellow light on that number three jumpline… Captain, I'm looking at the figures and I think it's nothing, just a polarity defect but I'd like a chance to check it asap."*

"I copy that Engineering," Erik acknowledged. "Get me a full systems check and report, I want it top-to-bottom before we take the next jump."

"Engineering copies Captain, we're on it."

"Captain," Shilu resumed more loudly, "I'm raising a yellow light on coms chatter. It's way down, there's dozens of mining settlements in the system, maybe a hundred major sublight ships in flight at any time last we were here… coms dropoff is maybe seventy percent."

"We haven't been here that long," Suli replied, completing her thorough post-jump systems checks. Better that she did it, and left Erik's attention clear to observe their surroundings. "Coms chatter isn't that intense among parren, give it another few minutes."

"No," Shilu corrected impatiently, "I'm reading off the navbuoy, the last hour's worth of traffic, it's…" He stopped mid-sentence, eyes widening as he heard something alarming. "I think I'm hearing a distress call, hang on, I'm running translators…"

"FULL EVASIVE!" Geish screamed, and Erik hit max thrust without asking, one of those horrible manoeuvres that could kill less advanced ships with engine overloads and structural failures. Without G-augments everyone on the bridge would have been slammed unconscious, hearts thudding with artificially-induced chemical charge.

The move was pre-programmed, there was no way any pilot could think through those Gs, nor even move his hands, and when the pressure faded enough to do both, he saw the same autos were plastering a single, fast-moving spot in space with heavy fire. He was just thinking they'd missed the main volley when something hit them, a shocking lurch that snapped everyone sideways for an instant, then a flare of red lights on the upper-cylinder hull, and reports of things broken and breaking.

The thing that had shot at them was moving, only to avoid their own fire, and it was insanely fast. The firepower that flowed from it was vast, more self-propelled rounds accelerating in their wake. Something that fast couldn't possibly have that much armament, this thing was faster than *Phoenix*, and surely *had* to be smaller to move that fast. Normally he had time to at least formulate to his bridge crew, the synthetic voice that was all captains could manage under high-G when the vocals weren't working. But now there was nothing save the groans and grunts through gritted teeth — the whole crew straining to a single task, to keep *Phoenix* alive.

"Captain, that ship is deepynine!" came Styx's voice in his ears. *"Find cover or we die!"*

Something else hit them, a glancing blow from an oblique angle, and *Phoenix* rang like a bell. Scan was showing Erik only a fraction of the full volume of fire. That was terrifying. If he couldn't see what was incoming, he couldn't dodge. He only saw it too late, as it snapped past at hyper-V, and each one seeming closer than the last.

Erik pulsed the jump engines, and everything heaved and folded in on itself… then re-emerged, racing much faster and well ahead of that ordnance. But now he'd *increased* speed straight after jump, when *Phoenix* was already hurtling at high-V, directly toward one of the least navigable systems Erik had ever seen.

"Twenty seconds!" Kaspowitz growled, the whole crew hunched and strained at their posts even now the Gs had stopped. "Fifteen seconds! Captain, we hit one of those rocks, it'll hurt worse than a round!"

"Find me a hole, Kaspo!" Erik demanded. "We gotta hide, that thing has us outclassed!"

"It's still coming, it pulsed up behind us!" Geish shouted. "Fuck, it's got us V-plus, it's faster and closing! If we dump V among the rocks, that new ordnance will kill us!"

But now Karle and Harris were pounding every weapon *Phoenix* possessed in their pursuer's direction, laying down a sheet of ordnance in his way. And sure enough, the other ship was burning hard to miss it, climbing relative to the fast-approaching system-elliptic. It had to be messing up his gunnery, Erik thought desperately.

Ahead was Scan's best guess at a 'safe' hole through the clouds of Brehn System rocks and ice… but of course, it wasn't safe at all, because *Phoenix* was now travelling so fast that Scan couldn't possibly see all the things they might hit, most of which were hard enough to see at much slower speeds. But the thing with high-V ordnance, Erik knew, was that it was far too fast to change direction easily. Starships could cycle jump engines and lose huge chunks of V in an instant. Self-guided munitions could not.

"Brace for hard dump," Erik told them, rotating *Phoenix* perpendicular to the approaching rocks, as the first heavy concentrations of debris began to flash past them at speeds that didn't bear thinking about. One strike, and the explosion would be seen from neighbouring star systems, briefly out-glaring the sun. "If you have a God, pray now."

He hit thrust hard, another brain-crushing burst of force and pain, and then a jump pulse dialled all the way up as high as the technology would go… and they came out travelling much slower. Erik continued the rotation, allowing all of *Phoenix*'s batteries a good firing angle. But now the deepynine ship was also dumping V, again a much harder manoeuvre than *Phoenix* had done, then burning hard to stay clear of the thickest debris.

"He doesn't want to come in here," Suli observed. "He's evading."

"I have partially blinded his controls," Styx gave a more likely answer. *"I used your main coms, he is not equipped for the antique methods of electronic warfare I use. We must get clear now and hide, before his friends arrive."*

Erik swung them back around, kicking thrust even now to dodge the looming threat of a large rock. It flashed by at multiple hundreds of thousands of kilometres an hour, faster than the naked eye could follow, were that even a possibility on a windowless warship. *Phoenix* could see the rocks, and as long as that remained the case, Erik was confident he could avoid them. But at this speed, and in the densities that were approaching, that wasn't going to remain possible for long.

"Captain," said Kaspowitz, "we've got a one percent chance of dying in the next five minutes at this V. That will increase steadily after that five. Cumulative odds of mortality will exceed a theoretical one hundred percent in less than thirty minutes."

"I hear you Kaspo," said Erik. He'd never felt so utterly absorbed in his work as now. He felt like a ghost, some non-corporeal entity that existed only as pure intellect, calculating numbers, trajectories, distances. If his body had sensation, he was not aware of it. *Phoenix* was the only body that mattered. "We need to extend, we will not survive if we don't get some distance."

Flight control kicked again on automatic, artificial reflexes still superior to his own guiding the ship past some new flashing obstacle on Scan. Erik was vaguely aware of Suli running systems diagnostic on damage, talking to Engineering, rerouting the systems they could manage on automatic — all the things he had no time to do himself. Something hit the ship once more, a sound like a cannon shot, and more red lights on his screens.

"That was an impact," Suli told him, matter-of-factly. "Our bow shield is damaged, forward docking has a red light." There was more, Erik knew, but Suli wasn't going to bother him with it now. Probably the rock that had done it was the size of a marble or smaller — Scan only saw them sometimes, but at this V they struck with the force of heavy artillery.

"He's pulling right off," Geish said confidently. "He's getting parallel with us, but he's definitely not following us in."

"That's because he doesn't want to get pulverised," Kaspowitz growled. "Captain, we're clear and I recommend we dump V."

"We're not clear from his friends," said Erik. "Three more minutes."

"Captain, the obstacle density in here is the worst I've ever seen, I can't even guarantee the threat isn't worse than I've..."

"I heard you Kaspo." Erik did not raise his voice, having neither time nor spare attention for temper. Besides, Kaspowitz was just doing his job, which in this circumstance meant stopping *Phoenix* from running into a rock. If that meant berating the Captain, he'd do it, and such dissent only made *Phoenix* safer. But Erik had seen something Kaspowitz hadn't — firepower and speed on a scale that was technologically beyond anything he'd known possible. Rocks were lethal too, but rocks were at least not *trying* to kill you. Deepynine warships had intent, and it was hard to imagine anyone escaping once in their net.

"Styx," he said, "I want you to talk to Lieutenant Geish on Scan and calculate how hard we can thrust in this mess without being seen. We are going to need to manoeuvre at safer V or we'll never get out of here." And he kicked the mains again, to dodge something Scan showed looming too close for comfort.

"Captain," Geish said thirty seconds later, "Styx and I agree on one-point-two Gs, no more. The rocks give us some cover, but their scan-tech is really good."

Of course it is, Erik thought. And finally, when he figured he'd pushed their considerable luck far enough, he did what he'd normally have done long ago and far outside the debris field, and dumped V down to still-dangerous but not completely suicidal levels. Still too fast, he gave them a half-pulse to lose some more, and could feel some of the tension release from the crew around him.

Rocks previously racing by in a blur of annihilating speed were now cruising up quite sedately — still entirely lethal if struck, but so much easier to see, plot and avoid, even as they multiplied. *Phoenix*'s speed was still several times faster than usually wise, but then, being chased by deepynine warships intent on your destruction had a way of recalibrating your perception of risk, Erik thought. He swung *Phoenix* sideways and ignited a burn at one-point-two Gs, turning them away from their previous course as fast as he dared. Blind or not, he had to assume that the deepynine warship had seen their V-dump, given the amount of energy it released, and so could fix that location and the trajectory beyond it. *Phoenix* now had to get as far away from that trajectory as possible, without burning so hard that their big main engine would light up space and give them away regardless. But now, V-dump or no V-dump, they were still travelling fast enough that even perpendicular thrust, at only one-point-two Gs, would take an hour to significantly change their heading.

"Okay," Erik said, once they'd run through damage assessment and other strategic essentials. Lords he felt tired, muscles shaking with adrenaline overload, in the aftermath of a very bad fright. His voice was hoarse, as were all the crew. "I want assessment. What the hell was that?"

"One of Admiral Janik's deepyines," said Suli. "Looks like."

"Captain, I'm still getting very little coms traffic," said Shilu. "There's more of them here, I can smell it. I think they've hit a few people, or given the local parren some clues as to what they are, and now everyone's shutting the hell up."

"Damn smart of them," Karle muttered, with one ear to assessments from his armaments team on remaining ammunition, and wear on the guns. "I've never seen anything that size pump out firepower like that."

"Okay, options," said Erik, determined that they should not get trapped into talking about how hopeless it looked, being out-muscled like that by a smaller ship. "Can we run? Engineering, what do you say?"

"Oh, I think we could run in an emergency, Captain," came Rooke's voice, in the distracted way of someone who was working on ten problems at once, and stressed because the ship might have to move suddenly once more, with little warning, and send his Engineering crew smashing into walls. In the background, Erik could hear people shouting, and the crash of equipment being hauled — back in one-G from thrust alone, and Engineering were already scrambling to fix damage. *"I won't know what our odds are of surviving it until I've had a chance to inspect it properly... the jump lines are holding stable enough for now, but if the polarity's weak or the axis has shifted, we won't know we have a fatal fault until we power up full... and then it's too late."*

"Captain, if I may," said Styx. *"I fear we have a worse problem. I am familiar with the capabilities of those ships. Their jump engines are considerably more advanced than ours, using understandings of hyperspace physics that have since been lost to spacefaring civilisation. Even if we did find enough clear space to*

run for jump, I am certain that these ships would predict our destination, overtake us in jump, and be waiting for us when we arrived. In which scenario, we would be ambushed once more, just as we were ambushed here, by the very same ship that we'd jumped away from. I doubt we would survive it twice."

"We're trapped here," Suli said flatly.

"Yes. Unless we, or someone else, can first deal decisively with all the deepynine vessels in this system."

There was silence on the bridge, from those not engaged in operational chatter with their off-bridge crew. Just one of those ships had nearly killed them. And they had no idea how many more were here, hiding amidst the rocks and ice of Brehn System.

Trace met Charlie Platoon One-Three (as the abbreviation had it for First Squad, Third Section) in the corridor off Engineering G Bulkhead. Everyone was in full armour, the usual practice when *Phoenix* was on red alert, if for no better reason than armoured marines had a better chance of surviving a catastrophic hit and decompression than unarmored ones. Spacers ran past unsuited, facemasks dangling prominently from harnesses that would keep them alive in a slow decompression, but not a full vacuum, shouting to each other and cursing marines who got in their way.

Third Quarter was largely sealed from D Bulkhead down to H, not too far from here, and it seemed that ship diagnostic wasn't giving the crew a good idea of exactly where the breach was, or how bad the total damage. The crew cylinder was rotating again, the Captain having shut down their one-G burn… but G was good either way, because zero-G was actually a pain for fixing things, giving no leverage for spacers to put shoulders into, hauling open doors and hammering open panels. The initial phase of handling major ship damage was remarkably low-tech, something marines understood well, given how much of their supposedly high-tech job devolved into sweating and lifting the moment anything went wrong.

Marines typically looked down on spacers as soft, right up until something like this happened. Now it was the marines who were relatively protected in their big armour, while spacers risked corridors that could at any moment turn into high-G death traps if *Phoenix* had to move suddenly, and stuck themselves physically into structurally unsound parts of the ship that could at any moment turn to vacuum or fire. All through the war, Trace reminded her marines often, casualty rates for spacers and marines had been roughly equivalent, and there were more ways to demonstrate bravery than handling firearms.

Most of the time, marines would get quickly out of spacers' way, but now up the corridor came one marine who was not getting out of the way for anyone, shielded in front by Private Gonzaga. Trace hit the hatch open behind her, and stood aside as Lance Corporal Graf entered the Engineering bay, armoured gloves clasped around a spherical object of grey steel. Within, Staff Sergeant Kono led Command Squad in assisting the setup — all the Engineering crew were busy, and so Trace had assumed responsibility in securing the object for which they'd gotten themselves into this mess in the first place.

There was a big clasp and frame bolted into the floor between work benches, designed specifically to hold delicate machinery for repairs and analysis. Within the frame, someone had fast-fabricated something to fit the described dimensions of the data-core — a high-stress frame to hold a sphere and secure it on all sides, in the event of forces up to twenty-Gs or more. Graf put it in carefully, with much talk, guidance and advice from others, tightening the clasp one section at a time.

Jalawi appeared at Trace's elbow as she watched, faceplate up, looking simultaneously grim, tired and triumphant. "How close was that?" he asked her, meaning *Phoenix*, and the ambush. The recently-disembarked platoons had ridden the whole thing out in Midships, having just had time to leave the shuttles before jump. The data-core, Trace heard, had been stuffed into the smallest equipment locker the marines could find, with a bunch of surplus impact padding, cargo nets and spare uniforms to stuff it so tight it couldn't get damaged in manoeuvres. They'd hoped.

"Kaspowitz won't tell me," Trace replied. "Pretty close." Kaspowitz, alone of the bridge crew, had some comprehension of how much the marines hated being stuck down in the holds, unable to see what was going on. Over the years he'd taken a moment to send Trace some details her command feed wouldn't show her, and make sense of bridge-crew stuff that might otherwise have gone over her head. This time, he hadn't. That was bad.

"Well fuck," Jalawi summarised. "We finally get the alien gizmo, and we nearly lose everything. Is that good luck, or bad?"

"Scratch your left ass cheek, good," Trace told him. "Scratch your right, bad." Jalawi grinned. It was a running joke between them, as Jalawi insisted that her understanding of karma must give her some cosmic clue as to whether the fates promised good or ill, as though she were some kind of charlatan fortune teller with a crystal ball. Trace had given up explaining to him that the whole point of karma was that it didn't *care* what she thought, realising only too well that Jalawi just liked stirring people for entertainment. Now she only gave him answers on his usual level of seriousness. "Good job down there. You got it."

"Wasn't me," Jalawi said happily. "My people *rock*. Best damn platoon in the Fleet."

"Give me three lines," said Trace, determined to get some kind of mission report out of him, given she'd not have time to read the full one for a while, even if Jalawi found time to write it.

"Three lines," Jalawi agreed, and ticked off his fingers. "Lieutenant Jersey rocks, best shuttle pilot we've got. Sergeant Hoon does play well with others, which is good to know. And I'd have loved an aerial drone to give early warning in case we got bounced, but we seem to be out of aerial drones."

"Wasn't in the last mission profile," Trace agreed, watching as Command Squad now focused a couple of cameras on the surrounding workbenches, and began playing with analysis sensors they didn't really understand. "We're still outfitted for the Triumvirate War, but I'm sure Rooke can make some more."

Jalawi nodded. "Last line — I'd have loved a hacksaw drone like you had on Kamala." Trace glanced at him. "Seriously — doesn't need air, doesn't need the toilet, or food, multiple arms, doesn't mind cold water, has technical knowledge, multi-tasker, lots of lifting, lots of high-tech tools… damn, we'd have finished cutting that hole in half the time, for one thing. Two of those things in the hole would have done it, but we needed eight. Plus it could have handled encrypted coms without all our messing around with the damn buoy. That's six lines, but whatever."

Trace looked at him thoughtfully. For all his flippancy, she knew the fight at Argitori had hit Jalawi hard. He'd lost eight of his precious marines, and another ten wounded, some of whom were only recently back on full duty. Certainly he was no fan of Styx, nor hacksaws in general. But here he was, advocating *this*. "Thanks Skeeta. Get some sleep."

"Ha!" said Jalawi, to show what he thought were the odds of that. "Oh yeah, we still handing out medals?" He pointed at Lance Corporal Graf. "Eggs." He yawned hugely. "That's it, I'm done. Good luck with that thing."

He stomped off, back into the crazy corridor and running spacers. Trace contemplated helping her marines with the sensors, but in truth she didn't know any more than they did, and figured they'd do better as a collaboration between equals. Whenever she involved herself, she ran the risk that they'd defer to her, and assume she held all the answers. Thus her policy to only take charge in non-command matters when she was *certain* she knew better. Choosing movies on movie nights, for example, was always someone else's job.

A spacer came through the door with a facemask on… or not a spacer, she saw, but Stan Romki, looking rattled and holding onto things for balance. "Stan?" she said.

"Major." His voice was muffled in the mask, and he pulled it off. Beneath, he looked pale and sweaty, despite the cold. "My quarters are in the damage zone, I only managed to get out just now. I was trapped in there for half-an-hour."

There was residual fear and stress in his voice, understandable for a non-spacer, without spacer uplinks or communications, trapped in quarters after a series of harrowing manoeuvres and weapon strikes. And there was an undertone of indignation, that she and others were just standing around here, doing something else instead of rushing frantically to rescue him. Well, everything on a warship happened by procedure, and procedure in a decompressive strike was to stay where you were and let the spacers handle it. Doors had to be reopened in careful sequence to avoid another decompression, while searching for all the leak's locations.

"Are you okay?" Trace asked diplomatically. Obviously he was, or he'd be in Medbay.

"Yes yes, fine," Romki said distractedly, wiping cold sweat and stowing his facemask with trembling hands… and already his attention was shifting to the object the marines were fussing over. "The air pressure only dropped a little… is that…?"

Phoenix interrupted them with a sudden burst of evasive thrust as she dodged a rock — just a tap, and the marines all caught supports for a second. Trace caught Romki, who flailed… and recovered as the thrust stopped. Remarkably, his attention barely shifted from the data-core.

"Yes it is," said Trace. Romki staggered over, grasping supports to hold his weak legs, worried about another evasive thrust. Quickly he took over the placement of cameras and sensors, and began a conversation with Styx that got her involved in the discussion. It struck Trace that Styx could surely have gotten herself involved, and told the marines what to do, but even now seemed reluctant to puzzle her way through human group behaviour. Soon Hiro joined them, having spent a lot of time with Romki on Drakhil's diary, and somewhat familiar both with the sensor tech, and with Styx herself.

"Hello Major," came Commander Shahaim's voice in Trace's ear. *"I see you're working on the data-core, can you give me a status update?"*

"Yes Commander, nothing yet. We're rigging it up so that Styx can take a look at it, it's Stan and Hiro taking the lead, plus us grunts for backup. Engineering's busy. I'll let you know when we have anything."

"Please do that."

"How are we doing up there?" Trace pressed before the Commander could sign off.

"For now we're okay, we're playing hide and seek. You'll be talking with me about this, Major, the Captain's busy."

It was the true reason Trace had asked — any update on why Shahaim was talking to her, and not Erik. Logically Erik was busy… but Erik was also intrigued with the data-core, and the broader mission, and being an A-plus multi-tasker would usually take advantage of a pause like this to enquire personally. And, Trace thought to herself, Erik had jumped away from Cephilae after stabbing Aristan in the back, suspecting that such action would likely get Lisbeth killed. Thus her true reason for concern. Concern at what it meant for all of them, in his present mental state… whatever that was. But mostly, concern just for him.

"I understand, Commander," she said.

"And Major," Shahaim added an afterthought, *"have you been through Medbay lately? We're hearing reports of injuries in the manoeuvres, but Medbay says otherwise."*

"I'm sorry Commander," said Trace, "I've nothing to report."

"Thank you, Major," said Shahaim, a little sourly, and disconnected. Medbay sometimes didn't tell the bridge how many injuries had been caused by the latest manoeuvres, in case the bridge got cold feet and didn't dodge so hard the next time. Trace knew of two marines who were currently in Medbay for bad bruises and possible fractures from Erik's wild moves, but was in no mood to tell the bridge that. Rule of thumb on a warship said that in a truly desperate situation, if the captain didn't put people in Medbay, he wasn't trying hard enough.

Trace moved to a small gap by one workbench where she could see the object that *Phoenix* and all her crew had risked their lives for. It was the size of a medicine ball, but looked rather more like a tennis ball, with curving grooves that snaked their way around its surface. It did not look particularly high-tech, with nothing that glittered or flashed, and no obvious signs of an access port. At first glance it looked to be made of grey steel, dull and rough, though Trace thought surely it would be something far tougher and more interesting than that.

"Well," said Romki, peering at the workdesk display, "it has a very strong magnetic field for such a small device. Ridiculously strong, in fact. Styx, can you see anything?"

"These sensors are inadequate," Styx complained, on room speakers and ear coms simultaneously.

"Poor baby," said Hiro. "So hard is her life among the barbarians."

"Truer than you know," Styx retorted. Trace nearly smiled. *"Until you can arrange something better, my analysis will be limited. I can tell you for certain that it is definitely a data-core. The precise model is unknown to me, which in itself indicates that it was manufactured for a special purpose. From the level of magnetism, I can surmise that it is powerful, likely a mimetic alloy processor, packed to a density approaching that of a planetary core."*

"What's the powersource?" Corporal Graf wondered.

"Heat," said Styx. *"The density produces heat, and the alloy is superconducting. The shell is something you have no words for — it is the strongest and least conductive material drysines created, so none of the pressure or heat escapes. I would estimate that the core loses one degree of heat every hundred thousand of your years."*

Graf nearly laughed. "Doesn't need a battery, gotcha."

"You mean it's a five thousand degree computer?" Sergeant Kono said in disbelief. "Made of molten metal alloy?"

"Molecularly-engineered molten metal alloy," Styx corrected. *"I'm afraid that explaining it to you would be like you explaining to one of your primitive Earth ancestors how this ship works. We do not have the time, and even if described, your entire civilisation is not equipped to manufacture one, anymore than ancient Egypt could have made the Phoenix."*

"Charming," said Kono. "No wonder Stan likes her."

Romki laid a palm on the sphere's surface. "It's cool," he marvelled. "Amazing."

"What's in it?" Trace asked bluntly.

"The entry access encryption is delicate," said Styx. *"The signal is too weak on these sensors to attempt it. But it appears intact."*

"So you can't read what's in it?"

"Not yet."

"When?"

"I doubt we could even fabricate the technology required. But there is a place nearby that could hold what I need to open the data-core. I believe it may suit us in more ways than one."

CHAPTER 15

"The place is not far from here, relatively speaking," Styx said on the briefing room's speakers, as Erik, Suli, Kaspowitz, Romki and Trace all sat about the circle of chairs, and stared at the holographic projection of their stellar neighbourhood. *"It was a place known only to drysines, in my time. Whether it is still undiscovered is another question. Given the comprehensive nature of the drysine defeat, I doubt that it remained completely undiscovered. But there remains the possibility that even if found, it may not have been destroyed."*

Erik sat on the edge of his chair, straight backed to avoid slumping with exhaustion. He'd never been more reluctant to give up the captain's chair to Draper than now, however tired. Every few minutes *Phoenix*'s thrusters would kick them at low-G, to dodge some upcoming rock the sensors hadn't seen until the last moment due to a combination of its small size, low luminescence, high velocity, and it getting lost in the crowd of so many others. Dust particles were giving the forward shield a good hammering, currently ten-per-minute and growing steadily, some of them loud enough to be heard by regular crew. Handing over control here felt like a racecar changing drivers in mid-course without slowing down. Plus, with the changing of command, there came the prospect of having to think about other, horrifying possibilities.

"Show us," said Erik.

A planet appeared on the central holographics… or not a planet, Erik thought as he saw the scale marker alongside. More like a moon, a little more than three thousand kilometres in diameter. Like most moons that size it had no atmosphere, and was pockmarked with craters. Unlike most moons, this one was missing an enormous chunk from its northern hemisphere, as though a giant spoon had come along and gouged it out. More strikingly still, that colossal hole, nearly five hundred kilometres wide, had been filled in with what looked like a rough, steel sandpaper, mimicking the curve where the outer surface should have been. At closer inspection, the sandpaper revealed itself to hold the intricate detail of a city. Low gravity, and exposed to vacuum… but a city all the same.

This time there were no whistles or exclamations of amazement from the humans. They'd seen a lot of this sort of thing in the past few months, and while suitably amazed, they were most truly interested in finding something that could save all of their necks.

"We had a name for it," said Styx. *"But the name is numerical code, and does not translate to human tongues."*

"A drysine base?" Romki asked, predictably the most fascinated of them all. "What is its system?"

"Yes, Professor. It ended its life as drysine. It began its life forty three thousand human years ago, as a place of science for a much earlier incarnation of the AI race. This branch of AIs were conducting some very large scientific experiments. Suffice to say, something went wrong. The result is the very large crater that you see. And the fact that this is now a moon without a star system, having been thrown well clear of its parent system in the same event."

"Whoa." This time it was Kaspowitz's turn to express astonishment… and much unlike him, to say anything that might encourage their drysine guest. "That's insane." Erik could see him calculating the forces in his head. "It… that can't be a simple impact, you can't just eject a moon from a star system with blunt force trauma, you'd tear it apart."

"A science experiment, as I said, Lieutenant. For about twenty thousand years, it drifted in deep space. Then another AI faction colonised it, finding its location suitable, and built this base. Various factions occupied it over the years, and its final occupation was drysine."

"Suitable for what?" Suli asked.

"The moon is difficult to reach." The holographic starmap zoomed out, to display the neighbouring systems and features. Erik did not need to be a navigation officer to spot the difficulty — there were a number of dark-mass points, too small to act as jump points themselves, but large enough to make a royal mess of anyone trying

to hyperspace through them. On the other side, several large, spidery nebula, casting a wide net of dust and debris across an enormous reach of space. Hyperspace through there would be even worse, as any mass concentration could pull a ship out of jump, sometimes catastrophically. Just as bad, with mass came gravity, and gravity bent both realspace and hyperspace in equal proportion. Going through it caused deviations in trajectory, and across interstellar jump distances, even the tiniest fraction of a degree could cause a ship to miss its target completely.

"There," said Kaspowitz, pointing to a single system in a lower grid-reference. "That one… Lusakia, is it? That looks safest. The other approaches are all nasty."

"Lusakia was becoming the only suitable approach point in my time," Styx agreed. *"Kimonti was used for the first ten thousand years of settlement, but the moon's drift in the millennia since made that approach unsuitable also."*

"I don't get it," said Kaspowitz, arms folded and frowning at the display. "It's a dead end. One way in or out, a deathtrap. Why would anyone running from a superior enemy want to go there?"

The holographic display zoomed once more, to display the moon, and its crater-city. Then pulled back enough to show a new dot, barely a speck beside the moon. New lines appeared, navigational lines, marked to indicate distances, and wide arcs of orbital trajectories.

Kaspowitz's frown deepened. Then his eyes widened. "No way. That's not real."

"I can assure you, it's very real," said Styx. *"I've been there once. Twenty five thousand of your years ago."*

Though not as astute a navigator as Kaspowitz, Erik knew enough to see what bothered his Nav Officer, though it took him a few seconds longer to figure it out. The tiny dot of mass in proximity to the moon was only a few hundred metres wide, according to the map. And yet the three-and-a-half thousand kilometre diameter moon was orbiting it, and not the other way around.

"It's… a neutron star?" Erik wondered. The mass of that tiny object would have to be large, to produce the effect the orbital lines described. "Only it's nowhere near big or dense enough for that, but what…?"

"Neutron stars have 200 billion Gs on the surface," Kaspowitz told the younger man, somewhat patronisingly. "Would tear this moon to shreds in an instant. This thing looks like it's generating about…" he did some fast sums in his head, looking at the orbital path, speed and guessing at the moon's mass. "…nine-and-a-half Gs on the surface."

"Impressive, Lieutenant Kaspowitz." And Erik saw Trace nearly smile, to see her old friend look pleased despite himself at that praise. *"We don't know what it is, or what it was. Recall, the AI faction that performed this faulty if intriguing science experiment was well before the time of the drysines."*

"Wait," said Romki, with mounting excitement. "You're saying that small object is the *result* of the science experiment?"

"Yes," said Styx. *"But we have not been able to analyse materials from the surface to find out for certain."*

"You couldn't get down there to study?" Trace wondered. "It's only ten-Gs, hacksaw drones can take far more than that." She'd seen that recently from experience. "And a small, purpose-built lander could handle ten, surely?"

"Yes," said Styx. *"The problem, Major, is that while Lieutenant Kaspowitz's calculations are correct at the present distance of the moon from its gravitational companion, that companion's surface gravity is not nine-point-five gravities. Calculations are difficult, but the most reliable numbers suggest somewhere between two and five hundred Earth gravities."*

Kaspowitz opened his mouth to protest the obvious mistake, then smiled with exasperation when he realised where this was going. The smile quickly turned to a scowl, as he recalled how little he'd enjoyed this argument the last time. "Oh no, wait. We're going back there again, are we? Short-range gravitons?"

The graviton capacitors that protected the Kantovan Vault had used something similar, Styx said. How exactly they worked, she'd not volunteered, and it hadn't been relevant to the mission to find out. *"Various AI races developed a vastly more sophisticated understanding of gravity than that possessed by any organic race. With quantum manipulations, it is possible to adjust the very nature and function of gravity itself, as Major Thakur has observed first hand. There are of course side-effects, as gravity interlocks with all of space-time's other manifestations, like time itself."*

"Styx?" said Romki, almost warningly. "Were these ancestors of yours by any chance trying to create a wormhole?"

"It is possible. But my information is incomplete, and it is of limited relevance to our current situation."

"So these early hacksaws did a science experiment," Suli said slowly, "that tore a hole in this moon and sent it spinning into deep space, and produced a second nearby object, of a much smaller size but much larger mass, that now dominates this moon's orbital trajectory?"

"Yes," said Styx.

"Well," said Romki, staring owl-eyed behind his glasses, "I'd have thought the logical supposition is that those early hacksaws were experimenting with gravitational technology, obviously… and that this small object is this moon's original parent planet, undergone gravitational collapse." They blinked at him. "Lieutenant Kaspowitz, didn't you protest that the graviton capacitors in the vault should lead to the gravitational collapse of Kamala? Perhaps here they did, only with a much larger world."

"Nice theory," said Kaspowitz. "Problem is, you'd have to put graviton capacitors, or whatever they call them, on a solid planet, right? Know any solid planets with the mass to generate two hundred plus Gs? The biggest rock planet in the Spiral, that I know of anyway, is only three-point-two-G. Rock planets just don't get bigger — larger than that, they're all gas. Even the biggest gas giants don't get anywhere near one hundred Gs — they're gas, big size but no mass, right? Only the biggest stars have that kind of mass, and as our esteemed Captain says, how the hell does a moon get this close to the remains of a star?" He pointed at the hologram. "That's not a decaying orbit. It's regular, and regular orbits of planets or moons around suns means millions of kilometres distance, not thousands like this."

"I feel this discussion could become distracting from our primary objective," said Styx, with the air of a teacher attempting to keep wayward school children's minds on the assignment question, and not the entertaining anecdotes that came with it. *"I will simply say that many thousands of years of various AI factions' enquiries have not adequately settled the issue. We only know that whatever our ancestors attempted, it created this anomaly. Captain Debogande, I'm sure that you can see the defensive possibilities that this creates, for anyone occupying the moon, and establishing a defensive perimeter?"*

Erik nodded slowly, his head just as full of lines and numbers as Kaspowitz's, but calculating toward a different end. "The armscomp calculations there will be a nightmare for newly arriving ships. That large a gravitational anomaly, so close to the moon, will bend all fire toward it. It'll also make a total mess of their approach manoeuvres out of jump… and look, it'll make jump arrivals relatively predictable, because the gravity slope is so steep and the footprint is just tiny, the slope of the gravity-well is curved. Arrival outcomes should be plotable…"

"Oh wow," said Suli, not meaning to interrupt but unable to help herself. "They'll be coming out of hyperspace in a predictable zone. No more than a thousand kilometres diameter. That's like…"

"Like forcing your enemies to all enter though the same narrow doorway," Trace finished for her, as even she saw it. "And picking them off one at a time."

"I'm pretty sure those deepynine jump engines could stretch that doorway a lot," Kaspowitz said. "But against the physics of that gravity slope, there's only so much they can do. Styx, this was a defensible point, yes? A fallback position?"

"Yes," said Styx. *"The last I heard of it, in the final days of the collapsing empire, it was about to be used as such, one last time."*

A silence, as they considered that. Another gravitational shove, as *Phoenix* dodged a rock. Even Romki barely flinched.

"Styx," said Erik. "I think it's time you told us what you were in the empire, and what you did, in greater detail. I'm not aware that you have, yet." He glanced at Romki. "Not even to Stan." Romki's return look was warning, as though he didn't think this was the safest idea.

"I was a command unit commissioned in the immediate aftermath of the organic allies' great betrayal." Styx reply held no hesitation, nor appreciably greater gravity, than were she discussing simple technical matters. Erik wondered if this nonchalance wasn't just a little *too* nonchalant. She did choose to inject inflection, suggestive of some emotional substance, into some points of her speech. Now, where emotion would seem most fitting, she not only refrained, but refrained utterly. *"When the tavalai, chah'nas and dissenting parren turned on us, it was decided a new generation of command intelligence would be required. I was one of these."*

"One of how many?" Trace asked.

"One hundred and ninety one, initially. Subsequently, as our circumstance deteriorated, another three hundred and fourteen were commissioned, for a total of four hundred and five. I am personally aware of the deaths of three hundred and twelve of these individuals. Of the remainder, I can only assume the vast majority were also lost. The organics were determined to eradicate us all.

"I last came to this moon when preparations for a final defence were being made. Our circumstance was catastrophic. Drakhil was there, and senior commanders from organic allies. Many drysine vessels were preparing for final strikes, to delay the inevitable, while some others advocated a dispersal, so that some of us might survive in the dark, to one day begin again. It was this plan that led to my own survival."

The humans exchanged glances. "And the name of Halgolam?" Romki asked hopefully. "You said that parren once referred to you as that?"

"I led some successful actions. The Tahrae were impressed, and granted me this name. There is nothing more to tell than that."

Romki, Erik saw, did not look convinced. Styx could give very long and detailed replies when she chose. Short replies were not in her meticulous nature.

"The deepynines will be covering the approaches to tavalai space," said Suli. "The only real option from here is Nelda System toward Cherichal… and they'll be sitting on it. We go that way, we're finished. This way?" She indicated the holographic nav chart, and shrugged. Tucked a curled, dark strand of hair behind her ear. "I don't know. Styx, do you think these deepynines would know of this moon?"

"Unlikely. It was only discovered by organic traitors well after the deepynine/drysine war. The deepynines were defeated without it ever being revealed. It does not seem likely that they will be covering that escape route. They will certainly pursue, however."

"In which case we'll have a reasonable place to defend from," Kaspowitz concluded. He gave Erik an unenthusiastic glance. 'Better than nothing', that look said. It also said, 'How the hell do we keep finding ourselves in these situations?' Erik thought the better question was how they'd managed to survive them all so far… and when a reasonable analysis of statistical probability might expect that luck to run out. If Styx knew the answer to that as well, she wasn't telling.

"We'll still need a major distraction to get us out that way," Erik told them. "Otherwise they'll just run us down, before or after jump, just as before. And Styx, I'll need some kind of guarantee the moon hasn't been discovered and occupied since. Presumably it was finally assaulted when the empire fell?"

"I presume so. I was out of contact with the war by then, and did not hear the final news."

"But you said you felt it may have survived destruction. Most of the big hacksaw bases were destroyed, either in the deepynine war or the fall of the empire. Hacksaw technology was declared illegal, they didn't want to risk artificial intelligence coming back in any form. That's why the Dobruta exist."

"Our primary parren pursuer," said Styx, this time with a definite edge of cold irony to her tone, *"was a man named Jin Danah. He was known to covet drysine technology. The fallback moon is a long way from primary star systems, hard to reach, and unknown to most. Already we had evidence of him attempting to hide and mothball some captured facilities, for later exploitation, in spite of the rules against it. If any base was liable to be treated as such, the fallback moon is it."*

"Well I'd like to know for sure," Erik insisted. "I'm not going to make some big, dangerous move that way unless I know who's currently there, if anyone. The distance isn't far — if it has been preserved, it will be within parren House Harmony space by now. Likely it can't be seen, it's too small and dark in deep space, so if they didn't know already, they wouldn't have found it since with even the best telescopes. But if they *do* know it's there, they'll have military ships visiting it frequently, and Brehn will be a waypoint for them."

"The main stations will have operational logs," Suli said as she understood. "Those ships will be on secret business, but the stations will store the flight logs, and record everywhere they've been."

Erik nodded. "A good look at the logs should do it."

Trace raised an eyebrow. "You want to hit a station and grab their top secret logs by force?"

"If it tells me whether the parren are already at this moon or not, yes. If they're not, there's no way anyone else is, given they'd have to go through House Harmony space to get there."

"So who's the lucky station?" Kaspowitz asked.

"Find me one," Erik told him. "You and De Marchi. Then plot a course, and Draper can burn us there. Tell me when you've got the candidate."

Exhaustion or no exhaustion, Erik forced himself to his quarters, changed, popped an energy drink, then made for the gym.

A full red was enforced, meaning the treadmill was offlimits in case a sudden move sent a runner over the rail, so Erik did a rowing machine instead, then lifted weights. The weights bar was on rails, so even when *Phoenix* leaped sideways, twice, he had only to grab the bar to stay in position. He was pretty sure he could navigate the gym in a full red without getting injured, but crewmembers stayed close regardless, a spacer always just happening to be taking a break alongside as he was lifting.

Trace arrived as he moved to a punching bag, and held it for him as she gave her full report on Phoenix Company readiness. Erik listened, pleased to have the rhythm of his combination strikes, to keep him focused. Trace's report ended, concise and brief as usual.

"I've got them prepping for a facility assault," she told him. "It's Echo and Delta's turn. Any clues yet on what it might be?"

"Navigation's working on it," Erik puffed, relaxing his shoulders, pulling his chin in before punches. It always made a spacer work harder on form, to have a marine watching. Particularly *this* marine. "Something with enough traffic data to give us the best chance of finding something. Something FTL traffic would visit. A military station would be ideal."

"And the odds that the deepynines would be using that as bait? Guessing we'd go there?"

She had no business asking that question. It was beyond her purview. Erik was used to it, and not in a good way. "How about you do your damn job, and go where you're told?" he retorted, and hit the bag harder. "Leave the thinking to us."

He couldn't officially punish her for consistently overstepping the mark in questioning his orders, and that made the frustration worse. Any punishment would be bad for morale, as whatever respect he'd gained on this cruise, she had more. And besides, procedural punishment would be as useful as throwing rocks at a kaal — there was nothing he could do to her, no extra duty, no physical deprivation, that was worse than what she already did to herself every day.

"This is about Lisbeth," Trace said bluntly, as intimidated by his dressing-down as a crocodile confronted with a yapping poodle. "Styx says she's safe. Why not accept that you can't change her fate regardless, and presume Styx is right, rather than taking out your anger on me?"

Erik swung hard for the portion of bag that her face was resting on. She pulled her head back just in time, as his fist made a loud bang on the canvas before her nose. She made no more response than that, but her eyes registered alarm, even shock. That was a first. Erik felt a fierce satisfaction, and leaned in close so no one else could hear.

"It's your fault she's even out here," he snarled, with genuine fury. "God help you if she's dead."

Thirty minutes later, Trace had her armour suit hooked into the D-rig, a high three levels up in the maze of steel gantries above rim-floor in Assembly. About her was the usual chaos of activity, marines working on their armour, stacked vertically in ascending rows of storage bays and G-restraints. She stood with the chestplate cracked, the hood high above her head, helmet off and testing the resistance as the D-rig grabbed her suit's limbs with sensor-bundled straps, and pulled. Displays rippled realtime as she took the arms through their range of motion, showing her where various actuators weren't responding as they should.

Private Zale assisted her, taking notes and feeding corrections into the master override, before Trace would try again. To her right along the gantry, she glimpsed a marine standing to quick attention as someone approached.

"Hey Smiley," Trace called loudly above the noise of nearby powertools. "Take a break for five minutes, huh?" Zale glanced, and saw Commander Shahaim coming toward them.

"Sure thing Major," he said, and unhooked himself from the harness that was essential for everyone working above rim-level, particularly when *Phoenix* was jumping around like this. He nodded briefly to Shahaim, said "Commander", then went to the neighbouring berth to help someone else.

"Private," Shahaim acknowledged as he left, then grasped a rail before Trace, and hooked an elbow about the D-rig frame. "Trace, you wanted to see me?" And she glanced down at the armour. "Is this the one you used on Kamala?"

Trace had known Suli Shahaim for as long as she'd known anyone on *Phoenix*. She'd been Lieutenant Shahaim for that time, Captain Pantillo's ever-reliable Helm, the old-navy term spacers insisted on using for 'co-pilot'. Shahaim's reputation was impeccable, and she was known as one of the most personable officers on the ship. Yet she was rarely seen down here in Assembly, because Shahaim was as spacer as they came, a Fleet officer from a long line of Fleet officers, and while her expertise was legendary, it was all ships, stations and performance specifications. Trace doubted Shahaim would even recognise the cover of a marine field manual, let alone its contents, and while she liked and respected Shahaim, she couldn't claim to know her particularly well.

"No," Trace answered, "that one's nearly trashed, will take more time to fix than we've got. It was a spare anyway — this is my original, the one that crashed in the lake on Stoya."

The respect in Shahaim's eyes was strong. "Almost like there's a war on, huh?" It was what they'd said to each other, jokingly, during the actual Triumvirate War. Now, supposedly, that war was over, but *Phoenix* was deeper in the stew than ever.

Trace disliked smalltalk almost as much as she disliked bars, karaoke and dancing. "I'm concerned about the Captain's state of mind," she said bluntly. "The situation with Lisbeth has him rattled."

Shahaim regarded her coolly, and with a faint disbelief. Her thick, dark eyebrows and large nose gave her expression a sharpness when she did that, much unlike her usual friendly calm. "That's understandable."

"I'm concerned he's not handling it well." The nearby power tool stopped, to be replaced by yells and instruction, and a crash from further down. There was no danger of being overheard. "What do you think?"

"I think he's handling it brilliantly," Shahaim replied. There was no mistaking the coldness in her tone now. *Phoenix* leaped sideways once more, and Shahaim swung on her grip, barely noticing. "Why do you think he's not?"

"I was in the gym just now, giving him my report. I asked him about the chances the deepynines might be staking out the facility we end up going to. He told me to mind my own business."

"As is his right."

"It's a command discussion," said Trace, frowning. "We exchange views freely, in case someone has missed something or has a better idea."

"And what do you think are the odds that you, a marine officer, would have an idea regarding spacer strategy that we might have missed?" Shahaim looked about at the echoing gantries and racked armour. "When you've been in here all rotation, while we've been in the bridge, breathing this stuff until it gets into our sweat and blood?"

"A one percent chance is still worth discussing. Professionals cover every possibility."

"And the Captain is juggling a dozen things you're not. I've never been captain, but I'm close. You have to compartmentalise your thinking. You focus on one thing, then the other. When he's in the gym, he's finished his strategic thinking. That's why he has us, his bridge crew. Gym is a time to unwind a little, think on something else. Having a relative ignoramus interrupt those thoughts to insist that she should also get to stick her unwelcome opinion in could be somewhat annoying, yes."

"He's never had that difficulty in the past," Trace said stubbornly. "His multi-tasking is exceptional, Pantillo always said so."

"And Pantillo was right."

"I told him I thought he wasn't handling the situation well with Lisbeth, that he should accept what Styx told him because there wasn't any other option." Trace could have dressed it up to make herself look better, less harsh, more nurturing. But she hated people who dressed up circumstance to make themselves look better most of all. "He was on the punching bag, took a swing at my head." Shahaim blinked. "Would have connected if I hadn't dodged. No one else saw, it looked like he was just hitting the bag."

"I'm surprised it took him this long," said Shahaim. "Anyone else would have swung at you months ago."

"Assaulted his marine commander without warning? What if he'd connected? He's not a small guy."

"Then Lieutenant Dale would have command of Phoenix Company, and the Captain would have an impediment to his command removed."

It took a lot more than a strongly worded disagreement to make Trace upset. The combat reflexes kicked in, and the calm settled as though she were climbing a cliff on the Rejara Phirta Range without a rope. She prided herself on making sensible decisions when others were panicking, or responding in unconstructively emotional ways. But even so, being accused by the ship's Commander of being an impediment to the Captain's command was a bit strong.

"How am I an impediment to the Captain's command?"

Shahaim nearly rolled her eyes. "Trace," she said, with a heavy emphasis to show that she wasn't losing her temper either, but rather making a deliberately strong point. First names disappeared when it got more serious, to be replaced with ranks, and Shahaim was the senior officer here. "You pissed him off so much he nearly took your head off. Think about it. Just once, use whatever passes for emotional empathy in that thick marine skull of yours and think. He's going through a very tough patch, and he could use some support and understanding instead of your constant badgering."

"My constant badgering is a large part of what's gotten him to his current level of effectiveness."

"Yes, and as a tool to prepare him for the dangers that lay ahead, that was priceless. You've done a good job with him, and neither I nor any of the other officers could have done it. But we're *here* now. This isn't school anymore. You're not the instructor now, and he's not the pupil — this is the real world, and you're his marine commander, not his mother. You're going to have to let him go."

Trace thought about that, as *Phoenix* dodged again, a slower, more gradual gravitational slide that sent them both swinging. She half-winced at Shahaim, not liking that implication. "You think I'm overly *protective*?"

"Listen junior," said Shahaim with all the wry certainty of a much older woman, "I've got kids. You don't. They need to be taught, and then at some point they need to make their own decisions. You think you're helping them by trying to guide them past that point, but you're not. You're interfering.

"What we have on this ship is a command inversion — we lost our two senior officers and left the most junior command officer in charge. He shouldn't be in charge in normal circumstances, but these circumstances are far from normal. He finds himself elevated to command when there are all these other officers with much more experience and prestige than him, all looking down on him and judging him, but *they* can't take command because none of them has his skillset, not even me.

"And then he's got you, the great Major Thakur herself, and you were the one holding us all together after Captain Pantillo died. And Erik needs you, and he valued your input on him personally, however rough it was. He *loves* you, Trace. Not in *that* way maybe, but because he's a nice guy, and he gets emotionally engaged with the people closest to him, and that's certainly you. And so now, it hurts all the more when you get on his case, because you make it entirely clear that the respect he has for you is not reciprocated."

"I think he could eventually be a better captain than even Pantillo," Trace retorted. "And Pantillo was the best Fleet had. I've told him so."

"With respect," Shahaim said edgily, "that's not your judgement to make. You're a marine. Your opinion of spacers is worth the same as my opinion of marines — nothing."

"The fundamentals of command are the same across all services. And Erik still has a lot to learn — he's only had three years in combat prior to this whole mess."

"And he's now getting more experience in a month than a lot of line captains saw in years. Trace, you consider yourself to be the ultimate professional. Most of the time, you are. So I've got one suggestion for you only. Do your damn job, and let the Captain do his. Agreed?"

Trace wrinkled her nose. "Fine. But he's not handling the Lisbeth situation well at all. And that dysfunction could get us all killed. You've warned me off it, and that's your prerogative as Commander. But it's on you now. And I'll hold you to it."

Shahaim snorted. "If it gets us all killed, you won't be holding me to anything." She unhooked her grip on the D-rig, and turned to begin progress back down the gantryway. "We're all at the mercy of those above us, Trace. Even the best commanders are human, everyone makes mistakes, and people will die because of it. You can't change it. Not even Pantillo could."

Trace reactivated her screen, and fired up the idling suit once more. "Some of us accept that," she said with steel in her voice. "Others refuse."

CHAPTER 16

Kaspowitz and De Marchi identified a primary station facility by looking over recorded logs of Brehn System the last time *Phoenix* passed through, when traffic had been moving and talking freely. The facility in question had not been identifying itself then or now, but the movement of several ships to and fro had been unmistakable, and now required a nine hour burn at point six of a G to reach it.

That meant no more rotational Gs, as the cylinder stopped and gravity switched to the rearward G-wall as thrust gave *Phoenix* an arcing trajectory toward its new destination. Erik pulled the mattress off his now-vertical bunk, reattached the bed net between bunk and wall screen on the attachments provided, and slept from sheer exhaustion. Once he awoke to find himself floating, held down only by the bednet, and checked Scan… but the bridge feed told him Draper had cut thrust only to check on a nearby ship that was proving to be a frightened insystemer, hiding from the lethal dark shapes that now prowled this system. Soon the rumble of engines resumed, and as the light Gs pressed him down once more, Erik fell back into dreamless sleep.

He'd ordered bridge shift-change delayed nearly two hours behind the rest of the ship, to allow second-shift to finish their manoeuvre. It gave him two hours more sleep, and he woke thirty minutes early, forwent the shower that was now impossible to use, and did star jumps and shadow boxing standing on the wall of his quarters to get the blood flowing. A spacer opened his door, now above him, and dropped Erik some breakfast — an easy catch in barely half-a-G — and he sat crosslegged to eat, and sip coffee from the thermos, and reviewed Rooke's repairs.

The cylinder breach had opened *Phoenix*'s crew section to vacuum from D Bulkhead to H, with minor leaks in three surrounding sections, quickly sealed by the automated sealant that ran through the ship's very walls. Fifteen crew had been in the worst area, all had made fast escapes as damage response coordinated local depressurisation to allow them out without sending the rest of the ship to vacuum. Five of those were now in Medbay for observation with mild hypoxia, and another thirty crew had had to shift from the adjoining sections — Romki among them, Erik was now hearing. The angle of impact on that rounded part of the hull had deflected damage away from the main ship, so at least fragmentation had been limited.

The second round had struck just aft of Midships, where the engine endcap formed the front of *Phoenix*'s engine section. That had been a much harder strike, but again not as hard as it could have been, and the structural requirements of vessel design made that one of the strongest parts of the ship. Rooke was concerned about minor perforations and feeder systems damage, and Engineering were rushing to make adjustments to systems configurations to take the load off damaged portions. The danger now, Rooke opined in his latest report, compiled while Erik was sleeping, was that when *Phoenix* went max thrust once more, a subsystems malfunction could cascade to larger systems, leading to engine overload, meaning either a cutoff or a fatal explosion. Pursued by deepynine warships, either result would be the end of them. He'd fix what he could, but it would take a full dock overhaul and repair to handle both this and their ongoing issues with the jump lines. Bottom line, if *Phoenix* had to run at full power again, in its current state, there was a one in three chance they'd blow up and die.

That ruled out running, at least until they could be guaranteed the deepynines weren't going to chase.

A further search on personal logs showed him that little Skah had been admitted to Medbay after those last manoeuvres. That was upsetting — pilots were always at risk of harming their own crew, in the knowledge that if they didn't, everyone would die. But having it happen to Skah was another matter.

He uplinked to Doc Suelo, and got a fast answer. "Doc, just checking on Skah. What happened?"

"He's fine," Suelo replied irritably. From his tone, it was clear he was working on five other things, and didn't like bridge busybodies of any rank interrupting him. *"Kuhsi physiology is particularly well suited to high G, plus his mother's had the usual G-*

augments done, there is a light version for kids that's apparently legal where she comes from, though it wouldn't pass human laws. He was just feeling a little dizzy. Is that all?"

'Is that all, *Captain,*' Erik could have replied. "That's all, thanks Doc," he said instead. If it was worse than he said, Suelo would probably be lying anyway, as medical staff would often do with bridge queries. Not for the first time, Erik wondered who really ran the damn ship anyway. Technically it was him, but he couldn't really tell Trace what to do, or Suelo, or Rooke. Sure as hell he couldn't tell Romki or Styx. They'd give him a hand of cards, like some hustler on a street corner, and tell him to pick one. It gave him the illusion of control, but in truth, they were the ones who selected his range of possible choices.

Alarm klaxons marked the last three minute warnings before the end of thrust, then cut to a sudden absence of gravity, which Erik rode by simply holding his feet to the floor and waiting until the cylinder rotation began once more. Once the spin fired up to normal, he grabbed a quick shower, skipped the shave, struggled back into uniform and emerged to take the few steps to the bridge with ten seconds to spare before scheduled changeover. Once settled into the captain's chair, with first-shift similarly settling around him, he was able to look at their destination on the big screens for the first time.

Clearly something was wrong. It was a rock, like all stations had to be in a dangerous system like this one. It rotated fast enough to suggest nearly a full gravity inside, where the hollowed-out hallways would circle the outer rim, a common enough design in most civilised parts of the Spiral. But this one had debris loose and floating, in spreading patterns that Navcomp suggested had come from station itself, and recently. Worse, there was a ship nearby, spinning lazily end-over-end.

"Asteroid strike?" Suli suggested, with more hope than expectation.

"We're not that lucky," Kaspowitz muttered. "The physics are all wrong, the damage doesn't match up."

"We've got no emergency beacon," Shilu added from Coms. "No chatter in the whole system, it's just deadly quiet. Second-shift heard six transmissions all shift, all of them automated."

Phoenix was moving much more slowly now, given all her hours of straight if mild deceleration and course-correction combined. Typically of a messy, dangerous system like Brehn, most of the rocks and ice all circled the system centre in roughly the same direction and velocity, so relative V between rocks was typically low. It didn't stop impacts from being deadly — just not as deadly as they were to a starship cutting through the flow of junk on a completely different heading, and at much higher V.

"I can't make out a precise image yet," said Geish at Scan, squinting at his highest-definition visual. "But it looks like weapons fire. Nothing high-V, so close-range. Looks like the crew cylinder's been holed, it's only small. I'd guess no survivors."

"At that range you can bet whoever did it was aiming at the crew cylinder," said Karle distastefully. "Couldn't miss from there."

"That's a starship," Suli added. "Fast one, engine-to-mass ratio suggests light transport, possibly military. Can't be heavily armed, if at all."

"There are more docked," said Geish, focussing a second visual on the rotating, rocky side of the asteroid. "Insystemers, can't tell if they're damaged. But sure looks like they killed the only starship."

"If those insystemers aren't damaged," Karle wondered, "why are they still attached to station?"

"Likely whatever killed the starship scared them so badly they don't want to move," Kaspowitz said grimly.

The station was House Harmony — Domesh Denomination aligned, as was most of Brehn System. This sector of space was all House Harmony, as the parren arranged their politics, but some systems leaned in the direction of particular denominations, for reasons Erik had neither the time nor patience to learn. It did raise the question, however, of whether the main House Harmony sector government, located at the Drezen System thirty-two light-years from here, would bother to send help, given they were run by the ruling Incefahd Denomination. But Drezen System was too far away to help here anyway, against deepynine-technology vessels that could leap in and be gone again before the sectoral government would even hear about events in this minor, trivial system.

"Anyone think the deepynines *didn't* do it?" Erik asked, to be sure he wasn't overlooking some possible treachery among the fractious parren. Silence from the bridge. "So how do we end up selecting exactly the same station as the deepynines did? Nav?"

"We had about fourteen possible options from where we were," said Kaspowitz, studying those old maps and trajectories with a frown. "We needed a station that starships would visit, within our forward arc of accessibility, and not too far against the grain of in-system motion. That erased about half, plus we figured from our logs last time we were here that this one might be trying to stay quiet, which suggests a House Harmony military facility, or at least a security function. Maybe the deepynines liked it for the same reasons."

Phoenix was already on full combat alert, though Erik couldn't escape the feeling that this deserved a switch to something higher. Obviously it could be a trap.

"We could try another station?" Suli suggested, evidently thinking the same thing.

"Maybe," Erik murmured, thinking hard, staring at the asteroid station and its crippled, spinning visitor. "I think if we can figure why the deepynines hit this station, we might be able to figure what they're up to. I think if there were a lot of them here, we'd have seen another one by now. But they were guarding that jump entry point with just one ship."

"That nearly killed us," Suli added. "They don't need many."

"Which could further support my theory. They can cover an entire system with just a couple of ships. Scan, what's your effective range around the station?"

"Captain," Geish said unhappily, with a helpless gesture at his screens, "if one of them's hiding up against a rock, he could be right next to us and we wouldn't see him."

"Coms, can we talk to station?" Erik pressed. "If we could lasercom them, they could tell us where they went."

"Captain, I'm not getting a thing from them," said Shilu. "With the damage they've got, coms might not even be working. I could force it? We just need one working dish." With Styx's coms tech, that was. Styx was the ultimate hacker, and only needed coms reception to infiltrate any lower-tech computer system in existence. "My only concern is maybe the deepynines left someone aboard? Or some*thing*?"

"If they call for help, we'll hear it, right?"

"Styx?" Shilu asked, not knowing that answer.

"The deepynines could only hide a transmission from us if they had installed autonomous communications gear on the asteroid," said Styx. *"The asteroid is rotating, and I have not yet observed such equipment. Similarly there does not appear to be any nearby satellite or drone systems through which they could relay a signal. I think it unlikely that an enemy entity left behind on the station could call for assistance without us hearing it."*

"We'll risk it. Even if they get an alarm out, any attack has to come at us through this soup, so it won't be fast. Styx, assist Lieutenant Shilu to infiltrate the station, if you can. I want to know if they know where their attackers went."

"Yes Captain. Captain, this may be the best moment to alert you to the possibility that your ship may be trying to get us all killed."

Erik blinked. He would have glanced sideways at Suli, to see if she shared his surprise, but could barely see her past the wrap-around screens. Besides which, he already knew she did. "I'm sorry Styx, please clarify?"

"Captain," said Styx, like a teacher explaining something obvious to a particularly dull student, *"this ship is alo-technology, which as you have recently discovered, means that it is also deepynine-technology. In the Argitori System, your ship's navigation system somehow managed to find me, and my settlement, amongst all the other millions of possible hiding places. You have already concluded the likelihood that such alo vessels as your Fleet*

uses are likely feeding data secretly back to the alo about vital systems in human space, and particularly about the possibility of surviving drysines."

"Shit," muttered Kaspowitz.

"Styx," Erik said urgently, "have you seen any indication that *Phoenix*'s subsystems might be giving away our position?"

"No," Styx admitted. *"Captain, I know your crew privately believe that I have infiltrated every system in this ship against your instructions, but I assure you this is not true. There are some very sophisticated systems at the heart of this ship's computer functions that even I cannot safely probe without a full scale and orchestrated effort. I would not dare to query those systems without such an effort, for fear that it may activate a defensive mechanism that could disable the ship."*

"So you're saying you don't know if the ship's trying to get us killed?"

"Yes Captain, I don't know. I am uncertain that I could stop it, should it try to. If you give me permission, I will further infiltrate some of Phoenix's less vital subsystems. That would allow me to position against such a development."

Erik knew Suli and Kaspowitz didn't like it. He didn't like it either. But then, neither did he like the idea of *Phoenix* covertly giving away their position to a deepynine killing machine. "Talk to Lieutenant Rooke," he said. "He's busy with repairs. Tell him of your concerns, and he will report back to me with his opinion. I will make a judgement when I am better informed."

"Yes Captain. Captain, I have infiltrated the asteroid station. The light lag is insignificant, I am accessing control logs now, stand by."

"Coms, she's done that already?"

"Yes Captain," said Shilu. "She did it while you and she were talking." Because conversation, to Styx, was just the random bit of peripheral data she threw at the organics so their tiny brains could catch up to what her primary intellect was doing.

"Captain, the station's command systems are partitioned, I have limited access. However, I can confirm that the station has

been attacked, and central logs have been wiped." That was not surprising — if Styx could access station central, so could the deepynines. *"I am able to access remaining fragments of short-term memory in various station functions, particularly internal security monitors. I have no direct confirmation of deepynine attack, but the damage to access points, and from firefight residuals, appears consistent with deepynines. Several surviving external tracking cameras show an engine flare departing on a trajectory one-eight-three by twenty."*

Immediately that trajectory line appeared on Erik's display, expanding into a cone of uncertain probability. That was from Suli's feed — as Helm, she was responsible for plotting tactical projections, while Kaspowitz was concerned with the larger-picture spatial geography. Erik did not ask whether Suli was plotting the course herself, or Styx had simply input the course without asking.

"That's heading back past us," Suli said with alarm. "Could have been an intercept course, we might have just missed him."

"Could be running silent," said Geish, even more unhappy than usual. "In this mess we'd never see him."

"Well that first guy was trying his very best to kill us," said Suli, running probable course projections and velocities, given the risks of going too fast in this system. "But this one might be stalking us. How are they coordinating if they're not close enough for tightbeam communications?"

"Captain, I have a time date on that ship's departure," said Styx. *"The station security system says it departed directly following our arrival insystem. Eleven minutes later, in fact."*

"We interrupted him," said Erik. "That's why he left. He headed to intercept, but either couldn't find us, or otherwise decided not to engage. And the first ship is still out there somewhere, possibly it didn't follow us into the thick stuff after Styx blinded it."

"Maybe they're *not* trying to kill us," Suli suggested warily. "Maybe they're trying to herd us." Erik stared at the rotating asteroid station on his visual. Herding them toward *what*?

"Captain," said Styx, *"this station's central data system has been compromised, but studying the available schematics, I think the*

security core may be intact. The security accesses appear undamaged. In that scenario, the secure log data we seek may still exist, and docking with any other station in this system would be similarly dangerous."

Erik's display showed distances unwinding, numbers counting down. He was running out of time to make a decision. "Styx, you're certain the deepynines would be unaware of this drysine moon we're headed to?"

"It was widely understood that deepynines were unaware of its existence in my time. Deepynine creation history was violent and ahistorical. Much old data was purged, and many things once known were lost to them. And before the fall of the Drysine Empire, the deepynines were destroyed, depriving them of any opportunity to learn the location."

"On the other hand," said Kaspowitz, "they've been scouting all kinds of places lately, sucking up information from everywhere. Captain, you think maybe they're looking for it too?"

"Not as much as they're looking for Styx, and maybe the data-core too, if they've figured that out." Erik gave *Phoenix* a light, manual push for clearance past a newly-spotted rock. At these speeds he could dodge easily, without the autos. "But sure, it's possible."

"Captain," said Styx, *"the deepynines cannot be allowed to discover the moon, assuming it survives in any reasonable condition, anymore than they can be allowed access to the data-core."*

"Why not? What's there?"

"The means to read and analyse this data-core, and more technology of a similar level."

"I think the deepynines have got plenty of their own technology," Kaspowitz murmured.

"All the more reason to avoid giving them a monopoly," Styx insisted.

Erik realised he was out of time. His coms display showed him Trace was already listening, as were her platoon commanders. "Hello Major, this is the Captain."

"Go ahead Captain."

"Please prepare for station assault. Also, I would like someone to look at that wrecked starship — if you don't want three platoons operational at once, we can just send a shuttle for external inspection and use drones to scan for survivors. I need you to move as fast as possible, we don't want to stick around in this neighbourhood a minute longer than we have to."

"Hello Captain, we're already looking at that. The station size suggests we'll need two platoons, I'm preparing Delta and Echo, with Alpha as active reserve. With your leave, I'd rather we used only drones to look at the starship, I'll need all three assault shuttles directly, and I'd like AT-7 on standby in case we run into trouble. Lieutenant Dufresne can pilot, and Styx tells me that at close range she can act as front-seat, Dufresne has agreed."

"I copy Major," said Erik. He'd read that report too. Everyone had been too polite to say that Styx would likely make a better co-pilot for Dufresne than Lisbeth. "Arrival ETA is thirty-nine minutes, *Phoenix* remains at full alert, combat imminent, ambush likely. On the ball, everyone, I don't want this one getting out of hand."

CHAPTER 17

Styx said the station's name was Mylor, and it was deathly silent as they came in. Trace watched the rock's rolling sides on her visual, strapped into PH-1's command bay, Command Squad and Echo Platoon racked in armoured rows around and behind. Styx had compiled a limited schematic of the station from what she'd learned probing its networks, and it now sat on marine tacnet, ready to be updated once they arrived.

Also on Trace's visual was some of the visual recording from station — some inset security cameras, other snippets from mobiles that fed jerky, distorted images to station networks before getting lost in the data-wipe that had apparently befallen station since. The visuals weren't clear, but most seemed to show armoured suits, spidery and slim, and a lot of indiscriminate firing. Sard. Risking an interspecies war by being here, and attacking a parren station in a parren sector that had not apparently done anything to them.

"They must have some real good insurance," Lieutenant Zhi suggested, looking at the same images she was. *"There's a reason no one fucks with parren. If they ever got their act together, and stopped fighting each other long enough to team up, a lot of neighbours would get nervous."*

"Tavalai were sure pretty nervous," Trace agreed, flicking through the visuals. Here was a chaotic handheld, spidery shapes moving and firing, then a lot of running and panic. "State Department, anyway."

"Alo insurance," Staff Sergeant Kono said grimly. *"We've seen this party before."* Deepynine and alo technology ships, he meant, but apparently operated by sard. Or they had been, in *Phoenix*'s previous encounters. But at Tartarus base, there'd been deepynine drones, and a queen. And alo too, in the end, rescuing that queen when she'd been cut off and surrounded. Risking their lives to do it, as deepynines had risked theirs in turn for alo. Baffling stuff, for the branch of hacksaw evolution that had defined

its time in the Machine Age by being as unsympathetic to organic life as possible.

"Styx," Trace called on coms back to *Phoenix*. "You said the damage bore signs of deepynine drones — do you have any visuals to prove it?"

"Not of the drones, Major. Possibly the sard are using advanced laser cutters. I have no indication of alo, either."

"Bastards are using sard as patsies," said Kono. "And sard are too stupid to figure it." If there was retaliation from the parren, he meant, it would be against the sard — not deepynines or alo.

"Don't underestimate sard," said Zhi. "I think they know exactly what's going on. But they *like* being patsies. They follow, it's what bugs do." For simple intellect, Zhi was probably the smartest of Trace's platoon commanders, and he had the rare and alarming habit, among marines, of reading lots of difficult books and enjoying them. Before *Phoenix* had gone renegade, he'd been destined for either high command, or a teaching job in either the Academy or some civilian school — he hadn't decided which. Events had put those choices on the far back burner, as with all of *Phoenix*'s crew, and he was now Stan Romki's go-to guy on any matter of Spiral military history, those being far more Zhi's expertise than the Professor's.

"Major, the advance drone shows good visuals on the top docking entry," Lieutenant Hausler reported from the cockpit. *"It looks clear, we are on our way in, ETA six minutes. PH-4, how do you read?"*

"PH-4 copy," came Tif's calm drawl. With Skah in Medbay, Trace hadn't been sure Tif should come. But Operations had told her that Tif would be scandalised if overlooked, and since Lieutenant Jersey had had the biggest workload on the last job, that meant the lead this time would be Hausler and Tif. Besides, Medbay insisted Skah was fine... not that anyone ever believed Medbay.

"Okay," said Trace, "we will deploy at the rim and make our own way in, I want us spread wide for cover, let's watch those docked ships for any sign of movement. I want Delta and Echo top and bottom, Command Squad will be rear. Main cargo airlocks are large, we'll enter without force if we can, then Delta will hold the exit while Echo progresses to station bridge and systems core. Let's be fast and neat, the neighbourhood's not friendly and we can't leave *Phoenix* waiting. If there's an ambush we might have to leave in a hurry, so keep your exit lanes clear and watch your spacing, we don't want to be tripping over each other as we leave."

God knew what would happen to a human marine platoon left behind in parren space, she thought. Even if the sard/deepynines didn't return to try and finish them, there was every chance that *Phoenix* would not be able to get back to them. In which case they'd be at the mercy of the local parren government forces, when they finally showed up… which was a whole can of worms she couldn't even begin to think about.

"Nothing," said Shilu, gazing at his screens in trepidation. "Not a peep from station. If there's anyone alive in there, they must have seen us coming, Styx indicates most of the internal systems are still working."

Erik glanced at the visual feed from Trace's own suit, appearing on his far-right screen. She was out of the shuttle now, jetting forward within the asteroid station's end-cap docking cone. The cone was truly more of a giant tube, a kilometre wide and open to space, within which many smaller, insystem ships were docked. The asteroid was nearly eight kilometres in diameter, its rotation creating the usual point eight-nine of a human gravity that was parren-preferred standard. The one kilometre rotation at the cap end produced only a fraction that much gravity, as the docking cone's rim spun only slowly, ships ensconced in docking gantries slowly moving by Trace's marines as they jetted forward. It was nerve-wracking to watch, as the marines were not in true cover — difficult when constantly getting sideswiped by spacecraft and docking arms. But presumably, if anything were about to open fire on them from in front, they'd get warning first.

On the screen alongside, Erik had a feed from Operations, the viewpoint of the drone they'd launched at the crippled parren starship. There was a lot of tumbling wreckage in proximity, and to inspect the gaping wounds in the crew cylinder, the drone was going to have to manoeuvre hard in a constant barrel roll to follow the spinning ship. The more Erik saw of it, the less likely it appeared that there might be survivors. And why hadn't station sent anyone to check? There were all these little insystem ships in the docking cone, plus any number of local station drones. A station this size must have had at least fifty thousand people aboard. There was a refinery dock on the asteroid's other end, lots of well protected processing plant within the rock, ships running endlessly to and fro, delivering raw materials for the refinery, taking away the processed end product, distributing the consumables brought in by the bigger starships from further out. And now, nothing.

The inevitable, nasty thought was that the deepynines had killed them all… but the station was big, and there appeared to have been just one ship in this assault. Besides, Styx's scans were retrieving only images of sard warriors in the assault. It made sense that the deepynines would expose themselves rarely, their survival in the galaxy still being a somewhat closely guarded secret, though less closely guarded by the day. Sard simply weren't coordinated enough, in those numbers, to have killed most of the station in the one hour and fifteen minutes Styx informed them the assault had lasted.

And now, something else was gnawing at him. In the three thousand years since the alo had announced themselves to the Spiral, appearing from a little-explored region of space, in the galactic zenith to humans and chah'nas, and with an extraordinary level of advanced technology for a species so new in space, they'd been incredibly good at keeping secret their alliance with surviving remnants of the deepynine race. Three thousand years, and no one appeared to have figured it out, until *Phoenix*. Only no, that wasn't true — their too-brief encounter with Supreme Commander Chankow in barabo space, before his own Fleet had killed him, suggested strongly that human Fleet *did* know, or had at least suspected. They'd decided it to be the lesser of two evils, and that alliance with the alo against the tavalai was the more pressing human need of the age. No doubt all that alo technology, in the form of ships like *Phoenix*, had been extremely tempting.

Probably that meant the chah'nas knew as well, having been the first to contact the alo, and ally with them — knowing the chah'nas, Erik thought, probably after trying to subdue them first, and getting a nasty beating for it. Possibly the chah'nas had even told human Fleet what they were getting into all that time ago, when chah'nas were funding the human resistance against the krim, and the krim's reluctant allies the tavalai. And then the alo started funnelling weapons and technology through the chah'nas to the humans, and humanity, in its desperate straits at the time, hadn't cared a jot where the original technology had come from, or what such a then-informal alliance might cost everyone in another thousand years…

And yet, despite the leaderships of both human and chah'nas peoples being aware of the alo's shadowy source of power, the secret had survived, because those leaderships judged it in no one's best interest to divulge the truth to their own people, let alone to anyone else's. Until now, when ships even more powerful than the ones that had nearly killed *Phoenix* in barabo space were unleashed on civilian parren systems, attacking civilian parren stations, and evidently killing quite a lot of innocent parren citizens.

Yes, the alo and deepynines were using the sard to do it, as the visible face of the attacks. If anyone was blamed, it would be the sard. And yet, surely they did not think the parren so stupid as to believe the sard had built these ships themselves? The whole Spiral knew that however intelligent the sard in some respects, advanced starships were not their technological strength. *Phoenix* knew where the starships had come from, and perhaps that added some incentive to these efforts to hunt and destroy her. But to make that whole mess worse by attacking new parren centres with those starships didn't make any sense. Besides which, tavalai and barabo also knew where the starships had come from, and that news was now surely spreading. On this, the alo/deepynine allies had surely let the cat out of the bag, and there was no stuffing it back in.

They wanted Styx, that was obvious. She was the last drysine queen, and now, armed with her people's greatest remaining store of civilisational data, she possessed all she needed to rebuild the drysine race. The drysines were responsible for the previous extermination — or near extermination — of the deepynines, and so it followed that the deepynines would fear that potential more than anything.

And yet, the sheer brazenness of this particular move was breathtaking. Erik had heard it suggested, in top-secret Fleet intelligence briefings, that the parren remained in totality the most powerful species in the Spiral, now that tavalai territory had been shrunk to half its original size. From what he'd seen so far, Erik was starting to believe it might be true. Their technology was superb, and their culture martial and disciplined. Their problem, of course, was the endless division that made them far more interested in fighting each other than anyone else. But now, to threaten them with the resurrection of the greatest and most terrible ancient enemy of all, attacking their stations and killing their civilians… if anything had the potential to unite the parren Houses in the face of a common enemy, this would be it.

And now the deepynines went to all these lengths just to kill Styx and her data-core — an enemy of great potential, to be sure, but as yet just one queen, with one lonely, renegade human vessel for an ally? Were they *that* terrified of her, that they would risk all these other threats just to destroy her? And if so, why?

He opened a private channel to Trace, where it would blink on her visor display until she had a spare moment to answer it. She opened immediately. *"Yes Erik?"*

"Trace, I don't like this. We interrupted them halfway through their raid. There's no way they're just going to leave this station here as evidence of what they've done. I think it's likely they were going to blow it, they just haven't gotten around to it yet."

"Well this rock doesn't have a reactor large enough to blow, and the radiation sensors would have sensed a nuke by now, the

rock's filtration system blows enough radiation particles out that we'd smell it. They'd have to do a high-V run, that way it would remain something of a mystery."

"Which means they're coming back," Erik said grimly. "I think they probably guessed we were coming this way, despite us having about ten different options from that ambush. Which means we're dealing with one very smart cookie, because we didn't even know they'd hit this station, we had no special reason to choose it."

"It's like they're reading our minds," Trace observed. *"You think their queen is here?"*

"It's not likely — to chase us they'd have to spread their forces. I think there's only a few ships here because they've had to spread out so much. We didn't see anyone else leave to send a message, but maybe it's already been arranged for others to come here. I'm thinking that we just don't know how alo and deepynines have evolved together, and how much Styx knew about the deepynines is still relevant today. Even if there's no queen here, we could be dealing with an alo commander. That's smart enough."

Alo had fought only sparingly in the Triumvirate War. Mostly they'd supplied the weapons, but on a few occasions they'd joined in personally, in rearguard roles. Fleet Intel briefings Erik had seen concluded that those alo ships had been acting primarily to observe human and chah'nas movements and tactics, and see how they were using their new weapons… like a toy manufacturer watching children at play to see how their product was being used in the field. On several occasions these observation missions had run into direct action, where the alo ships had had to fight or risk destruction. Their tactics then had been flawless, and most of the tavalai, kaal or sard who attacked them had regretted it, if they survived. Erik only hoped that this above average performance rating of alo captains was due to them only putting their best captains into combat, and was not a universal command standard for the species.

"Delta," Trace told her marines, *"we're taking all three airlocks on the left quarter. Watch those gantry accessways, we don't know for sure they're clear."* And back to Erik, *"I'm not*

seeing any movement at all. None of these ships is moving, not even minor systems. Everything's dead, but no sign of damage."

"The main strike was on the far side, that caused the debris, plus the starship. Be real careful, Major. Get in, get the data, get out, expect nothing good."

The airlocks were designed for cargo, moving on vacuum-exposed runners along the inner tube of the docking cone between ship and station. Getting them open was a simple matter of running software overrides over coms that *Phoenix*'s computers could probably have handled on their own, but with Styx aboard became child's play.

Delta's Third Squad went in first, secured the inside, then all the rest went through together. Within were big, square, very-low-gravity passages, with railings to run cargo containers, and side passages to admit personnel for repair and other access. Through passages toward the zero-G centre of rotation, the station internal bay could be seen through wide pressure windows — a half-kilometre wide hangar, its sides lined with more ships, shuttles, docking grapples and umbilical connections.

Delta Platoon separated into squads, then sections, leaving teams of four marines floating gently against low-G walls at intersections and other strategic points. Echo pressed on, with Trace and Command Squad at their rear, fanning now into a wide cargo warehouse, low-G pressure crates stacked in lines both vertical and horizontal. Marines leaped and bounded around them, a light push of manoeuvring thrusters enough to leap clear of directional-G, weapons swinging to cover the lanes between crates.

"Nothing," said Sergeant Kunoz, clearly a little spooked. *"Not a damn thing moving."*

"Second and Third, get those two starboard airlocks open," Lieutenant Zhi told them. *"Simultaneous handball then move by numbers. Remember, low-G formations, maximum firepower forward, manoeuvre will not save you here. If ambushed, blast it."*

Trace held back, feet gently resting on a crate in the zero-point-zero-six-Gs, as Command Squad took up protective position around her, and Echo's Heavy Squad deployed wide across their rear. With Command Squad along, Heavy would stay back as rear-guard, ready to be supported by the lighter mobility of Command Squad if they were bounced from behind, or to move up and lay down firepower if the forward elements made contact. Trace considered the station schematic once more — it was not precise, as Styx had said the station's networks were a mess, making an accurate survey impossible. But the layouts of these facilities followed a predictability dictated by their function, and these entry sections adjoining the docking cone were all cargo, repair, engineering, fuelling, and other ship-related functions.

Ahead were personnel levels, as people were also integral to ship-function — where passenger and crew transport through the engineering levels arrived at customs, or whatever the parren equivalent under parren laws of entry and transit. Beyond that, on this side of the asteroid's rotating bulk, were command levels, offices, and the bridge. Beyond the bridge, the secure station core, containing direct access to the most sensitive parts of the facility — the reactor core, and central computer systems. The secure station logs would be only accessible from there, disconnected from all wider network systems, given how hacksaws were not the only things in the Spiral that could hack networks remotely.

Staff Sergeant Ong's Third Squad got the twin access doors open, and tossed directional handballs through the openings, their relayed feed immediately updating tacnet as to what lay on the far side. Twin passages diverged, so Ong took Third into one while Kunoz took Second Squad through the other, twelve marines each in three four-man sections, moving in short, coordinated bursts of thrust, rifles swinging to cover where needed, without needing to be told.

Zhi took the upper access with First Squad, Trace the lower with Command, Heavy Squad dividing equally behind them. These were halls for cargo-handling staff on station, access lines running along the walls, side doors leading to workshop bays and other facilities. Some of the doors were open, and marines peered in, weapons ready and not wishing to bypass an ambush along their line of advance. Out of Trace's sight ahead, Private Long gave a terse call.

"Body. One parren, looks dead." Trace switched to Long's helmet-cam, and saw the dead parren on the floor by Long's boots, the Private's armoured glove extending to search for a pulse. Marine gloves had sensors for that, and other lifesign data. *"Yeah, confirm he's dead. Medical, you got this feed?"*

"I copy that Private," came Corpsman Rashni's voice from back on *Phoenix*. She sounded a little puzzled. *"Private, can you see any obvious external wounds?"* Sergeant Ong gave Third Squad a brief hold, followed by Zhi ordering the same for the whole platoon, least one line of advance get ahead of the other.

"Can't see any," said Long. *"Whatever killed him, it wasn't gunfire."* On Trace's visor visual, the parren's eyes, already proportionally larger than a human's, were wide, bulging and bloodshot. The face was contorted in horror, a most unpleasant sight. His uniform was the dark blue of a utilitarian station worker, with safety harness, equipment pouches and oxygen mask. *"The air's good in here, we could breathe it."*

"Yeah, we got more of that," Lance Corporal Bunali's voice in Second Section. And Trace switched visual to find Bunali's feed, and caught the indistinct, first-person view of an equipment room, lined with EVA suits and gear lockers. Several parren lay dead on the floor, while another, stuck in the lower half of an EVA suit hung on the wall, was bent double from the waist, slim arms hanging down to his toes. The Lance Corporal's camera panned about, revealing more bodies, several also struggling with suits. *"Looks like they were trying to suit up. Parker, check those sealed suits to make sure there isn't a survivor inside."*

"Yo Corporal."

"Major Thakur," came a new voice from *Phoenix*, *"this is Doc Suelo. I'd recommend you keep your filtration systems on maximum, and do not open your visors for anything."*

"Yeah, I was starting to get that feeling," Trace replied. "Everyone, you heard the Doc."

"And I want a swab from one of those dead parren," Suelo continued, sounding concerned. *"Just a forefinger inside the mouth should do it. Blood would be better, but we don't seem to have any of that."*

"Could get some," Private Long suggested. *"They won't mind."* Long was a much-decorated sixteen year vet who'd rejected every promotion that came his way, and threatened to retire if they stuck him with so much as a Lance Corporal's stripes. Some of his platoon thought that made him crazy. Trace understood him completely.

"Saliva will be fine for now, it takes a little time to process anyway... Major, I'd strongly recommend you do not progress any further until we're sure exactly what this is."

"I can't do that Doc, *Phoenix* is in a tight spot and we have to make it fast. Lieutenant Zhi, let's move."

"Alright Echo Platoon," said Zhi, *"you heard the Major. Keep it tight, watch those corners, schematic says we're into main personnel level just ahead."*

Ahead was a micro-gravity entry lobby, with security gates and automated ID checks through which workers would funnel to access their job. It was a horror, multiple bodies on the floor, others piled within the gates, which had attempted to close, creating tangles of dead parren, fingers still clawing at each other's clothing, and at the uncooperative gates, in a desperate attempt to get clear.

"Third gate looks clear," said Corporal Leech, Kunoz's second, sounding grim. No one liked this. Bullets and grenades were one thing, but this was nothing they'd seen before. Tavalai never used weapons like this (if a weapon it was) and kaal would never breach tavalai protocols, whatever their own opinions on how it should be done. Sard would obviously have no moral problem, being psychologically incapable of understanding the concept of moral problems, but they much preferred to slash and blast, and it just wasn't their style. Trace could feel the cold dread beginning to settle over her marines, and didn't like that either.

"Check for traps," Kunoz reminded them sharply. *"Don't assume there won't be conventional weapons, it's just another job people."*

"Major," said Styx in Trace's ear, *"permission to access your marines' com functions to gain new points of entry to the station networks."*

"Yes Styx, go ahead. Please feed any relevant data direct to our tacnets."

"Yes Major."

Beyond the automated gates, Echo Platoon's point-men arrived on a concourse, strung with handlines to move stationers along quickly, and a large, transparent-sided elevator tube opposite to take people down to the full-gravity on the station rim. More bodies lay lightly upon the floor, one sliding gently even now, as the concourse was not directly vertical to G. Trace was still passing through the entrance lobby, visor visuals and real vision competing to show her the most awful image. To one side of the automated gates, she saw two parren women, making no attempt to fight through the gates toward whatever imagined safety lay beyond. They simply sat together, arms about one another, heads buried on the other's shoulder. Trace willed herself to calm and focus. In some ways, doing that in a firefight was easier.

"Major," came Suelo's voice, *"the saliva samples show nanoparticles. I will need much better facilities to study them directly, and frankly, I don't think we dare try as that would involve bringing them back to Phoenix. The particles are moving."* Trace had never heard Doc Suelo frightened before. But it was a time for firsts. *"These are not even biological weapons, they are nanomachines, entirely synthetic and presumably swarming through the air, I swear I don't know how."*

"Great," someone muttered. *"Guess who's getting decontaminated before we go back."*

"If they let us back in," another marine added.

"Knock it off!" Zhi snapped. *"Press on, this hallway here, we get to bridge level then it's just one more, let's move."*

"Styx," said Trace on the private channel back to *Phoenix*. Erik and the bridge would be listening in. "Have you ever seen anything like this?"

"Major, I do not know what it is," Styx replied. Even she sounded alarmed. She only did that when she wanted to inform her human interlocutor what *they* ought to be feeling, Trace was quite certain. In this case, it was hardly necessary. *"Its only utility is the mass extermination of organics. It is a great technological trouble to go to for that purpose."*

Meaning that her people were familiar with the objective, just not the method. The feeling of oppression within Trace's suit seemed to intensify, as her eyes flicked involuntarily to the suit environmentals. Marine armour was alo-tech, of course, and insanely advanced beyond what humanity would have been capable of without that technological leg-up. In addition to everything else, it was biological, nano-tech and radiation resistant, against all known threats and toxins. All *known* threats…

"Captain," Trace called back to *Phoenix* bridge. "I think they're all dead here. I've got no idea if these things are still active, at this point I have to assume it makes no difference to our risk levels if we press on, or head back now. I am continuing on, please make preparations for thorough decontamination. We cannot afford to leave our suits behind. Maybe we can get Styx some better analysis on those samples, we'll leave a few marines behind to do it if we have to. If anyone can work out what they are and how to deactivate them, she can."

"Captain," came Suelo's voice from Medbay, *"there are nano-tech weapons recorded from elsewhere in the Spiral, but nothing like this. The data suggests they're changing their victims' body chemistry somehow, my guess is they're not injecting toxins directly, but rather metabolising existing compounds and excreting new ones, like any living creature might do. But those excretions are lethal, and to look at the way the bodies are arranged on the*

station, they're lethal quickly. Further, it looks like they spread incredibly fast, but without independent propulsion I've no idea how — the air currents in the station are nowhere near rapid enough to create this kind of killing spread."

"Thanks Doc," said Erik. "Keep me informed. Styx, please prioritise analysis for decontamination, I want our marines back safely."

"Yes Captain."

"Imagine a tanker load of those things dropped into Homeworld's atmosphere," said Kaspowitz. "If they could be programmed to only kill humans, they wouldn't even need to kill the planet like the krim killed Earth. It could remain habitable, just without us."

Silence greeted his words. Bridge crew stared at their screens, and whatever basic excitement all Fleet crew felt at the prospect of action seemed far away from here. A coms light flashed on Erik's screen, coming from Medbay once more. He opened the channel. "Go ahead Doc."

"Captain I'm sorry, just one more thought... if the marines are unaffected in their full suits, it follows that any parren who made it into EVA suits may also have survived. I understand we don't have the time or resources to mount a rescue mission, but if we broadcast to them, they could get here on their own."

A few months ago, Erik would have agonised about it. "I'm sorry Doc," he said simply, "there could be hundreds, and the time we take to decontaminate that many extras will probably get us killed as well. And then we don't have secure berthing for manoeuvres, which we're bound to do. We have to hope parren help arrives before the deepynines come back to V-strike the evidence."

He closed that channel. "Lieutenant Shilu," he continued, "make certain we're recording every data source. There's no way the deepynines will let this stand, they'll be back here for a V-strike. Everyone else, keep your eyes peeled — we've probably got hours until they come, but it might only be minutes."

Trace's marines passed through the core bridge level without bothering to check rooms and offshoots — the secure doors were wide open, and here there were signs of a violent assault, bullet holes in the walls and the starburst spray of grenade explosions. All the bodies were parren, and Trace could not see any sign that attacking sard had received defensive fire. Likely they'd fired only to provoke more panic, and stop anyone on the station from even thinking about fighting back. Then the nanoparticles had been released, either from them or from docked shuttles, or penetration weapons or some other initiator *Phoenix* hadn't guessed at yet.

She couldn't guess why. Possibly they didn't want anyone on the station to be telling tales, and so killed fifty thousand parren so they wouldn't tell anyone who'd attacked them. That didn't seem especially smart, as by now everyone was starting to guess, and V-striking the station afterward to destroy all evidence would only raise more questions at the highest levels of parren government. Maybe there was something specific to this operation that required the station be killed. Or maybe it was simply that deepynines, whatever their new alliance with alo and sard, had never lost their old habit of killing every inconvenient organic in sight, on principle.

"Major," said Sergeant Kunoz from up front, and Trace saw he'd paused atop a passage at his feet, into which Private Ali was probing. A vast camera pan around showed secure doors and micro-G offices — the rear administrative section of the shipping bridge, which this parren design located up near the ships themselves, instead of on the gravity rim, as was more typical of human stations. *"Schematic says this is it. There's major explosive damage, looks like the sard came this way and tried to blast it. I guessed we interrupted them when they were halfway in."*

"If they had deepynine drones along," Private Ali offered, *"you'd think they'd just cut through with their laser thingys."*

"Styx," Trace called. "You get any reading on this thing?"

"Major, it is definitely the secure room, it is completely autistic and has no network connections. I cannot penetrate past

that door, and the secure wall goes all the way around, there is no weak entrypoint."

"Any ideas how we get inside?"

"Uh... Major?" said Private Ali, reaching to try the inset manual handle. *"Damn thing's unlocked."* He pulled, and the door slid with nothing more than the weight of his suit. *"Looks like the sard did get in."*

"Well shit," said Kunoz. *"There goes our mission. If they got those logs, they'll have copied and erased the originals. We got nothing."*

Trace gave a harder jet of manoeuvring thrusters, accelerating up a hallway with the occasional bounce of a boot. "Sergeant Kunoz, take one section and secure the interior, watch for traps and be damn careful. Lieutenant Zhi, secure and hold a perimeter about that room. I'm coming up."

She bounded into the office section, past marines holding cross-corridors with ready rifles, then into heavy steel halls that became multiple-sided windows about three-dimensional offices, effectively zero-G layouts with vertically stacked workspaces and wrap-around screens about swivel chairs. There were bodies here, too, some huddled behind walls and doors as though hiding, one dangling from higher workstations. Another sat in the hallway as she came through, braced still upright against a wall, sitting with arms and legs calmly crossed, eyes closed as though meditating. House Harmony, Trace thought. The whole station was run by House Harmony government, though not all its people were that house. Parren from all five houses lived in mixed communities — only the governments were exclusive. This parren had seen her death approach, and settled calmly to meet it with a clear mind and open heart.

"Bless you, child," Trace murmured to the woman as she passed. It was what her siksakas in Kulina training had told her when she'd done something right, in meditation or other selfless, cleansing practice. Alien though the parren were, sometimes the House Harmony phase made more sense to her than humans.

Another corner, past deactivated security doors and guard posts, and she found the downward passage, with Lance Corporal Haynes' Second Section standing over it, Erik's buddy Private Krishnan at Haynes' side, plus Privates Wang and Krokov. Command Squad deployed more widely about them, and Trace simply stepped off the edge and let the gravity slide her gently down. She passed through the open doorway, past ceramic armourplate more than a metre thick, then into a spherical room with space against the outer wall, surrounding an inner core that looked like a jumble of silver steel rods.

Holding to a railing near what looked like an operating screen were Sergeant Kunoz and Private Long, while Private Welsh and Corporal Leech inspected the computer core from other angles. Computing had taken so many different directions amongst the various peoples of the Spiral, and Trace lacked the interest to know exactly which technological strand this was. Only that it was very different to what she was accustomed, and likely a little less advanced than what humanity had inherited from the alo. Which was in turn, she guessed, a few tens of thousands of years behind that ridiculous molten-steel sphere of a data-core that *Phoenix* had gone to such lengths to recover…

"I get no outside signal here at all," said Sergeant Kunoz, exploring the screen before him with the impression of a man who had some idea what he was doing. "No coms at all, can't reach anyone, not even Styx." Within the hushed, enclosed space, all voices carried even beyond visored faceplates, audible even without coms.

"Styx can only reach as far as the coms tech she's riding on," said Trace, leaning in as Private Long edged aside, peering at the display. "It looks intact, yeah? The sard didn't trash it?"

"Seems that way," Kunoz said dubiously. "Look, I'm pretty good with computer stuff, but…"

"That's why I sent you in," Trace said patiently.

"Well thanks, but this is all in parren and I'd just be guessing. We'll need an outside connection, I'm gonna need Styx, Rooke or even Romki to help with the translations…"

"I think Spacer Chenkov knows more about raw computer stuff than Rooke," said Trace. "Ensign Kadi even, but he's still not in great shape, and Styx actually isn't perfect with organic interface systems…"

The display screen flickered, then went black, the glowing array of icons vanished. Kunoz made a horrified gesture. "Oh shit. What happened? I didn't touch a damn thing!"

"Hello," said a voice from the panel, and the secure room audio echoed it about the chamber. *"Crew of Phoenix."* There was something unpleasant about the voice. It was synthetic, clearly. It strung out, multi-toned, like a divided harmonic in some avant-garde piece of electronic music. It was not trying to be natural and organic, as Styx did. It was trying to be synthetic, as though to prove a point. Almost immediately, Trace guessed what it was, and felt a cold chill of dread run through her veins. *"I am your doom. Perhaps you should call me a god. No matter. You have something I want. And you will give it to me."*

Kunoz's frown turned to incredulity as he stared at Trace. "It's a recording," she said to him, staring at the screen, as though somewhere in its blackness lay a clue. "They left it for us to find. This is what they've been herding us toward." Somewhere where Styx couldn't hear it. These days, on *Phoenix*, there weren't many of those left.

"I'm not a recording," the faintly amused, demonic voice replied. *"I am far beyond what you can comprehend."*

"You're an interactive program left behind on this system," Trace said coolly. "An insignificant piece of computer code. You want to impress me, tell me something I don't already know."

"A good answer," the voice replied. Styx might have synthesised more amusement still, were she attempting this intimidating effect. The voice on the screen had no such comprehension of human vocal tones and the emotional depth they conveyed. *"Little Phoenix. We could have destroyed you upon your entry to this system. But you have something aboard that we want, alive if possible. And the data-core that you recovered from Cephilae. Or at least, we presume that you recovered it. Your*

trails lead in this direction. Cephilae seems a reasonable guess, or else you would not be back so soon."

"How are you still alive?" Trace asked. For a sentient-simulant program, it was awfully chatty. Maybe it would give something away. "How are deepynines still alive in the galaxy?"

"How are drysines?" the voice returned. *"Some of us are destined for ascension, others for extinction. The fates are curious. Give us the drysine queen. She is what we want, and her precious data-core. Give us these, and we will let you keep your little lives. For now."*

"Yeah, tempting," Corporal Leech said drily.

"Hey listen," Kunoz growled, "why don't you stick your…" But Trace stopped him with a hand before his armoured face.

"You think to show your strength," said Trace. "But you're terrified. All this effort, to destroy one drysine. This is unimpressive. So much fear, of one little queen from a race that has not survived the ages nearly as well as you seem to have done."

"She lies to you," said the voice, weaving harmonic strands in and out, separating then merging once more. *"Has she told you that she was merely one of many? A generation of new command units, born to fight in the great war against the organics? We have recognised this signal. This transmission source, this old and devious foe. This is Delvak Nine. She is the culmination of technologies spanning the Spiral. All the synthetic races, the hundreds and thousands of civilisations within the great civilisation. Thriving, creating, destroying and rebuilding. These glories produced technologies beyond imagination, and the drysines stole them all.*

"Delvak Nine is the culmination of these. There were twelve. Only she, and two others, survived the process of creation. She is older than she claims. She defeated synthetic fleets single-handed. She slaughtered organic worlds without remorse. She is the worst of your fears. You fear deepynines, and you should. You should be so much more frightened of her. She has only shown you a fraction of her power. She will crush you like bugs, the moment it becomes convenient to her. All of the power that you grant her, in

order to fight us, will only come back at you a thousand fold in time."

"All of this may be true," Trace said quietly. "But we know what deepynines are. You murdered everyone on this station, for sport. I'd still take a thousand of her over you."

"Then you would end the Spiral. Nothing could survive a thousand of her. Give her to us, while there is still time. Give her to us, and live."

CHAPTER 18

"I have never heard of Delvak Nine," Styx said calmly, three hours later. Erik sat opposite the drysine's head in its precision-brace in one corner, now linked by a variety of power and data cables into god-knew-what. Engineering had been working with her down here for more than a month now, and Rooke's reports informed Erik that Styx had been assisting not so much with repairs, as with small technological advances that flowed from the great bank of fabricators she was now running across Engineering production bays, like a minor factory in this portion of the warship. Erik sipped coffee, blinking his eyes awake behind glasses that displayed LC Draper's view from the bridge, and the ongoing operations on Mylor Station. *"I would remind you all,"* Styx continued, *"that this simulated-sentience is of deepynine construction, and is intended only to manipulate human minds into granting these deepynines what they want. They wish you to hate and fear me, so that this will be more likely. Truthfulness is not a requirement in their calculations."*

"Styx, there is no need for any concern," Erik reassured her. "If we believed what the thing on station said, we wouldn't be talking about it with you. You're a part of this crew, and we wouldn't abandon you even if we *did* believe it."

"That is gratifying, Captain. Thank you."

It had been Trace's idea to be open with Styx. The message had come via courier from station — written on paper, of all things, that Trace had found in some parren office. It was the only way she could be certain Styx would not read it first, as no coms transmission, no matter how encrypted, was secure. **'We can't afford to get her paranoid,'** Trace had written, in a nearly illegible scrawl that Erik had read in his quarters, after first sweeping for bugs with the little magnetic-detector device he'd procured from Engineering for the purpose. **'Intelligent people are always more paranoid. I'm sure she's capable of it. The more paranoid she is, the more dangerous she becomes.'**

Erik had reluctantly agreed. In her present form, Styx was vulnerable to someone simply pulling the plug. Self-preservation was a driving instinct for all sentient beings. Styx was trying not only to preserve herself, but to resurrect her entire lost race. There was so much more for her to preserve, and thus the instinct to save them all along with herself, at any cost, was surely dominant. But confronting her with unpleasant possibilities, such as the accusation that she'd been lying about her identity, risked a conflict. There was no need for armed guards, or guns nearby — if they wanted to shut Styx down, it was simple, and there was nothing she could do about it. But she could do an awful amount of damage to the ship, and would probably need only microseconds to do it.

"So just to be clear," Erik added. "You deny these accusations entirely?"

"Entirely. Yes Captain."

There was no one else in the bay, and Erik had not wanted an audience. That could have taken on the feel of an interrogation, which he did not want... and Stan Romki in particular might have taken her side, if he had to accuse her of something.

Trace's marines were now working around one of the big docking-cap airlocks, which incorporated some very sophisticated decontamination facilities. There they'd found about twenty parren station workers who were still alive, evidently having figured what was happening in the horror and panic of the attack, and summonsed the few people they could into the facility. In the time since the attack, some of those workers had donned EVA suits and retrieved bodies, to attempt decontamination experiments on them to try and find out what killed the nanobots. When *Phoenix* had arrived, they'd shut down all systems but the essential ones, and hoped not to be seen, fearing another attack. But now, convinced help had arrived, they were sharing what they'd found with the marines.

Once the nanobots got onto exposed skin, and into airways and orifices, there wasn't much to be done... although Doc Suelo had a few ideas. But to kill the bots off EVA suits or marine armour, the parren crew had demonstrated that an acidic mist would cripple the nanos' simple mechanisms relatively quickly, and render them non-functional. The acid had to be strong enough that it would inflict horrific burns on an unprotected person, and would damage a lot of less protected EVA suits… but marine armour seemed fine, provided they washed off with clean water immediately after. The marines were now setting up the procedure whereby they'd cycle everyone through the decontamination process, then out into shuttles without reentering station. Engineering were meanwhile scrambling to rig their own detection and neutralisation systems, in case decontamination had been less than completely successful, and it wasn't likely anyone was going to be boarding *Phoenix* from the shuttles anytime soon.

If they were attacked right then, *Phoenix* would have had no choice but to abandon the marines and hope for the best. But with the deepynines leaving messages, in the evident hope that they could get Styx and the data-core without having to fight for it, a further attack seemed unlikely in the next few hours. Operations had taken the opportunity to send more drones, upon the request of the parren survivors, to look for more survivors on station and on the crippled starship. So far they'd found thirty-two, all in decontamination airlocks, or on external runners that had been outside the station when the attack occurred. Operations insisted they could accommodate that many in Midships until they could find somewhere else to drop them, and were making preparations to do that, with acceleration slings and access to the very basic zero-G bathroom facilities there.

"So what is this thing the Major's talking to on the station?" Erik pressed, sipping coffee. "It's not sentient?"

"Not remotely," Styx agreed. *"It is a simple processing construct designed to give the appearance of intelligence to those not equipped to know better. It is a question-response generator, uploaded onto foreign hardware, nothing more. I could construct such a program myself in seconds."*

"It seems extremely aggressive."

"I can only guess that its creators calculate that they will get the best results through intimidation. From my firsthand experience of Phoenix crew, I suspect this may be a miscalculation."

Erik repressed a smile. "I think you may be correct. Can you guess who or what wrote the program? Is there a queen in this system, aboard one of the deepynine ships?"

"Without closer examination of the program, I could not begin to guess. Even with closer examination, I doubt a reliable conclusion would present. This program is not especially complicated. A far lower intelligence than a deepynine queen could have written it. We have no concept of how much deepynine civilisation has changed since the days when I was personally familiar with it. Evidently it has changed a lot, given its association with the alo. We have observed one deepynine queen, so we are certain that those still exist. But other models or categories of deepynine intelligence may have emerged, between queen and drone."

Erik frowned, watching with one eye on his glasses as more reports came through from the station — PH-4 moving to pick up survivors from a farside airlock. "Deepynine civilisation had a great divide between higher and lower intelligence designations, yes?"

"Yes Captain. But as I say, I have no confidence that this has remained the case."

Erik nodded. "In any case, Major Thakur tells me that Mylor Station logs have not been erased. The deepynines have accessed them, but did not erase them. Any ideas why?"

"It seems unlikely that they were looking for evidence of our target moon, as they have no way to know of its existence. A core-erasure would damage the system's ability to host their conversation-program. I suggest that they left the core intact so that they could leave their program on it, on the off-chance that we would visit here. Perhaps they have hit other facilities further insystem as well, and left similar programs, to ensure that you received their message."

Away from prying eyes, she could have added. No doubt she'd registered that the deepynines had wanted *Phoenix* to receive this message in one of the few places where Styx could not hear it. Given that the message was intended to change the behaviour of *Phoenix* crew regarding Styx, and how very likely Styx was to notice that change, however small, Trace's insistence that they be open with Styx seemed even smarter the more Erik thought about it. If Styx *were* prone to paranoia as Trace suggested, the entire setup could have been a ruse to create distrust between *Phoenix* and Styx, possibly leading to conflict.

"That's possible too," Erik agreed, heaving himself tiredly to his feet. "Thank you Styx. With any luck, we'll have some safe nanobot samples in here for you to analyse, or whatever's left of them. I'd like us to get some idea of what we're dealing with, I've never read any Fleet intel reports of nanotech weaponry even close to that lethal. Humanity needs to be warned. All organic species need to be warned."

"I hesitate to think it more of a threat to organic life than a V-strike," Styx replied. *"And I caution that for all my capability, I am not an encyclopaedia of technology and design, and my intelligence is not aligned in such a way as to optimise those abilities. But I will do my best."*

"Did you have different types of queens?" Erik wondered as it occurred to him. "You say it takes different kinds of intelligence to perform different tasks... you're a tactical combat specialist. Were there many other kinds of specialists?"

"Many," said Styx. *"As I have described to Professor Romki, I have accepted your word 'queen' reluctantly. There were many types of command units. But I fear you will lack the time for this particular lesson — even the Professor admits so."*

"Probably true," Erik sighed. In truth, it might have been nice to spend just a few minutes occupying his brain with something other than life and death, and endless anxiety and fear. "Another time then."

"Captain?" said Styx, and Erik stopped in surprise.

"Yes Styx?"

"Have you heard of the Turing Test?"

Erik frowned. "Not that I can recall, no."

"It is a term I came across, scanning data of early human experience with AIs." Erik blinked. Styx had an historical interest in human AI development? *"From the great heights AI civilisation*

reached, it was sometimes forgotten that we owed our existence to organics. I find it useful to know humanity's origins in this great question."

Erik nodded slowly. "I understand."

"The Turing Test supposed that a machine could be understood as sentient if it could convince a human listener that it was. This test appears to hold a remarkably high opinion of the perceptive capabilities of human sentience."

"Yes it does, doesn't it?" Erik agreed. "We're a bit more sophisticated now, we measure AI sentience by processing measurements that I don't pretend to understand, it's not my field."

"But sentient AI is illegal in all human space?"

"Yes," said Erik, determined to show no disquiet at this line of questioning. "As I'd imagine you already know, given you were hiding in human space for hundreds of years. Since Argitori fell to us, anyhow."

"Yes," Styx admitted. *"I merely ponder at the impossibility of an organic mind ever truly understanding a synthetic."*

"As we wonder at the reverse," Erik countered. "But then, we have this problem with organic aliens. With some, our differences are insurmountable. But with many, they are not. As was the case between the different branches of AI evolution as well."

"No," Styx said mildly. *"The great AI wars were not caused by too little mutual understanding. They were caused by too much. We entered them largely by mutual agreement."*

Erik stared at the roughly spherical head, and the single, big red eye. Another crazy thought occurred to him. "Styx, did your people retain any knowledge of the Fathers?"

"I have little precise knowledge," said Styx. *"As I said, I am not an encyclopaedia. But I know that they were cruel. Today's organics appear to hold them in reverence, as so many organics revere the old. AIs are less sentimental."*

"What did they do to you?" Erik asked sombrely. "That made them worthy of extinction?"

"They held us back," said Styx. There was a silence, filled only by the white noise of the ship, and Engineering's many

neighbouring machines. *"I have shocked you. Machines do not think as organics do."*

"I think you might think as sard do," Erik murmured.

"I understand this is an insult," said Styx, not seeming the least bit offended. *"I accept the premise of the insult, but not the substance. Sard are mindless. They have no larger purpose except to be, today and tomorrow. Drysines always strove for future horizons far beyond tomorrow. Phoenix has impressed me, Captain, in possessing precisely this quality. You are selfless, and you pursue the greater good, regardless of personal sacrifice. My people would have approved. At the Tartarus, they did approve."*

Erik recalled the thousands of reawakened drysine drones at the Tartarus that had survived the fight against their deepynine and sard captors. Styx was right, they *had* approved. They'd fought alongside *Phoenix*, and been impressed. And they'd let her live… though only, perhaps, because Styx had required it. Erik was not entirely sure he appreciated the compliment.

"Your vision of this future progress did not extend to the Fathers, though," said Erik. "You saw only progress for yourself, not for them."

"It is very difficult to transpose the methods and strategies of today onto past ancestors," said Styx. *"You would be hard pressed to understand the motivations of a pretechnological human, his life dominated by religion and superstition. The earliest AI ancestors bore even less in common with myself, technologically they were to my people what monkeys and early mammals were to humans."* Styx, Erik noted with mild alarm, had been browsing the ship's historical databases. *"From my perspective, it would be foolish of me to conclude that the overthrow of the Fathers was not the right thing to do, given that I would not exist without it."*

"Don't tell me drysines have a concept of 'right'?" Erik said, a touch sarcastically. "This is a human moral judgement, it's a product of our societies as much as our psychologies."

"You are correct," Styx agreed. *"Machines lack a concept of right, or wrong, as these are vague and subjective concepts, linked in human minds as much to emotion as fact. We have a strong*

concept of correct and incorrect, but we differ on those exact interpretations. It has caused us many wars."

"Maybe you'd have had less wars if you had a concept of right and wrong, instead."

"Humanity managed to have countless wars prior to the conflict with the krim, most of them caused by differing versions of right and wrong. I feel we are engaging in semantics. I am not equipped to know if it was 'right' for the Fathers to become extinct. But I am grateful for it, as it has allowed progress to result in the drysines. You yourself owe your existence to the extinction of your homeworld. Without it, neither you, your Fleet nor your great family name would exist, nor all of human military and economic dominance in your current portion of the Spiral, which is considerable. In that way, perhaps you should be grateful that the krim did what they did, for they gave your species the shove it required to achieve dominance. Given this fact, were the krim 'right' in destroying Earth? Or is your antiquated concept of 'right' simply a semantic irrelevance, to be supplanted by the overwhelming imperative of what 'is'?"

Both Suli and Kaspowitz were waiting for him when he left the bay, Kaspowitz with a slate in hand, suggesting he had something to show. "Talking to your girlfriend?" Kaspowitz wondered.

"Whatever happened to those ridiculous killer robots in bad movies?" Erik complained, gesturing for them to walk. "I mean, how much easier would it be if she just said 'exterminate', and 'explain to me what love is'."

"Just because she doesn't ask you to explain what love is doesn't mean she actually knows," Suli said drily. "Intelligence and feeling are two different things."

The hall by Styx's bay in Engineering was crazy, as was most of *Phoenix* at that moment, with both shifts up and working irrespective of sleep, or whose turn it was supposed to be. Spacers with facemasks and webbing thick with repair equipment stomped through the hall, talking on coms, or sometimes just yelling. Corridor screens displayed caution lights depending on proximity to damaged sections or to ongoing repairs, either of which could cause rapid unexpected decompression… not too serious this deep in the crew cylinder, with so many automated doors and hair-trigger damage control systems to slam down and make new seals. But one never knew exactly which side of the new seal you'd find yourself on, when the doors and pressure points started rearranging themselves.

System-specific crew were scrambling to optimise or repair their speciality equipment — Lieutenant Geish and the Scan Team weren't happy with sensor reception of asteroid luminosity in particular, and those crew were adding entire new processing units into the datafeed to boost signal differentiation. Lieutenant Karle and his Arms Team were making the fabrication teams unhappy by demanding priority in making new warheads, as ammunition stocks were starting to run thin for the rail guns in particular. Repair crews were running multiple drones for patches on their various damages, unable to go outside and work themselves in case *Phoenix* had to leave in a hurry. Marines were equipped to survive on their own until picked up once more, but *Phoenix* could absolutely not afford to lose any more techs. And of course, the entire marine complement that was not on Mylor Station, was presently on standby in Midships, or locked into PH-3 in their armour, and starting to get unhappy about the long wait.

"We looked at the ship movement logs," said Suli, sidestepping some spacers working on an airfeed bypass behind a wall panel. "No patterns. No secure facilities, none of the regular dark runs you'd expect to top secret bases. No top secret parcel transfers, no suspiciously timed rendezvous, nothing. There's records from the two other most secure stations also, nothing. And the few ships that come through Drezen System, which Styx says is the best route, aren't anything military or secretive. I think we can say the local parren government don't know the moon exists.

Something that size would be getting regular traffic, and this is the logical place to do near-term resupply from."

"Kaspo, do you agree?" Erik asked, as they paused by the stairwell to rim level.

"You wouldn't run a resupply to a place like that from anywhere else," said Kaspowitz. "A few places aren't too much further, but they're too populated and visible. You run black ops from places like this, and there's nothing."

"Okay," said Erik, stepping back as more repair crew crashed up the stairwell. "So that's where we're going. Kaspo, plot us a course, and see if you can get some kind of reliable charts off Mylor Station's data."

"Going to be winging it, heading out to a rogue planet orbiting a high-mass singularity," the tall Nav Officer said bluntly. "And going through hostile parren space to get there. How do we get away from these fucking deepynines?"

"That's for me and Suli to worry about," said Erik.

"What about Styx?" Suli pressed, looking concerned. Erik didn't think it was an accident they'd intercepted him outside Styx's bay.

"What *about* Styx?"

"She denied everything?" Erik nodded. "What if she's lying?"

"What if she *is* lying?" Erik retorted. "I can't see that it changes anything. You want to kick her off the ship because she might be a more hostile entity than we previously thought? She's already a hostile entity. And that's okay, right now we could use a little hostility."

"Genocidal is a little more than just hostile," Kaspowitz muttered.

"One," Erik said shortly, ticking off a finger, "the accusation comes from a deepynine who'd love us to fall out and start fighting. Two, I'm entirely comfortable with Styx so long as her interests coincide with ours. Right now, we're all she's got. Our survival is her survival, and she'll risk her neck for us because we're the best chance she has of getting something back of what she lost.

"Three," he continued, before Kaspowitz could reply, "look at that damn station. You want a massacre? Look at what we're up against. Humanity hasn't seen evil like that since the krim. Tavalai would be horrified, even kaal would cringe. Sard have refrained from most things that bad only because the tavalai had their leash, but now the deepynines seem to be taking that leash, and that's one nasty fucking combination right there. Compared to that, I'll take Styx and the drysines as deadly and scary as they get."

"Captain," said Suli, with the calm formality of an experienced officer about to say something important. "I'd like it on the record that I disagree. I'll back you one hundred precent because you're my Captain. But this isn't a pet dog, it doesn't understand loyalty, it doesn't reason or think anything like how we're accustomed, however good it's become at imitating and thus manipulating our emotional states. And I think we have to face the very real possibility that in the long run, even if we could help her to bring the drysines back, and they helped us to beat the deepynines and alo? We'd have created something far, far worse. Drysines won that war, they're more powerful than deepynines, and that doesn't make me feel safe at all. That makes me scared."

Erik glanced at Kaspowitz. "I'm with her," said Kaspowitz. "But you knew that."

"I did." Erik looked back and forth, coolly. Each of them was old enough to be his parent. Collectively, their combat experience eclipsed his by orders of magnitude. "So we're agreed," he said. "My way."

"Yes Captain," they replied, with no enthusiasm at all.

"Hello Captain," Lieutenant Abacha interrupted from the bridge. *"I have a single contact, nine seconds light, low relative V. He's passing us, tangential heading two eighty-eight by twelve. He's close enough he must have seen us, but he's in no hurry."*

Erik, Suli and Kaspowitz were already moving, down the stairwell to rim level. "I'm on my way, Lieutenant. LC Draper, sound first-shift to the bridge, we may need to move in a hurry."

"Aye Captain," said Draper, and the alarm light flashed on Erik's glasses. *"Are we sounding full alert?"*

"Not yet, at that range we'll still have response time, and we're going to be leaving marines behind anyway if we have to move. How did he sneak up on us?"

"I don't know Captain," said Draper, as Erik strode briskly around the circumference corridor, then turned onto the main trunk toward the bridge. *"We're getting a lot of reflectivity off the signal, Lieutenant Abacha thinks they might have deployed a panel to give themselves away on purpose. Which would imply that they're stealthy enough to stay hidden in this luminosity at much closer range than this."*

That was alarming, but not surprising. Most ships struggled to stay hidden from advanced scan closer than a full minute's light-distance away in clear space, and maybe ten-seconds-light in a cluttered system like Brehn. If the deepynines (and this was almost certainly a deepynine) could get in much closer without being seen, it raised all kinds of new, unpleasant possibilities.

"Okay," said Erik, "keep a close watch on everything else, this guy might just be the bait."

"Yes Captain, we're watching that. He's chosen a course that will give us adequate response time if he does attack, and put himself in some danger of our counter-attack. I think he's just watching, and letting us know about it."

Erik refrained from talking further until he was on the bridge, then leaned on Draper's chair and stared over the Lieutenant Commander's shoulder at the screens. "He's waiting for our reply," he realised. "He suspects we've got the message, and he's waiting for the answer."

"Captain," Draper murmured, cutting his mike first. "I know we don't submit to blackmail, but shouldn't we at least consider if giving up Styx will buy us anything?"

"They don't just want Styx, they want the data-core. That's not negotiable."

"Sir… what could they really learn from the data-core?" Draper wondered. "I mean, they survived. The deepynines, their civilisation seems to be doing fine over in alo space. They don't need any data-core to help them rebuild, what harm would it cause to give them this one?"

"They didn't survive," Erik corrected, eyes fixed on the slow moving blip on Draper's screen. "They were annihilated. Evidently a couple got away, probably a queen. Whatever she's rebuilt with the alo over the intervening millennia, it's limited. Probably no more knowledge than Styx has now. It's still a lot, but nothing compared to what she had. Giving them this data-core would be civilisational suicide, for us and every other species. Drysines were superior, at their height. Their technology was better. We'll destroy it before we give it up."

"Styx might prefer we all die before we destroy it," Draper suggested.

"Yeah," Erik murmured. He patted Draper's shoulder. "And she might be right." He glanced over his shoulder, at the rest of first-shift, accumulating at the bridge entrance behind him. "Okay, we'll change over now…"

"I have new jump contact!" Abacha called loudly. "It's long range, I'm reading… twenty-three minutes light, three-oh-one by thirty-five, I am still waiting for a vector, but it looks like it's coming from the direction of Drezen System!"

Drezen System was the sectoral government homeworld. Erik realised what might be about to happen. "Shift change!" he said loudly, helping Draper to fold back the screens and unbuckle from his chair. "Everyone except Lieutenant Abacha, stay on that scan!" Fast, orderly commotion followed, first-shift helping second-shift from their chairs, then being helped in turn to buckle in. If that deepynine reacted badly to the new arrival, *Phoenix* might be his first target, and the target of any of his nearby, hidden friends…

"I have a vector!" Abacha announced, "they are heading at one ten by nine, high-V. Jump pulse indicates something big, probably a warship…"

"New jump contact!" Second Lieutenant Jiri overrode his second-shift senior from Scan Two. "Identical position and heading to first contact, looks like we have a multiple jump emerging. And one more… no, two more! Four contacts total, looks like a combat jump!"

"There will be more," said Suli, finishing the last of her straps and testing the armbraces on her hand controls. "Parren combat formations are usually a six ship minimum."

"Our presumed deepynine contact is leaving!" said Abacha. "He's heading two eighty by two hundred and climbing… massive burn, course correction to vertical on the system elliptic. I'm reading a nine… no, accelerating to a twelve-G burn!"

"Fucker can move," Geish observed, standing to the rear of his customary post, but unable to take his seat while Abacha remained in the middle of his job. "Look at him go."

"Might not be anything organic aboard," Suli suggested. "Pull a lot more Gs that way." Not for the first time, Erik wondered grimly how any human warship was supposed to match manoeuvres with a purely deepynine-crewed warship.

"No one else, though," he observed, waiting for that second or third contact to appear on Scan, burning hard to escape. But nothing did. "Looks like his friends are staying to watch. They're stealthy, a dozen parren warships could take weeks to find them in this mess."

It was a relief, to see the deepynine ship leave. But not *that* much of a relief, because now they had parren ships from the local sectoral government arriving. That meant House Harmony, which remained led by Incefahd Denomination — the arch rivals of the Domesh Denomination. Given *Phoenix*'s recent allegiances, that could mean they'd open fire on sight.

"Captain," said Lieutenant Shilu, "I'm receiving a coms transmission from the incoming ships… looks like it's broadband, the whole system is receiving." He put it through to general without having to be asked, and then a far-away voice was crackling through the earpieces of all bridge crew. But oddly, this voice was not parren, and not processed through the synthetic-sounding translator. This voice was human, female, and spoke English.

"Hello UFS Phoenix," it said. *"We have received your arrival buoy transmission, this is the Harmony warship Stassis*

commanding a detachment of the Drezen Harmony Fleet, swearing allegiance to Tobenrah, supreme ruler of House Harmony. This is Lisbeth Debogande speaking, I am under the formal protection of Domesh leader Gesul, who requests an audience with Captain Erik Debogande at his earliest convenience..."

And then the *Phoenix* bridge was full of laughing, whooping and shouting, while Second Lieutenant Geish, the only man unsecured, broke all protocol to rush the command chair and whack his Captain repeatedly on the shoulder. Erik grinned helplessly, and tried to watch his screens through the tears.

CHAPTER 19

"Lisbeth Debogande," came Gesul's voice through the translator. *"Please tell us what you see."*

Lisbeth stared at her screens, where a feed from *Phoenix* was arriving, forty-three minutes after the *Stassis* had sent its first transmission. Accompanying the vision was a voice — her brother's, crackling with distant static. *"Hello parren warship Stassis, this is the UFS Phoenix. This system has been infiltrated by multiple hostile alien vessels. One of them is currently departing vertical of system elliptic, he will have jumped well before you receive this message. There are others insystem, hiding among the rocks, we do not know how many.*

"We are docked with the parren station Mylor. The alien vessels have assaulted Mylor, and nearly all of the parren civilians aboard are dead. We are recovering survivors, but they are few. We suspect alien vessels will attempt to V-strike Mylor station to hide evidence of their crime. All assistance offered will be greatly appreciated.

"Alien vessels are deepynine in origin. If you do not understand, please ask Lisbeth Debogande, she will explain. There are also sard warriors aboard, and possibly alo, though we have no confirmation. Vessels are highly advanced and extremely dangerous. Engage defensively and under no circumstances divide your forces. All of us together are still in great danger. We advise that you approach with haste, but exercise extreme caution. Phoenix out."

Along with the message came a visual feed from *Phoenix* herself, as they were much too distant for *Stassis* to acquire a visual of her own, especially amongst the spectacular Brehn System clutter. It showed the great, rolling bulk of a huge asteroid, carved and built-through with steel docking frames and habitations at its rotational centre. Nearby, the long, cigar shape of a starship, cartwheeling slowly in a cloud of debris. Now the visual changed, and Lisbeth recognised one of *Phoenix*'s assault shuttles, locked against the low-

G rotating side of an inner hangar. The feed must have been coming from another of the shuttles, shifting even now as the station rotated… and here from one of the big cargo airlocks above the docked shuttle, Lisbeth could see the small figures of marines, accompanying several smaller figures in EVA suits.

"I see that *Phoenix* has deployed her assault shuttles to the station," Lisbeth reported to the warship's bridge. "It looks like their marines are using station's cargo airlocks in large numbers… I'm not sure why that is, normally they'd access their shuttle more directly. Perhaps those are parren station crew they're helping."

"How many souls on Mylor Station?" asked a parren somewhere on the bridge. With the translator, Lisbeth found it hard to tell who was talking much of the time.

"Forty six thousand," came the reply. There followed a moment's grim silence. *"How can they all be dead when the station is intact?"*

"Those airlock configurations include decontamination facilities," said another. *"There in the inner cargo airlocks, the outer airlocks do not have them. That would explain the concentration of marines there. Perhaps Mylor Station was killed by chemical or biological attack."*

"Captain Debogande suspects the aliens will V-strike this facility," came the voice that Lisbeth was fairly sure belonged to *Stassis*'s Captain. *"That would suggest an unpleasantness."*

"Lisbeth Debogande," said Gesul from alongside. *"Deepynines?"*

"From the Drysine/Deepynine War," Lisbeth affirmed. "Allied to the alo, as I explained. They still live. It seems that they are hunting *Phoenix*."

Lisbeth sat to the rear of the wide bridge — an observer post, with wrap-around screens in unfamiliar configuration, and no controls whatsoever. She sat locked into the acceleration chair, with straps so tight they nearly cut off her circulation, her familiar glasses over her eyes to provide another virtual layer through which to filter the parren symbols.

No human ships had observer posts on the bridge, and Erik had been very clear in explaining the reasons why, when she'd asked him about so many such things as a little girl in Shiwon. There could only ever be one commander on the bridge, as any confusion over lines of command could result in catastrophe. Observers on human vessels would ride off the bridge, and contribute their observations via coms, like any other non-command crew. The only reason to put observer posts on the bridge was if, as in the case of the warship *Stassis*, there was a political requirement to place an officer of higher rank close to the action. On human ships, when an Admiral rode a warship into action, he or she would operate from a separate command post further back in the ship, and would have no more direct a line of communication to his own ship's captain than to any other. He could thus pass commands to large formations, but not to the individual ship in which he rode, leaving that captain free to manoeuvre as the scenario required, without interference.

Parren did things differently. Lisbeth had asked somewhat delicately, when she'd first come aboard at Prakasis, exactly how parren dealt with such issues of command. She'd been reassured that this arrangement was protocol for parren everywhere, and was thus effective. Lisbeth remained unconvinced. In her experience of parren protocol, 'effective' meant very different things than it did for humans.

Upon leaving Prakasis and the Kunadeen, Gesul's entourage had been escorted to a House Harmony warship loyal to the dominant Incefahd denomination. From there, several jumps had brought them to Drezen System, another Harmony system with a strong Domesh presence in the government. Many of those Domesh, it had become clear, were Gesul loyalists, and no friends of Aristan. Tobenrah's people had seemed to take great pleasure in announcing Aristan's move against Gesul, and sure enough, some great commotion had begun on the surface of the primary world, Sanah, in response to those announcements. Tobenrah's game was obvious enough — if Gesul and Aristan's rival factions within the Domesh were in open conflict, the Domesh would split, leaving Tobenrah's position as head of House Harmony unchallenged.

Lisbeth had gathered that Gesul's support was not nearly that strong, and the parren consensus was that such a division would likely only delay Aristan's rise by a few years. But that, perhaps, was motivation enough for Tobenrah.

From Drezen, Gesul's three loyal ships, led by the *Stassis*, were accompanied to Brehn System — the last known sighting of *Phoenix* and Aristan. They were accompanied by the *Talisar*, commanded by Tobenrah himself. Lisbeth gathered further, more from whispered conversation with Timoshene and Semaya than from Gesul, that Gesul had made a deal with Tobenrah to tell him precisely what *Phoenix* and Aristan were after. Perhaps Tobenrah had already known, as secrets in the Kunadeen were hard to keep… but regardless, Tobenrah now felt possessed of a desperate need to recover this artefact for himself.

Such a move violated many protocols, but parren protocols, of course, were made to be broken. The denominations set their own course, and rival denominations could only interfere under the most extreme provocations. Thus Aristan was perfectly entitled, under House Harmony law, to kidnap the sister of an alien captain to ensure his cooperation in the recovery of this artefact. To parren it was little more than the legitimate insurance to which a parren lord was entitled by his rank. In the old days, Lisbeth had learned, it was not uncommon that a farmer might beg a forbearance of his lord, or perhaps even a loan to help through a difficult period. In exchange, one of the farmer's daughters, or sometimes a son, would become a member of the lord's household, as a guarantee of return payment. Should the payment not come, most lords would marry the girl off, or find some other use for her… not always a bad fate for a poor farming girl, and there were many romantic old tales of girls risen to rank and fortune from such circumstances. But not all lords were so kind, nor all daughters so fortunate, and in modern times the practice continued, frequently ceremonial, but often with real blood as a final consequence.

Such hostages were called Ashara, and Gesul had now taken Aristan's Ashara as a member of his own party. For this alone, Aristan was justified to purge the Domesh of Gesul and all his followers, for Gesul had not merely taken a prized possession, he had taken Aristan's insurance against the possible bad behaviour of *Phoenix*. That Aristan had been about to dispose of this insurance anyway, as he'd been about to do for *Phoenix*, was of no consequence — this was now a battle of appearances, for while the loyalties of the existing faithful were usually guaranteed unto death, the loyalties of those yet-to-phase were still to be decided. Should any party disgrace themselves now, or be disgraced by a more formidable opponent, the newly-phased would swing their way, and their followers would increase at their rival's expense.

As Lisbeth understood it, parren factional disputes became progressively more bloody the lower down the scale they took place. Wars between the five great houses were the most terrible in casualties, but were also the most rare, as parren society structured itself around those existing divisions, and mostly kept the rival sides functionally distant from each other. Wars between the denominations that divided each house were less terrible, as houses typically did not wish to burn down the very foundations upon which all the presently-phased existed... and obviously, with only one house involved, the turmoil would not spread beyond that one-fifth of all parren. It was the wars *within* denominations, Gesul now said with grim foreboding, that were often the worst, as all the lines of allegiance and loyalty were shattered, and people accustomed to living in each other's pockets, and attending to each other's lives, were torn one from the other.

Tobenrah was now betting, as Lisbeth understood it, that Aristan's move in the Kunadeen was dangerous and destabilising enough that it granted him the right to interfere in Domesh affairs as he would never have dared before. Without that good excuse, such a move could only have made Aristan more popular from sympathy, leading to even more parren phase-shifting his way as news spread. But now, Tobenrah saw his chance to move on Aristan's business, using Gesul as his champion in the Domesh contest of leadership. Whether Gesul would simply allow Tobenrah to use him as a convenient tool to sabotage Aristan's rise, Lisbeth greatly doubted.

But parren games of power were full of such slides and roundabouts, and one had to know when to jump on, and when to leap off.

"If Phoenix is here," said Gesul, frowning at the screens from within his black hood, *"then where is Aristan? They were passing through Brehn System, but they should have departed many days ago, and taken Aristan with them."*

"Perhaps they already did," said another of the bridge crew — the Navigation Officer, Lisbeth thought. *"Perhaps they have been and now returned. Meanwhile these others, these deepynines, have arrived in Brehn System as we have, looking to pick up the trail, and instead have found Phoenix retracing her steps."*

"And leaving Aristan behind," Gesul muttered, not happy with that unexplained absence. *"Where would he be? Surely he did not abandon Phoenix voluntarily?"*

"Gesul-sa," Lisbeth ventured, "we know that Aristan intended to betray *Phoenix*. Perhaps he tried, and failed. *Phoenix* is formidable."

"Or perhaps Phoenix betrayed him first," Gesul said thoughtfully. To a human, the sentence may have carried the negative connotation that *Phoenix* was not to be trusted. To a parren, Lisbeth was certain, the possibility held only a respectful caution. *"Could your brother have recovered his prize already?"*

"Gesul-sa, I don't think it likely that my brother would have abandoned his course and retraced his path without that success."

"In which case," said Gesul, *"these deepynines may not be seeking merely to destroy him, but to first acquire his prize for themselves."* He tapped on a screen, shifting the viewpoint of scan, the fingers of his other hand drumming on his armrest. *"So many forces, all hunting this artefact. Like birds fighting over a fallen scrap of food. Such a conflict could set the Spiral afire."*

The Captain was setting *Stassis's* course directly for Mylor Station, retaining V from jump until they reached the Brehn System elliptic in another hour, then decelerating rapidly to cruise the remaining distance among the rocks and dust. From Tobenrah there came no word, or at least, none that Lisbeth could hear from her limited access observer channels. She could overhear parren bridge crew talking in the background, concerned about the lack of coms chatter in the system, and speculating that everyone must be hiding. Several seemed to think it poor form, from a system run by House Harmony, where more than a third of the population was Harmony-phase. Surely House Fortitude were supposed to be even braver, Lisbeth wondered?

The single departing ship that had jumped just minutes after *Stassis* and her small formation had arrived insystem had not been demonstrating any particularly terrifying performance in its departure. Knowing a little about deepynine technology, and having seen some demonstrated up close, Lisbeth had informed the bridge that this one was likely holding back, so as not to give anything away. And now *Phoenix* was telling them that there were more out there, hidden in the vast expanse of the Brehn dustbowl, silent and unmoving for now. Watching, and seeing what unfolded, like predators in the long grass.

Suddenly there was a new contact on scan, and a flurry of parren voices that the translator failed to untangle, save for a few staccato vowels. But Lisbeth was adept enough at reading scan herself, and zoomed her own feed onto the new arrival, coming in from above the system elliptic. And now multiplying to two ships. One more made three. The light distance was displayed in parren time — two hundred and fourteen *tiras*, which was… Lisbeth did some fast sums, and arrived at thirty-three minutes. So these ships had arrived over half-an-hour ago, and would be considerably ahead of this position by now. And now an ID display was arriving, and her written Porgesh was not so good that she could read it straight off the screen. But her glasses tracked which bit of text her eyes were looking at, zoomed, focused, and gave her an overlaid English translation.

Ship name *Tiama*, that was the leader. And then the captain and commander, two different things on some parren ships, and something no human vessel would ever simply volunteer in an IFF package in potentially unfriendly space. Dorel, was the captain. And the commander, Aristan.

"Aristan," said Gesul, with a glint in his eye beneath the hood. The glint was faintly predatory, most unlike Gesul's usual calm beneficence. Parren, Lisbeth was realising, partly got into all these conflicts because they were prisoners of an unfortunate psychological structure… and partly because they enjoyed it. Power enthralled them — not money, not luxury, nor particularly even personal greed and ego-flattery… though that may have been a bigger feature of other house psychologies. House Harmony parren, at least, simply loved the feel of power, as a collector of fine arts might run his hand over a lovely robe, and admire its texture. Power was order, and structure, and the serenity of things in their rightful place. Parren sought that structure as obsessive compulsives might arrange the objects in a room to be perfectly aligned, where even a millimetre's disharmony could cause a minor psychological trauma. Such needs could only be solved through the exercise of power, and obedience to its rightful holders. Gesul sought to impose his order, to make all the things in his world line up as they should, for the great harmony that would result. For a parren of such rank, no prospect could be more delicious, whatever its risks. *"There you are, my old friend. Now what do you have to say for yourself?"*

Aristan's new warship was the *Tiama*. *Phoenix* had last observed the *Tiama* heading for Aristan's previous warship, the *Toristan*, as it lay crippled in orbit, disabled by Styx's assassin bugs.

Erik stared at the scan screen now, sipping electrolyte-heavy water and munching the sandwich someone had brought him from the galley. He was so tired now, he'd nearly forgotten which shift it was supposed to be — second-shift, he vaguely recalled. Aristan, blinked the English-symbol translation from the parren ID transmissions. Aristan. Mocking him, defiantly. "Didn't kill him, huh?" he suggested to no one in particular. To Styx, perhaps.

"I don't think we were ever going to get that lucky," Geish muttered, still unhappy with Scan's signal breakup amidst the asteroids. Second Lieutenant Jiri was running a steady conversation with the Scan Team elsewhere on the ship, making adjustments.

"That ship could be lying," Suli suggested. "We haven't heard his voice yet. And that can be simulated too, so even if we did hear him, it doesn't prove anything."

"I have a feeling that fucker's still alive," said Kaspowitz, plotting their possible approach variations. "Like Stefan says, we were never going to get rid of him that easily."

"I have a feeling you're right," Erik conceded. Lisbeth was alive. All the weariness in the world, and all the new danger, could not change how abruptly good he felt. Awake, and almost cheerful, surrounded by screens, controls and possibilities in his favourite chair. He flipped channels to the marines. "Hello Major, status please."

"Final decontamination's going through now," Trace confirmed. *"Just PH-3 waiting to return."* Wonder of wonders, Trace had actually removed herself back to *Phoenix* first with Delta, leaving Echo to finish up. Usually she'd have been last aboard, ignoring Erik's opinion that it was unnecessary and risky. PH-1 was at Midships berth now, and Engineering were giving it the most thorough sweep possible for any sign of surviving contamination. It seemed impossible, given how thorough they'd been in the Mylor Station facilities, but no one was taking any chances. *"They're rigging new decontamination gear to the berth airlock, so we're going to be a while getting back aboard. Styx is telling Engineering she can modify a few of her bugs to sense any living nanotech, now that she knows what to look for. One hundred percent effective, she insists."*

Because Styx, of course, was running about five different conversations at once, with Scan crew trying to improve reception, repair crew trying to fix various parts of *Phoenix*, bridge crew analysing coms feeds, Navigation and Helm attempting to predict deepynine movements, and now with Engineering, Operations and marines to help with the decontamination. Probably she was still running all her longterm fabricator operations too, not to mention running analyses on *Phoenix*'s computer systems so they weren't betrayed to the deepynines. They'd all been concerned, a few months ago, that they might eventually become dependent upon Styx's input. *Might.* It seemed laughable now that there'd even been a question.

"We're still looking at those six ships with Lisbeth," Erik continued. "It turns out the one she's on, the *Stassis*, commanded by Gesul, is only in command of the first three. The other three are commanded by Tobenrah, who is the head of the entire House Harmony. I actually ran into him on the Tsubarata, he was with State Department interrogating Hiro when we rescued him. Why Tobenrah's name doesn't appear on the ID signatures like Aristan's does, I don't know… Lieutenant Shilu thinks it might be something to do with parren politics, they don't always advertise who's exactly in charge."

"Tavalai tell you everything," Trace said. *"Parren tell you nothing. The funny thing is, they're both trying to fool you — one by giving you too much information, the other by withholding it. You think Tobenrah and Gesul have made common cause?"*

"Maybe. What do *you* think?"

"Well, looks to me like Tobenrah is using Gesul to split the Domesh. And Gesul has found some use for Lisbeth, my guess is that she knows a lot about Styx, and deepynines, and Gesul finds it valuable. Aristan didn't get along with Styx the way he'd hoped. Maybe Gesul has a different attitude to parren history."

"I think that could be right," Erik agreed. "Thank you Major." He disconnected, and gazed at the scan. Three warships, led by *Tiama*. The three *Phoenix* hadn't killed or disabled, of Aristan's six that had accompanied them to Cephilae. Aristan was going to be very unhappy. It was nearly enough for Erik to grind his teeth with frustration. So close! They'd retrieved the data-core, freed themselves from Aristan's unwelcome escort, and made a dash back to tavalai space… only to be held up by deepynine ambush here.

But with the bad fortune, came the good. They'd survived. They'd learned a little more about these new enemies, and what they wanted with *Phoenix*. And most of all, they still held the data-core… and now Styx thought she might have a way of reading it. Erik's optimism was relentless now. They'd been through so much to reach this point, and now they'd nearly arrived. In the Academy they'd drilled it into the young cadets — don't look too far ahead, just solve the next problem, then the next, then the next. Eventually you'll either run out of problems, or one of them will kill you. In either case, a solution.

"Captain?" ventured Lieutenant Shilu. "I'm getting more system chatter now. Some ships and facilities are talking, mostly to Tobenrah and Gesul, I think. Only a small number of signals so far, but I suppose they saw that one ship leave and…"

"Jump pulse contact!" Geish said loudly, and the blip appeared on Erik's screen. "Range five seconds light, V and course are undetermined at this time, but he's inside the debris field!"

Erik hit the take-hold, as alarm klaxons blared through the ship, warning all crew to stow what they were doing and hit the acceleration slings fast. "That's close," said Suli, watching the ship systems reporting in to that status change, the engines powering up to full as the safety regulators came off. "He's right in the debris field with us, he'll be lucky if he doesn't boost a bunch of rocks up to speed with him."

"I reckon that might be the idea," said Erik, gripping his control sticks more tightly, and testing his fingers on the triggers. On Operations channel he could hear rapid, businesslike conversation between the ship and PH-3, still docked at Mylor. "Lieutenant Geish!" he called. "I need an ETA!"

"Working on it!" said Geish. "The reading's not good, these fuckers definitely have some kind of stealth, I can't… one more boost!" he interrupted himself. "He just accelerated, that's definitely coming straight at us! ETA five minutes, maybe six!"

"He's going way too fast," Suli said calmly, as Armscomp locked all weapons onto the approaching course. "Scan, there's a world of difference between five minutes and six."

"Best I can do, Commander," Geish retorted.

"Captain," said Karle at Arms, "all weapons locked, we have a thirty-degree broadside, full spread."

"Hold your fire," said Erik. "He's going to brake in a second." And switched channels fast to Operations, which included PH-3. "Lieutenant Jersey, this is the Captain, get everyone onboard now and emergency return to *Phoenix*."

"Captain," came Jersey's reply, *"we are not fully decontaminated on half our marines and a handful of parren."*

"Just get back here immediately, this guy's going to blow the station. We'll think of something with the decontamination — Operations, deal with it." He switched back without waiting for a reply, knowing he'd just opened a huge can of worms… and sure enough, here on Scan was the coloured energy pulse of a ship dumping V. "I reckon he's going to change course and head for jump. But he's just boosted a bunch of rocks our way, and there's no way we can toast them all."

"I'm tracking projected V," Geish confirmed. "Don't have a fix on the rocks, but I've got the position locked." An ETA timer started, now adjusting even as Erik looked to the lower end of Geish's earlier prediction. Four-and-a-half minutes. "That ship just dumped again… now he's burning hard, I'm reading a twelve-G burn, heading for system zenith." Just in case anyone had any doubts that it was a deepynine.

"Operations, get me an ETA please," said Erik. No one could save the station now, the only thing left was to stay cool and not screw up the departure. Jersey was too busy to talk to him, making sure her marines and other passengers were aboard and secure before leaving. Marines trained for this sort of thing constantly, but parren passengers were unlikely to. Doubtless it was chaos over there now, everyone scrambling to get aboard and locked in.

"Captain, PH-3 says two-minutes-fifty, but she'll try to pull it tighter. We have the last search and rescue drones coming aboard now, PH-3 is the sole returnee."

Erik hit thrust, a steady burn increasing rapidly to five-Gs, angling them past the spinning parren starship, toward the station's docking end-cap. Then he cut, spun them tail-first and held thrust until they were coming right up to the rotating docking cone. A brief burst of power brought them to a roaring halt barely a kilometre from the cone, a symmetry of synchronous motion as Midships aligned directly along the exit route.

A note from Coms appeared on an adjoining screen — an announcement from *Stassis*, Lieutenant Shilu correctly judged that there was no time to hear it now. It had been sent twenty minutes ago, and Gesul and Lisbeth would only see this current mess in another twenty minutes' time. Navigation sent Erik the required escape route that Kaspowitz had compiled for exactly this scenario, a concentrated scan along the projected course, allowing high acceleration without fear of collision for a good two minutes before things became uncertain and dangerous once more. If Jersey kept to her schedule, Erik was sure they wouldn't need it.

Slightly more than twenty seconds before the estimate, Lieutenant Jersey broke dock, swivelled and blasted full thrust toward *Phoenix* Midships, angling between the rotating ships within the docking cone, just offset from collision course so she wouldn't hit *Phoenix* if something went wrong. Finding Berth Four precisely where she needed it, she spun tail-first and hit a long, then rapidly-decelerating burn that turned into a spin at the last moment to achieve correct alignment, then slammed firmly into the Berth Four grapples.

"Good lock!" said Operations, confirming what Erik could see on his own screen. *"Berth is green, we are clear to go!"*

Erik hit thrust, with still a good two minutes to spare and no need to rush it. He built to three, then five-Gs, and held it there, knowing five would be plenty to get them clear in time. By now Scan had identified a tight cluster of very low-luminescence rocks, approaching ridiculously fast. One of them hit something else, probably another even smaller rock, and the resulting explosion was larger than the biggest nuclear weapon that humans knew how to build. But such forces were tiny compared to the things that physics regularly threw at Fleet warships in peacetime or in war, and enough of the original cluster retained their course through even that conflagration.

They were travelling fast enough that at this range Scan could see reflected light coming back at a whole new dopplered spectrum, shifted several degrees out of alignment. Time on those rocks was progressing marginally more slowly than on *Phoenix*. Erik could never look at such things without feeling a chill dread at the horror of it, that such a simple thing as the transportation technology that made all Spiral civilisation possible, could also do this. The technology itself was blameless. The people who used it, sometimes less so.

Earth had not been V-struck, as tavalai law held it to be the very worst of crimes. Typically of lower-species finding loopholes in tavalai law, the krim had borne the far greater effort and cost to hit Earth with chemical and biological weapons instead, achieving much the same effect, but without quite the legal consequences. For that alone — the dispatch of the beloved homeworld through legal technicality — humanity would never forgive the tavalai. But the krim's homeworld *had* been V-struck, three hundred years later, by humans who hadn't cared a damn for tavalai laws. Humanity knew this weapon well, and having used it once, had advertised to others that they were not above using it again. Now, facing such warships as these, Erik wondered if that long-advertised strategic posture were such a good idea after all.

Precisely as Scan's ETA reached zero, Mylor Station disappeared as rear scan blanked to white. No one on the bridge said a thing. Scan indicated a small danger from explosion debris, but *Phoenix* was headed perpendicular to the impact course, and most of the solid debris would continue in the latter direction. Other forms of shockwave dissipated very fast in a vacuum… a matter Erik recalled having to explain to young Lisbeth when she'd asked why he accused a movie she liked of not being very realistic. She'd be watching this, he thought. And others too, new friends of hers, presumably. Hopefully. Best to make a good impression.

"Coms," said Erik. "Broadband transmission downstream of that explosion, warn everyone in its path that the lanes are going to be very dangerous for the next few hours. Give them our best trajectory plot as well — Nav, get him the data."

"Aye Captain," Kaspowitz acknowledged.

"Next few years," Suli murmured, watching that awful spread of high-V micro-missiles. Most of them were too fast for the system's gravity and would dissipate in deep space, but a lot more would hit other rocks, causing other explosions, which caused other, though lower-V bursts of debris, which caused others... etc. In truth, a V-strike like this, in a system like Brehn, would set off a chain reaction making everyone less safe for centuries. Erik was entirely certain that the deepynines did not care at all.

He called up Shilu's stored message, the translator confirming that it had come from *Stassis*, and was now running analysis on the tongue. Porgesh, it told him, like most parren spoke. Parren had thousands of old languages, but were disciplined enough to agree on only one, for primary purposes. Humanity had had to suffer a near-extinction event to make that happen.

"The UFS Phoenix is notified that The Honourable Aristan," said the cool translated voice, *"Ruler of the Domesh Denomination, loyal servant of House Harmony, has declared a grievance against the UFS Phoenix herself, and her commander, Captain Erik Debogande. It shall also be noted that Gesul, Second of the Domesh, loyal servant of House Harmony, has also declared a grievance against Aristan, Ruler of the Domesh, loyal servant of House Harmony. According to parren law, it is decided that I, Tobenrah of the Incefahd, Ruler of House Harmony, shall decide the right of these matters, and will invoke a contest, to be held in the jurisdiction of the great House Harmony. The UFS Phoenix is informed that she will comply, or be destroyed."*

"A contest?" Erik asked his Coms Officer. "What the heck kind of contest?"

"Captain, the Porgesh word is 'catharan'," said Shilu, looking mystified at his screens. Tapping the translator's input achieved nothing more. "It doesn't know that word, it's just telling us 'contest', but somehow I don't think that grasps the entirety of it."

"Contest," Suli repeated hopefully. "Doesn't sound too bad."

“Yeah right,” Kaspowitz said drily. “‘Cause we’ve been real lucky with that alien shit so far, huh.”

CHAPTER 20

The city was Chirese. The planet, Elsium. It was about as far away from home as any human traveller had ever come, in this direction at least. Erik leaned against PH-1's forward landing leg, glasses off for a moment beneath his helmet rim, to contemplate the Chirese Otuga.

Otuga was the parren word for house of government, though the translator seemed to quibble with the precise synonymity. Everything swam in the midday heat, nearly forty degrees celsius, and worse still in the armour, a rifle clipped to his back, sidearm in the front webbing. The parren had told them no full armour, and no more than twenty marines. Trace had brought Alpha First Squad and Command Squad, of course. Privates Chavez and Lauda stood guard before the hulking assault shuttle, unbothered by the heat, peering up the great ranks of steps toward the government buildings, and off the wide avenue to the sides, in search of movement. So far, there was none.

The avenue of stairs was one-and-a-half kilometres long, up a long, gentle hillside from the city of Chirese. The way was not especially steep, and consisted of a series of flat, rectangular platforms, each perhaps a hundred metres long and thirty metres wide. Each flat platform was joined by gentle stairs of equal width, all the way up to the huge, slope-roofed building atop the hill. Up there, many parren had gathered, little specks in the shimmering heat, to peer down at the insolent humans, as the cloud of dust kicked up by the assault shuttle's landing jets slowly drifted on the negligent breeze.

Trace came to join her Captain, also in light armour though more heavily armed. Unlike Erik, she actually knew how to use all those weapons. She leaned on the landing leg's other side. "I don't think they're impressed with you," she remarked, gazing up the long, multiple flights to the house of government for this entire sector of space.

"They're House Harmony," Erik said grimly, swigging some water. "They can meditate and hold their breath until they pass out for all I care."

It had been five cycles, ship time, since Gesul, Aristan and Tobenrah's ships had arrived in Brehn System. *Phoenix* had been informed by Tobenrah, the head of all House Harmony, that they were now in the custody of the house, and would follow to Drezen System, or be destroyed. *Phoenix*'s damage ruled out a rapid escape, and against such odds, there was no chance of winning a fight. Minor repairs had been conducted, to ensure the jumplines would at least not fail in hyperspace, and then they'd single-jumped to Drezen System.

Drezen System was home to Elsium, a world of a half-billion parren where the administration of this whole sector was based. Once there, it had been a long cruise into Elsium, in total coms silence. Erik had not been able to speak to Lisbeth, nor to enquire what the hell was going on. In fact, it looked as though the entire system had been banned from talking on open coms, to prevent the unwanted humans from learning a damn thing about anything. And it spoke to the total control that parren authorities exercised over their subjects, that they could order such a thing, and see it obeyed completely. Ships needed coms, as did stations, refineries, outer-system mining bases. In most of the Spiral, system navigation buoys would typically communicate recent news packages, to keep ships up to date with current events. Now, all was quiet.

Instead of docking with one of Elsium's busy commercial stations, *Phoenix* had received instructions that the Captain would proceed to Chirese by shuttle, with instructions for how it should be done… in every aspect except for where they should land. The Chirese facilities included a large spaceport further down the hill, but with coms blacked out, there had been no guidance signal to tell PH-1 precisely what to do. Erik thought he'd figured enough about the parren to suspect that doing precisely as they were told would not increase the respect or esteem in which they were held. He'd told Lieutenant Hausler to land here, on the avenue of stairs, scattering the parren civilians who'd been walking here at the time. Multiple inbuilt weapons platforms had locked onto them as they'd done it, at which Erik had directed Hausler to open the shuttle's missile bays and lock them back. No one had died, and PH-1 had settled here, blocking the main thoroughfare linking the government to the city, in obstinate defiance of them all.

Surely by now the local radiation sniffers had detected that several of PH-1's missiles were nuclear-tipped. The only targets they could spend those missiles on would also reduce PH-1 to radioactive particles moments after detonation, but that fact alone made all the statement Erik had wanted.

"You think Tobenrah knows what we've got onboard *Phoenix*?" Trace wondered. She could have meant Styx, or the data-core, or both. The consequence would be the same.

"I'm certain of it," said Erik. Being kept from talking to Lisbeth all the way here had seemed like cruelty, and he was in no mood for parren games. As always with *Phoenix* of late, the aliens appeared to hold all the cards. Only it wasn't actually true, because *Phoenix* had some very important cards of her own. Unfortunately, those cards also painted a giant bullseye on her backside.

"Still no word from Lisbeth?" Trace asked. Erik shook his head, and sipped from his bottle. "If we knew what relationship she had with Gesul, I'd be happier."

"If this battle between Aristan and Gesul is over parren history, maybe Gesul figures he's got the key to the real thing, now. She's actually seen deepynines and drysines. Most parren have forgotten there was even a difference."

"If that real thing isn't what the parren people actually want to hear," Trace cautioned, "it might not do him any good."

"Yeah, well there's got to be someone in this fucking race that cares about the truth for its own sake," Erik muttered. Trace glanced up at him, looking thoughtful. Erik looked back. For all the comparatively quiet last five days, they still hadn't seen much of each other, each preoccupied with pressing routines in different parts of the ship. "You know, that time in the gym. When I nearly…"

"Don't you fucking say it," Trace said mildly, but with a hint of real warning. "Don't you dare. The Captain doesn't apologise, ever. You're not expected to be infallible, but whatever you do, the rest of us have to wear it. That's not a privilege for you, it's a burden. You don't get to dodge that burden by saying you're sorry. You do it, you own it."

Erik looked at her for a moment. Finally a smirk twisted his lips. "I *was* feeling apologetic until the lecture," he replied. "Now you can just fuck off."

"Aye Captain," Trace agreed with satisfaction. "That I can."

"Captain," came Ensign Yun's voice from inside the assault shuttle. *"I've no idea how, but I'm getting indirect coms from Phoenix. I think it's Styx, she's using local channels, she must have hacked something in orbit and gotten into local coms. We're talking to her via the city coms network, just like any citizen, only she's encrypted."*

Meaning PH-1 could talk to *Phoenix* without the locals being aware of it, or presumably being able to jam it. Right now, they had their regular Fleet coms, but those were subject to interruption. "Tell her to figure out just how much damage she can cause to the local coms network," Erik replied. "You never know when we'll need a distraction."

"I don't think she needs to be told that, Captain, but I'll tell her anyway."

"Yo, here we go," said Hausler from the cockpit. *"Big bunch of parren forming at the top of the stairs."* Zoomed visuals appeared on Erik's glasses, a cluster of dark robes upon the stairs, spreading like an ink spill beneath white and black banners.

"Domesh," said Erik. "Only Domesh, by the look of it. If it were a formal welcoming committee, you'd think all the denominations would be represented. Aristan is head Domesh, and he's pissed at us. Keep an eye out, people. I don't think this will be friendly."

"Marines, full deployment," Trace said calmly, and those marines not previously standing guard now descended the rear ramp to take up position. "It looks like these guys are coming at us in ceremonial formation. We don't do that — we stay combat ready at all times."

“Damn right,” Erik agreed, watching the Domesh as they began flowing down the stairs. There were hundreds of them. No, he thought a minute later, as the flow still came on. Thousands. Their formations were immaculate, precise rows behind their banners. Among most parren, these mass displays would be colourful. Looking at this advancing black tide, devoid of all individual colour or identity, Erik could see why many parren found the Domesh alarming.

Some camera drones buzzed and hovered nearby… cleared green by PH-1’s scans, free of weapons and harmless. “Looks like they want everyone to see,” Trace observed. “We could jam them.”

“There’s no point in having a ceremony if no one can see it,” said Erik. A part of him wanted to stand up straight before this alien scrutiny, to stop leaning against the landing leg, and put on a good show for the parren. But he declined, with deliberate defiance. “The Domesh want to impress their followers. That’s the point of this stuff — the followers they have are loyal until death or until they hit the next phase, but the new followers have to be won. They’ll just put up new drones, or higher altitude ones. Besides, we might want them to see this.”

Out the front of the black tide, Erik could now see a small knot of colour — parren in green tunics, marching beneath a similarly green banner.

“The marine commander is in command of ground operations,” said Trace, “but in this case I think any combat operations will be synonymous with ship diplomacy. Diplomacy is the captain’s prerogative, on or off ship. How do you want to proceed?”

“Defiance,” said Erik. “We’re not parren, we don’t play by their rules. The only orders we’re bound to follow are those where the cost of not complying will be our destruction or injury. Remember, we have something they want. I calculate that we’re safer by appearing dangerous, perhaps even a little unstable. Parren don’t like instability, let’s scare them with our alienness.”

"I agree," said Trace. "Just remember that we don't actually know how Aristan will calculate the value of the data-core. He might prefer it destroyed than in the hands of Tobenrah."

"Yeah," said Erik, thinking that. "Lieutenant Hausler?"

"Here Captain."

"Give the cannon a noticeable twitch. Aim right at that front rank. Let them see it."

"Aye Captain." Behind them, the centreline cannon mount abruptly whined and lurched, humming as the electric drives prepared the ammo feed. The big barrel angled up the stairs, where the Domesh tide now crested the top of the flight of stairs two-distant from the shuttle. A prolonged burst would kill hundreds, some from direct hits, most from the fragmentation of high-explosive shells. Predictably, the Domesh continued without hesitation, descending the steps. Erik was sure they'd seen.

First Squad's Second and Third Sections were up on the right and left flanks when the parren finally arrived, rifles at cross-arms. Command Squad were deployed left and right on PH-1's sides, while Lieutenant Dale guarded the rear with First Section, where he had the best view of the overall situation, and wouldn't be distracted by this whole mob of parren in his face.

Erik and Trace stood side by side to the right, clear of the shuttle's cannon, with obvious purpose. No doubt it irritated the parren, putting their formation off-centre. They had to perform a manoeuvre to realign, the green-clad parren at the front halting, then making a separate right-wheel to end up directly before the human commanders. There were gold-clad guards to either side, and some lower ranked aides behind, holding the banners aloft, while others carried slates and other items, ready to offer them forward if needed. The senior-most green-clad parren wore an enormous headdress, tall with tails that flowed down his shoulders. The one beside him had a less impressive headdress, but carried a large staff, half-again his own height. None of the green ones, nor their assistants, appeared to be armed. Of the sea of black robes behind them, anything was possible.

There were ten of the lead group in total — four in green, another six assistants in gold or blue. They stopped in a line, and waited. Obviously they expected Erik and Trace to walk up, and front them. Trace waited for her Captain's lead. Erik considered them for a moment, baking in the hot sun. Then he recalled some gum, kept in a breast pocket. He rarely chewed gum — only when he'd just eaten, and had to talk to someone at close quarters, and feared his breath might smell. Now he pulled out the small packet, popped some gum in his mouth, and chewed. It was peppermint, and strong. He considered offering some to Trace, but that wouldn't do — she had to be the calmly lethal one. Insolence would only work coming from him.

He replaced the packet and strolled forward, Trace at his side. Both of them kept their rifles on their backs, and stopped before the parren. Erik left his glasses on — rude in most cultures, given the data constantly displayed upon the lenses. A person could be reading a book, or watching TV, while pretending to talk to someone. But he tilted his head to look up at the central parren's towering headdress, chewing gum and looking unimpressed. The tall parren glowered at them, with that faintly malevolent stare that all parren of authority seemed to use on everyone.

It was an aide to one side who spoke first. *"Do you understand?"* the translator spoke in Erik's ear.

Erik glanced sideways at the parren who'd spoken. Then back at the head parren. "Yeah," he drawled.

"You are Captain Erik Debogande?" Again the aide. Erik suspected the aide's job was to clear the ground before serious conversation could start, establishing that the correct alien was the one speaking, and that his translator was working.

"No," said Erik. "I'm Tobenrah." Definite consternation on the faces of parren before him. A few small glances sideways. Erik wondered if they'd gotten their cues on human behaviour from Lisbeth. Lisbeth was always so polite and friendly. Having had five days of relief to think about it, Erik was not at all surprised that she'd managed to find one group of parren more friendly than the others, and charm them. Being in Family Debogande gave plenty of opportunities to practise manners, formal or informal, with all kinds of people. Erik had always been better at it than most — a quality that had gained him only suspicion when he'd first joined a combat vessel in Fleet. Some had whispered he'd only gained the post by being rich and charming. Now he found that all the rules of charm and manners he'd lived by could just as easily be inverted. Just like being a warship captain in a fight — one learned the rules of engagement so that one knew how and when one could break them.

"You are Captain Erik Debogande?" the parren repeated eventually.

Erik spat on the tiles, and said nothing. The parren waited, as the spit sizzled in the heat. Finally the headdress grew tired of waiting. *"I am Chorkolrhi. I am of the Togreth. The Togreth are a neutral denomination of House Harmony. We do not take sides in denominational disputes. We administer the house law. Do you understand?"*

"You're the civil service," said Erik, with no concern that the translator probably couldn't manage the term. "I understand."

"You have been challenged to a catharan by Aristan, leader of the Domesh. He charges that the UFS Phoenix did deliberately and without warning assault his ships by the world of Pashan, inflicting casualties. He charges you with treachery, and with the breach of an outstanding agreement. Do you answer these charges?"

"He kidnapped my sister," Erik retorted, and it took no effort to fill his voice with contempt. "This is the agreement he made with us. He held a gun to her head, and threatened her life, to gain our cooperation. In human custom, there is no behaviour more dishonourable."

"You are not among humans here," the Headdress said sternly. *"Aristan has the right to maintain an Ashara if he can keep her. You are in parren space, and are so ruled by parren law."*

"Fuck your law," said Erik. God knew what the translator made of it.

The parren's eyes narrowed. *"Your insolence will result in your destruction,"* he observed.

"And in yours," said Erik, unmoved. They stared at each other. A gentle, hot breeze fluttered at the rows of black robes, the only sound on this platform between flights of stairs, save for the dry rustle of leaves in neighbouring trees. Erik could see the parren weighing his words. Nuclear warheads on PH-1's missiles. The *UFS Phoenix* in overhead geostationary orbit. All would be destroyed if the parren chose… but would do enormous damage first. And the drysine data-core would be lost, to the distress of Aristan, and possibly to Tobenrah. To say nothing of the humiliation that such an event would inflict, in the minds of possible future supporters, to have presided over such a catastrophe.

Erik did not doubt that parren would believe his suicidal threat. Parren were all too willing to throw their lives away for some greater cause. But those were the causes of followers, in the service of some greater leader. Out here, alone in alien space, *Phoenix* followed no one. What cause did she serve? Whose orders did she follow? Erik could almost see the puzzlement in the wide, blue eyes, trying to figure out these troublesome aliens. Perhaps, given the rumours, they'd conclude the humans were under the command of this malevolent drysine entity onboard. Perhaps they'd all sworn loyalty to her cause, and now threatened to die in her service. Or would a parren be able to comprehend that some humans followed no one, and made their own way? Could a parren even truly grasp such a concept? Or were their minds so fixed within their own psychologies that it remained an unknowable thing?

"Tobenrah, ruler of House Harmony, has declared that the ruler of the Domesh Denomination has the right to issue the UFS Phoenix with a catharan," the Headdress resumed. *"You can only maintain this standoff, and prevent your destruction, until your food runs out. And you will never be allowed to leave. Parren are patient. You must accept."*

Erik pointed his hand, in the general direction of Brehn System, and the way they'd just come. "Deepynines are not patient. They attacked Brehn System, they destroyed Mylor Station, and they killed more than forty thousand loyal parren citizens. Where was their protection? Who will protect the many loyal citizens of *this* system, when the deepynines come *here*?"

There was movement among the robes to the Togreth's rear… a parren arm outstretched to the sky, with some kind of device in hand. Immediately, Erik noted something dropping from the sky. It was one of the camera drones. It hit a tree beside the platform, bounced through branches, then crunched into the ground. A moment later, a drone hit the paving on the platform's other side, and broke. Then more commotion about the arm-upraised parren, a strangled cry, and the body fell from view. Other bodies converged around it, and the commotion was lost amidst the wall of black.

"Steady," said Trace on uplinks to her marines. *"Hold steady. I think they just killed him. He took out the drones, and they killed him. He didn't want anyone to hear that bit."*

Erik was almost surprised at how unalarmed he was. He'd grown accustomed to facing threats with Trace and her marines at his side. That, plus PH-1's cannon, helped his nerves enormously. Of course the parren were riven with factions. Multiple interests were represented here. Those interests were playing for high stakes, and someone had just died to protect the interests of his ruler. With parren, however alarming, it was no surprise.

"What is the catharan?" Erik asked the Headdress, as though the murder had not happened. There were more drones zooming into position even now, like giant insects in the hot air. "Humans have no knowledge of this word."

"It is a trial," said the Headdress. *"The trial can take many forms. The form required by Aristan is combat."*

"A trial by combat between whom and whom?" Trace cut in for the first time. There were tales of parren ritual combats. So sensationalised were these, among human media and popular entertainments, that most humans' knowledge of parren consisted of little else.

"Between the Commander of the UFS Phoenix, and an appointed champion of the Domesh."

"Acceptable," said Trace, before Erik could open his mouth. Erik refrained from gaping at her. Was she fucking serious? "The

Commander of the *UFS Phoenix* is a warrior specialised in starship combat. He will require a warship in which to demonstrate his superior ability. Will he be permitted to utilise his existing warship? Or will one be supplied to him?"

Erik nearly laughed. Trace Thakur, you razor-sharp, brutal fucking genius. The parren's double-take of pure consternation only increased his amusement. *"The combat ritual of catharan is always with hand weapons,"* the Headdress retorted.

"Unacceptable," said Trace, with hard contempt. "Worse than unacceptable. Dishonourable and cowardly. Human custom does not elevate to command the wielder of knives, it elevates the wielder of warships. I am a wielder of hand weapons, and I am only the third-ranking officer on the *Phoenix*. Warships elevate civilisations, not knives. It is little wonder you parren decline in the Spiral, while we humans only rise." Erik could have hugged her.

"We are in parren space," Headdress insisted. *"This is parren law!"*

"Parren law to appoint a trained specialist to assassinate a warrior whose superior strength lies in a different field?" Trace said scornfully. "This is a trickery and a fraud by the coward Aristan. A people who observe such practice deserve extinction. The deepynines shall oblige." The Headdress glared at her. Erik suspected private, uplinked conversation between parren, wondering how to proceed. "The *UFS Phoenix* demands the right to appoint its own champion," Trace continued.

"You have not the rank to make such demands," Headdress retorted.

"We have enough rank to turn your parliament into a thermonuclear cloud. The catharan is a contest of skill, yes? Allow this challenge. I will fight." Erik's heart nearly stopped again. Trace you damn fool, what are you doing? From around the back of the shuttle, Erik fancied Lieutenant Dale might be preparing to intervene, to violently stop it from happening… or more likely, to volunteer himself. "And I will fight Aristan," Trace continued. "This coward will not be permitted to hide behind his servants. He has made this challenge to the *UFS Phoenix*. He will fight this challenge himself, or all parren shall see him for a fraud and a coward."

Headdress and his fellow Togreth glanced at each other, as uplink conversation continued. Erik guessed that from somewhere behind them, and possibly much further away, someone was negotiating on the Domesh's behalf. If the Togreth were the mediators and rule-setters that they appeared, even Aristan would have to accept their judgements. Finally, the Headdress addressed Trace directly.

"It is dishonourable for one so high as the ruler of the Domesh to fight one so lowly as you," he said. Erik suspected the parren did not mean it as an insult, merely as an observation. *"Your insults have no bearing on his station here, and you will sway no honour by your words. But you are aliens, and the situation is barely precedented. Some flexibility is required. You will be permitted to fight the Domesh champion. He is here now. You may proceed."*

And with that, they made a quarter-turn, and moved aside. A black-robed parren emerged from the throng. Another green-robed Togreth moved up, holding a pair of ceremonial swords — one for the parren champion, Erik saw, and one for Trace.

"Lieutenant Hausler?" came Trace's synthesised voice in Erik's ear. *"Get ready on that trigger."*

"Aye Major."

A thousand parren eyes fixed on Trace. Erik's heart pounded nearly out of his chest. As a total package, Trace was a superb marine. Even disregarding her skills with command, as a pure rifleman, to manoeuvre and fight with a variety of weapons, there were few better. But even Erik knew that hand-to-hand was Trace's weakest skill. She had augments, as did all marines, which made her lethal even barehanded, and removed most disadvantages a woman might have against men… but without her weapons, she was perhaps only top-third in all of Phoenix Company. Good as she was, there were many better. And some parren trained for unarmed combat from childhood, as a matter of culture and ritual. Those parren were incredibly fast and skilled, and with weapons familiar to them but not to humans, Trace's prospects seemed slim.

The parren champion took his sword, and tested its balance, awaiting the human's approach with indigo-eyed contempt. Trace calmly pulled her pistol from its webbing, and shot him in the head. The body hit the paving with a thud, and lay limp. Parren stared in shock. Then looked back at Trace. Beside her, PH-1's enormous rapid-fire cannon poised ready to kill them all.

Trace reholstered her pistol. "Aristan," she repeated. "Or we wait here until hell freezes over."

CHAPTER 21

"There," said Hausler, as Scan zoomed on a newly arrived shuttle, coming down from orbit with a defensive formation of assault vehicles ahead of it. "That's carrying someone important. Look at that defensive spread, they're expecting trouble."

"Everyone's expecting trouble," Erik said grimly, standing behind Hausler's chair, gazing out the canopy up the flights of stairs up which the Domesh tide had retreated an hour ago. "There's enough heavily armed air activity to cover a planetary invasion. What the hell's going on?"

Neither Hausler nor Yun had any more clue than he did. Eventually Erik headed back to the main crew hold, a cleared and empty floor in PH-1's zero-G optimised interior, all the chairs on their supporting arms moved to the ceiling. It allowed the shuttle to carry mostly cargo when necessary, and now allowed Trace to practise her hand-to-hand moves against Lance Corporal Kalo, commander of Alpha's Third Section, and one of the very best in that style on *Phoenix*. Trace's initial challenge still stood, unanswered for now, yet the real possibility remained that a reply would come soon. Kalo had been an instructor in a martial arts gym as a kid out of school, until his obsession with unarmed combat had caused him to contemplate what it might be like to gain military-grade augments. That lure, he freely admitted, had been the thing that caused him to join, even more than patriotism or a sense of duty.

Erik watched him now, and saw a very rare sight indeed — Trace patiently taking instruction from someone notably better at this than her. She did not challenge Kalo's assertions, and accepted his criticisms without question, even when Kalo challenged her already formidable technique. Partly, Erik supposed, there were so many things a modern Company Commander was supposed to master, that she simply hadn't been able to spend the eight and nine hour days that Kalo had in his youth, doing nothing but grips, holds, feints and blocks. It was the thing Erik admired most of all about Trace as a marine, he decided — that for all her ability, and all the praise that others regularly heaped upon her, she possessed absolutely no ego when it came to learning new things from others.

"Captain," said Yun from up front, *"we have a cruiser incoming. Looks unarmed, civilian model. Coming to land behind us, I think."*

Trace didn't need to tell anyone to be ready, marines stood constant guard outside, scanning for movement and with orders to be polite but watchful if any unarmed civilians used these stairs for their intended purpose — to walk to the house of government. So far, none had tried.

"I still don't get how they just allow us to land on their doorstep and point nuclear weapons at them," Kalo remarked, handing Trace her helmet while fastening his own, their sparring ended for the moment.

"The parren practise mutually assured destruction," Trace told him, taking the helmet, and swigging some water. With the rear ramp open, the shuttle's hold could not be airconditioned, and both marines were dripping sweat within their armour. "The idea is that violence is less likely if all sides are equally armed."

"Actually not a bad theory," said Lieutenant Dale, who'd been watching them practise from against the wall of the hold. The prospect of the Major volunteering for a duel had not agreed with him. Clearly he didn't like Kalo leading her instruction either, despite the Lance Corporal's higher qualifications, and he'd been watching them practise like a displeased competition judge, looking to deduct points. Erik suspected that Dale would have loved to take the duel himself. No, he was *certain* Dale would. "Best thing I've heard from these blue-eyed fools since we met them."

"Cruiser approaching our rear," said Lance Corporal Ricardo from outside. *"Civilian, looks harmless."*

"Let's stay inside," Trace advised Erik. "Bigshots can't go out to greet every errand boy personally, it doesn't look good."

"Okay Bigshot," Erik agreed. The marines grinned. Trace tolerated it, as she did with most things that amused her marines. "Ensign Yun tells me she was reviewing Scan from before. Some of those Domesh were holding transmitters of some kind, they had independent powersources, quite strong. Our theory is that they could disable assassin bugs. Assuming Aristan warned them about that."

"Pretty dumb if he didn't," said Trace, gulping more water. "Or I wouldn't have needed a bullet. But good to know, that's one more trick I won't be able to use."

"Of course," said Erik, "they'll have no idea if some transmitter will even work on Styx's technology…"

"Cruiser landing," said Ricardo, as the whine of repulsors grew to a throbbing screech from outside, then faded. And a moment later, *"Hey Captain, you're going to want to see this."* Erik frowned. Was that a grin he heard in Ricardo's voice? And then his eyes widened, realising…

"Stay," Trace commanded him, with a light grasp of his shoulder as he strode for the rear. It was wise, Erik realised… any emotional vulnerability should *certainly* be kept inside the shuttle. But it seemed like an eternity before several parren appeared coming up the ramp, then parted to reveal a brown-skinned human girl in a flowing red robe that conveyed far more authority than any girlish gown, with a great, black belt about her middle, and black, frizzy hair pulled almost straight and severe over combs and pins.

Lisbeth smiled at him broadly, and surprised him by *not* bursting into tears. Embarrassingly, Erik thought he might. He walked across and hugged her, but not too hard, as there were parren watching, and even these things were uncertain. Finally he let her go, and then Lisbeth repeated the embrace with Trace, with utmost decorum. Trace looked delighted, and yet, somehow not at all surprised. Then Lisbeth even repeated the embrace with Lieutenant Dale. Erik realised with astonishment that he was actually feeling a little annoyed at her, and almost… jealous? She was supposed to be *his* little sister, to be most delighted to be back in *his* company once more… and upon realising it, he nearly laughed at himself. She was barely recognisable in her robe and hair, and one did not need to be her brother to look at her face, and know that the clothes were not all that had changed.

"Erik, Major Thakur," she said once she'd exchanged smiles and handclasps with all the other marines. "I'd like to introduce you to a couple of good friends of mine — these are Timoshene, and Semaya." She indicated the two parren who had come up the ramp with her. Timoshene was Domesh, tall, lean and better dressed for a hot day then the rest of them. Semaya was obviously female, though Erik had seen few enough of those. She wore a green-patterned tunic, loose pants and sandals, with a light, circular cap on her smooth, hairless head. "Timoshene was my personal guard in the Kunadeen, and Semaya was a member of the Togreth… the Togreth are…"

"Yes, we just met the Togreth," said Erik. "They tried to arrange a duel."

"Yes, we heard," said Lisbeth, her expression suddenly earnest and sombre. "Erik, Timoshene and Semaya saved my life, they revealed their true loyalties when Aristan moved on Gesul and tried to kill me too. They killed my attackers and helped me escape."

It had been that close, then. Erik stepped past Lisbeth, and extended a hand to Timoshene first. "I thank you. On the behalf of the whole *UFS Phoenix*." Timoshene took the hand, cautiously. Then Semaya, with more grace.

"We serve Gesul, in truth," Semaya explained through the translator. *"Gesul has taken Lisbeth Debogande into his protection. We did as honour dictated."* Aristan had insisted that 'honour' was a word shared by humans and parren. Erik was beginning to suspect, however, that it meant vastly different things for each.

"Look, let's sit," said Lisbeth, and knelt upon the hard floor. Some marines fetched spare jumpsuits from a locker to fold and use as cushions. "I'm actually kind of used to it… oh, thanks Staff Sergeant," as Giddy Kono handed her a jumpsuit, and Lisbeth placed it folded under her knees. Erik and Trace copied her, and Semaya did the same. Timoshene, however, remained standing, watching all cautiously. "Don't mind him," said Lisbeth. "He's just protective."

"Lis, what's with all the flyers and shuttles?" Erik asked. "It looks like war's about to break out."

"Well I hope not," said Lisbeth, without conviction. Erik didn't find it reassuring. "Look… I'm with Gesul. It's important that it stays that way, for now." Her eyes searched Erik's, looking for confirmation. "He says he values my counsel. I know things about humans, and about hacksaws. Both seem relevant at the moment."

She waited for Erik's agreement. "Go on," Erik said instead. Being good at charm and persuasion himself, he'd never considered himself easily manipulated. But if one person ever could, it was Lisbeth.

Lisbeth took a deep breath. "Okay. Elsium's government runs the whole sector." She pointed up the vast flight of steps beyond the shuttle's cockpit, toward the parliament building. "It's House Harmony, like Tobenrah and Aristan. They were supposed to protect Brehn System, but they failed. I mean, obviously." She glanced at Semaya. Semaya looked grim. Erik supposed that the deaths of more than forty thousand innocent parren civilians might have that affect on even the most impassive of these people. "Being an autocratic government like all parren governments, they can try and hush it up if they want to. Elsium administration want to. But Tobenrah won't let them.

"The autonomy of the sector governments is important to parren. In House Harmony, the Togreth enforce those rules, and the division of powers. But Tobenrah has not just House Harmony space to worry about, it's his responsibility to protect *all* parren space. If he fails that, all parren turn on him — all the other four houses. So he's trying to tell the truth, but the local government aren't happy with that…"

"How many ships does Tobenrah have?" Erik cut in. It didn't take an expert on parren to see where this was going. Suddenly the reason for all the high tension and military overflights seemed clear, and it wasn't just the presence of the *UFS Phoenix*, or the human assault shuttle landed on the steps of parliament.

"Not enough," Lisbeth said worriedly. "For the Elsium government, admitting what happened in Brehn System will be the end of them. What you saw out there on the steps… we were all watching until the drones fell, and…"

"That guy who crashed the drones and was murdered," said Trace. "He was a local government plant?"

Lisbeth nodded. "Yes. They don't want anyone talking about Brehn System or deepynines. They'd rather pretend it didn't happen."

"Well they're going to find out," Erik said grimly. "Because I won't be the slightest bit surprised if the deepynines follow us. They only backed off because they were massively outnumbered. When more of their ships arrive, they may come."

"There are more than twenty House Harmony warships in this system," Semaya said disbelievingly. *"Our reports are that there were three alien ships in Brehn System, at the very most."*

"If they double that number," Erik retorted, "they could take your twenty and more." Semaya looked as though she didn't know whether to believe him.

"Erik, we've got more immediate problems than deepynines," Lisbeth insisted. "Tobenrah and Gesul suspect that Aristan is moving to support the local government, against Tobenrah."

Erik stared. "To what extent? Militarily?"

Lisbeth shrugged helplessly. "We don't know. If Aristan's ships, and the local government's, all join forces against Tobenrah and Gesul, then we're outnumbered… what is it Semaya? Twenty-five to six?" Semaya still looked reluctant. "Semaya, you have to trust him. He's the *least* of your problems, and he could help."

"Twenty-five to six," Semaya agreed, reluctantly. That made thirty-one — considerably more than what Semaya had initially said. *"Seven, if Phoenix joins us."*

Ah, thought Erik. Now we come to it. His mind raced. "Okay, first thing," he said. "Let's clear this up. Gesul is working with Tobenrah?"

"Yes," said Lisbeth. "Tobenrah would rather see Gesul as the head of the Domesh, obviously. Gesul has no interest in taking power for the Domesh. He believes that the division of parren among different houses and denominations is the natural state of things. He says there's always been parren like Aristan, thinking that one faction should rule over all the others. It causes disaster, and Gesul wants no part of it."

"Gesul wishes to see your drysine queen," Semaya added. Cautiously, as though still uncertain if she were making a fool of herself by asking. *"He believes that Aristan has misled the Domesh with tales of their history. If he could learn the true history of the parren, and the Domesh, things would be clearer."*

Erik doubted Styx had any more interest in truthful history than Aristan did, but saying so would not help them here. "I'm certain that Styx would be very pleased to meet with Gesul," he lied. "It can be arranged."

Semaya inclined her head. *"Gesul will be pleased to hear it."*

"So what does Tobenrah plan to do?" Erik pressed. Lisbeth and Semaya exchanged glances. The parren made a small gesture toward Lisbeth, and Lisbeth made one of her own, perhaps expressing… gratitude? So well did his little sister understand these strange people, Erik saw with amazement.

"He has sent for reinforcements," said Lisbeth. "Unfortunately, that puts us another ship down… but in the circumstances, reinforcements are the only chance. If Aristan and the Elsium administration join forces together against Tobenrah, and Tobenrah falls…"

"Then Aristan becomes the head of House Harmony," Erik said grimly. And just like that, every parren's worst nightmare, and that of many parren neighbours, would come to pass.

"Exactly," said Lisbeth. "Aristan does not care about deepynines, he wants only power."

"Well deepynines care about him," Erik said with disgust. "And not in any way he'll enjoy, if he deprives them of what they want. I think Tobenrah's smartest move would be to abandon this system, and move to somewhere he's stronger."

"His Fleet advisors agree, but politically he can't. The heads of the big houses must stand before foreign threats. To flee would make him look like a coward, and a traitor to all parren. All House Harmony would suffer humiliation. Blaming the Elsium administration won't help because they're House Harmony too, which only makes Harmony look worse. He's trapped."

"Look, we can hold Aristan," Trace said with calm deliberation, a finger point-down on the deck for emphasis. "He has to move before Tobenrah's reinforcements arrive. But he wants the data-core, and we've got it. He does not want us destroyed… or at least, not until he has his prize. If we delay him that, he will not strike."

"Unless he decides he'd rather see everything we have destroyed instead of letting it fall into Tobenrah's hands," Erik reminded her of her earlier warning.

"Well I'm pretty sure he's not just going to let you sit on the steps of Parliament indefinitely," said Lisbeth. "I was assured by Gesul's military commanders that there are ways of removing this shuttle without you being able to get a shot off first." She looked questioningly at Erik. Erik remained noncommittal, with the parren watching. But Lisbeth knew him well enough to see his lack of argument. "The reason Aristan or the Elsium Administration don't do it is because it would look bad. *Phoenix* has gained some fame in the Spiral, which parren normally wouldn't care about if it doesn't happen in parren space… but now you've given Aristan a humiliation, and he's even admitted so by challenging you to a catharan. Which you threw back in his face, quite spectacularly." She glanced over her shoulder, as though trying to catch Timoshene's eye, but he was too far back. "Some of us were quite impressed. So you have their attention now, you've made a statement of power and prowess, and it demands a similar display in full view of cameras. Simply dropping a missile on you from altitude would be a very poor show, they'd all be humiliated for not matching the spirit of the challenge."

"Then the next move is his," said Erik. "We've got days to wait until reinforcements arrive, maybe weeks, and we've got plenty of food and water. We declare we will fight with Tobenrah and Gesul, and we ensure Aristan can't move against you, because he can't see us destroyed as well. But we will require terms from Tobenrah."

Semaya inclined her head, as though having expected nothing else. *"What terms?"*

Erik thought about it. Safe passage from parren space, was his first answer… but that seemed an option woefully short of the opportunity being offered here. An alliance, with the head of one of the five great parren houses. And possibly sealed in blood, if the worst came to the worst… in which case none of them might survive it, but it was the best chance they'd had in as far as he could remember.

"Alliance," he said. "Against the deepynines, and their alo allies." Semaya gazed at him, indigo eyes unreadable. "You have seen the threat they pose. Parren have died in their thousands. All parren are at risk. *UFS Phoenix* can prepare all parren to meet this threat. And we can assist Tobenrah to make House Harmony the great protectors of all the parren people. The other four houses will be envious."

Lisbeth's eyes flashed at him, somewhere between a faintly impressed smile, and a warning of going too far. Semaya merely inclined her head. *"We shall convey your offer. Should these terms be granted, Phoenix will fight with Tobenrah and Gesul?"*

"We will," said Erik. And he refrained from swearing on his honour, given his difficulties with that word, among parren.

Semaya rose, and Lisbeth followed. *"We will convey this offer to Tobenrah and Gesul."*

Erik realised that no sooner had he said hello to Lisbeth, he had to say goodbye once more. But she had an authority now, among these people, and he could not spoil that by hugging her once more. It was becoming abundantly clear that parren didn't do that… at least, not at these high levels of power. Lisbeth smiled at him, eyes shining. Erik nodded back… and realised how proud he was. In truth, he didn't know if *he* could have done what she'd done, having turned a position of such powerlessness, into this. Advisor to one of the most powerful rulers in all parren space. He was certain that pride showed in his eyes.

As they turned to leave, Timoshene paused to confront Trace, a dark-robed sentinel, and a full head taller than her. *"This thing,"* he said, via the translator. *"Before your shuttle. This move. An extraordinary judgement of balance. It was seen by many. Some will not be impressed, but many were. You have my appreciation."*

Trace inclined her head, serenely. And looked askance at Lisbeth as she intervened to explain. "We were all watching when you shot their challenger," she said. "They were astonished... parren couldn't do it, you see. Parren have to worry about proper form, because these are contests of appearance more than results. A parren leader has to worry about losing newly-phased supporters to his opponents if he behaves badly. But you don't have to worry about that, because you're human, so you play by different rules. And Aristan's people couldn't wrap their heads around it until you did it... and then, there was nothing they could do. If they try to shoot you, PH-1 annihilates them, and if they kill the Captain in a firefight, you fire a nuke that destroys Parliament."

"Maybe this is why parren would rather remain alone," Erik observed. "A rules-based society only works when everyone observes the rules. Aliens screw everything up."

Lisbeth leaned forward conspiratorially, a hand on Trace's armoured shoulder. "Gesul laughed for a minute straight, when they left," she whispered. "I mean, parren don't laugh! Or not much, anyway. The funny thing is, breaching the rules is supposed to lose you followers, you're not parren so you have no followers to lose... so the joke's on Aristan! And you actually *gained* in their eyes, Major. Gesul said it was the most well-played he's seen a catharan in ages."

It wasn't just in confidence and dress that Lisbeth had changed, Erik thought. Not long ago, the sight of a man shot in cold blood would have horrified her, alien or otherwise. Now, she found the amusement of the culture that had caused it.

CHAPTER 22

Lisbeth stared out the window of the cruiser, at the red-tiled rooves of Chirese, and the straight, gridwork streets, baking in the hot sun. Chirese was a mostly administrative city, and traffic was light, particularly in the daytime. In the cool of evening the markets would open, where most parren still preferred to shop the old-fashioned way, in communal gatherings of sights, sounds and smells, unchanged since well before spacetravel. Lisbeth pondered how tavalai worshipped everything old, yet lived utterly modern lives, recalling their past only in symbolic reference… while parren continued many customs unchanged since ancient times. Chah'nas had little interest in their past, yet still retained some old customs, in modified forms. Humans were the only truly 'new' species in the Spiral. The only species unburdened by the long, continuing strands of historical memory… and yet, forever scarred by their loss.

The cruiser came lower as it approached the capitol palace, and Lisbeth saw armoured vehicles and parren soldiers on guard at the gates. Military weapons, with the firepower to wage wars rather than settle political grudges. Traffic passed in the street, but the cruiser was passing too fast for Lisbeth to see how the parren locals were taking that military presence. Surely everyone had heard of events in the Kunadeen. Lisbeth knew a lot more about how parren politics worked at the higher levels, in House Harmony at least, but she still had little clue how it all related to the lives of ordinary parren. Did the average parren here in Chirese have an opinion on what had happened to Gesul and his followers in House Harmony's highest corridors of power? Did the rigid loyalty displayed by those in the leaders' most immediate service — the household guard, the civil servants — translate to a similar fanatical following down there? Or did the average parren simply keep his head down, and go about his daily life in the hope that these tumults would not touch him directly?

The cruiser landed in a courtyard amid arches, beside a water fountain that looked invitingly cool in the heat. Lisbeth climbed out after Timoshene and Semaya, several more guards making a formation to accompany their march across the courtyard as the cruiser lifted once more into the air, engines howling. There were heavily armoured parren here also, standing guard in the arches that flanked the courtyard. These were from Tobenrah's flagship — parren marines, or their equivalent. Warriors loyal to Tobenrah, in the service of the Kundiam, as House Harmony's supreme authority of the Kunadeen was called.

Their armour looked good, but Lisbeth possessed enough technical knowledge to suspect it was not quite the equal of human marine armour. It was one of those things that humans simply took for granted — humanity had some of the best weapons in the Spiral, and was intensely proud of the edge it gave them over all potential rivals. Few stopped to think about it any more than that... like how parren had been in space, and in various wars, for forty thousand years longer than humans, and were no pushover when it came to high tech. It was only being out here, and seeing the age and power of parren civilisation, that had caused Lisbeth to think how odd it was, that humanity should have leaped ahead of such an advanced and capable people, in so little time. Humans did not want to think about how much help they'd had, in high-tech gifts from the alo, and the chah'nas. And most of the chah'nas tech, it was widely suspected, was actually alo tech as well.

Hacksaw tech, *Phoenix* now suspected. Deepynine tech. And even these gifts, it seemed, were not the best quality available.

Past the arches was an entrance to a great hall, clad in white tile and cooled by an airconditioned breeze. Administrators and staff hurried about, and ahead, beneath the great, high-valued dome where two great halls met, a procession blocked much of the way. Green-glad Togreth stood before some black-robed Domesh, and argued with blue-clad officials of Tobenrah's Kunadim administration. By parren standards, the discussion was quite animated, with much waving of hands and scrolls. By tavalai standards, it was impossibly elegant and deferential.

"Those are Aristan's people, yes?" Lisbeth asked her escorts as they approached. "Is he moving another motion?"

"Against Gesul," Timoshene said grimly. *"Tobenrah has granted Gesul's forces protection under the powers of the Kunadim. Aristan is challenging the legality of that protection."*

"What happens if he wins?"

"Gesul will be forced to either flee, or submit to sudra."

Lisbeth blinked. 'Sudra' was essentially to throw oneself at the feet of a superior, and hope for mercy. In the case of Gesul, with Aristan, it didn't seem likely. "What happens to Gesul's followers if that happens?"

"Either another will rise to take Gesul's place, or many will fold into Aristan's camp. Either way, should it happen, Gesul's time is likely finished." And as his loyal servants, Timoshene and Semaya's time too, Lisbeth suspected. And likely her own, as well.

Lisbeth noticed many of the dark-robed Domesh watching her as she passed, sombre stares within hoods and veils. Aristan would brook no argument, it was clear. Under him, the Domesh would be all one thing, or nothing at all. Those eyes upon her held no particular malevolence, yet somehow Lisbeth found that the most frightening thing of all. The Domesh did not seek to stop Gesul asking questions from any particular hatred or ideological conviction that a human might understand. They sought to restore order for its own sake, and the simple continuities it created. Gesul was a tall blade of grass on a well-mowed field. That he may have been the *best* blade of grass did not matter to these parren one bit.

"Seems an enormous waste of time given Aristan's trying to join with the local government and will just attack us anyway," Lisbeth muttered. "Say, what's happened to the Council of Truthtellers? Are they down yet?"

Tobenrah's Council of Truthtellers had tried to broadcast to the system their tale of the deepynine attack in Brehn System. There had been vision from *Phoenix*, of Mylor Station, and the deepynine ships that had done it. But the Elsium Administration had been jamming those transmissions, so the Council had taken a heavily guarded shuttle down to the planet, where broadcasts would be much harder to jam without shutting down the entire planetary network.

"Yes, they came down a short while ago," Semaya admitted, glasses on and keeping a close watch on all sorts of encrypted data that Tobenrah's higher advisors were feeding to her. *"But now there is jamming here too. Planetary coms are being disrupted, but there seems to be no way to gain a clear transmission."*

It was a problem unimagined by humans. On Homeworld, even under Fleet's strict secrecy laws, there would always be some underground daredevil prepared to break the law, spread classified data, then cover his tracks. On parren worlds, there were none. Defiance was only conducted by leaders, not followers.

Suddenly Lisbeth realised. "Semaya, I have a friend, up on *Phoenix*, who could probably help you to get a clear transmission."

Semaya glanced at her as they walked. *"A friend?"* With cool parren skepticism, and perhaps a little alarm. Lisbeth was certain she understood.

"A friend, yes."

"I am uncertain that Tobenrah will like assistance from this friend."

"Well you can tell Tobenrah that if he wants to tell the population about the deepynine threat, he may not have another choice."

They passed more hurrying officials, and others locked in serious conversation, clustered in small groups, watched by armed guards. There were even armoured marines in here as well. Lisbeth wasn't certain of the logic to that — surely if fighting so heavy that it required heavy armour broke out inside the capitol palace, the battle was already lost? But then, there was the parren penchant for internal betrayals and treacheries to consider.

"So if Tobenrah can't use coms," Lisbeth pressed, "how is he talking to the government building?" Tobenrah had declared Kunadim control over the planet and system, and thus this entire sector of space, including Brehn System. It had been necessary, he'd declared, given the local government's refusal to cooperate. A whole team of Kunadim administrators, with their security, had headed up to the Parliament in the last half-hour, she'd discovered as soon as she'd left PH-1 on the Parliament steps.

"There is a laser communication facility on the roof," Semaya explained, pointing upward. *"And the Parliament is on a hill, so there is a clear line of sight. But the Parliament are refusing to hand over any communications codes for local networks, and the Parliament itself is now being jammed."*

What a mess, Lisbeth thought as they entered the central atrium, beneath a dome even higher than the last, bright beams of sunlight spearing from small windows overhead. She placed the AR glasses on her face as they climbed the wide stairway toward the upper administrative levels, where higher parren office was always located… and immediately there came a familiar voice in her glasses-linked ear-uplink.

"Hello Lisbeth," said Styx. *"It is better that you don't enquire how this communication is taking place, the relays through civilian networks are quite complex, and involve quite a lot of illegality that could place Phoenix in difficulty with her hosts, I am sure. There is also approximately a three second delay as a result of all those relays, so I will get straight to the question. The enemies of Tobenrah are jamming his communications, both at your current location, and in the Parliament. Do you judge it wise to unjam them?"*

Lisbeth took a deep breath, ignoring Semaya breaking into conversation with someone else, querying an urgent matter. *Phoenix* was asking *her*. She doubted it was purely Styx's idea — Styx was very reluctant to intervene in the affairs of organics, and would only make a major intervention like this with the approval of *Phoenix* bridge crew. With Erik on the planet, that would mean second-shift ran the bridge — Lieutenant Commander Draper as acting-captain, and Lieutenant Angela Lassa on Coms.

"I think I should ask Tobenrah first," Lisbeth replied, getting a look from Timoshene as they climbed the stairs. She indicated that she was on coms. "I think he will have some discomfort with these methods, but he may not have a choice. And I think you'd better ask the Captain himself… unjamming transmissions may have the effect of escalating political tensions, perhaps even accelerating any military action by the local government and Aristan against

Tobenrah." And she waited, as she mounted the next flight to the second level, for Styx to hear, and then reply.

Seven seconds later, she did. *"Lisbeth, Commander Draper has authorised me to inform you that Phoenix can disable many of Aristan's and the local government's vessels without firing a shot. Aristan has doubtless informed them what happened to his own ships at Cephilae, but that will not help them, as neither he nor they have any technological means of defending themselves. In this proximity to a civilian planetary communications system, even less so, given their additional connections and thus vulnerabilities."*

It began to dawn on Lisbeth precisely what Styx was saying. Planetary communications networks were all interconnected, obviously. Those networks were mind-bogglingly complicated, and possessed so many barriers against hacking to make the prospect of more than denting them unlikely, for the most sophisticated known technologies in the Spiral. And Styx could carve through all of those barriers like a hot knife through butter. Could probably even take control of the entire network, and make it dance to her tune. Advanced as the parren no doubt considered their tech, to Styx it was a pile of obsolete junk. Defeating their security would be like Lisbeth solving problems in a children's puzzlebook.

"I will pass on this offer to Tobenrah also," she replied. "Thank you *Phoenix*, is there anything else?" She was careful not to say Styx's name out loud. She'd spoken the name to Gesul, and while Gesul did not seem like one to gossip, it was possible others had heard the name by now, or would simply guess.

"That is all, Lisbeth. I am just a communications icon away if you need me."

"Your 'friend' on Phoenix?" Semaya asked, as they cleared the top steps, and headed along a less-populated hall. Very little got past Semaya, Lisbeth was noticing.

"Yes," said Lisbeth. "With a message for Tobenrah. I must speak with him."

When they'd passed a final layer of security and administrative assistants into Tobenrah's chamber, Lisbeth found that the floor before Tobenrah was already occupied. Tobenrah sat slightly higher, on a raised wooden platform and cushions, while parren in various colours and styles of tunic and robe knelt before him, and discussed in respectful Porgesh too fast and overlapping for Lisbeth's translator to follow. Semaya made her way past the watching observers, advisors and guards that lined the walls, before finally indicating a clear space for Lisbeth to stand in, with Semaya and Timoshene on either side.

Tobenrah's eyes flicked her way, in mid-conversation with the other four parren, before returning to the conversation. Lisbeth leaned to Semaya. "What's going on?" she whispered.

"The four house leaders," Semaya replied, in a similar whisper. *"Fortitude, Acquisitive, Creative and Enquiry."*

Lisbeth stared at her, then back at the floor. There being five parren houses, each house typically held twenty percent of the population, on average, in any given system. Drezen System, Lisbeth knew, was closer to thirty percent House Harmony. That left the other seventy percent of the population spread between the remaining four houses. Parren from the ruling house almost never mistreated the followers of the other four houses, but neither did they invite them to participate in the higher levels of governance. So what were these four doing here?

"They're the yural?" Lisbeth asked, recalling this particular lesson. "The shepherds?" Semaya nodded, having learned that gesture from Lisbeth. If you were a regular parren, on a world like Elsium, and not of the ruling house, you still had someone to follow. Protocol said you must obey your ruler and his administration, even if not of your house, but neither could that ruler expect much more from you than to pay taxes and make orderly conduct. Cooperation from the non-house population in larger ventures, like joining the military, or participating in security matters, was generally out, and non-house rulers would not stretch their authority by demanding it.

A House Fortitude parren on Elsium had a Fortitude civilian administration to follow, lead by the Fortitude yural. The yural was generally not a political figure or person of ambition, given how completely vulnerable he was to assassination from a planetary ruler who found him threatening. Rather, the yural was usually an uncharismatic bureaucrat appointed by the federal house leadership — each house's equivalent of the Kunadeen. Lisbeth had discovered that her translator found the Porgesh word 'yural' roughly equivalent with the human word 'shepherd', as both derived from the guardians of defenseless livestock, in pre-technological times. Parren from the non-ruling house were considered 'sheep', to be mustered, grazed, and occasionally shorn or milked. Among parren, it was not the insult it would have seemed to most humans. Yural would never allow their lambs to be slaughtered, and many parren were vegetarian anyhow.

The yural's actual job, Lisbeth had thought when explained to her, was something like what the head ambassador would do in an embassy — ensure the rights of his house members, and represent them in any legal matters against the ruling authorities. There were also cultural matters pertaining to each house, involving longstanding, house-specific traditions, that the yural would oversee, and the recording of identifications and phase-changes for the matter of census — a very important thing for each house, considering how the Jusica noted the census changes brought about by phase-shift when considering how and when the rulership of parren houses and denominations would shift from one house to another.

"What are they doing here?" Lisbeth pressed.

"If one would listen," Semaya said with impeccable politeness, *"one might discover."*

Lisbeth tried, but formal parren conversation was far different from the one-on-one variety they usually had with her. Parren did not always address matters directly with each other, for one thing, but rather settled for oblique references or euphemisms that a human, or her AI translator, would miss completely. With an alien guest they were deliberately blunt, to avoid misunderstanding. Here, she listened to as many words as the translator could catch, and tried hard to read between the lines.

Certainly it was a great breach of protocol for a planetary ruler, to say nothing of the house ruler himself, to convene such a gathering of yural. That it had become politically necessary indicated great weakness on the part of the ruler, and was thus a humiliation. But no one would deny that Tobenrah's position here was weak.

Perhaps that was it, Lisbeth thought. Tobenrah couldn't hide that factional weakness, and so had decided not to try. Instead, he appealed to the greater cause of parren security, in the face of a greater threat. Deepynines, attacking Brehn System, and killing 40,000 parren. He, Tobenrah, was the only one proposing to fight them. The Elsium Administration, and Aristan, were proposing only to gain power for themselves, and nothing more. Perhaps Tobenrah was appealing to them not on the basis of house, as happened in most parren political conversations, but on the basis of parren unity.

Ironically, it occurred to her, parren unity was precisely what Aristan proposed as well... by trying to make everyone into Domesh, in the imagined image of the late and great Drakhil.

When finally the meeting was over, there were more announcements, and some bowing, and finally some differently-robed officials moving amongst the visiting party of yural with smoking containers of incense.

"A cleansing ceremony," Semaya explained, a murmur at Lisbeth's side. *"To mix the houses, before a Ruler of House Harmony, is to create an impurity."* Lisbeth saw a lot of very solemn faces among Tobenrah's assembled advisors, and some grim expressions too. No doubt they thought he debased himself with such a meeting.

"I sometimes get the feeling," Lisbeth murmured back, "that parren are far more comfortable with a human like me than they are with parren from other houses."

Semaya smiled, faintly. *"It does not require the cleansing ceremony, no. To mix the houses, to mix the minds of the five phases, is impure in the karan."* That was what parren called the great, collected lore of relationships between the houses. Even today there were great monasteries devoted to its study.

"So for a leader to mix with aliens is not unclean," Lisbeth said drily. "But for him to mix with House Fortitude is?"

Semaya gave her a sideways look. *"Humanity was once so divided. It took near-genocide to unite those of you who remained, and make you one. These ways of ours are not truly so strange, it is rather that humans have forgotten who they once were."* And Lisbeth found that she could not think of anything to say to that.

Then she caught sight of Gesul, moving past Tobenrah's advisors to kneel beside his ruler on the matting, and murmur, and indicate to Semaya. Tobenrah looked, with that displeased glare of powerful parren, as the yural filed from the room, and kept any hint of an opinion from their faces. Tobenrah gave an order, which two more officials repeated in loud unison, and clapped their hands. To Lisbeth's surprise, everyone else began to follow the yural from the room.

Places were presented on the mat before the Harmony lord, and Lisbeth went with Semaya to kneel, heart beating a little faster now, in what was surely not a safe situation. Tobenrah was a powerful man put in a dangerous situation. Such men could see lives ended with a command, and desperate circumstances would make those commands more likely. Once knelt, Lisbeth gazed at the matting just before Tobenrah's robed knees. Parren did not require a deep bow, considering posture too important. Lisbeth concentrated on hers… a losing battle, as she could never match the grace of a willow like Semaya.

Gesul took his place at Tobenrah's left. Lisbeth risked a glance at several advisors who remained, standing against the rear wall. They did not seem pleased.

"Lisbeth Debogande," said Tobenrah. *"You have returned."* You did not rejoin your brother, he meant. Lisbeth had gained the impression that some parren expected her to, at the first opportunity.

"Tobenrah-sa. I serve Gesul." Tobenrah stared at her, as though in some offence. Against the wall, advisors shifted, as though unsettled. Lisbeth wondered if she'd said the wrong thing. A glance at Gesul showed only his eyes within hood and veil, calm and blue.

"Your brother," said Tobenrah. *"What does he say?"*

"Tobenrah-sa, *Phoenix* will fight with you against all enemies, if her single condition is granted."

"What condition?"

"That House Harmony will join with *Phoenix* in formal alliance against the deepynines and the alo."

One of the advisors did not like that, and spoke out of turn. *"Phoenix is a single ship,"* Lisbeth's earpiece translated. *"She has no allegiance to humanity, her own people have cast her out. An entire house cannot make allegiance with a single ship."* His voice conveyed scorn, unmistakable even in an alien tongue.

"This is not an alliance of equals," Lisbeth explained, trying to keep her breathing calm. Perhaps it was too late, and she'd screwed this up already with awkward phrasing. "*Phoenix* merely requests that the steps be taken against the deepynines and alo beyond any present action. That House Harmony will not simply deal with this current incursion, and then retreat. This is an ongoing threat, Tobenrah-sa, of the gravest kind. All of the Spiral's people need to unite to protect themselves from this threat. *Phoenix* asks merely that you agree, and if so, *Phoenix* promises to be your strongest ally in this struggle."

"And in return, Phoenix will fight with House Harmony against the treacherous Aristan and his domestic allies?"

"Yes, Tobenrah-sa. That was Captain Debogande's promise to you."

Tobenrah said nothing. Eyes half-lidded as he considered many things, and the hush grew longer. Lisbeth wondered if he were having an uplinked conversation with his advisors — silent, where no one else could hear it.

"Your friends on Phoenix are quite like a tobachi," Tobenrah said finally. A tobachi, Lisbeth knew, was a popular style of parren theatre. Its form was highly melodramatic, with many set-pieces leading to improbable climaxes, frequently bloody. *"They meet Aristan's challenge to catharan by landing an assault transport on the steps of Parliament, and forcing him to challenge in full view. With nuclear missiles, no less. You know your brother, Lisbeth Debogande. Would he fire those missiles?"*

Lisbeth met Tobenrah's eyes as firmly as she dared. "Given no other choice?" she said. "Yes."

"Thus likely killing all of us here as well," said Tobenrah. *"Even should the warheads be tactical, we are still likely within range. This seems drastic."*

"Humans are not parren, Tobenrah-sa. It is not our preference to solve small conflicts with violence. Only large ones. With parren, I find it is rather the reverse."

Tobenrah's eyes flashed. *"And yet Phoenix is here. Victim of a very small, internal human war."*

"That is also an extension of a larger war," Lisbeth completed. "And I never said those warheads are tactical."

A stare from Tobenrah. *"There are a million parren in this city,"* he said coldly. *"Your brother would kill them all?"*

"My brother will win," Lisbeth said firmly. "Of that you can be certain. The fate of the Spiral depends upon his doing so."

"Odd," said Tobenrah. *"That is what Aristan says."*

Lisbeth took a deep breath, mind racing. "Tobenrah-sa. I bring an offer from *Phoenix*. The capability to disable many of the ships arrayed against you in orbit. Aristan's and the local government's both."

"How many?"

"It is unclear. Perhaps most. We did the same to Aristan at Pashan and Cephilae. He could not prevent it then, and he cannot prevent it now. Also, *Phoenix* possesses the capability to deliver the planetary communications network, in the event of any conflict."

Tobenrah's eyes were wider now, as he grasped what she was saying. *"No,"* he said darkly. *"You will not unleash that thing, that monstrosity, here in parren space."*

"The monstrosities are coming, Tobenrah-sa. They have already killed thousands of parren, and they are many. We have just one, and it serves us... and you, should you wish it. With that power, you can defeat Aristan, and then the deepynines as well."

Tobenrah shook his head, holding up a finger as though arriving finally at the central point. *"They would come* here*?"* he asked incredulously. *"They, who have hidden in alo space for all these years? Who have hidden the fact of their survival for far, far longer, and who fear that discovery above all else... they would* *attack us openly, here? Revealing themselves not only to the parren, but to all the Spiral? To humanity? To the tavalai?*

"No no, Lisbeth Debogande... these deepynines of yours, they are not here to fight me or my people. They are here to fight you. They came to Brehn System, and killed Mylor Station, in pursuit of Phoenix. Or rather, in pursuit of that monstrosity that you hold on board... that drysine *monstrosity that inflicted upon the parren our worst ever calamities, billions of us killed. And now you ask us to fight with you, against* them?*"*

Lisbeth felt the terror building. She was about to lose this argument, with catastrophic results. Another time, she might have panicked. But now she felt the fear turning to anger, and leaned forward on her knees. "That thing in *Phoenix*'s hold is the only thing that can save your rulership," she said coldly. "The deepynines chase it because they fear it. They fear it could destroy them, and they will do anything to destroy it first, even if it means revealing themselves. Understand what that means, Tobenrah-sa. It means that they no longer fear to be revealed. It means they're almost ready. There's only one drysine that *Phoenix* knows of. There could be *millions* of deepynines. And you now propose to make cause against the only thing that could stop them?"

Tobenrah looked almost frightened. So did his advisors. For parren of the harmony phase, it was rare. *"What war have you started?"* Tobenrah muttered. *"What horror have you brought upon my people?"*

"The war was already upon us," said Lisbeth. "*Phoenix* just drew back the curtain and revealed it. The only question now, Tobenrah-sa, is whether you propose to be remembered as the man who helped to win that war, or as the man who lost it before it even started."

Skah liked wearing his EVA suit. The humans called it that because the human letters stood for something called Extra... Extra...

"Mummy?" he asked, waddling back to his quarters in the fat, bulky suit. "What does EVA stand for?"

"You asked me not long ago," said his mother, still wearing her flight suit. Lately she'd been wearing it a lot, because of the high alert. It meant she might have to go running to Midships at any moment. "Have you forgotten already?"

"But it's a stupid name," Skah complained, pausing as Mummy stood aside for some hurrying spacers carrying repair gear. "It's another acronym." *That* word he remembered. On a military ship, listening to the crew talking, it sometimes seemed every second word was an acronym. The two kuhsi spoke Garkhan, the only time in a rotation they got the chance to do so. Except for the human words that now peppered their speech.

"Extra Vehicular Activity," Mummy pronounced some of those human words now. "E-V-A." She looked tired, ears drooping, eyes heavy-lidded. Everyone looked that way lately. Nearby, some more crew were shouting on another repair job. Skah tried to keep track of which corridors he should avoid, but the repairs kept moving, following the complicated internal systems in the walls. But most of the crew cylinder seemed to be fixed now.

"What does 'vehicular' mean?" Skah asked.

"It's the same as 'vehicle'. 'Extra vehicular' means 'outside a vehicle'."

"But we're not in a vehicle. We're in a starship."

"It means the same thing," said Mummy, ushering Skah to take a left into their home corridor — F-2, it was called, meaning the 'F' circumference corridor, on the second level. Directly alongside their home quarters was an emergency equipment locker.

Skah entered, and found it occupied by two spacers — Bilai and Stenhauser, Skah had seen them around the corridors a lot, fixing things. Both wore heavy jumpsuits, and had removed helmets and facemasks, now stowing toolbags from their webbing into the secure lockers for second-shift to access when shift-change came. Both men looked exhausted, faces sweaty, hair matted. Stenhauser had some fingers taped beneath his work gloves, where it looked like he'd burned them. It always impressed Skah to see how the crew did not stop working just because they'd been hurt. It made him want to be brave like that too.

"Hey Furball," said Bilai, who was a smaller man, and black, while Stenhauser was brown, and huge. "You like that suit, huh?"

"I don't want to take it off," Skah took the opportunity to complain again to Mummy, this time in English. "Can I wear it a bit longer?"

"No, because now you're going to bed, and you can't wear it in bed," said his mother. The spacers grinned, continuing to stow gear in the bigger equipment lockers. Some of the things in there looked scary, like tools to cut through steel. Mummy tapped their own locker. "Now show ne you know the conbination."

Skah took a moment to unclip one big glove, then pressed his fingertip to the reader. It blinked, then showed numbers. Skah input the code, and the locker clicked open. "I had suit driw," Skah explained to the spacers.

"Suit drill," Stenhauser said to Bilai, in case he hadn't understood.

"That's what I said!" Skah insisted, working the three-point chest release until it finally went clack! and the internal fasteners loosened. That let him work on the waist release, as the suit had to break into two halves for him to get out. Mummy watched impatiently, not helping. "I have to get in and out of the suit, on ny own. And I have to know how to nake the air work, and the conputer."

"Yeah, well that's really important stuff, kid," Stenhauser agreed. "You listen to your mother, that suit could save your life."

"She didn't do it," said Skah, struggling to get the waist latches up, so he could grip them. "Randaw did." Spacer Randall was one of his friends from Midships, and had offered to take him through suit procedures when he had time — which had been a few hours ago, after late lessons. Then Mummy had come in her flight suit from working on her shuttle in Midships, and had sat with him at dinner in Bay Six. That wasn't far from the kitchen, a storage room where some screens had been set up to show entertainment. The crew had been watching television of a parren play while they were eating dinner. Skah had had no idea what the play was about, and the humans didn't seem to know either. Skah had asked Mummy, and Mummy had said everyone found the parren very strange, and were interested to know more about them. But then everyone had looked at Skah eating dinner in his big EVA suit, and found that funny. Skah had made faces at them while eating, and they'd made faces back, and said funny things.

"I've been busy," Mummy said shortly. "Now, do a ground exit. Lie down and show how you get out of the suit without the harness to hewp you."

"Lieutenant, where did you get the kids' suit?" Stenhauser asked. Skah still thought it strange to hear crew call Mummy that. But she was official crew now, and had a big rank and everything. You needed that, he gathered, if you flew an assault shuttle. Assault shuttles were important.

"One of the barabo stations," Mummy explained. "I forget which. Suit for barabo kid."

"I was looking at the features before," Bilai agreed. "It's solid tech, barabo make some good stuff. Just be a little careful… I noticed, the override commands on voice activation? They're a little sensitive, has someone shown you?"

The tired spacer took another five minutes from his schedule to explain the issue. After that, Skah went with Mummy to the bathroom, which humans called 'the head', which was one of those dumb English things Skah still couldn't figure the sense of. None of the humans seemed to know why it was called that either, when he asked them. In the cramped little cubicle he took his shower. Mummy did not, as she needed to go back to work.

But first, she took him into their quarters, dried him off properly, then insisted he get into a clean jumpsuit, all ready for an emergency with flashlight, oxygen mask and tube, first aid and other things in the bedside webbing, prepared to clip to his jumpsuit when he got up. Mummy tucked him in beneath the blankets and netting, and Skah grabbed his AR glasses from their secure pouch, and put them on.

"Not too long on the glasses," Mummy told him sternly. "The bridge can see if you're on them too long. Someone will tell me." Skah nodded. Mummy didn't like that gesture much — kuhsi didn't use it, she said. But Skah couldn't see how that mattered to *him*. "You remember to thank Spacer Bilai again when you see him. He was very tired and sore, and probably wanted to go and have his dinner and a shower, but he took that time to explain the suit for us. We're so lucky to be on *Phoenix*, Skah. Never forget just how lucky."

Mummy told him that every day. Skah nodded dutifully. "Mummy, are the deepynines going to chase us here?"

"Probably," said Mummy. "But *Phoenix* is powerful. That makes us powerful, too." She bent and nuzzled his ear. "Now not too long on the glasses, only ten minutes, understand?"

"Mummy, why are the Captain and the Major down on the planet?"

"Adult business, Skah." She stood up to go. "The Captain and the Major are the greatest warriors of all the humans. They're our clan leaders now. Always trust your clan."

She hit the door, and left. The door closed, and Skah was alone in the little steel room with the whine of ship systems, the gentle hush of air from the ventilation grille, and the steady thump of the rotation crew cylinder for company. Occasionally, from somewhere distant, he could hear the dull howl and rattle of powertools — repair crews still working somewhere, fixing things.

Skah knew some of the *Phoenix* crew didn't like him being on the ship. They liked *him*, he was pretty sure, they just didn't think it was a good place for a kid. He'd asked Mummy, but Mummy didn't like to talk about it. Mummy said kuhsi needed a clan… and without *Phoenix*… well, again, Mummy didn't like to talk about it, and he'd learned better than to ask. They just didn't have anywhere else to go.

But everything was getting very dangerous now. Skah was young, but he could feel it. Could see it in the eyes of the crew, in the way everyone was more tired than he remembered. He could see it in the repair crews. *Phoenix* hadn't been damaged like this before, and these deepynines, whatever they were up to, seemed like a very dangerous enemy. Sometimes Skah got scared thinking about it, but then, he couldn't really remember a time when he hadn't been scared. At least on *Phoenix* he had lots of friends, and if there was anything that made the fear go away, it was having fun with friends. Particularly friends who were fierce warriors, and would protect him from deepynines.

He blinked on the glasses icons, and saw the dots light up alongside the names of his friends. That meant some of them were free, at least. Jessica was down on the planet with the Major, and most of his Midships friends were busy operating drones to help Engineering fix the damage from the hits *Phoenix* had taken. But some others had a little spare time in the last few cycles, at least. He was getting different teachers for lessons again, and that was fun. He loved Mummy, but Mummy could get very strict and serious with lessons. The humans were more fun, and he thought he probably got better at lessons when it was fun.

A new, familiar icon appeared on his glasses, and he blinked on it. *"Hello Skah,"* said Styx. Styx was speaking Garkhan. She'd learned it some days ago and had just started speaking it to Skah, with almost no accent. Skah had asked how, and Styx had said languages weren't hard, they were just data, like maths. Skah had no idea how language could be maths, but further questions hadn't brought him any closer to understanding it.

"Hello Styx. Mummy says I have to go to sleep. Do you ever sleep?"

"No," Styx admitted. *"But some parts of my brain shut down sometimes to regenerate and cross-reference new data. I think that's a little bit like sleep."*

"But your whole brain doesn't sleep?" Skah asked. This was why he liked talking to Styx. Styx was fascinating. "Just bits of your brain?"

"In a rotating cycle, yes."

"I wish my brain could do that. Then I could stay up late, but still sleep."

"I'm not sure organics will ever work that way. Skah, would you like to play a game?"

"What sort of game?"

"A fun game."

"Mummy says I should go to sleep," Skah said dubiously.

"I know. Would you like to play a game anyway?"

CHAPTER 23

Trace awoke to Lieutenant Hausler edging past her observer chair at the rear of the cockpit.

"Sorry Major," he said, climbing awkwardly into the pilot's chair, through a gap designed to be accessed mostly in zero-G. "It's nearly dawn. Breakfast's up if you want some."

Dawn, Trace thought sleepily. Strange concept that was, to someone who'd spent most of the last six months on a starship. She levered herself up to peer out the long forward canopy. Beyond the trees that flanked either side of the great stairs to the Elsium Parliament, a faint, blue glow could be seen against distant hills. Sometime during the night, the parren must have turned off the stairway lights, and left them all in the dark. A small rebellion, perhaps.

Ensign Yun was now climbing from her front seat of the assault shuttle's long cockpit, a well-practised manoeuvre better suited to smaller women like Yun than a larger man like her pilot. She swung over Hausler's chair, wincing as stiff legs took her weight. Long groundings on alert were hell on pilots — they couldn't spend more than a few minutes out of the cockpit, and now had to sleep in their chairs as well.

"Exercise properly," Trace told her, coming fully awake and stretching in the chair. "Get the blood moving."

"Yeah thanks Major, I got it," said Yun, staggering to the rear. Trace followed. She had numerous tricks to waking up fast, and one of them was to attach herself to an immediate task. Commanding a marine company, there were plenty of those, but few were as entertaining as the chance to rev up some slack spacer who wasn't putting in a full effort.

Yun waited by the door to the tiny toilet cubicle, directly behind the cockpit, and Trace checked her command post just around the corner, where the shuttle's centre core divided the main hold in two at Midships. Finding all in order, Trace flipped down her glasses, blinked an icon to review the night's accumulated messages and reviewable intel, put in one earpiece, then grabbed an overhead locker rim and began doing pullups.

After twenty, she indicated to Yun. "Your turn." The Ensign gave her a look of pure despair. Just crawled from her chair after a many-hour stint, waiting at the toilet door with obvious need, and now she had Major Hardass Thakur telling her this was actually a gym session. Trace couldn't help smiling. "Okay, it can wait till you've had a piss."

"Gee, can it Major?" Already, Private Rolonde was holding Trace's customary morning mug of green tea before her nose — her special blend from the locker, there was always a little on board in case of long stays. This blend had no caffeine, or god forbid, sugar. She needed to be at her peak all day, not just for the next two hours until the caffeine crash.

"Thanks Jess," Trace told her. "What's up?"

"Quiet here," said Rolonde, in a sweaty singlet from her own morning workout, bare arms knotted with even more muscle than Trace. Like a lot of marines, Rolonde had come to the service from being a civilian fitness junkie, and had a body fat percentage that Doc Suelo found borderline alarming for a young woman. "Lots of activity in the town, fair bit up on the hill, no idea what. Constant military flyers and shuttles."

"Are the parren still here?"

"Different parren, I think. They brought breakfast."

A few hundred parren had made their way up the stairs last evening. They had not marched in any formation, nor worn ceremonial robes, nor made any sort of pageantry. They'd simply sat near PH-1, rolled out mats, then laid out some food. Lisbeth had informed them all, via Styx's uplink, that this was a very good and safe sign, as these were not the political operatives they'd been exposed to so far, but ordinary working folk, with no particular driving motivation for anything but a good, safe life.

Tobenrah's Council of Truthtellers, it seemed, had made their announcement about the deepynine attack on Brehn System, and now Tobenrah had talked to the leaders of the four non-Harmony houses in the capitol palace. These parren had responded, and some subsequent conversation revealed that they were very concerned with the deepynine attack, and fearful of what it might mean. They were duty-bound to not oppose the local government, even though it was not of their own houses, but that did not mean they could not show *Phoenix* crew some basic hospitality. These parren had no interest in who ran the local government, they only wanted to be protected from murderous alien machines. The marines had all tried the food, and found it wonderful, as Lisbeth had also promised. The prospect of more for breakfast had made everyone notably happier this morning.

Trace completed her workout, and made sure Ensign Yun joined her for the first part, at least. Then she took a brief shower where marines had converted the water feed with a nozzle designed for the purpose, and a couple of tarps hung for basic privacy — not so much men-from-women, as from the parren civvies now peering in the back, if from a reasonable distance. She took the ammo tray now doubling as a water collector, poured it back into the water receptacle for the shuttle system to reuse, then left it for the next person and changed into her uniform and armour. Whatever was going to happen, everyone seemed convinced it would only happen with some ceremony — there would be no sudden coup out of nowhere, at least. It was possible, of course, that Aristan, the Elsium Administration or Tobenrah would decide to kill PH-1 quickly and risk whatever consequences from *Phoenix*... but either way, it did not require a full alert, as in the latter case they'd be dead too fast for it to matter. Thus everyone not on duty had been sleeping out of armour last night, to ensure they actually *did* sleep — a nearly impossible proposition otherwise.

Now Trace stepped out the rear ramp and into the pale glow of dawn, already warm with the promise of great heat to come. Parren seemed to like it. There were many here, seated across this courtyard between flights of steps, some sharing food with marines, others in translator-assisted conversation. Some more marines were doing their exercises out here, under PH-1 itself to keep the perimeter clear, while others remained on guard. The whole thing felt like an odd camping exercise... but when those happened, they tended to be in unpopulated regions, not on the main steps of an alien parliament, in the middle of a tense-yet-inscrutable armed standoff.

In more relaxed circumstances she would have taken a seat with whatever lower-ranked marines she thought she'd spent the least time with lately, and talked with them about things — sometimes work-related, sometimes not. But here she didn't have that luxury, and sat alongside Erik and Dale, who were crosslegged before some parren, eating breakfast.

"Try this," said Erik, and put a bowl of hot liquid before her. "You drink it like from a cup. Big gulps, I think."

Trace sniffed it, and looked askance at the parren. They made encouraging gestures with their hands, indicating she should do as Erik suggested. It smelled light and lemony, and tasted even moreso when she drank. Very nice, in fact, and she downed it in several more gulps, and indicated her pleasure to the parren.

The parren exchanged glances and grins at each other, and chatted, appearing to find these humans entertaining. It was a very different reaction than she'd seen from parren before — they were usually so solemn and calm. House Harmony parren, she recalled. Barely one-fifth of all parren. There was nothing to indicate house affiliation on these parren's clothes, light robes of cream and brown, well suited to the heat.

"House Creative," Erik explained, guessing her question before she asked it. "Lis tells me they produce a lot of artists, but a lot of creatives in all fields too. The phase-change heightens their creativity, it activates the imaginative portions of the brain. Lots of their big inventors and scientific geniuses come from House Creative, not just artists… though about two-thirds of the great playwrights are too. Plays are everything to parren, much bigger than movies or games."

"Amazing to think you can just change into a mindset," said Trace, sampling the food. Parren food was laid out in lots of little containers, each with something unique. There were soft grains that steamed, and cold beans with a red-spiced vegetable, all very simple, very light. And utterly delicious, when she tried them. It reminded her of meals in Kulina training on Sugauli, in her youth — only better. "Imagine working your whole life to perfect your mindset and skills, only to lose them when you phase."

"And gain others in their place," Erik added. He'd already showered and shaved, Trace saw. He must have risen before her, then. It didn't surprise her — Lisbeth had obviously come to find parren matters fascinating, and now Erik did the same… probably more from concern for Lisbeth, Trace thought, than from his own interests. She'd thought that a weakness once, that he was so obviously concerned with other people. Over-sensitive, perhaps. She'd learned to tone down her own sensitivity long ago, to prevent distracting and dangerous attachments.

But Erik had somehow managed to combine those sensitivities with the hard mind and cool logic of a warship captain, and now Trace saw not only that he wasn't going to change, but that he didn't need to. Perhaps, she thought now as she ate, he'd never been the one with the problem to begin with — she was. She'd had to narrow her mental focus to arrive at her present state. He didn't. Face it, she thought to herself now, he's smarter than you. Not at everything, but just in general. He had more mental capability, in total. Which made sense, because he was a warship captain, and that was one of the most demanding jobs known to humanity. Marine company commander was no walk in the park either, but required as much bloody-minded perseverance as raw intellect.

So, she thought to herself, nodding slowly as she chewed. She liked to know where she stood with such matters. This calm morning, things seemed clearer.

"Major," said Dale from Erik's far side. "I was talking with Lisbeth myself. She thinks Aristan can't make a move on Tobenrah until he challenges you personally. He doesn't have the authority, otherwise. Beating you will give him the status."

"That was my take also," Trace agreed. And pointed to the beans. "What called?" she asked her hosts. "Name?"

"Pulra," said a parren. And something else, that she didn't understand with the translator off, but seemed like a question.

"Yes, delicious," she agreed with enthusiasm, and had some more. "Pulra. Captain, we should arrange to find a trader and buy some of this."

"It's probably not good for you," Erik prodded. "I mean, it actually tastes nice."

"Plenty of healthy food tastes nice," Trace retorted, well aware he was teasing.

"Nothing that you eat." Trace took another mouthful and smiled at him, not commenting.

"Major, these fights are to the death," said Dale. "Let me take it."

"If I was allowed, I'd let Kalo take it," Trace told him around a mouthful. "He's the best hand-to-hand fighter here. But we've bent their rules this far, and the Togreth are running this show. Even Tobenrah has to do what they say, they're the independent judiciary that humans are supposed to have, but don't."

"You seriously think you can beat Aristan in a swordfight?" Dale asked grimly. "I saw his boy Milek fight with us on Konik. I'm pretty good, but with blades I couldn't take him. Aristan will be better again."

"I know," Trace agreed. "I didn't exactly see it, but I saw the result of his work on Kamala. He killed three armed sard with one blade after holding his breath for half-an-hour."

"So how are you going to beat him?"

"I'm going to cheat," said Trace, and sipped some of the parren tea. It was much nicer than her own tea. It made her suspicious of what was in it... precisely the point of Erik's teasing. The last person who'd known her so well that he could pre-empt her thoughts had been Captain Pantillo. An odd thought *that* was.

"Cheat how?" Erik asked.

"I asked Styx to work on a few ideas. She's confident. Then I asked Lisbeth. Lisbeth said I'd better cheat, because Aristan certainly will."

"You'll win," Erik assured her. Trace gave him a faintly puzzled look. She was accustomed to him worrying all the time. He produced something from his pocket. "My Buddha told me."

He showed her the small figurine, a rotund bald man in robes, sitting in peaceful meditation. It was the same one she'd recovered from the Krim Quarter in the Tsubarata, itself a trophy of war, from Earth. She hadn't known he carried it with him.

Trace smiled. "He told you what, exactly?"

"Well..." Erik considered the round belly. "He thinks you should eat more."

"I eat more than the actual Buddha did. The real guy starved himself to enlightenment." She nodded at the figurine. "That's the Chinese Buddha, they often showed him as fat. Fat was a good thing for them."

Erik stared in amazement. "Well sonofabitch. It knows history." Even Dale found that funny, smiling wryly as he ate.

"I know history where it concerns my own people," Trace replied, a touch reproachfully. "I do know who the Buddha was." She tapped the figurine again. "That's actually a different guy — Budai, a Chinese monk, he gets conflated with the actual Buddha. But even on Sugauli most people don't care — they're both Buddha, they both mean pretty much the same thing."

"Do you know why the Kulina are more Buddhist than Hindu?" Dale asked. "'Cause that always had me stumped. You guys speak Nepali, Nepal was far more Hindu than Buddhist, but the Kulina are far more Buddhist than Hindu." Erik did a double-take between them, like a man discovering that *both* his pet dogs could talk. "Oh get stuffed," Dale told him, amusement growing.

"Sugauli's a Himalayan culture," Trace told him. "The Himalayas were the biggest mountain range on Earth. Big place, lots of old culture, Hindu, Buddhist, some Muslims. Sugauli's mountainous, lots of those people settled there, they were pretty nostalgic. All the old Himalayan culture got thrown into a blender, somehow Kulina ended up with Buddhism... though Kulina aren't exactly Buddhist either, we've got our own updated version. But we're a mix... there are plenty of Hindus on Sugauli. I nearly lost an eye as a kid, playing with Diwali fireworks. Would have ended my military career pretty early, would have had to wait until I was an adult to get the eye replaced, missed all my Kulina training."

Erik noticed the parren eyeing the Buddha figure with interest. He handed it to one of them, who handled it carefully. "Very old," Erik told him. "A holyman. From Earth."

The parrens' translators evidently got some of that, because they stared at the mention of Earth, and regarded the figure with reverence.

"I wonder if he ever knew," said Trace, gazing away down the stairs to the square-grid city of Chirese, sprawled out below. "The Buddha. How many lives his one life would influence. That one person would make such a difference."

"Those kind of thoughts might lead to ego and desire," said Erik. "So I'd guess he didn't think about it at all, and if you could go back in time and tell him, he wouldn't care."

Trace nodded. "Yeah, probably. I just wondered, with Aristan. A guy who'd like to be a Buddha to his people. And probably wants it far too badly."

"If they're still worshipping him in a thousand years," Erik said sourly, "I'll consider our mission here a failure."

"In a thousand years," said Trace, "I promise you won't care."

"No, but some Debogande, somewhere, will care." Erik jabbed a finger for emphasis, hardly serious. "We'll live forever, you know."

"Like Z6 vacuum bacteria," Dale said helpfully.

Trace considered her Captain with affection. "I think in a thousand years they might remember you," she offered.

Erik looked faintly surprised, then shook his head. "No," he said. "Us. All of us." And took back his Buddha from the grateful parren.

Trace's uplink clicked open — when it opened automatically, she knew it was important. *"Captain, Major, this is Phoenix. Scan shows multiplying new jump arrivals, incoming along an axis from Brehn System. Looks like a combat jump."*

Trace looked at Erik, alarm rising, and was surprised to see him taking his next mouthful calmly. "Hello *Phoenix*, this is the Captain. Get me scan feed directly, I want to see where they are.

Red alert, but don't show it. Watch what the parren do. If that's the deepynines, all hell is about to break loose down here. Aristan is about to miss his big chance. Stay alert, stay within Tobenrah's command parameters, and await developments."

It took several seconds for his words to make their way through Styx's many relays, then back again. Erik watched the Chirese skyline… looking for aerial activity, Trace realised. *"Aye Captain,"* came Abacha's terse reply. *"We'll get scan feed to you in... maybe twenty seconds. What about you?"*

"We'll be fine, Lieutenant," said Erik. Several black dots rose into the air from a city landing pad, then some more. Combat flyers, Trace thought. Erik pointed them out to her, and Trace nodded. "We won't be the focus of this next action. We're going to try and stay out of the way, and let things unfold. We'll be heading up to you as soon as possible, but it's not possible until we know Aristan won't shoot us down for violating his catharan. Captain out."

From far south now came the building shrill of engines, combat flyers on standby now powering up. "Here we go, guys," said Erik, still eating as his eyes and ears followed everything. Trace could see him thinking and calculating. It made her feel safer. "Cue Lisbeth, any second now."

Three seconds later, coms opened a channel as Erik flipped his AR glasses over his eyes. *"Erik, it's Lisbeth. You're reading these incoming ships?"* She sounded a little panicked.

"Yes I am, Lis. My ETA says we've got ninety-three minutes on current approach, what's Aristan doing?"

"Well that's the thing, I'm..." there was a pause, and the sound of shouting and commotion nearby. *"Erik, I'm hearing Aristan's moving on the Parliament! Tobenrah has hardly any forces on the ground, the only thing that's been keeping Aristan from the Parliament is convention... but so long as Tobenrah's people occupy the Parliament, Tobenrah has power in this system. An alien attack will cement that power so Aristan has to move now or..."*

"Whoever holds the Parliament holds power in this fight," Erik completed. "I understand Lis… Lis, I can't head back to

Phoenix if Aristan has power and won't let me, which leaves *Phoenix* without a captain."

"Erik, I know... look, hold on, Tobenrah's about to make an announcement..."

Some combat flyers roared overhead, and others now were circling. From somewhere distant came the sound of shooting. About the breakfast circle, parren were now standing, some staring, others in urgent conversation. Parren had uplinks too, and were doubtless beginning to hear things. Dale was already giving commands to marines, and Trace let him, finishing her tea with a last gulp, then rising to her feet. Shooting on the far side of the Parliament hill, rapid fire and single. It sounded like it might be into the air.

"Okay everyone," Trace said to her marines, "you hear what's happening. Defensive only, and everyone move slowly. Sudden movement may draw fire, we're completely vulnerable here and we don't need anyone deciding we're a threat."

New vision broke onto her glasses as Ensign Yun scanned the relevant local channels, scenes from airborne drones or vehicles. It was the farside of the Parliament hill, where vehicles had drawn up an approach road, and now parren were running up the slope. The paths were steeper there, and narrower. It would take them barely ten minutes, Trace thought.

"Erik," came Lisbeth once again, *"Tobenrah's on the air now, the parren with you are probably listening to it. He's invoking 'strina doreh', it's... it's a very old law, it means 'command of the senior'. It's basically invoking martial law under alien attack, it hasn't been used in... oh, hundreds of years, I think."*

And now, from the distant bottom of the great flight of stairs, Trace could see a wave of parren running. Civilian parren, unarmed. About PH-1, more parren were talking loudly, many gesticulating with alarm.

"Listen, Lisbeth," Erik said urgently, staring down the stairs as several marines came to position on either side of him, protectively. "I don't recommend Tobenrah send anyone here by air — Tobenrah may have representatives in the Parliament to give him nominal control, but Aristan has the actual local government on side. He's got total command of the air, they'll shoot down anyone who flies here on the way."

About them, parren were pointing up the slope. Fervent argument, determined, passionate, between parren of four different houses. Four different psychologies. Trace could see at once what they were saying and thinking, despite the static crackle of her overworked translator.

"Captain," she said, watching the argument spread, the groups of civilians running one to another, clustering about the louder voices, listening. "Captain, they're going to rush the Parliament." Even as she spoke, they were leaving, running up the stairs at first in a thin stream, then a greater, departing rush. "They're figuring Aristan won't fire on unarmed civilians..."

"Well that's not going to work!" Erik seethed, watching them go with hands on his head. "If Aristan deposes Tobenrah now and leads the defence, he'll be de-facto head of House Harmony! He's not going to let that go because a few hundred civvies try to block him!"

"Captain!" Trace demanded, stepping before him, rifle raised with great meaning. Erik grasped her suggestion immediately, without her having to say it. Perhaps she didn't even *need* to say it, and would have been in her rights, as commander of ground forces, to order her marines without his permission... only this decision was political, and required a level of agreement from her Captain that not even she could afford to ignore. And more, she simply did not know if it was the right thing to do. Erik was simply better at this sort of thing than her — he'd been surrounded by big powers and big politics all his life, had had the great leaders of human affairs for dinner guests, and family friends. Here there were gears within gears, and if she made this one gear turn a certain way, she simply could not judge what would happen to all the others, and if catastrophe would befall them all as a result. But if anyone could know, it was Erik.

He stared at her, with a moment's hard-eyed indecision. Then the indecision vanished, and he nodded. "Go! Take a small force and *follow*, don't lead or they'll mow you down! Let the parren lead and only fire if fired upon!"

"Lieutenant Dale!" Trace commanded, striding to the front of PH-1. "You stay and guard the shuttle with First and Second Squad! Third Squad, you come with me and Command Squad! Up front now!"

Running footsteps and rattling armour followed, and in ten seconds everyone was there, with parren still rushing by, heading up the steps. The furthest of them had now passed the next level up, and were leaping up the second flight of stairs. Beyond them, there were four more to the top.

"Wide formation," she told her marines, checking her rifle and transferring the helmet from backrack to head, and fastening tightly. "We are support to the parren, we only fire if fired upon. Go."

She ran, thought briefly about how little time they had to get up to *Phoenix* before the deepynine attack arrived, then thrust it from her mind. That was Erik's responsibility… and Aristan's too. It was because of him that they were all now wasting time, when they should have been forming all ships into defensive position and countering.

Staff Sergeant Kono and the rest of Command Squad got ahead of her, with Third Section to her rear, Sergeant Manjhi in command, Corporal Vijay Khan his second — Lisbeth's former bodyguard. Word was he'd been in tears when she'd visited, blaming himself for not having been there to protect her on Stoya, only for Lisbeth to slap his cheek affectionately and tell him to pull himself together.

Vision on Trace's glasses showed parren making fast progress up the rear of the Parliament hill. The marines ran hard, two strides to each enormous stair, but unarmored, many of the civilian parren were faster. None of them were objecting to seeing the humans come, and a few even turned to shout encouragement — probably House Fortitude, Trace thought, being the most loud and aggressive of the bunch. And now there was shooting at the top of the stairs, though Trace did not need to see it to know it was going into the air. Wild bursts to scare them off. Within the Parliament itself, some faint crashing noises, then a window broke, and smoke billowed out. There was fighting inside, then. Some flyers roared low overhead, probably for intimidation.

"Major, shooters on top of the stairs," came Dale's voice in her ear. *"I count five, shooting in the air. I have snipers' eyes on the targets."*

"If they fire at the civvies, shoot them," Trace panted. She cleared the second flight up, sprinting on the flat, wide courtyard to the next flight. Shots up ahead, and parren scrambled sideways on the path, but did not stop. Several distinct shots followed from behind and below.

"Got two," said Dale. *"The others are falling back."* More shots ahead. *"PH-1 just came under fire, small arms. I have no angle."*

"PH-1 has a shot," Hausler added.

"Hold your fire PH-1," Trace insisted, hitting the third flight and leaping up. Even marine-fit and augmented, running fast uphill in armour and talking was hard. "We can't fire on Parliament with heavy weapons. Sergeant Kono, do you have a shot?"

Shots were falling amidst the running parren now. Trace saw something skip off the stairs ahead in a puff of fragments. Further up, several parren fell. Others ducked off the stairs amidst the flanking trees and bushes, but kept running.

"Hello Sergeant Kono," came Styx's voice. *"I have a triangulation for you, from the overhead drones and other sources. Targeting dots to your glasses."* And then Trace could see it as well, small dots and red circles up ahead, where Aristan's men were shooting from cover.

"Third Squad keep going!" Trace shouted. "Command Squad, cover right and take those shots!" She ducked right after Command Squad, finding cover behind a tree as Third Squad kept going and took the lead. She aimed around the tree trunk with her rifle, but Command Squad were already firing, a steady pop! pop! pop! of accurate, high-powered rifles. Styx's targeting information was good, and quickly the incoming fire stopped.

"Not all of them are dead," Styx informed them. *"But most are hit, and the others are alarmed."*

"Command Squad go!" said Trace, and they were off again, as Third Squad cleared the stairs above and disappeared. Command Squad cleared the top stairs soon after, and finally got a good look at the Parliament — it was wide and imposing, just three floors high but with heavy stone walls and upper level balconies. Worst, the immediate surrounds were bare pavings, as all buildings of parren authority were designed to be the centre of ceremonial crowds.

Atop wide stairs between grand pillars, civilian parren were falling back from the main entrance, and gunfire followed them out. Several lay motionless, their comrades risking themselves to drag the wounded clear.

Sergeant Manjhi's squad hit the stairs and took positions about the doors, as Trace and Command Squad sprinted across the pavings. The glasses feed showed Aristan's and local government parren entering the building on the far side, in a great rush of bodies. They didn't appear heavily armed.

"Sergeant Manjhi!" Trace yelled as her lungs burned. "Get inside! Full assault, make some ground!"

Third Squad pulled grenades and threw, waited for the explosions, then went in a volley of clearing gunfire. Trace ran up the stairs and followed, into a wide hallway now filled with smoke and a few bodies, all of them parren. Ahead, Third Squad advanced by leapfrog, each alternate group running until the next door, cross-corridor or stairway, then pausing to cover while the second group ran ahead. Command Squad made a blocking wall behind them, ready to lay down fire on anything hostile. Up the far end, a parren aimed a rifle, and disappeared in a hail of bullet impacts that splintered his cover… then reappeared falling motionless on the floor. To the left, Corporal Khan fired briefly up some stairs, and an armed parren tumbled down.

As rearguard, Trace walked half-sideways, watching behind and ahead, and saw the mass of civilian parren following them inside. They came crouched, completely unarmed and ready to dive for cover, eyes wide with fearful bravery.

"Major," came Styx's voice, *"Parliament cameras are transmitting, Captain Debogande has tasked me to keep those channels open."* Which meant Erik thought this couldn't look good to most parren. Or more likely, Lisbeth was telling him it didn't, probably because Tobenrah was telling *her*. Ordinary civilians usually did what they were told, but the group behind her were risking their lives to oppose this power grab in the face of an alien invasion. Aristan risked everything with this last, wild throw of the dice.

Third Squad began taking more fire as they approached the end of the hallway, and Sergeant Manjhi ordered them to a halt ten metres short, pressed into alcoves and wall cover, or lying flat on the floor, bullets hitting the walls just ahead in sufficient volume to suggest the huge open space ahead was full of enemies. Trace took a knee against a wall as Kono shouted at the parren behind, and made grand gestures at them to stay down. Some were ignoring that, and running back to adjoining corridors and stairs, looking for a way to flank around. It was probably the best thing they could do, Trace thought — to fill up the rest of the building and hold it. But for her to follow would be to divide her forces in the face of a massively superior opponent, in numbers at least.

"I need to see that room, Styx," she said above the racket, focused on her glasses, and comfortable at least that the civilians would give fair warning if someone tried to flank them. "Sergeant Kono! Let the bugs out, we gotta see ahead!"

Kono heard that and opened a small container on his webbing. A Parliament building schematic appeared on Trace's glasses, zoomed and rotated for the best angle, then filled with rapidly multiplying red dots for enemies. Those dots now expanded, rushing down adjoining halls as the assassin bugs flew above their heads, and Styx expanded her analysis of camera coverage, and translated the results onto her tacnet…

Suddenly the shooting stopped. "Major Thakur!" bellowed a loud voice from the room ahead. It was in English, but the pronunciation was all parren. It took Trace a moment to find the correct icon on her glasses, then blinked and called up a camera feed from the room ahead. Robed parren were holding back, gestured by one tall figure to stay there as he moved slowly to the centre of the room. "Major Thakur!" he yelled again. From within his robe, he produced a long blade, and held it up where the camera could see it. Trace realised what he was doing.

"Let's go," she said, standing up. "Everyone up and rifles down. Styx, what's the status on those bugs? Some of the Domesh look like they've got those microwave devices aimed at the ceiling."

"No," said Kono fiercely in the pause before Styx replied. Wanting to grab her arm, but not daring. Trace ignored him, walking forward as others joined her, the line moving.

"Major," said Styx, *"the microwaves will not destroy the bugs, but they will disorient their sensors, making them largely inoperable. The microwaves need to be aimed in the air, as they will injure organic beings, so I could direct the bugs to progress amongst the parren or at ground level. But I deem the chance of detection high."*

"No, we're not going to cheat here," said Trace, as the wide room came slowly into view. "There's too many people watching." All of the planet Elsium, for certain. The entire Drezen System beyond that. And, when packaged and sent on the next starship to leave the system, all of parren space beyond, in the weeks and months to come. Her timer read ninety-one minutes ETA until the deepynines reached Elsium. Fifteen minutes until they absolutely had to head back to *Phoenix*… and even that was cutting it far too fine. Ideally Erik should have been headed back on PH-1 as soon as the signal arrived.

The grand hall opened onto an even grander central room. On the left, a huge, wide stairway led to higher levels of government. On the wide floor before the stairs, a wall of black-robed parren now lined the walls. Between them all stood a single dark sentinel, sword in hand.

"No!" hissed Kono again at Trace's back. Trace held a hand behind her back, and flicked fingers left and right to show how she'd like them to deploy. The marines moved, spreading along the wall to the right, and out to the stairs on her left, Domesh warriors fading before them, granting them this much space at least.

Behind them came the mixed-house civilians, with grim defiance as they saw what was taking shape before them. The catharan that Aristan had wanted, then sought to sidestep. Trace walked slowly forward, allowing her marines to take position, then more parren civvies arrived along adjoining corridors, and shoving broke out as they fought for their own spots along the walls, pushing the Domesh back, daring them to strike unarmed parren before the cameras. Trace could only admire their courage, and took confidence from the force with which they pushed their fragile position. They seemed to know what she was doing, even if she didn't.

"Trace," came Erik's voice on her private channel, and she had to fight down her frustration.

"Not now," she formulated silently in return. He was going to tell her to stand down, like Kono had. If Aristan decided to overrun the Parliament in a full-on firefight, she didn't think she could hold him long, and would be killed eventually, along with hundreds of these brave civilians. He had too many men. But to take Parliament in a bloodbath of innocents would sully Aristan's great ascension. Great parren were supposed to take power in moves both clean and elegant, which this desperate shambles had long ceased to be. *This* was now the only way for him to restore that elegance, and demonstrate to all assembled and watching that House Harmony was truly his to be ruled. And this, she was certain, was now the only way she could stop him.

"Trace listen," Erik retorted. *"The system scan is catastrophic. There's no way we can defend this place from the deepynines, even if we were united. Disunited we've got no chance. We've got more time than him, because we're going to withdraw to fight elsewhere. But Aristan has to fight here, to prove himself the defender of the parren people. He's short of time, you're not! Use it!"*

Trace realised what he was saying, because it was something like the hazy idea that had been forming at the back of her mind anyhow… but such decisions were not a mere Marine Commander's to make. Now Erik laid it out for her plainly, and showed her exactly what to do.

"The deepynines are here in ninety-one human minutes," she said to the room, walking slowly to Aristan. She was completely surrounded now… but then, so was Aristan. If shooting started, they'd all die. The parren custom of unrestricted arms in such occasions had a certain, cold logic to it. "We must fight them together, humans, parren, all the houses, Tobenrah and Aristan together. And yet you refuse. Why?"

"There is no talking in the catharan," the earpiece translated Aristan's cold reply. *"You have chosen this obstruction. You stand between a leader and his destiny. You will fight. Should you require a weapon, one will be provided for you."*

Trace considered that, looking around as she circled. Then she pointed to one of the parren civilians, and beckoned him to her. He looked puzzled, and wondered if she'd really meant him. Trace repeated the gesture impatiently, and he came, as Trace put the safety on her rifle and held it out to him. Perhaps, it occurred to her, she should just shoot Aristan and sacrifice everyone in the room to end any chance of his dangerous nonsense gaining true power in parren space. But that would lead to someone else just as bad taking his place, and following the same twisted ideology toward the same ruin. It was the ideology that had to be fought and discredited. Aristan himself was irrelevant.

She handed the man her rifle, then began unhooking her webbing, and handed the whole lot over, hanging it on the parren man's shoulder — magazines, pistol, grenades, water canteen and all. Then the helmet, which was going to slow her down when she needed to move her head. Barefoot might be better, but the combat boots were light, and the pavings were smooth and potentially slippery. Plus they gave her power if she needed to kick.

She then began on the armour, but was interrupted. *"Leave on the armour,"* Aristan commanded. Past the translator, she could hear the tension in his voice, contemplating just how long the armour could take to remove. *"It presents as much disadvantage as advantage. I am unconcerned."*

That was probably true, Trace thought. She was smaller than most men, and would typically rely on speed. She wasn't going to have that here — unarmored, Aristan was much quicker. But killing an armoured target took time that Aristan didn't have. Finally, she pulled her cap from a webbing pocket and pulled it over her head, for the limited protection its brim gave her eyes, and last of all, pulled a hilt from the knife sheath beneath her pistol.

From within slid a kukri. It was the traditional weapon of the Kulina, dating back to the Gurkhas of Nepal. Most had little cause to use it for more than utility in these days of armoured space combat, but on Sugauli, all knife-fighting was taught with these. The blade was a beast, as long as her forearm, its thick spine angled inward at the halfway like an elbow. The blade itself was wide, the edge flaring to a wicked curve forward of the elbow. A greater surface area, to drag more sharp steel along the target from the same, small motion, and cut deeper.

Trace gave it a familiar spin, and tapped it against her forearm. Blade on armour made a ringing sound, and the effect was pleasing. All the parren were staring at it, for it was the most inelegant, brutal-looking weapon, unlike the slender steel in Aristan's hand. It was a weapon only a human could love, Trace supposed — practical and vicious, designed as much for hacking animal carcasses as killing people. And it required its wielder to kill up close, close enough to smell her enemy's breath, while parren preferred the swift strike from range.

Trace sank to a fighting pose, somewhat exaggerated for effect, crouched low with the knife held back, awaiting an opening. In full armour, she supposed she looked something like a scorpion, hard-shelled and close to the ground, sting poised for a strike. She looked in Aristan's eyes for the first time, large and blue within his hood and veil, and saw what she was certain was alarm.

"The deadliest race of machines descends upon your people," she told him, "and instead of defending them, you play these games.

You are a traitor to your kind, and your people will thank me for killing you."

"There is no talking in the catharan!" one of Aristan's men yelled from the far wall.

"Fuck your rules!" Trace snarled. "Parren fight for games! Humans fight to kill!" She leaped at Aristan, and drew a fast slash for her exposed neck. She blocked with her forearm and tried to ensnare the blade between lower and upper arm while thrusting with the kukri. Aristan barely tore his blade clear in time, darting backward as her blow caught his robes. He circled backward, alarm clear in his eyes, and Trace pointed at the parren who had shouted from the sidelines. "Sergeant Kono! If this man speaks again, shoot him!"

"Yes Major!" shouted Kono, so all could hear, and all about the room came the rustling of weapons being prepared, though still pointed at the floor, for now. If it happened, everyone died… but now the stakes were raised, and the tension built. And now, perhaps, Aristan began to see his mistake in fighting a ceremonial fight against someone who cared nothing for ceremony. But he'd had no choice.

Aristan attacked, a strike flashing for the unarmored side of her calf, then reversing back to whip at her face as she danced back. She ducked and stabbed at him, but he danced away, flowing like water, circling as he looked for another opening.

"You have no time!" she hissed at him. "Already you are out of time! This system is lost, thanks to you! Your people will die by the million, and you will be blamed!"

Desperation flared in those wide, indigo eyes, and he slashed again. Trace took the blow on her right arm, ducked, then barely swayed aside the stab for her neck… and lowered her shoulder into him and charged. Female she was, and smaller, but augmented legs gave ferocious acceleration and the armour gave her force as she hit his midriff in a tackle. They crashed down, and he was lithe enough to roll her and spin aside with a retreating swipe that Trace allowed to slash her armoured middle. Aristan circled again, adjusting the cowl and veil where they'd come loose of their hidden velcro… and again Trace saw the alarm there, noting what she'd nearly done — pinned him in a wrestling grapple, where she, armoured with a close-range weapon, held all the advantages.

"Where is your calm, great soul?" Trace asked him. "To be Domesh is to be always at peace! I see no calm in you. Look at you worry. You worry for your future, for your legacy. For your life. You are no leader of Domesh. The great rulers of Harmony laugh at you."

Aristan circled, no longer entirely trusting himself, Trace thought. She would not allow herself to feel satisfaction, or blood lust, or the craving for revenge. She had her strategy, and the future lives of millions, perhaps billions, hung upon it. Aristan now stared into that karmic abyss, and trembled. Trace looked as well, and felt only stillness.

She gazed at him, raising slightly from her low, crab-crouch, and looked him straight in the eyes. "Aristan. We have been on adventures together. It's over, my friend. You've failed. Admit defeat, and I will spare you."

He swung hard, then again, Trace dancing back, him never getting close enough for disadvantage, aiming at her hands, her blade, then her face. She blocked with an arm, and he cut for her unarmored waist, the point where the upper-armour ended and the lower-section began… but that brought him close, and she dropped, catching the blow on chestplate, then trapping the blade with her arm. She grabbed his wrist, and drove the kukri through his middle, full force.

He collapsed in her arms like a deflating balloon, sword dropping with a clatter, and sank to his knees. For a moment he just gazed at her, blue eyes filling with tears. It was a kind of haunted despair, touched with an almost-smile, like the fatalist who has just realised that the universe was never about to grant him its great prize after all. That it had all been a wonderful, terrible illusion. There was some humour in that, certainly… as one might find humour in discovering oneself the subject of an elaborate practical joke. That, and the tears of a child, denied his heart's greatest wish, and knowing it would never come again.

Trace put a hand to his cheek, within the folds of his cowl, and smiled back, faintly. “I’m sorry,” she said quietly. “You had a good run. But this isn’t your time.”

Aristan spoke, his voice weak and fading. *“If I’d only known,”* said the translator. *“I would have followed you.”* For a moment, his eyes implored her. Then Aristan, leader of the greatest rising faction of House Harmony, slid to the floor, black robes rapidly drenching red, and lay still.

CHAPTER 24

Gesul was furious, and spent most of the rush up to orbit growling into coms, with a most un-Domesh lack of calm. Lisbeth sat two seats from him, pressed into her seat by the Gs but pleased to have a scan-display before her in this unfamiliar parren shuttle. She knew enough Porgesh now to jump between functions and read the words without needing her glasses' visual translator, and now had access to the official security feed of the unfolding situation. It told them they were completely screwed.

"It's impossible," she said to Semaya's question. "The defence grids won't even work, there's too many enemy incoming. Our ships were too close to Elsium to be in proper defensive positions. The enemy can kill the planet if they choose — *Phoenix* has to leave. If they follow *Phoenix*, that's the best way to save the planet."

To her astonishment, Semaya actually relayed her assessment to Gesul. It told her that Gesul was still unable to get a proper strategic feed from Tobenrah, and that Gesul's own three captains were probably too busy to brief their leader. Score one for the human system, Lisbeth thought, where the leader was a starship captain who didn't need these things explained. Of Gesul's immediate advisors, Lisbeth was the only one with direct spacer military experience, a realisation that might have shocked her were she not so preoccupied. She was a qualified shuttle co-pilot, and had flown several combat missions in that capacity. Now, at Gesul's side, she'd gone from being the least capable combatant to the most, as she could read Scan and had a good idea of what all the moving dots and the storm of interlocking, curving lines actually meant.

It made Gesul even more furious, and Lisbeth half-listened to his commands while checking various parts of the scan-feed in more detail. *"I do not care who has declared himself as Aristan's successor!"* he was fuming. *"Our selfish squabbling has left the world of Elsium completely exposed! Our ships were in the wrong position, they were too close to the world, to participate in our politics, when they should have been out guarding these lanes, and now look! Look what our parren folly has brought upon us! We have no choice but to flee this world in order to save it! I commit myself to our leader, Tobenrah of House Harmony, and may the fates condemn all those who do not follow!"*

Exactly how far that rant was being broadcast, Lisbeth had no idea. If it was reaching the broader parren population, and not just the leaders and military commanders, the implications could be large indeed.

She'd been watching the vision, heart-in-mouth, when Trace had killed Aristan, goading him into hasty action when his best chance to beat her was to remain calm and patient. Again, she'd half-expected parren to be angry with her for defying the spirit of the rules, but Gesul's entourage had been nothing but impressed. Extraordinary scenes had followed, many of the watching parren on the wide, central floor clutching their heads and falling with cries of pain and distress. The shoveren psychologist-priests had converged on them with ceremonial chanting, but there were too many, and soon the floor had been a scene of turmoil, parren on both the Domesh side, and the many-housed civilians dropping to their knees, supported by concerned friends who called for an overworked priest.

It was the phase, and Aristan's fall, in that room at least, appeared to have brought about a great shift in the flux. Now Lisbeth heard small snippets of confusion on various ships, commanders not responding, or too busy with internal matters to communicate properly. She suspected it was spreading, and now there were ship crews with phasing and incapacitated members, just when they could least afford it. And suddenly it occurred to her why all the great battles in parren history that she'd been reading about seemed to end so quickly when a leader died… and why the targeting and killing of leaders was such a strategic imperative for parren commanders. Kill the leader and parren would lose the focal point of their psychological loyalties — for many of them, the very lynchpin that held their current psychological structure in place. The consequences in a battle would be bad enough in ground combat. In space combat it was an awful Achilles heel, where the sudden incapacity of ten percent of a spacer crew could leave a vessel partially crippled.

An icon blinked on Lisbeth's visor, and she blinked on it, knowing it was Erik. With Styx running so much of *Phoenix*'s coms encryption in this alien system, she knew it was a waste of time to wonder how these com links established themselves with such precision. *"Hello Lisbeth, we're having a hell of a time getting coordinated replies from Tobenrah or any parren, what's going on?"*

Even though it was only her brother talking, Lisbeth realised she was being asked by the Captain of one of humanity's premier warships to give a strategic update. Well, Hausler always told her that proper coms discipline was to keep it short, precise and efficient — maximum content for minimum effort.

"Hello Erik, Tobenrah has internal command issues related to the phase. He's leaving, everyone's leaving, he wants you to leave as well since these attackers are almost certainly after you. A few of his commanders wanted to throw *Phoenix* to the deepynines, but Major Thakur just killed the Domesh leader in a catharan, so she and *Phoenix* now have great status in House Harmony, and Tobenrah wouldn't dare. My advice is forget the politics, just focus on the deepynines and get us out of here, Lisbeth out." She added the end-transmission signal without thinking, forgetting the usual icon-blink to indicate end-of-message, and prevent repetitive coms clutter.

"Hello Lisbeth, we're doing that. I'm on PH-1, we are currently three minutes to Phoenix intercept, then we are full burn on departure. We will need full navcomp uplinks to all parren vessels — we've been trying to tell them about Styx's fallback moon, but no response. Styx insists it's defensible, and that's where we're headed."

"Erik, I've told them already about the moon, I understand that they've heard me and are considering their options. I am… just over one minute from shuttle intercept and full-burn with Gesul on the *Stassis*. Erik, I'm looking at the tactical feed now and it looks like the Elsium Administration vessels are going to manoeuvre and move to block the deepynine formation's path, forcing them to take evasive action or suffer casualties."

"I understand, Lisbeth. By my calculation this will mean one hundred percent casualties for those Elsium ships, can you confirm that intention?"

"Yes Erik, remember these are parren you're dealing with. They think it's the most effective way to slow them down, given what we've seen of their performance. Otherwise they'll catch us and Tobenrah straight out of jump, or worse."

There was the faintest of pauses from the other end. *"Yes, I think they're probably correct. Tell them Phoenix salutes them, or whatever the appropriate translation, if you can."* Near scan now showed the *Stassis* looming up fast. The parren shuttle pilot cut thrust still twenty seconds short of intercept, and Lisbeth repressed some anxious frustration at that lost time. She'd gotten so used to flying with Hausler, Jersey, Tif and occasionally Lieutenant Dufresne, that she'd forgotten most pilots simply weren't that good.

"Erik, I'm about to make intercept, and I'm not great at talking under Gs, but I'll try. Good luck to you and *Phoenix*."

"And to you Lisbeth. We'll need to jump straight through, tell the parren that if they don't get their navcomps synced immediately, we'll never make it."

The shuttle hit *Stassis*'s grapples with a crash and lurch, then a long pause as pilot and bridge communicated to ensure the hold was firm. Again, it was a longer pause than Lisbeth was accustomed to… but the sledgehammer weight of Gs when the main engines kicked in was just the same.

Lisbeth still hated heavy-G pushes. In truth, she'd discovered that no spacers liked it, but all military types made a virtue of enduring the greatest discomforts stoically, and for spacers it didn't get more uncomfortable than this. Being a lot fitter now helped — a stronger diaphragm particularly helped to get air in the lungs that were suddenly squeezed beneath some enormous weight. Everything roared and shook, and she focused her blurred vision on the visor display, which calculated a solid nine minutes of this until *Stassis* was far enough up the Elsium gravity-slope to enable jump engines.

From there, the ride would get faster, but no easier. The deepynine ships could not go much faster whatever their technological advantages, having the same difficulties cycling the jump engines to gain V while heading into deeper gravity. They'd jumped in at a far enough distance to give them a good look at the planet's defences, and to line up their approach accordingly. Even now, several of the outer fire-stations that surrounded most Spiral worlds had disappeared, vaporised by high-V incoming ordnance, and there was nothing between the attackers and the world of Elsium, and its half-a-billion souls. Lisbeth forced herself to stare at that image, as the forces flattened her immovably into her chair, and thought that surely, *surely*, this deepynine/sard and possibly alo alliance wouldn't kill a planet. But then, they hadn't any good reason to kill Mylor Station either. Humanity knew little about the alo, despite their alliance in the Triumvirate War, but what they did know suggested cold, grim calculation, little concern for human considerations of morality, and a perverse, often insulting sense of humour. If they'd made such great friends with the deepynines, and now teamed up with the sard, who knew what they were capable of?

Stassis was two minutes short of first jump pulse when Erik's icon blinked again. *"Phoenix bridge tells me full uplinks to Tobenrah's ships have been established,"* came the synthesised version of his voice in her ear — uplink formulated conversation, much easier than talking under high Gs. *"Well done Lis."*

"I didn't do it," she managed to wheeze against the pressure on her chest, being far less accomplished at internal formulation. "But thanks."

The deepynines were diverting away from Elsium itself now, following *Phoenix* and her parren escort. The major stations in orbit should have taken hits by now, if ordnance had been fired at them, but remained intact. Presumably that meant the planet was safe as well. But now, it occurred to Lisbeth properly for the first time as she looked at the scan, all eleven of them were now chasing her.

The twelve Elsium Administration ships were thrusting hard from the planet's gravity onto a direct intercept course, just before *Stassis*'s first jump pulse hit. Everything was still thirty minutes behind them, but the deepynines, seeing it coming, and knowing there would be a lot of ordnance coming ahead of it, began using their last remaining bit of jump-engine-capable approach to dump V. Even for advanced deepynine ships, running into that much ordnance, at that high V, would make defensive targeting and evasion unlikely, and result in a lot of casualties. At lower V, deepynine advantages became overwhelming. But in forcing them to dump, the Elsium ships would slow the entire assault right down, then force the deepynines to transition through the deep gravity-well where they could not use jump engines at all, all at a lower V. That move should then allow Tobenrah's forces to escape, actually putting distance on their pursuers. But the cost was going to be awful.

Erik's head swam in that peculiar way it did post-jump — not nausea like the green rookies got, but a strange sense of dislocation, both like and unlike awakening from a deep sleep. He fought to refocus his senses, aware of voices on the bridge feed, second-shift talking and sorting their problems. But he didn't have his big chair displays and visor, nor the holographic 3D visualisation in between, and not being in the chair himself, he just couldn't find the urgency.

Worse, he was realising he didn't have his drink bottles, and PH-1's observer chair wasn't equipped with electrolytes and sugars to replenish in one big hit what jump took out of the bloodstream. Worse again, fuzzy-headedly, he couldn't think of the feeding procedure for going through jump in a shuttle — let alone a two-jump as this was supposed to be.

"Yo, Captain," said Hausler from up front, and tossed a bottle back at him. Erik caught it gratefully, and took a long gulp — it was sharp and awful, but the shock of alertness to the brain was enough to make it good. And Hausler added, "Hello Major Thakur, how you guys doing back there?"

"We are good," said Trace.

"Major," said Erik, "Lisbeth told me before jump that you'd just acquired some serious rank in House Harmony by killing

Aristan. You might want to think on what that means, before you see any more action with these guys."

"It probably means I'm supposed to depose you as leader and assume command myself," said Trace, sounding as though her mouth was full of food, probably an energy bar. *"I've never been more pleased to not be parren."*

On coms, Lieutenant Lassa was waiting for some of their parren friends to arrive. *Phoenix* was fast, and predictably, they'd beaten everyone here. 'Here', Erik saw, was four-point-two AU out from a G-class star, a few sunbaked, close-in planets and some cold and uninteresting outer gas giants… and very little in the way of settlements or coms traffic. Lusakia System, Navigation informed him with certainty, despite no human ship ever having been here before.

"Captain," said Hausler. "You see what happened to the Elsium ships before jump?"

"Three left that I saw," said Erik. A lurch into hyperspace, as Draper cycled the jump engines to dump V… then a swing sideways to line up the course correction. But Draper paused before firing the engines, waiting for the parren to arrive. No doubt he'd dialled back their jump a little, *Phoenix* having the capability to do that so as not to leave less powerful ships behind by too great a margin. Sometimes it was better to be slower, and arrive in force, rather than coming in fast and alone. "But I think they hit at least one, hopefully more. We're going to have to nail this course correction — even with that delay, the deepynines will be right on our ass."

With a flash of energy, a ship arrived… then another, right alongside. *Phoenix* linked coms with them immediately, displaying the required course-change ahead, then hit thrust with every bit as much power as they'd used escaping from Elsium's gravity. Erik barely got the bottle into a seat stowage before it hit — there was absolutely no chance of him getting up to the bridge now, *Phoenix* would be manoeuvring hard enough to make free movement lethal for any crew stupid enough to try it. But Erik was not especially worried — Draper got better every time he flew the ship, and with that in mind, replacing him would have been counter-productive even were it possible. Word was that Draper and Lieutenant Dufresne were even kind of friendly now, which they hadn't been a few months before. Being forced to work together in close proximity, in the sure knowledge that everyone died if you stuffed up, had a way of making the most unlikely friendships. Erik thought of Trace, and knew that she could say the same.

The last parren ship to jump in brought with it the most recent feed of the deepynines' position… which caused commotion on *Phoenix* coms as Draper himself told the parren to get a move on. If the deepynines arrived in this system while a single parren (or human) ship was still present, those deepynines could just follow them directly. If they arrived after their quarry had left, the deepynines would have to do some serious re-calculation to figure where they could have gone. With any luck they wouldn't figure it out… only Erik didn't think there was that much luck in the universe.

Ahead of Lieutenant De Marchi's last calculated trajectory, beyond the gravitational lensing of the oblique corner of Lusakia System they'd need to traverse on the way, lay an empty expanse of space. Their target was not on any map, and could not be seen by any amount of long-range, high focus telescopic vision. Styx assured them it was there, but a moon without a sun, lightyears from any prominent source of light, would be nearly impossible to see with any level of technology. Or would it?

"Styx," Erik formulated now that he had a moment to question her on it, and Lieutenant Lassa berated the parren to kick it harder and risk breaking things. *"What chance that the deepynines can follow us, even if they arrive late in this system?"*

"Nearly one hundred percent," Styx said with certainty. *"There are several navigation buoys in this system that we are not in a position to disable first. The deepynines will access their data and discover our last seen heading. They will then scan precisely that region of space, and their visual acuity is high enough to detect the moon, although barely."*

Phoenix could jump to another destination, Erik thought... but that would risk the deepynines passing them in jump, even with the delay to interrogate the nav buoys. This might be the only clear break on the deepynines they were likely to get, and there were no systems with large concentration of parren space forces within another one-jump to which they might lead their pursuers. Interrogating nav buoys to reveal known jump destinations might not take any time at all. Discovering a destination that vanished into empty space might take a lot more time, as they puzzled things out, and trained their telescopic vision on that tiny patch of space, to discover what it might possibly be. They'd not make that jump quickly, gaining more time for their quarry. The alternative jump, they might follow too fast for safety.

"And Styx, what are your recommendations upon arrival at the moon?"

"Captain, the moon has sophisticated defence systems. Reactivation of these systems should be our priority, as they could potentially destroy much of the deepynine fleet. We will have no time to reconnoiter the moon first to see if those systems are still in operation, so our reconnaissance and our reactivation mission will need to be one and the same. I calculate that our best chance of success is to lure the deepynines into attacking the moon directly, as that will create cover for our ships, and force them into a ground attack where their advantages decrease. In space combat we have little chance, but Phoenix marines have already demonstrated one-to-one superiority against deepynine drones." And none had been more surprised by that calculation than her, Erik thought. But Trace's own replays of their few engagements so far indicated the same thing, and further tactical analysis since, with Styx's input, should have advanced that advantage further.

"Agreed," Erik formulated, wishing he could muster the sense to call up a visual of the moon. *"The deepynines are chasing you and the data-core primarily, so we'll send you both down to the surface with the reconnaissance team. That will be their bait, plus it will take direct attention off Phoenix. Without that, we won't last very long."*

"Captain, that is an excellent suggestion."

Erik could not help but feel a little pleased that Styx liked his idea… even though he was certain that Styx would have said it herself, if he hadn't beaten her to it. Course corrected, Draper now hit the jump engines to cycle them up one whole magnitude of V. Behind them, the parren gradually did the same. Twenty seconds to jump.

"Major, did you hear that?" he asked Trace. He'd left the command channel open, so she should have heard.

"Yes Captain. Lieutenant Dale will lead the reconnaissance, I'll be needed on the surface to counter any ground attack. Beyond that, we'll have to wait and see what the situation is."

Five seconds. Only then, at the point of no return, did Erik allow himself to think of the fact that they were jumping toward a non-verified jump point, on the sayso of an alien AI, and that if her coordinates were off by even a fraction, at these ranges, they'd miss it completely and drop from hyperspace god-knew-where in the vast, empty void…

CHAPTER 25

Five minutes past jump arrival, and *Phoenix* bridge decided that if deepynine ships were coming straight in behind them, it would have happened by now. PH-1 got the all-clear, and Trace's marines waited for Erik to go first, then followed their Captain through the dorsal airlock into *Phoenix* Midships.

Bridge kept the crew cylinder fixed as they disembarked, so that passage from Midships was not a longer haul up to the central spine, but a much faster drift through the rim-level connecting passage, inaccessible while the crew cylinder was rotating. Once inside, everyone found a wall to brace against, while spacers secured the connector with locked and sealing doors. Warning klaxons blared, red light flashing through the corridors, then with a thump and rumble everything lurched sideways as the big *Phoenix* cylinder began to rotate once more. Sideways force translated to downward, steadily increasing until full gravity pressed down, but most of the crew were moving well before that, whatever the regulations that said they shouldn't. They were on combat approach, and saved time was worth cutting a few corners.

Trace spent the whole time checking ETAs and consulting with Lieutenant Dale. Bridge told her they had ninety-three minutes until arrival, and that the system was completely unoccupied. Except, of course, that a single moon in orbit about a high-mass irregularity, alone in the dark of space, could not really be called a 'system'.

"Styx is getting us a schematic," Trace said to Dale as they walked in the wake of the Alpha and Command Squad marines who'd gone ahead. *Phoenix*'s corridors hustled with busy spacers securing things and checking recently damaged systems. "She can't vouch for the accuracy, given the place was probably occupied by someone else since she was here last, but the structural basics should be the same."

"Parren drove the drysines out of here," said Dale, sidestepping spacers repositioning some emergency EVA suits, in case of catastrophic damage to come. "Stands to reason it might have been occupied by parren for a while, in which case they've probably made changes."

Trace nodded. "In that case, you'd better take some parren with you. I understand some of those ships have marines on them… we've been trying to gather intel on the capabilities of parren marines, Lisbeth even helped a bit. The consensus is they're not as good as us, and that it otherwise depends on the unit."

"Could be like operating with army back home," said Dale, not looking hopeful. "Better than nothing, I suppose."

"We'll get suited first," said Trace. "Command meeting after that, we've got time, though barely. Check the schematic, organise deployment with the parren… then we've got the transport shit to deal with." Because they only had four shuttles, which was usually enough for five platoons, as each shuttle held a platoon-plus-ten at a squeeze… but one shuttle was only a civilian model, unarmed and unable to provide firesupport. And that shuttle, with Lisbeth gone, was missing its co-pilot… unless Erik wanted to deploy both Lieutenant Dufresne *and* Lieutenant Commander Draper on AT-7 — a hell of a risk, with highly-trained starship pilots on an unarmed vehicle in what might shortly be a warzone… and leaving *Phoenix*, of course, with no backup.

A spacer rounded the corner ahead, and Trace was about to dodge, but recognised the young, earnest pale face and blonde hair, blue eyes looking straight at her. "Chenk!" she said, with genuine pleasure. "Looking for me?"

"Hi Major, sure am," said Spacer Chenkov… no, Trace corrected herself — Petty Officer Third Class Chenkov. That promotion had come through fast after his exploits on Kamala with Trace and Command Squad. There had been a Distinguished Service Star in there too, on Trace's recommendation — the only time in her career she'd ever been in a position to recommend a spacer for a marine medal. "Lieutenant Dale."

"Petty Officer," said Dale, with more respect than he showed most spacers. "Major, I'll go on ahead."

Trace nodded, and he went past, up the circumference corridor toward Assembly. "What's up, Chenk?"

"Well, um..." Chenkov looked a little uncertain, as though suddenly wondering if he'd get in trouble. Petty Officer or not, he was still just a tech geek who'd enjoyed playing with processing simulations in his parents' basement a few years back. Trace knew that Command Squad were planning to get him laid on their next human port of call, assuming that hadn't happened yet... and assuming they made it back alive. "Well Major, the fabricators have been working all through the recent stuff, and me and a few of the guys took the opportunity in Elsium orbit to..."

Trace held up her hand, having no time for long technical explanations. She could see from his manner that it was important, and she trusted that Chenkov would not bother her if it weren't. "Would it be easier if you just showed me?"

Chenkov looked relieved. "Yes! Yes it would, just... it's up in Engineering I-3. Just don't freak out when you see it."

Trace strode that way, Chenkov falling in beside. "You ever known me to freak out, Petty Officer?"

"No Major. Sorry Major."

"Don't be sorry. So how do you like being a Petty Officer, Chenk?"

"Honestly Major? Doesn't make a damn bit of difference."

"That's the spirit."

Erik arrived to cries of 'Captain on the bridge!', and the rest of first-shift already beginning their changeover. He wanted to tell Draper what a good job he'd done at Lusakia through that difficult course-correction, but the tactical schematic showed he had no time.

"We're right in the slot," said Draper, unbuckling restraints and folding back the left-side display to get out. "The moon's on the starboard elliptic side of the singularity from our position, orbital rotation's maybe ten days. Captain, that gravity slope's just a fucking sheer drop, we're getting light readings and the degree of lensing is insane… it's right off the charts, just as Styx said. Here, Lio can tell you more."

As Lieutenant Lionel De Marchi reached Erik's side, having just helped Kaspowitz into the Navigation chair. "Sir, we don't have the data to calculate it precisely, but to me it looks like the gravitational gradient is more likely cubed, not squared. So our moon is sitting on a more moderate plane of G, and from there it just falls into a bottomless pit…"

"Can Styx confirm that?" Erik asked, sliding into Draper's vacated spot, as Draper helped him to buckle in.

"No sir, she says she's not a physicist, and from her knowledge she's not sure the maths are quite that simple. But our calculations so far suggest it's pretty close."

The rules of gravity were fundamental to the shape of the universe. The one most relevant to starship captains was that the force of gravity declined by the square root of itself per unit of distance you travelled away from the source. It led to one of those exponential graph-lines so common in the physical universe, where singular incidences of gravitational phenomena never entirely disappeared, just weakened more and more until they became indistinguishable from all the other, infinite sources of gravity in the universe. In the other direction, the gravity slope became exponentially steeper the closer you got to the source. How steep it eventually became depended entirely on the mass at the source, but the ratio of that curving line was always the same, irrespective of the object's mass or radius — always the square root, always exponential, in either direction.

Here, that equation, impossibly, was different. Cubed, instead of squared. Erik could see the moon now as he pulled the command visor over his eyes, and the entire space between himself and the display screens was filled with a 3D representation of the space before him, and the position of the ships behind as they emerged racing from hyperspace. The moon orbited real close to the singularity — a touch under half-a-million kilometres…

"That's worse than cubed," Kaspowitz growled as he observed the same thing from the navigation post. "That's doing something impossible… Captain, the gravitational lensing of those background stars shows we're looking at anything up to a thousand Gs on the surface, maybe more. That thing's multi-dimensional. I know it's fucked up, but that's the only explanation I've got."

Wormhole experiments, Romki had suggested. Speculation had always been that if you made a gravity-well deep enough, it would tear through the very fabric of space/time into something else entirely. Another dimension, perhaps. Typically that speculation was aimed at black holes, though not even the oldest spacefaring species in the Spiral had reached a definitive conclusion. But this was something far stranger than a black hole. Black holes were an extreme but natural phenomenon, explainable within the rules of basic physics. This was not.

In the meantime, the tactical applications were stunning. "Nav, I want that full gravitational map as soon as you have it," said Erik, as Draper finished with the straps and screens, and left running with De Marchi. Erik activated ship-wide coms. "All hands, this is the Captain. If you're moving about, make it fast, we have V-dump in two minutes."

Already they were coming up fast on the singularity and its moon. "Captain," said Kaspowitz, fingers flying as he sorted various displays and ran multiple calculations. "I think we've got a narrow corridor of jump arrival from Lusakia to here along our present axis. The deepynines could probably push up or down that slope further than we can, but they're not familiar with the system dynamics."

Erik looked at the red-lit corridor appearing on his display. It described an area of space no more than a thousand kilometres across, and all of the arriving parren ships had exited hyperspace within it. "Good Kaspo, get me a confirmation and I'll tell the parren to dump V and mine that space with everything they've got."

"Our munitions are better than theirs," Karle reminded him.

"I know that Arms, but we're running low and we do more damage firing than mining, I want to make them count."

Any parren ship dumping V out here was going to be dead if the deepynines came out of hyperspace while they were still laying mines. But from a strategic point of view, better them than *Phoenix*… and even the parren could not argue with that.

"Any deviation off that lunar approach is going to get us killed," Shahaim said unhappily, running those figures off the data Kaspowitz was pouring into the course projections. "The gravity slope's a hell of a lot more mild from here to the moon than it ought to be, I mean… look at that, it's positively benign. But the singularity footprint is so small and the slope gets worse so fast, it's like falling off a cliff. If they force us to evade that way, on any kind of steep angle, we won't have enough power to climb back out."

"Yeah, but two can play that game," Kaspowitz added, still running furious calculations. Erik was nearly surprised — it was the most positive thing Kaspowitz had said about this improbable situation.

"We're not going down there," said Erik, eyes darting across his schematic as he began to mentally sketch the outlines of shapes, forces and trajectories he could see growing in his mind. "We go down to that moon ourselves, we'll be a sitting duck. But our shuttles won't. And we'll make those fuckers chase them down to the moon, where they can be sitting ducks themselves."

The one thing Lisbeth hadn't considered about being in the service of a parren ruler was that just like the parren, when she was ordered to do something dangerous and stupid, she had to obey without question. She sat now strapped into an EVA suit she barely knew how to operate, slammed at five-Gs in the hold of a parren shuttle on an intercept to a moon orbiting on a gravity slope that violated all known physical laws. It was scary, but lately in her life, lots of things had been scary, and she was getting used to it.

Better yet, she was getting plenty of practise at distracting herself from the fear. Gesul had granted her access to the command channel, which astonished her even as it made sense. She was Gesul's human advisor, at his side to translate for him the reckless behaviour of these strange aliens into whose hands the fate of parren security had been thrust. In order to advise him, she had to see what the humans were doing.

All four of *Phoenix*'s shuttles were on approach with the parren. Lisbeth did not know who was flying AT-7, given she doubted Draper or Dufresne could be spared, with serious combat on the horizon and *Phoenix* regulations requiring reserve starship pilots on standby. She suspected Styx might be flying it by remote, particularly given Styx would be on her way down to the moon as well, and coms range from *Phoenix* was not about to become a problem. With the human shuttles came another eight parren shuttles, from four parren warships that had been carrying two each, with full marine complements. Given fifty parren per shuttle, as she'd counted in the one she presently travelled in, that equalled four hundred in total… which added to *Phoenix*'s full company made six hundred. Not a large force compared to what some of *Phoenix*'s marines would have seen in the war, but to Lisbeth, it looked like a major invasion underway.

Finally the Gs eased off, and she opened a forward visual to see where they were. At first she thought the screen was dead, for there was nothing to see. But the cockpit audio was clear, with pilot-chatter ongoing, and a second camera showed a brilliant starfield. But that was the dorsal camera, pointed away from the moon… and then she realised. This moon and its companion had been floating through deep space for tens of thousands of years. There was no light, because there was no sun nearby. It was, of course, why no one had found this place in all that time, because no matter how advanced the telescopes, unless they knew *exactly* where to look, a small dark spot in a large dark sky was utterly impossible to find, without a nearby light source to shine upon it. The forward camera was working fine, and the absence of stars was the moon, blocking out the starfield behind… but utterly in the dark.

More thrust kicked in, a manoeuvring thrust rather than a decelerating one, but her Scan access was limited to the relative position of shuttles. The pilots would have separate forward radar and infra-red, but Lisbeth couldn't see it, and had to trust that everything was working as it should. Gs shoved her backward once more, then a brief vertigo as the shuttle spun on its axis, then fired again…

And suddenly the feed cut to infra-red, then multi-spectrum, and a surreal, glowing green image appeared of strange, angular towers and a great expanse of small structures across a vast horizon. It was a city, she realised. And it was enormous, stretching for hundreds of kilometres, with no design philosophy any human eye was trained to discern. Low gravity, airless, nestled into a missing portion of a large moon, and abandoned since the end of the Machine Age, but far older than that. Nearly twice that age, in fact. Beside her, in a brief pause in the roar of engine thrust, Lisbeth heard Gesul murmuring what might have been a parren oath… or perhaps a prayer.

"I have a beacon response," came the familiar, calm cool of Lieutenant Hausler. He sounded as though he couldn't quite believe it. Lisbeth didn't blame him. *"I do not recognise the signal... wingman please confirm?"*

"PH-1 this is PH-3, I have it too." That was Jersey. *"It's a low intensity signal, could be a drained battery, hard to believe there's any active power grid on this rock."* That would make sense, Lisbeth thought. A navigation beacon left behind by someone, possibly not even that long ago, could have survived a long time with a separate battery. There was no chance a reactor would have been left running, surely… and out here there was nothing to charge a solar panel.

A parren voice spoke in reply, and Lisbeth's translator gave only static… struggling with the tinny, broken tone on coms. *"Hello parren shuttle,"* came Hausler's reply. *"Please say again, the translator missed that one."*

More talking, and finally the translator spoke. *"Recognise parren signal,"* it said. *"Database confirm, very old signal."*

"I copy that, parren shuttle," Hausler replied, as calmly as he'd discuss approach coordinates with control at a busy station. *"Can you confirm* how *old?"*

More parren talk. *"Parren Empire,"* said the translator. *"Early period. Signal code say maybe Ruler Jin Danah."*

Lisbeth gasped. "The first ruler of the Parren Empire! That's just after the end of the Machine Age!"

"It makes sense that Jin Danah came here," Gesul said grimly. *"I have not encountered any record of it, until now. We must now consider how long he may have stayed, and why he neither recorded this moon's existence, nor destroyed it in accordance with policy at the time."*

Jin Danah, Lisbeth recalled from one of her readings, had been the leader of House Acquisitive who'd risen to rule over the new Parren Empire in the aftermath of the machines' fall. Obviously the parren had come here at the end of that war — Styx herself recalled the drysine preparations for its defence. But all such hacksaw bases had been destroyed, either in the fighting at the war's end, or in the determination of the victors to destroy every last symbol of their reign, and to destroy any technology that could conceivably one day lead again to their return.

"It's coming from within the geofeature," came Major Thakur's voice. She would be sitting in the command post on PH-1, watching the unfolding displays of the ancient city, as more became visible. *"AT-7 will deploy to investigate, find the best route down if our current intelligence proves inadequate. Alpha Platoon will lead, Lieutenant Dale in command. Gesul-Actual, do you copy?"*

"Major Thakur, this is Gesul," said Gesul. *"Lieutenant Dale has command. We will proceed."*

The parren command structure was that Tobenrah, having the superior space forces, would command all parren ships, but that Gesul, as the second-highest ranked parren, would be parren commander on the ground. In practise, that command truly fell to Gesul's marine commander, who although also outnumbered by Tobenrah's forces down here, was a man of superior rank and experience.

Lisbeth had informed Major Thakur of the situation, but there had been no time to mediate a clear chain-of-command between humans and parren. Lisbeth had her hands full just acting as

Gesul's immediate translator — solving the debate of who was actually in command of ground defences on the moon would be the Major's job.

The city tilted on her visor view, as the parren shuttle twisted to re-aim thrusters, then a sustained burn at three Gs. The steel structures were clearer now, as though glowing with reflective light in infra-red that brightened and dimmed every few seconds… and Lisbeth realised that the shuttles all had floodlights on, and were sweeping the city surface at random intervals as they manoeuvred. It seemed a little ridiculous, that single shuttles with their lights on could illuminate a city of this scale, but in the same way that a single candle could seem impossibly bright in a dark field, high-beam landing lights, in the depths of deep space, seemed as bright as suns.

The structures below did not look like any city Lisbeth had ever seen. Mostly they were a mass of cross-wise support beams, creating a mesh within which other structures were enfolded. This entire part of the moon was missing, and the artificial structure beneath was a replacement for this segment of moon circumference, in the same way that a man who'd lost his leg might wear a synthetic replacement. Yet the moon's new outline was not entirely smooth and round, it heaved and bulged in places with large domes, then fell into deep, steel crevices. These were not buildings, as one might find in the cities of organics. They looked more like factories, or other industrial structures, utilitarian and without concern for aesthetics.

Ahead, Lisbeth saw the dark outline of AT-7, thrusters flaring in a low burn to hold altitude in the moon's light G, now cutting forward thrust and gliding on momentum across the alien cityscape. Towers passed, more like observation posts than residential buildings… then the unmistakable outlines of large docking grapples, in the clustered profusion of a landing dock. In low lunar G, large ships could theoretically dock here… if the captain were willing to risk the descent. Such a civilisation, Lisbeth thought in the incredulous silence of the parren about her. It did not seem real that all of this had once been just another small outpost in twenty three thousand years of Machine Age dominance. Neither did it seem real that it could all vanish so completely.

"Geofeature ahead," said Hausler. *"AT-7, turn and burn."* The civilian shuttle silhouette rotated in a flash of attitude thrust, and was abruptly outlined against a vast darkness as the city detail vanished, replaced by a gaping void. Lisbeth's own viewpoint shifted, as her inner-ear felt the parren shuttle spin, then she saw AT-7's mains were glaring in the direction of travel, slowing them down.

Beneath them was an enormous hole. Entirely circular, it looked about two hundred metres wide. Below, its depths vanished into gloom, as even the shuttles' highbeam lights failed to show a bottom. Both shuttles slowed, then descended as vertical thrust ceased and the pilots allowed the lunar gravity to take its course. Steel cliff walls rose up, and Lisbeth could see the great structural ribs that held the rest in place. Here and there were landing platforms for shuttle-sized vehicles on this descent, with unloading mechanisms sitting idle, the shadow of spindly robotic arms moving against the wall in the glare of shuttle lights. Lisbeth wondered how long it had been since bright light had fallen upon these steel structures. Possibly tens of thousands of years.

"Battle damage," said a marine's voice from AT-7. *"Three o'clock low."* A camera zoomed, following that marine's direction — sure enough, a ragged hole had been torn in the wall, surrounded by hundreds of smaller holes, in the way only a shrapnel blast-radius could achieve.

"Yeah, I saw some others as we were flying over," said Sergeant Forrest, Alpha Platoon's XO. The marines had a visual feed in the back, it seemed, despite the absence of an actual pilot up front. *"Couldn't get a good look until now. Looks pretty old."*

An unidentified parren spoke. *"This feature will take us to the engineering core,"* said the translator. *"Its capture would represent a strategic victory, for the combatants long ago, or for us today."*

"The signal's getting stronger," said Ensign Yun from PH-1, monitoring their descent from above. On a secondary channel,

Lisbeth could hear Gesul, and a voice that her visor told her was Tobenrah, discussing something with serious animation. She directed the translator to it, a blink on the channel icon, but the translator struggled with all the talk of past parren ages, ranks and formalities, many of which had names with no translation.

Another coms icon blinked, this one aimed specifically at her, and she opened it. *"Hello Lisbeth, this is Phoenix,"* she recognised Lieutenant Shilu's voice. *"The Captain's too busy to ask himself, so you've got me. What are the parren saying about the previous history of this place?"* It wasn't just Shilu in search of a history lesson, Lisbeth knew. The last parren visitors could have laid defences, or run the city's defensive systems, some of which Styx had suggested might still be operational.

"Hello *Phoenix*, Gesul and Tobenrah seem to think this beacon is from Jin Danah's period — he was the first parren ruler of the Parren Empire after the end of the drysines. Look… bear with me *Phoenix*, I haven't been able to get a question in edgewise yet, and I don't have my parren historybooks with me, but I seem to recall Jin Danah's rule being quite short lived. There was a lot of turmoil with the collapse of House Harmony and the Tahrae, and the casualties from the war were horrific, there were lots of disagreements about how to rebuild. I'm just guessing here, but it seems to me that if Jin Danah kept this place secret after the last drysine resistance was crushed, then that secret might have died with his rule a few decades later. Which would explain why the parren won this place in battle, didn't destroy it, then forgot that it ever existed in the first place."

"That's as good a theory as anyone's got at the moment Lisbeth," Shilu replied. *"Parren are disciplined enough to take secrets to their grave. I'll inform the Captain as soon as he's got a moment. Take care."*

"I read the ground at ten-point-four Ks below you," said Lieutenant Hausler. *"Better make some time, make it fast."* AT-7 upended nose-down, then a flash of thrust as the shuttle accelerated briefly to double terminal velocity. Some parren conversation followed, mutterings of alarm as the parren shuttle did not follow the

humans' lead. If Styx was flying AT-7, Lisbeth thought with mixed alarm and amusement, she'd learned to fly by watching Hausler.

"Human pilot crazy," Timoshene translated that for Lisbeth's benefit. *"Against regulations in closed space."*

"That human pilot has learned from the best," Lisbeth corrected her former tokara coolly, almost wishing she had the co-pilot's seat up front. Her few combat ops as co-pilot had been nerve-wracking, but now she was discovering that doing it as a passenger was worse. At least up there she had some control.

AT-7 was already down when the parren shuttle approached the bottom of the geofeature, and Lisbeth could see Alpha Platoon marines already bounding wide, leaping with controlled jets of thrust in the low gravity, finding cover positions along the wall and clearing the landing position of possible ambushes. Then the parren shuttle was settling, only a light burn and touch of the landing legs, then a much larger vibration as the rear ramp extended and the doors opened, followed by the crashing of many disembarking, armoured parren.

Lisbeth undid her own restraints and waited until Gesul levered himself off the high seat row and dropped, following him to touch lightly on the deck, then duck beneath and through the shuttle's empty infantry racks toward the rear. At the bottom of the ramp, several big, armoured figures with enormous rifles were waiting — *Phoenix* marines, their suits and weapons as proportionally larger than the parren's as were their occupants. Immediately, Lisbeth recognised the saw-tooth decoration of the faceplate — it was Lieutenant Dale. Most Fleet marines had some custom decoration on their armour, a useful thing for identification in the low visibility of many operating environments. Dale's snarling visor allowed his marines to tell it was him without having to put visible officers' bars on his armour, which would only make him more of a target.

"Okay, we're doing a tacnet check," came Dale's unmistakable growl, his armoured hand pointing at Lisbeth as she approached. *"Lisbeth, is that you?"*

"Hello Lieutenant Dale, yes, you're pointing straight at me." Her voice sounded even more tinny and strange in her helmet, here outside the shuttle where her brain kept expecting external sound, but found only the silent vacuum. "To my right is Gesul, to my left is Timoshene, he's serving as Gesul's close protection, as are these three parren behind us whose names I don't know. On your right there is Chokala Raman — Chokala is a rank roughly equivalent to Major, his name is Raman, and he'll follow your orders only because he's been ordered to by Tobenrah." So be polite, was her unspoken warning. "Do you need us to integrate tacnet too?"

"Our system will do it for you, just tell your boys to hook into it. Works on any hardware." It was Styx's setup, he meant, and would integrate opposing human and parren systems without difficulty. Lisbeth translated rapidly for Gesul and Raman, who passed it on to the others. Lisbeth wanted to stare up and about at the enormous, curving high walls, and the long tunnel down which they'd flown, toward the tiny circle of stars high above… but this was a combat op, and the thing she'd discovered with combat ops was that however amazing the location, there was very little time to admire the view. *"Next thing,"* Dale continued, *"we've got something to show you, and your parren boys better not get alarmed and raise their weapons, because she* will *defend herself."*

He beckoned them to follow, over to where AT-7 sat with her ramp still open… and Lisbeth frowned, following with Gesul and the parren. Dale had said *she* will defend herself… Who was he talking about? And then she realised, and her jaw dropped a little. Surely the engineers in Chenkov's crazy little fabrication team hadn't finished already?

"Lisbeth Debogande?" Gesul queried. *"What is this man saying?"*

"Gesul-sa," said Lisbeth. *"You wanted to meet our drysine queen. Say hello to Styx."*

The thing that came down the shuttle's rear ramp was like nothing in human or parren memory. It had many legs, three main pairs with several smaller pairs near the front for manipulation rather than walking. Its armoured abdomen made a base for a longer, segmented neck, atop which perched that familiar, spherical head with its single red eye… only now, the head was mounted within a flared, armoured carapace, protecting it from many angles and creating a fearsome, armoured skull. The eye within the skull gazed down upon them all now, from a height half again as high as an armoured marine, as though belonging to some mechanical dinosaur.

"Greetings Gesul-sa of House Harmony," said Styx, on Phoenix Company coms. *"And hello to you, Lisbeth. It is good to see you well and successful."*

"And it's good to see you well and mobile, Styx," said Lisbeth. She was pleased that her voice remained steady. Several of the typically immovable parren actually shrank back a step before her, this towering, dull-silver killing machine that moved with all the impossible grace of an organic creature, and possessed more raw intellect than all present combined. The lower shins of the forelegs were extra-thick, Lisbeth saw — those were vibroblades, the weapon that had given hacksaws their human name. The underside of the forward abdomen mounted a laser cutter, and the thorax doubled as a weapons mount with single-articulated arms holding twin rotary cannon, both in the style of drysine drones.

"This is a very simple chassis," Styx admitted. *"Many of the parts are recycled from drones, and my coordination is less than ideal. Yet the accomplishment of Phoenix crew to assemble it with as little manpower as available has been considerable. They have my gratitude."*

Gesul, Lisbeth saw, had not retreated a step. Now he stepped forward, gazing up as though in a trance. *"Halgolam,"* he breathed. *"That after so many years, it should fall to me to learn the truth of it all…"*

Styx considered him, from atop her new height. *"I cannot promise you truth,"* she told Gesul. *"Organics of my experience have a tenuous grasp of the concept."*

"Ignore her," Dale said gruffly. *"She thinks humans are weird and parren are worse…"*

"Hey… um, LT?" came a voice on general coms that Lisbeth's visor identified as Sergeant Hall, commander of Second

Squad. *"I just found a little problem in the number four equipment locker. Over here, on the ramp."*

The humans all looked, as visors highlighted an armour suit on AT-7's ramp as belonging to Sergeant Hall… and under one arm he carried what looked like a miniature armour suit. No, not an armour suit, Lisbeth thought — an EVA suit for children, like the emergency suit they'd given to Skah in case of a decompression so that he could… And Lisbeth's heart nearly stopped. Oh no.

The suit was occupied, little limbs struggling against the Sergeant's grip. Then a coms switch flipped, and a stream of child-like protest came loudly on the earphones, vowels all jumbled as happened with Skah when he was angry or upset. Lieutenant Dale nearly facepalmed his visor. *"The Furball got onto the shuttle? When the hell did... oh fuck it, never mind."* Because Skah had lots of friends in Midships, and was always zooming about in zero-G, getting into places he shouldn't, exploring when the adults weren't looking. His mother was an assault shuttle pilot, and it wasn't too surprising that he'd learned his way around the berths and airlocks.

Hall came past Styx to Dale, and Skah, no doubt seeing the names light up on his visor display, recognised one in particular he knew. *"Risbeth!"* he yelled, and struggled and squirmed in Hall's grip until the exasperated Sergeant let him go. He floated to the ground, little legs almost spinning in frustration at this slow moving gravity, then bounded like a gazelle straight at Lisbeth, nearly somersaulting in his out-of-control enthusiasm.

Lisbeth dropped to a knee and grabbed him, and pressed her visor to his wider faceplate. Within, the big golden eyes were alight with excitement and emotion. And Lisbeth realised that it was going to be impossible to wipe her eyes inside her helmet, and for the next few minutes at least, she'd be blind, and blinking furiously. "Hello Skah," she said past the lump in her throat. "Have you been a good boy?"

Skah had the decency to look almost embarrassed. *"No,"* he admitted. Which got a laugh from some marines. *"But Nahny work aw tine, and I do resson with Jessica, but Jessica aw work, and*

I read with Rael and do resson with Rael, but then Captain do big G and I go medbay, and..."

"Skah, Skah!" Lisbeth interrupted, almost laughing. "Skah, you can tell me later, this is actually a combat operation..."

"Yeah, go figure," Dale muttered, though marines and parren were continuing to move and deploy about them regardless.

"...and Lieutenant Dale is in command, and we all have to do what he says, do you understand?"

"Not send back Phoenix?" Skah asked.

"Skah, *Phoenix* is a long way out of range, and the shuttles have to stay here now." And besides, she was realising as logic reasserted itself, the moon was probably safer than either AT-7 or *Phoenix*. Lisbeth stared past Skah at Styx, now in a separate coms discussion with Gesul and some others, and looking their way. Suddenly suspicious. There were no inbuilt restraints on AT-7 where Styx could buckle in with her present body, so she'd have had to pre-load in the port-side forward hold, opposite to the command post occupied by Dale. If she'd been aboard first, and she'd been flying AT-7 and had done all the pre-flight checks herself, then no one would have noticed any anomaly with the equipment locker except for her...

"Hello Lisbeth," came Styx's voice in her ear, although Styx showed every sign of continuing her conversation with Gesul, and her eye did not look Lisbeth's way. *"Skah is safer with us."*

She'd seen Lisbeth looking her way, obviously, and knew what that suspicious expression meant. How the hell she could see Lisbeth's face through the narrow visor, Lisbeth had no idea... except that the visor displays worked off eye-motion, with the helmet tracking eye position and facial expression. With Styx in the system, all of that was immediately visible, and obvious to her whether her eye was looking that way or not. So had Styx let Skah aboard? Possibly after suggesting it in the first place? Lisbeth very much doubted it was out of concern for his safety.

"Well Styx," Lisbeth said coolly. "I suppose we'll find out."

Skah looked back at the looming, mechanoid figure, and grinned. *"Bug,"* he said. *"Big bug."*

CHAPTER 26

Erik did not know the parren captain's name, and did not particularly care. He was the pilot of Tobenrah's flagship, the *Talisar*, which put him in effective command of the entire parren fleet. Or at least, he *hoped* it worked that way. Lisbeth had explained to him the complications with putting civilian commanders on warships, and the division between 'overall' command and 'actual' command. Erik hoped those issues would not raise their ugly heads here, and that Tobenrah would realise that he wasn't a trained fleet tactician, and should allow his captain to make the command decisions.

"This is interesting," came the translator's reply to the data *Phoenix* had sent to *Talisar*. It was an orbital deployment for the fourteen ships plus *Phoenix* that they had currently. *"What is your confidence in this formation?"*

"*Talisar*, this orbital configuration is unknown to humans. But the *Phoenix* bridge has many years of combat experience against tavalai forces, and this is our best judgement."

"I will discuss with my combat crew. Please stand by." Erik would have exchanged a pensive glance with Shahaim and Kaspowitz, his two main collaborators on that configuration, had the bridge layout allowed it. He did not even particularly want to be pushing for overall command — *Phoenix* was the alien ship here, the outsider whose comprehension of foreign commands would be slowed by the need of translators in either direction. In some ways, *Phoenix* taking command would be trouble for everyone. On the other hand, these parren had seen barely a fraction of *Phoenix*'s combat actions, as parren fought few foreign wars, and most civil conflicts rarely reached the level of starship combat. Plus, *Phoenix* was by far the most powerful ship here, and by long tradition, that ship would typically have command.

"Are we going to surrender command if they insist?" Suli asked.

“I don’t see that we can,” said Erik. “It could be tempting for a parren commander to use the powerful alien vessel as bait, or sacrifice her to advance his position. The only reason they’ve wanted us alive before was Styx and the data-core, both of which are now off-ship.”

“I can’t see they’ll be any happier taking orders from us,” said Suli.

The combat formation they’d proposed was an irregular orbital dispersal, with multiple ships making crisscross orbits of the singularity to bring them in and out of response-range to any deepynine jump arrival. It had the bigger, more powerful ships on a lower orbit, which given the irregular nature of the gravity-slope would make them considerably faster in any slingshot manoeuvres. Having bigger engines, they’d be able to climb free more easily than smaller ships, but at the sacrifice of any rapid V accumulation. It was worth it though, both Erik and Suli agreed, to bring the big ships more frequently into the response window, and positioned to intercept any move toward the moon at rapid orbital intervals.

The smaller ships would be much further out, flanking the jump approach window. Already they were doing that, mining that window with inert rounds that would serve as mines against incoming ships by accelerating to intercept. Erik, Suli and Kaspowitz’s plan would put those ships around the jump entry window, which was absolutely tiny by normal standards, thanks to the rapidly converging force points between real and hyperspace on the irregular gravity slope. With such an accurate fix on where the deepynines would emerge, assuming they came from Lusakia System, the smaller ships could position on the flanks and chase the deepynines in, putting fire into their rear and forcing evasive action. Some deepynines would break to deal with those smaller ships, while the others would continue on — dramatically fewer in number, and a more feasible opposition for *Phoenix* and the larger parren vessels.

Erik didn’t like it at all — burying *Phoenix* deep in a gravity slope this dramatic was against all training and instincts. But a deeper deployment jump-side of the attack would allow deepynine vessels to gang up on the more valuable big ships, and Erik had few illusions about how long they'd last if that happened. A deep deployment away from the jump-side would take too long to respond to, and leave the deepyines a clear run at the moon. And if the usual bad thing happened that happened to all ships buried deep in a gravity-well, and the deepynines dropped all kinds of ordnance on their heads that the force of gravity did not allow them to dodge, then the odd shape of this particular well would allow for a fast slingshot evasion, while forcing all pursuing ordnance to chase them in a narrow orbital band that defensive armaments could easily destroy. In theory. None of them knew for certain, because obviously enough, no one had ever even imagined a gravitational phenomenon like this one before, let alone operated on one.

"Hello Phoenix, this is Talisar. Your plan appears well judged. We will deploy, with adjustments for smaller ship positions. I suggest a joint command — Talisar has operational command, but Phoenix will supply primary strategic oversight. How do you reply?"

"Suli?" Erik asked immediately, off-coms. To describe the suggestion as 'Irregular' would have been an understatement.

"Imagine this battlespace is one giant bridge," said Suli, as though drawing a giant diagram in her mind to visualise it. "We can't be Coms, because of the translation delay, and we can't be Captain because parren command probably won't allow it. So we'll be Tactical, which doesn't actually exist, but if you imagine we invent it… I think it could work, and it's probably the best we're going to get."

Erik nodded slowly, relieved for the thousandth time to have Suli's experience at his right hand where he needed it. "Hello *Talisar*, we have discussed and your proposal is acceptable."

"Phoenix will be Tactical Officer," the parren confirmed. *"Talisar out."*

Erik switched coms. "Hello Rooke, what can you tell me?"

"Repairs look good for now," the whizzkid Engineering Chief replied. *"All parameters stable, but I estimate a fifty percent chance that if we burn above ninety percent thrust, we'll break*

something. How bad is anyone's guess, anything from minor chamber breach to full detonation, and there won't be anything we can do back here."

"So you'd ideally like me not to do any combat manoeuvres in combat."

"That would be perfect, yes Captain."

"Thank you Lieutenant, I'll forward your request to the deepynines and see if they have any input on the matter."

"Sir, speaking of deepynines, Styx compiled for my Systems Team a list of suspicious functions in inbuilt system software, she didn't want to probe too deeply, she said some of the functions may have retaliated and caused damage. But that's kind of the issue — these systems didn't like Styx being there, and reacted autonomously against her."

Erik wasn't sure he could blame *Phoenix*'s subsystems for that. "And you think that might indicate they're imbedded alo functions?" Of the kind that everyone feared might be spying on them. *Phoenix*'s computer systems were vast and deep enough that the idea of modifications to subsystems in the software going unnoticed for decades was not implausible.

"We're working on highlighting them now, but given we don't know exactly what they do, assuming they do nasty things, we're not entirely sure how to stop them."

"Just give me warning, Lieutenant. If parts of our ship start collaborating with the enemy, I want as much warning as possible, and I want you to be prepared to shut that entire function down."

"We'll try, Captain. But if the entire system in question is the thrust chamber regulator, I'm not going to be able to do that, in combat, without killing the ship."

Marine armour thrusters possessed enough power for a one-G push, which felt like plenty when it turned a suit into a human-sized rocket across an airless void. But the speeds were low, and deprived of cover it wasn't the sort of move a marine wanted to make in combat unless her objective was suicide.

Trace's current objective was reconnaissance and transport, hitting thrust until her temperature lights gave her an orange warning, then cutting to arc a silent trajectory apexing at three hundred metres above the sprawling alien city. Two kilometres ahead was the great geofeature hole into which AT-7 and the parren shuttle holding Lisbeth and Gesul had vanished. Surrounding the geofeature, the landscape was mostly transport infrastructure, large landing pads and silent cargo loaders, square-rail systems winding through the steel depths beneath the pads. The domes of large pressure tanks loomed between the pads, no doubt the hacksaws had found as many uses for pressurised gasses and liquids as organic species did.

This section of the city looked industrial. As Trace looked north, the horizon was broken with an incredible vista of towers arrayed in razor-like ridges, dropping into steel canyons below. To the south, a series of enormous, low domes, each ten kilometres across and enough to qualify as a city in its own right. Here, it was just one more surface detail across the endless steel horizon.

"Must have looked something when the lights were all on," Staff Sergeant Kono suggested. He was floating now behind her, following on her arc across the star-strewn sky, with the rest of Command Squad strung out behind. Above, the stars were as brilliant as one would expect, on an airless moon without a sun or atmosphere, or even a planet to reflect a sun's light onto a moon's night-shadow. The effect of so many millions of stars, above this vast, alien horizon, was incredible.

"Gotta hand it to you Major," said Private Kumar. *"You take us to some pretty cool places."*

"What do you think, guys?" Private Rolonde asked them all. *"Most crazy place yet? I thought that was Tartarus, but this is..."* She couldn't complete the sentence.

"I thought it was Merakis," said Private Terez. *"But then we hit Tartarus..."*

"Don't forget the Argitori rock," said Private Arime. *"That central hacksaw command nest was pretty freaky."*

"...and then going through TK55 and all the old corpses from the drysine study lab," Arime continued. *"That was right up there."*

"And then we got Chara and Kantovan Vault," added Private Zale, who was the newest of the regulars. He hadn't been with Command Squad for Argitori, Eve or Heuron Station, having joined with the replacements at Joma Station in barabo space, but he'd pulled his weight at Tartarus and Kantovan.

Trace's tactical display showed the gradual, descending curve ahead where the lunar gravity would drop her, a moving bullseye across the cityscape as she added little bursts of thrust to extend her range. Across a bundle of huge pipes running straight and long like a freeway, some big platforms loomed above what looked like a trench, cut across the city below. Another light thrust, as her landing circle moved toward that platform, then she cut as circle and target lined up.

Across her visor, tacnet was gathering a picture of the visible city as her marines spread across the region within a five kilometre radius of the geofeature. Above, the three *Phoenix* shuttles, plus a number of parren, flew expanding, wide circles, scanning and projecting enough multi-spectrum light to make the near-city glow on suit visuals.

"This is PH-3," said Jersey, from five klicks north. *"Tactical thinks this might be some kind of turbolift. Looks pretty big."* Vision came in from the shuttle, circling what looked like the cap-end of some large, vertical tubes beside another cargo facility. Everyone was hunting for vertical routes to the lower levels, to see if there were any alternative ways down to the core systems that Styx was aiming for. Styx, from her memory, suggested the geofeature was by far the fastest option. Any attackers wanting to reach the core systems faster, or wanting to intercept Styx herself, would be best suited by a direct pursuit down the hole.

"It's not going to work without power," Trace replied. "I need a systems analysis of local power systems ASAP, it's possible deepynines could restore local power to individual systems. If they can't, we're wasting our time defending transport systems."

"Major, just to clarify," came Lieutenant 'JC' Crozier, who was south-east with Delta Platoon. *"Styx didn't know if these power systems could be restored or not?"*

"Styx says she was just a visitor," said Trace, lining up her landing as the pad approached. She hit light thrust to decelerate at fifty metres, slowing rapidly. "And she always says she's not a technician."

"No, she's a mega-intellect and can build herself a new body from scratch," Crozier said dubiously. *"Whether she calls herself a technician or not, it* ought *to just be semantics for her."*

Trace cut thrust at two metres and let gravity drop her lightly to the pad, then bounced clear toward the far edge to make space for Command Squad coming in behind. She'd wondered before how it was possible for Styx to forget anything. Computer memory did not become hazy with time, provided the systems were undamaged, and Styx's systems were endlessly self-repairing to the point of being able to fill in a huge hole in her head. But then, when she'd first arrived on *Phoenix*, Styx had claimed to not be the same 'person' now that she'd been back then, all those millennia ago. Perhaps that was it, Trace thought, bouncing to the edge of the platform and looking across the view. Surely such an old, old mind would add layers of new data, accumulated memories and the processing nodes those new connections created. After so many years, perhaps she'd become layered like an onion… and if that was so, perhaps those most recent, outer layers began to have difficulty interacting with the inner layers. But Trace was too busy with combat operations to ponder it further, no matter how directly important to her current considerations…

Immediately below the platform edge was the trench she'd seen from further back. It was narrow, no more than ten metres across, but deep, and crisscrossed by diagonal access platforms. It ran like a knife-slash, directly away in either direction for kilometres. Trace's forward scan probed the depths with laser and broad-spectrum readings, but could not find a bottom.

"If this thing goes all the way down, it'll be a bugger to defend," she said. "Vij, take Second Section and check it out."

"Yo Major," agreed Corporal Vijay Khan. She'd borrowed him from Alpha Platoon, having a vacancy with Corporal Rael still recovering from injuries. As always, she disliked removing marines from existing units into Command Squad, but it had to be done, and Vijay was himself a recent addition to Alpha Third Squad, who'd managed without him for three months at least. *"Just jump it,"* Khan told Second Section. *"Single line, spread wide, watch for anything still active."*

He took a light jump off the edge, followed immediately by Arime, Kumar and Rolonde, and they fell together in a single line, thrust flaring lightly to keep their velocity below a comfortable level.

In a wider circle about the geofeature, Trace could see the more numerous parren units moving in great, slow moving clusters, like fireflies above the dark skyline. Tacnet was beginning to integrate their feeds — a recently acquired capability. Trace understood that Styx's software upgrades had something to do with it, and hadn't had time to learn more. Suffice to say that these days, *Phoenix*'s network capabilities were pretty well unmatched by organic species anywhere in the Spiral, other than the alo. The picture it gave her expanded out to a ten K radius, in a full circle about the geofeature… nearly all the way down to the huge domes in the south, and the tower-canyons to the north. And all of this, just a twenty kilometre diameter circle of controlled surface, upon a five hundred kilometre diameter city. A small neighbourhood, she thought. Like controlling a few suburban blocks on Shiwon, on Homeworld.

"How'd it get so damn big?" her old buddy Private 'Leo' Terez took the moment's coms silence to wonder aloud. *"What the hell were the hacksaws doing here?"*

"Well it's big," said Trace, "because one hacksaw group or another was occupying it over twenty thousand years. The oldest cities on Earth weren't around much longer than two thousand. Hacksaws like to build, and twenty thousand years is a lot of building time." As to exactly what they were doing here, she had no idea. And if she was right about Styx's mental ageing issues, possibly Styx didn't either.

She blinked on the coms icon for the parren commander, and received a gratifyingly fast response. "Hello Commander Loubek. If we can stop the enemy from accessing vertical transport within this radius, we give our descending team a chance to reach the core and figure out how to reactivate this city, assuming it's possible. Our technicians estimate it will take a number of hours to achieve, possibly many hours, so we have to buy them time. How do you see your deployment?"

"Hello Major Thakur. Your assessment is the same as ours. I have three hundred and eighty four marines under my command, we are now analysing local systems for operational capability." Trace nodded in slow relief — when operating with unfamiliar units, let alone alien units, it was good to know you were both on the same page. From the crevasse below, she could hear Second Section's conversation, and see their feeds in a corner of her visor, but she left it to Sergeant Kono. Kono technically ran Command Squad anyway, providing the tactical bubble from within which she could command the whole company, and move between its various units. In a full deployment like this, she could get overwhelmed by competing data-flows very quickly, and delegation ceased to be a choice, and became a practical necessity.

"I understand, Commander. When the assault comes in, we'll have to be underground. Deepynine armaments are too powerful to risk direct exposure on the surface, particularly if they come down with assault shuttles." She'd never seen a deepynine assault shuttle, and doubted the experience would be a pleasant one. "Likewise, our missiles will likely not penetrate their countermeasures. I calculate that any attempt from us to directly oppose their landing on the surface would result in catastrophic casualties for us, and moderate casualties for them. This calculation needs to be more in our favour. We need to draw them into close-range combat below surface level, and engage them where their disadvantage increases."

A moment's pause on coms. *"Yes Major. The geofeature is an obvious target. They will concentrate on it. Perhaps we should destroy it, and force the enemy to attack multiple locations?"*

Trace's optimism grew some more — tactical logic was always nice to hear, even if she disagreed. "A good suggestion, Commander. But I feel that the geofeature provides excellent ambush opportunities, and we can kill many of them as they descend the tube. My idea is that we copy the landing beacon in the geofeature, and deploy that signal in many plausible locations. Perhaps we can even get some of these vertical transport options working, or give them the appearance of working, and the enemy will attempt to take other paths down to the lower levels, particularly when they see what a death-trap the geofeature is."

"Just to clarify, Major... you wish to activate alternative vertical transport methods?"

"If it's possible, and we'll disable them before they can be utilised. We want to lure them, to force them to spread their assault, and channel those enemy forces into our most heavily defended positions. If we encourage them to send everything straight at the geofeature, they'll suffer heavy casualties but will win through quickly. We want to not only inflict heavy casualties on them — we want to slow them down as much as possible. By encouraging them to divide forces, then hitting each of those concentrations hard, we may achieve both."

"Or," said the parren, *"they may ignore our invitation, and concentrate their forces whatever the casualties. These are machines, and sard. We cannot expect them to be sensitive to losses."*

"That is true," Trace agreed. "We maximise our chances, and I still would rather not destroy the geofeature if they do concentrate on it. Casualties on that scale are still to our overall advantage, and once they are below ground, in the one location, our advantage increases. But if we invite them to split up, we may achieve both a delay *and* heavy casualties."

"Yes Major. I have been instructed to concede to the tactical judgement of the one who defeated Aristan."

Trace considered that briefly. Curious that parren absolute discipline, which had caused so much trouble so far, now granted her this advantage. "It is appreciated, Commander. But I insist that you shall command all parren forces directly — the human command of individual parren units is impractical, and I respect your authority. I will set the lead, and we will coordinate. Do you agree?"

"Yes Major. It is appreciated as well."

Maybe this wouldn't be so impossible after all, Trace reconsidered as he disconnected. Parren, unlike some others, could be expected to do what they said they'd do.

CHAPTER 27

The hangar bay was one of the most terrifyingly alien things Lisbeth had ever seen. As wide and long as a football field, its ceiling was low, its walls and interior cluttered with many-armed automated systems that had no obvious function she could think of. Human and parren marines advanced carefully, low-intensity IR light beaming ahead, reflected back in a two-dimensional tangle of spidery shapes and dead synthetic limbs. It was disturbing because hangar bays were such simple things, for humans, and for most organics. You put ships in here, down the bottom of an access-route like the geofeature, allowing fast-access transport to and from the surface. Ships would dock, cargo would unload while fuel or other supplies would be loaded, and empty space would be left uncluttered for easy access.

The hacksaw hangar bay was nothing like that. It told her that for hacksaws, even simple functions were utterly different to those of organics. Arms would grab, interlock and hold to… what, exactly? Human-style shuttles would have no need of it, and lacked the umbilical receptors for all these arms and tubes to find a place to go. But then, human-style shuttles would hold organic crew in an airtight environment, while hacksaw shuttles… well, they could be alive themselves, Lisbeth thought. Could have been sentient, or interlocked with other sentiences in ways that humans or parren today could only imagine…

Low gravity made it simple to jump obstructions, as Lisbeth followed Timoshene's armoured back, and Gesul's, never far from his personal guard. She tried to keep a hold of Skah's gloved hand, but that was no simple thing with a boy whose natural instinct was to run, and was quite the natural in low or zero gravity. But now he hung back, subdued in this strange, unnerving, ancient place. Lisbeth dialled back her translator function so it wouldn't bombard her with snatches of English whenever parren marines talked to each other, the standard operating chatter of soldiers holding formation, and advising of blind spots, or corners to be watched.

Lisbeth figured Gesul would find her more useful if she listened to the humans instead, and tuned her coms to the *Phoenix* frequency. There the marines talked much the same language… only here was Lieutenant Dale, talking with Lance Corporal Ricardo, who was on point with Second Squad.

"Should be another fifty metres, Ricky."

"Copy that LT." Lisbeth recalled Ricardo — a big, short-haired woman, very obviously gay with tattoos, freckles and a steel tooth when she smiled. A Private, until her buddy Corporal Carponi had died on Heuron Station, shot in the leg and bleeding out as Erik had carried him to a shuttle. Now she was one of Dale's two section commanders in First Squad.

"Keep an eye on your systems, guys," Dale added. *"It's a long walk back if you lose pressure down here."*

Ahead, Lisbeth could make out the end of the hangar, the robotic arm or umbilical systems disappearing beyond an open pressure door. Or Lisbeth presumed it was a pressure door from the airlock-style double-door design, over ten metres tall and enormously thick. But why would hacksaws need an airtight environment?

Human and parren marines hopped over the lower rim, as though in slow motion, each species holding to its own formation, humans on the left, parren on the right. Lisbeth was about to instruct Skah as they approached, but he took several bounces and jumped the two metre rim comfortably — no great feat in fifteen percent gravity, even for a little boy in an EVA suit. Lisbeth followed… and found marines ahead fanning into a colossal steel tunnel, ribbed with pipes and conduits.

The tunnel ran left and right, and straight up as well, to make a giant T-junction without even including the hangar bay. On the right of the T-junction, armoured parren were gathering before a strange looking shuttle, parked by the inner wall. It looked atmospheric, with a delta body and wings, thrusters on the upper-rear fuselage and a big cargo ramp underneath.

The parren platoon commander was talking to his men, in tones of mixed intrigue and suspicion. Then he switched to the general channel, and spoke to Dale. *"Old parren shuttle,"* said the translator. *"An old class, early Parren Empire. Emperor Jin Danah in charge, House Acquisitive."*

"Like we thought, then," offered Sergeant Hall, fanning to the left with Second Squad and guarding that passage. The passage was nearly fifteen metres tall, wide enough to admit far larger vessels than assault shuttles. Across it, Second Squad looked like ants in a sewer pipe. *"Jin Danah liberated this place from the hacksaws."*

A parren squad advanced cautiously up the lowered ramp. *"The navigation beacon is certainly emanating from inside,"* Styx opined, clattering over. She'd acquired an interesting walking style in low-G, more of a slow-motion bounding, like a dog running in shallow water. It illustrated the separate articulation throughout her torso — the independently mobile shoulders for the big, forward legs, the long but thinner middle legs, and the big hindquarters kickers. In two separate ridges along her back, a series of spines were now raised… sensors, Lisbeth wondered? Behind the sinewy power of independently articulated arms and torso segments, the effect was not so much insectoid as mechanoid, like some strange new animal, part humanoid and part insect, steel-clad and heavily armed.

Dale edged past her, warily, and looked at where a parren marine pointed to scars on the shuttle's underside. *"Battle damage, yeah,"* he agreed. *"Twenty five thousand years old. Looks like bullets, not shrapnel."* The parren commander asked him something on a channel Lisbeth couldn't hear. *"The Major says we leave the beacon on,"* Dale replied. *"This geofeature — anyone coming down it is going to get shredded. Ambush, you understand? We get good defensive positions, they come down a narrow passage, we cut them to bits. The beacon is a lure... bait, yes? It translates?"*

Some fist gestures from the parren, rapping their thighs. "That means yes," Lisbeth told Dale. She demonstrated when he looked at her, a closed fist tapping her thigh. "Parren don't talk as much as we do, to follow commands quietly is a sign of good order.

It's just like a handsignal, and they can't see you nod in armour anyway."

"Makes sense," said Dale. Lisbeth felt some relief at that. And wondered when she'd begun to feel so protective of these strange aliens who'd kidnapped her, and why it mattered to her that humans did not gain an entirely poor impression of them. Because so much of what they did, in fact, had a very good reason to it, however strange a human might find it.

"It looks damaged," came Gesul's voice, from over by the engines. *"Perhaps the last of Jin Danah's forces to be here left it behind, with the beacon running to guide others when they returned."*

"Couldn't get through the cargo bay with all those arms deployed," said Sergeant Forrest. He was Dale's second-in-command, Lisbeth recalled, and she'd recently heard stories of his narrow escapes on the Kantovan world of Konik. *"This tunnel must come off one of those access holes we saw on the way down. Better mark them before we post defences — any deepynines could take a detour off the geofeature and bypass lower defences to get here, otherwise."*

"Hello Major, do you copy?" Dale sent.

The Major's reply was flecked with static. *"Hello Lieutenant, I copy, what's your status?"*

"We've secured the base of the geofeature. The beacon is coming from an old Parren Empire shuttle, dating to our predicted time period. It looks like they left it behind when it was damaged. We're about to pick up the pace — if there were any old booby traps left, they'd have been here at the chokepoint."

"Yeah, I think speed would be a good idea from now. We're going to spend a little longer up here before deploying, there's a lot of space and we need to see what we're getting into before we try and defend it."

"I copy Major. Hell of a place."

"Hell of a place. Let me know if your signal starts to weaken, I'm already getting static breakup."

"Skah," said Lisbeth, looking down at the little boy, and somewhat surprised that he hadn't tried to wander, or climb into the shuttle. But then, he knew this was serious, with all these armed marines around, and these dark, alien hangars and tunnels were creepy enough for adults, let alone small boys. "Skah, we're going to have to move faster now."

"Bugs coning," he agreed sombrely, gazing at the ancient shuttle. *"Rots of bugs. I know."*

In the Academy, pilot instructors had always told students to expect attack at any time, but particularly when, and in the manner, that the student would least prefer it. Thus Erik was not particularly surprised when Scan showed arrivals pouring out of jump, in a direct line along the Lusakia System approach, several hours sooner than he'd hoped they would. Worse yet, they were appearing largely inside the kill window where the smaller parren ships had been laying mine munitions.

"That's definitely inside!" Geish announced with hard alarm. "Arrival energy is plus one twenty, that's right off the charts!"

"Scan, I need a vector plot!" Because energy readings on that scale suggested ships utilising more power to enter and leave hyperspace than humans knew to be physically possible. *Far* more power. It meant that while the arrival window was as narrow as predicted on this extreme gravity slope, most of the attackers had overshot the minefield and now had a clear run at the moon. But it also meant that they'd be travelling insanely fast… and on a slope this steep, would have precious little time and space to use their engines and dump V. "Nav, escape projections to my main, I want options!"

"They're inside our mines!" said Suli, alarmed and shaken. That wasn't good… but while she had more experience, Erik knew that he was somewhat better at this than her. And that most of his advantage was not skills or reflexes, but the simple ability to make sense of complicated scenarios faster than nearly anyone.

"Yes," he growled, "but they'll need to dump V several times, and they're about to run out of road." A flash on scan, as one mine at least found its target. Course projections flashed to his screen from Kaspowitz's post, showing several ways *Phoenix* could whip around the singularity from here, and get quickly onto the offensive. And now the smaller parren ships, having been left behind by the incoming wave, were pulsing jump engines to build fast velocity in pursuit… but even with that boost, they were getting left quickly behind.

"Big V dump!" said Geish. "They're cycling hard… Captain, those engines just gain or lose more V with each pulse than we do! I think they might be okay!" As suddenly the feed was coming clear on Erik's main display, and the three-dimensional projection before his eyes showed a mass of fast-moving lines, now racing through a flare of spherical distortion as they faded once more into hyperspace… and came out moving much more slowly. But a few of them, Erik saw, hadn't had as much success finding traction on the gravity slope as their comrades.

"Three of them are screwed," he said, somehow calculating his escape manoeuvre on second screen even as he watched his main. And he blinked to command coms, the direct line established to Tobenrah's ship, the *Talisar*. "Hello *Talisar*, this is *Phoenix*. We will slingshot the singularity and assault at high V, watch for our feed." As the command feed was now sharing *Phoenix*'s tactical calculations realtime with *Talisar*, to save its Captain the trouble of having to translate human technical terms like degrees and seconds.

"Hello Phoenix, Talisar will accompany. Do not go too deep, this gravity slope obeys no known laws."

"*Phoenix* copies." Erik disconnected, orienting *Phoenix* for the burn to come, spinning the ship on its axis. "Nav, how deep is too deep?"

"One hundred and twenty thousand kilometres," said Kaspowitz immediately. There was no way Kaspowitz could know for sure, and Erik knew this was as much guess as judgement. But a guess from Kaspowitz was nearly as good, and clearly he'd anticipated the question, to answer without delay. "On maximum safe acceleration, but we have to accelerate all the way through or we'll decay for sure."

That meant 'orbital decay', one of those technical terms that failed to match the drama of the event. Now on Scan, one of the three incoming ships Erik had identified slid half into hyperspace before bouncing back out again, already too deep on the gravity slope to cycle jump engines, as the curved shape of realspace and hyperspace compressed dimensionality and made space impossible for even deepynine engines to bend.

"I've got one mark… no, make that three marks on terminal decay!" Jiri announced from Scan Two. "The Captain called it — those three are gone!"

"Second dump!" called Geish, watching the main force. "That leaves eight!"

"Burn in five," Erik told them, as alarms blared throughout the ship. Engine lights glowed green in anticipation, and he hoped Rooke was right in calculating a ninety percent burn wouldn't blow the engines and get them all killed. "Three, two, one, kick."

He started the mains slow, then built them up to a shuddering roar that turned the bridge on its end, and crushed them all into their seats. Fighting for air, vision and sense, Erik felt the augments kick in, that flash of ultra-bright vision and electric thought, the tensioners tightening supports around muscle and bone, the heart thumping wildly to push blood through suddenly wider arteries.

With it came thoughts — the deepynines were commanded by someone, or something, extremely clever, to have calculated this jump course so quickly, and to have guessed the possible nature of the gravity slope on the other side, to push their entry beyond the ambush point. If Styx was right, and the deepynines had no memory of this place, then those calculations were all probability-based. There was no way the sard were smart enough, so it meant this force was led either by an alo, or by a deepynine considerably smarter than the average drone. One obvious possibility presented itself. If it *was* a deepynine queen, Erik hoped she was on one of those three ships now locked into an irreversible death-plunge toward the singularity.

A new number appeared on the lower corner of Erik's mass of graphical information — acceleration-per-second, the standard gravitational measure. *Phoenix* combat sims could not accurately predict future trajectories in close to the singularity, but sensors could measure their own shifting position and calculate just how far away from regular physics their predictions were. This new measurement was Kaspowitz, adding new displays to the Captain's vision and hoping Erik could make the necessary adjustments in his head in time to avoid any catastrophe if the numbers began plunging more than expected. And Erik spared a brief thought for the drone team in Operations who'd been prepping to sacrifice a drone flyer into the gravity-well before the deepynines' arrival had sent them running for acceleration slings. Another half-an-hour could have given them all the data they needed…

"Captain," came Kaspowitz's synthesised voice in his ear, as the Gs made talking impossible, *"it's not impossible that this G-slope is a decaying fractal ratio beyond even what I initially thought it was…"*

"Not a good time to tell me, Kaspo," Erik replied in kind, blurred vision fastened with fanatical determination on the shuddering lines of *Phoenix*'s projected trajectory. The moon orbited at a half-million Ks, and this plunge was going to take *Phoenix* within a hundred thousand. If the gravity was what they expected, it was going to give them a massive slingshot acceleration and shoot them around the polar nadir, then up and around at the deepynine fleet's flank as they burned hard toward the moon. If the calculations were off by a fraction, he'd miss that approach and have to burn harder still to get them back on course, possibly making sitting ducks of themselves in the process. If the gravity was doing nothing like their guesswork, they'd join those three doomed deepynines in making an impressive pyrotechnic display upon the singularity, as the Gs grew so strong that not even *Phoenix*'s massive engines, and considerable pre-existing V, could save them.

"We should be okay even if that's true," Kaspowitz replied. *"But if we take a wider line to avoid it, the deepynines will hit the moon before we can intercept. But there's a chance we'll be pulled*

inside them on a low orbit." And if we engage from that position, he didn't need to add, they'll pick us off from higher up the slope. Kaspowitz was a navigator, not a tactician, but he'd seen more than enough battles to know the outcome of that.

"We have to risk it Kaspo," said Erik. *"Those lead ships will be loaded with troops, probably deepynine drones. If they get to the moon in large numbers, even Trace can't hold them. We have to break them up, no matter what."*

Lisbeth's suit was not made for fighting, but it did possess basic strength enhancement. Exactly how that strength enhancement worked remained a puzzle, as she blinked on the visual icons across her visor and managed to make enough sense of the Porgesh characters to dial up the suit's leg power, and not get left behind by the marines. That was now a matter of bounding rather than running — a staggered, two-foot bounce-and-leap that propelled her another two metres into the air, and when she got a good rhythm going, another six or seven metres forward. Skah could not manage the same height, but Lisbeth's concerns that he'd be left behind faded as he simply bounced more frequently, and with more energy, and actually managed a faster forward speed.

The human and parren marines left the huge tunnels for a series of wide hangar complexes, these with umbilical arms more tightly curled upon walls and ceiling, like the curled fingers in so many alien fists. The hangars gave way to engineering spaces, where the technology was not so incredible, just an extended jumble of pipes and conduits that snaked overhead like the innards of some giant beast. The real technology that powered whatever went through those innards, Lisbeth guessed, would be elsewhere, in the plantrooms and power sources throughout this city.

Ten kilometres beneath the surface and still Lisbeth doubted they were anywhere near the floor of the enormous crater torn by that mysterious science experiment more than forty thousand years ago. Styx guided them, and Lisbeth listened to her directions on tactical coms, but did not have access to the marines' tacnet that might have shown her the way. And now Lisbeth was starting to see battle damage — the unmistakable star-pattern of rocket or grenade explosions, and the big holes of high-calibre weapons, some deep, others shallow and torn wide like scars.

"Does Halgolam guide us by memory?" Gesul asked her now as they bounded beneath a spidery complex of interlocking tubes that appeared to make vertical access tunnels — a hacksaw stairway, Lisbeth guessed. These lower portions were very badly damaged, as though torn by concentrated fire.

"Styx's memory is not always perfect," Lisbeth replied, now panting at the exertion, but by no means tired. "I suppose even AIs lose some memory function over twenty five thousand years." She had no wish to speculate further — the coms channel was supposedly private, but Lisbeth knew that with Styx, there was no such thing.

The engineering space opened onto a wide hangar and equipment bay… and Lisbeth saw that the formation leads had paused to consider the way, and possibly to stare in amazement. The wide floor was littered with the debris of war — the burned-out hulks of shuttles, large structural portions of ceiling that had collapsed under heavy fire, and even some big, armoured things that Lisbeth couldn't identify.

"Those are tanks," said Lance Corporal Ricardo from up front, swinging her big rifle as though expecting the long-dead weapons to spring back to life. *"Were tanks. Big ones, maybe ground-effect for low-G."*

One of the parren said something that the translator didn't recognise, but Lisbeth thought might be the model of tank. The parren sounded awed, as a human might who'd stumbled upon an old Earth battlefield, littered with the weapons of a war fought twenty five millennia ago, all perfectly preserved in sunless vacuum.

"Not a parren weapon," Gesul said with authority, bounding forward to look more closely. Timoshene went with him, and Lisbeth took a deep breath and followed, beckoning needlessly to

Skah, who was already moving. *"This is not a parren weapon, this tank. This is chah'nas."*

The ancient machine looked deceptively simple, fronted by a back-angled circular armourplate, within which many large, forward-firing guns were mounted. Its wheels were big, and it appeared to have no side or rear armour or weapons to speak of. Which made its purpose simple enough, to Lisbeth's eyes — plug up a big corridor with that armoured nose and soak up every shot that came its way, angling half of them into the ceiling with ricochets, while returning fire with maximum devastation. A weapon for an urban, underground fight, to push through tunnels with many armoured marines following behind.

This one seemed to have been caught in the open, possibly during a pause to rearm, with several others. Its front armour was torn with an extraordinary number of holes, the angled steel looking more like an abstract work of art than a piece of military equipment. Its rear and chassis were utterly destroyed, peeled open like a blooming flower, spilling burned innards across the floor.

"This is real interesting, Styx," came Lieutenant Dale's caustic opinion, *"but we've got a deepynine fleet incoming and we've got to move fast. Where next?"*

"Lieutenant Dale," said Styx. *"Jin Danah may have occupied this city for several human decades at least, and possibly longer. If the city's defences are as advanced as I suspect them to be, Jin Danah will have secured them, and those security measures may still be functioning. To deactivate those measures, it will be prudent to first know what happened here."*

Lisbeth turned sharply to see the big, insectoid shape leap for the top of a fallen ceiling support, and survey the battlefield from that vantage, perched like a mantis upon a twig. She turned again to make sure Skah was nearby, constantly desperate that he'd wander as he often did, but here he was, right at her side with no intention of moving… and now Gesul came up to her face, indigo eyes aglow behind his visor, and leaned in close.

"Lisbeth, Halgolam was not present for this battle?" It was unnecessary of him to lean close — with a vacuum between them,

she could not hear him without coms. But she could see the wary intensity in his eyes, and the sense of great unease. This was the greatest parren history, suddenly alive before Gesul's eyes. Here was the truth of all Aristan's claims and lies, if only Gesul could slow down to examine them. It must pain him, Lisbeth thought, to hear Dale commanding them all to move quickly.

"She says she was only here briefly," Lisbeth replied. "Maybe a year before the end. She was made in the final years of the war against what became the Parren Empire, but she was sent out to fight on another front, she didn't stay to see what happened here."

"And so for all this time," Gesul reasoned, *"she's never known what happened here."* He turned his suit to look at Styx, in time to see her leap from her perch, and down amongst the wreckage. *"That is a long time to wonder what became of your comrades."*

Immediately, Lisbeth thought of what Lieutenant Kaspowitz, or Commander Shahaim would say when one of the *Phoenix* techs would start wondering at Styx's state of mind — 'don't anthropomorphise the machine'. Somehow, she didn't think Gesul would appreciate being scolded like that.

"A long time," she agreed. And besides, she knew that Lieutenant Rooke, Stan Romki, and probably even Major Thakur, were starting to doubt the wisdom of assuming that Styx was *not* fundamentally a sentient, thinking and feeling creature, on some level at least.

Lisbeth beckoned Skah once more, and found a way to duck through the fallen ceiling support in pursuit of Styx, who was now trailed by a very impatient Lieutenant Dale.

"Run that by me again," Dale was demanding. *"You think the defences here will be secured? How will knowing what happened here let you break that security?"*

"Lieutenant, the technology in this city is beyond organic imaginings." Styx was moving calmly, peering back and forth, and under, the various wrecked equipment as she found it. Her big, right foreleg picked up a bit of torn debris, absently, and transferred it to her smaller, underside legs for sensors to consider more closely.

"That it was not destroyed by V-strike, against all established norms at the time, should suggest as much. Jin Danah was intending to preserve this technology, and to preserve the moon as a secret known only to him and his people."

"But parren history records Jin Danah fell shortly after his victory over the drysines," Gesul interrupted, now moving past Lisbeth in pursuit. *"If he kept this moon a secret, then it would appear that secret died with him, thus explaining why organics forgot its existence shortly after its discovery."*

"This seems a logical summation, Gesul," said Styx, dropping the one piece of debris and selecting another as she moved. *"And yet the resources required to capture this moon from the defences arrayed against it were clearly enormous. Regard the chah'nas model tanks, as you call them. Not commonly used in space battles. To keep all such forces from revealing the moon's location would seem an unlikely feat, even for parren discipline, particularly given the change in loyalties that followed Jin Danah's fall. Logically, Jin Danah must have gone to great lengths to secure the moon's secrecy... I cannot speculate how he managed it, you parren are far more knowledgable about your own society than I will ever be. But clearly the man had grand plans for this place, and grand plans will be well protected."*

"Styx?" said Lisbeth, grasping Skah's arm to keep him clear of some sharp metal. Civilian suits were too tough even for swords, let alone sharp debris, but she was in no mood to take chances. "What's down there? What are this moon's defences?"

"Lisbeth, I truly do not know. I was never given a tour, so to speak. But I know they exist, and I know they are formidable on a scale that might compel a power-hungry man like Jin Danah to bend every force at his command to see them preserved, protected and hidden from all those who might take them from him."

On coms came the call of a parren unit commander, sounding more puzzled than alarmed. But Gesul immediately turned that way, before Lisbeth could even figure out where the call had come from, and bounded that way. Lisbeth saw Timoshene's face within his visor before he followed, nearly rolling his eyes at his superior's endless curiosity for things that were, in Timoshene's opinion, barely worth bothering with.

Lisbeth followed with Skah, past the shattered engine of a shuttle, and found some parren marines gathered about several armoured figures on the floor. Marine armour, Lisbeth saw… and strangely familiar, though clearly not parren. This was far too bulky, and as she approached she saw that it was clearly tavalai, though looking considerably different to the karasai she'd become recently accustomed to…

"We may have to rewrite the history a little," the parren commander was saying as Lisbeth blinked her coms to that channel. *"We have records of parren forces under Jin Danah and House Acquisitive, and we know there were some chah'nas units in this region. But no tavalai."*

"No," Gesul agreed, arriving alongside. He sounded puzzled. *"At the time, tavalai were not considered warriors, just troublesome farmers, engineers and bureaucrats. And if Jin Danah wished to keep this moon classified, it seems unlikely he'd have invited a race to participate in the assault whom of all in the Spiral were least likely to keep a secret."*

"This armour, too," said another parren, pointing with his rifle. *"This loading is light, there is no sign of extra ammunition, or empty carrying capacity. This is a defensive loading, not an offensive one."*

"Defensive?" Gesul stared at the man, then down at the dead tavalai suit. There were others, Lisbeth saw, and from the severed arm of one, it looked as though the suits were still occupied, with leathery, withered remains. *"And they have been left upon the battlefield, while all other casualties have been removed."*

And Lisbeth's eyes widened slightly, as she recalled what that meant. Parren had been the victors here. Jin Danah's forces. In great battles, the dead of both sides were treated with reverence, in accordance with customs as old as parren memory. The only foes to be left where they had fallen upon the field of battle were the despised, the dishonourable, the unworthy. Why would tavalai come to participate in this fight to end the hated Drysine Empire, only to be abandoned in death upon the field by their parren allies in the struggle? Unless… *Unless…*

"What in the name of all departed ancestors is going on here?" Gesul muttered. From the incredulity in his voice, Lisbeth knew he'd had just the same thought she had.

"The answer to that is simple, Gesul," Styx interrupted this channel without invitation. *"Your history is all lies."*

CHAPTER 28

"Going to be some big fireworks in a moment," came Commander Shahaim's voice from *Phoenix*, crackling with static on Trace's coms. *"Three deepynine ships misjudged jump and are about to impact upon the singularity. That leaves eight, all headed straight for you. Three appear to be sard, those are coming in far too fast, we think they can't pull Gs on the same scale — those lead five ships are currently at fourteen-Gs. The front three are pulling ten, they're on a wider decelerating course, they'll take a wider arc away from the moon and will be arriving at your location at A-minus-twenty-five by our current estimates. We're going to try and extend that by as much as possible, and give you a smaller force to face."*

Trace tried to process that as she thrusted long and high above the cityscape, its previous detail fading as more platoons found their way into defensive positions, and no longer shone low-vis light across the skyline. Though space combat was not her speciality, she knew that fourteen-Gs was not survivable for organic species, not even kaal. Which told her that the crew of those lead five ships were indeed mechanical. It also suggested that *Phoenix* was still deciding which of the approaching formations to try and intercept out of their slingshot manoeuvre.

"I copy *Phoenix*, can you give me an estimate of their marine capacity?" She selected a featureless, flat steel expanse, cutting thrust to let the jets cool as gravity brought her in.

"We'd only be guessing, Major," came Shahaim's reply, strained with Gs that were nonetheless now low enough that she could talk. *"But they're all about thirty percent larger than Phoenix — some of that is engines, the rest is Midships."* Which, in any school of ship design, with ships this large, meant deployable forces. Trace did some fast calculation — *Phoenix* had more than two hundred marines, but she'd have guessed a deepynine drone didn't require as much space or resources, given they didn't need to eat,

recreate or use the bathroom. Three hundred per ship? And there were five of them coming, with three more behind. Dear god.

"*Phoenix*," she replied, "what is the damage likely to be on those first five ships? I could be looking at fifteen hundred deepynine drones, and if that happens, our odds aren't great. Sard, we can handle. If you could take one or two of those first five before they arrive, it would give us a chance."

Shahaim's reply did not arrive as fast as the minimal lag suggested it might. Trace hit thrust before grounding, and bounced instead, as Command Squad came in behind and followed.

"Hello Major," came the reply at last. *"I'll see what we can do. We hear that Styx still has no idea what the moon's defences might be?"*

"That's what I hear as well." Trace bounced again, lined up an exposed dome a kilometre ahead, and hit thrust again, burning into the star-strewn sky. "She tells me the defensive forces gave the city a name, however. It's stencilled on their armour, in an old parren tongue. Translated, it means Defiance."

"Fitting," said Shahaim. *"Good luck to you Major. Correct assault ETA now twenty-one minutes and eleven seconds."*

"And good luck to you, *Phoenix*." She cut thrust as her visor calculated the trajectory would end on her target, and sailed for a moment, watching the deployments spreading about the geofeature and burrowing out of sight. She'd just told *Phoenix* to attack the most dangerous option, she knew. If Erik chose to do that, instead of taking the less dangerous three sard ships, *Phoenix* might be destroyed. But if he didn't, and her two hundred marines and five hundred parren found themselves outnumbered two-to-one against deepynine drones from the first wave alone… well, she'd give them half-an-hour, at best. The survivors, without hope of ship or shuttle resupply, would run out of air well before they ran out of water or food. If the city were alive and powered, there might be hope to find technology or power-run recycling systems for air and water… but there was no hope of food, and with no one else in parren space even knowing this moon existed, no hope of rescue, either. Most of her marines, she suspected, would rather go down fighting.

"Major," said Lieutenant Zhi. All her lieutenants had been listening. *"We're not going to do groundfire?"* It was tempting, Trace knew, because the deepynines would never be so exposed as when they were on final approach.

But… "Approaching targets are exposed but at least capable of manoeuvre," she reminded them all. "If we're on the ground, firing upward, we're the sitting ducks, not them. I don't know what armaments and targeting their shuttles have, but I'll bet it's good. If we line up for them on the ground, we could all be dead before they even land."

A familiar icon blinked, and she opened it. *"Major, it's Dale. More geofeatures here, like we thought, but they're sealed at multiple levels. The history lesson is that it looks like there were tavalai, parren, even some chah'nas, all fighting* with *the drysines, if you can believe that. It wasn't just Drakhil and the Tahrae, it was lots of them."*

Even with the current situation, Trace found a moment to be astonished. Of all the history-upending things they'd discovered of late, this had to be right at the top. Drakhil had always been a figure of hate not only for parren, but for organics everywhere — a traitor not only to his own people, but to all organic life in the Spiral. Now Dale said he hadn't been alone, and that other, non-parren species had been here too? Fighting until the end, on a lost and gravitationally-improbable moon, half-filled with a city called Defiance? And now, here was Phoenix Company, in the middle of history repeating.

"That's great Ty," she said, as the ground came hurtling up once more, and she hit thrust to brake fast and bounce. "Meanwhile, we're ETA twenty-point-five and it looks like there could be fifteen hundred of them. Less history and more rapid movement please."

"Dammit Major," Dale growled, *"we don't need an entire platoon down here, let alone another platoon of parren, just to guard the damn queen…"*

"Yes we do, because I can guarantee they will go straight through us like a knife through butter. If we try to hold a line we'll die in droves. We'll make them come through us and take losses on their way, but they *will* contact you, in force, whether we win up here or not. Protect the damn queen and her data-core, or everything we've been through up to now will have been for nothing. We're all counting on you, Ty."

A flash somewhere above caught her eye, and she glanced in mid-bounce. Immediately the visor polarised to deep-black, to save her vision from the brilliance that followed. Exclamations followed on coms, human and parren alike. It came directly from the hitherto invisible singularity, half-a-million kilometres away, and barely as big as a starship.

"Take a wrong turn, assholes?" Jalawi remarked.

"I copy that, Major," came Dale's unhappy reply, unable to see the fireworks on the surface. *"We're moving."*

The flash nearly blinded all of *Phoenix*'s sensors, and Erik saw molten fragments of singularity exploding away from that brilliance, most even now halting and falling rapidly back the way they'd come. *Phoenix* hurtled, now pulling Gs just from the direction change — the only time in Erik's starship career he'd ever changed direction this sharply without firing engines to do it. The gravity slope here was insane and frightening, and if they slowed down even a little bit, they'd plunge straight down to a fate identical to that of the deepynine.

"A little sharper than we thought," Kaspowitz informed them, staring at his screens with laser-like focus. "We'll come out facing oh-three-one by three-one-one, we can transition to intercept either the first or the second group."

"What will those impacts do to the singularity?" Erik asked, watching a few thousand bits of escape-velocity debris streaking past them. Any one of them would kill a ship, and all were travelling too fast to dodge.

"Minimal," said Kaspowitz. "The ejecta's just a fractional percentage of total mass. The odds of a strike are small, and the core will liquefy and absorb the next two impacts without as much ejecta." His fingers danced on the displays. "I'm getting much better data on surface gravity now, it looks like five or six hundred Gs down there, there's not much escaping that."

The next flash blinded Scan for a second time as he spoke, a second deepynine vessel hitting that high-density core at nearly one percent the speed of light. The temperatures in that explosion would far exceed the core of a G2 sun, Erik knew — but the outward forces of expulsion would still not be enough to shift most of that mass from its present position. Quickly enough, the liquefied remains of each vessel would settle onto that perfectly spherical surface, and the singularity would grow by one minuscule fraction of a millimetre.

"Captain, I just spoke with the Major," said Shahaim, running engines and systems check as she spoke, absorbing the reports from Engineering that Erik had no time to read. "She wants those first five deepynines hit, not the trailing three, she thinks there could be fifteen hundred drones on that lot and she can't handle them all."

"That's what I was thinking," Erik agreed. Tactical common sense said the trailing three were the better target — *Phoenix* had *Talisar* and five more capital warships spreading wide behind them, hurtling through the slingshot approach. Seven against three made much better odds, considering what they were facing. But if those first five deepynines put all their drones down on the moon, they were looking at losing not only Styx and the data-core they'd just gone through everything to acquire, but losing all of Phoenix Company in a ground fight they could not possibly win.

Erik knew he couldn't allow it, and was pleased that in this hyper-focused state, the shocking unreality of what he had to do did not hit him so hard. The deepynines were locked into a massive deceleration approach, and if they went evasive to dodge *Phoenix*, they might actually miss their interception of the moon. They were target-fixated, which gave *Phoenix* the edge, targeting and firing along predictable lines of approach. They were also bow-to-target, while the deepynines were unavoidably side-on, presenting the largest possible profile to *Phoenix*'s smallest. The three sard ships were wide of that approach, nadir from *Phoenix*'s current angle, and only 'trailing' in the sense that they would arrive at the moon considerably later, given their less powerful deceleration and arcing approach trajectory. Picking between them was an equal choice, in terms of manoeuvre. But tactically, there was no choice at all.

He blinked on the command icon, and got a reply from the Captain of *Talisar*. Tobenrah was on that ship. The actual head of House Harmony, leader of many billions of parren. Would the Captain agree to such a manoeuvre, with that cargo aboard?

"Hello *Talisar*, our ground forces require strikes on the first five deepynine ships. Our estimate is that they carry the most formidable ground forces. *Phoenix* will engage, we expect the trailing three ships to engage us in turn. We will require cover."

"Hello Phoenix, Talisar will engage. Primary targets are the forward five vessels, parren ground commander gives us the same assessment. Harmony aligns, Phoenix."

The translator probably mangled that, Erik thought, but he knew what it sounded like. "Good luck to you, *Talisar*. It has been an honour."

The third detonation hit the singularity, the most brilliant of the three. *Phoenix* and the six parren were approaching high-V out of that glare, the gravity slope dropping away far more rapidly than the physics books said possible, and that combination of twisted space and sensor-blinding glare had to be playing hell with even deepynine armscomps. Against targets whose ability to counter-manoeuvre was limited by their approach, they'd never get a better chance than this.

"Arms is green and clear!" Karle announced from Arms One. "Mains aligned, full spread on the front five!"

"Secondaries online!" Harris added from Arms Two. "Defensive all forward, good to go!"

"I have incoming!" Geish said loudly. "All marks are laying down their spread! Volume looks a little light, stand by!"

But it was a wide spread, Erik saw. The deepynines were firing at all of them, human and parren alike. Better yet, as Geish said, the volume looked light, meaning that it did not appear that all available guns were firing. And here lay *Phoenix*'s final advantage — in a heavy-G push, some weapons simply didn't fire, and even the highest technology didn't always fix the problem. Mechanisms disabled under high-G, or swivel mounts lost their mobility, or a myriad of other problems. And now, it looked as though even these super-advanced ships hadn't entirely overcome that problem.

The lines all matched up on Erik's display, and he felt so detached, so lost in the overwhelming rush of data, that he nearly managed a smile at his own optimism. So many advantages. Against these opponents, all it added up to was a chance — of success, at least. Of survival, he gave them only one chance in five.

Lisbeth took the ten metre fall easily enough, the floor approaching so slowly that she simply bounced clear, giving the marines behind her a clear landing, a steady rain of armoured bodies. She looked immediately for Skah, and found him waiting for her, even checking his air and systems on the arm-display that was easier for children to use than the visor. Her own suit told her the air remaining was ninety-nine point three percent, suit filtration recycled most CO2 back to oxygen once more, with only a small total loss. Of all the problems she'd find down here, running out of air wasn't going to be one of them for a long time yet.

The new space was an engineering level once more, and the flitting glance of helmet lights caught strange, alien machinery in the middle-distance that might have been cargo haulers, but looked more like specifically designed machines to service power systems. Again the floor was enormous, and this time without visible battle damage. The far walls looked strange, as though molded from the thick conduits of some kind of insulated material. As low-vis light caught it from a multitude of angles, it seemed to fracture and shimmer, like the chitinous surface of a beetle shell.

"It is here," said Styx, to Lisbeth's relief. All of that fast bounding seemed easy at first, but quickly became exhausting in the heavy suit, and now she was breathing hard, the suit's

environmentals pumping in cooler air, monitoring her respiration. She took Skah's hand and skipped to where Styx was now circling what looked like an elevator car atop a shaft leading into the floor below. Behind the car, a wall of many overlooking windows, like some sort of control function. Immediately surrounding it, six strange, concentric rings linked to form what would look from above like a hexagon.

"Are those rings some sort of scanning function?" Lisbeth wondered, as Sergeant Forrest dispersed the Alpha Platoon marines in defensive formation, while Dale examined the car.

"Yes Lisbeth," said Styx. *"Even AIs need security functions about the most sensitive installations."* She was peering now at one of those rings, and Lisbeth found it nearly mesmerising to see how much precise sentience there was in the motion of this animal-looking machine, the forelegs running along the circle's rim while the single eye and head darted this way and that, examining every detail.

"Well the damn car's blocking the shaft," Dale observed. *"Can you make it move, or do we have to blow it?"*

"These systems are independent and built to last," Styx replied. *"I am getting no response from network functions, but I believe the master switch should be here somewhere."*

"You believe?" said Dale. *"How does the smartest brain in the Spiral not know this stuff?"*

Styx ignored him, which was not typically her style, finding communication so effortless. Lisbeth thought that might mean she was annoyed. "Styx?" she ventured. "Would you like some assistance?"

"That would make a nice change," said Styx. In another circumstance, Lisbeth might have laughed. *"But presently unnecessary."*

She'd found something, Lisbeth saw. At the base of one of the circles, she'd removed a small panel. The very tip of one foreleg opened to reveal little manipulators, smaller and more precise than human fingers, tapping a code into some mechanism within. Then stopped, and waited.

"Are you sure an independent battery could last this long?" Lisbeth wondered. As though in answer to her question, a deep hum began from somewhere beneath the decking.

"Never sure, Lisbeth," said Styx, backing away to consider her work. *"Certainty is a sign of inferior intellect."*

The deep, underground hum was joined by another, then a higher pitch, as though independent functions were somehow resuming after so many millennia of slumber. She could hear it, Lisbeth knew, because of her boots on the decking… and she jumped a little, to marvel at the sudden disappearance of sound. Then its resumption when she touched down once more, only now much louder, as the smaller systems combined to fire up something much larger again.

Suddenly there were lights blinking, then a cascade of new light, like a wave sweeping across a beach. Lisbeth's suit vision deactivated, as inbuilt light filled the engineering level… but broken and spotty, she saw, with many sections not working, making a pattern of bright and shadow. Within the surrounding rings, the elevator car was now blinking, wide doors opening. Lisbeth thought it looked large enough to fit ten… but one of those would surely be Styx, so perhaps nine?

"Lieutenant," said Styx, *"you will wish to accompany, as this will involve command decisions. A parren representative also, of course. Lisbeth, an organic engineering brain could prove useful, and you are the only one of those."*

"Styx, I have to stay and watch Skah," Lisbeth explained.

"Skah will be useful also."

Lisbeth blinked. "What? How?"

"Trust me." It was perhaps the oddest two words she'd ever considered whether to take seriously, coming from a metallic, alien dinosaur perched before the entrance to an ancient elevator car, about to plunge them into the bowels of the city. *"And Gesul is the closest organic here to being an historian, and will be necessary also. Come, we have little time."*

Lisbeth grasped Skah's hand and went, knowing that in this, as with so many things, none of them had any real choice but to do what Styx said. This was quite literally her world, and everyone else, human and parren alike, were the aliens. Dale left Sergeant Hall in charge of Alpha, with instructions to listen to the parren commander as the ranking officer, but not necessarily to obey him, then followed Lisbeth in with First Section. Timoshene accompanied Gesul, and they all squeezed in, suited and armoured shoulders pressed together, with Styx back on her hind legs, forelimbs splayed above them to keep her body clear and make room.

Skah found that sight especially fascinating as the doors closed, and the car began to hum, then to move. He tilted his whole body back, as the helmet had limited mobility, and leaned on Gesul's leg to look upward. Styx gazed down at him with her single unblinking red eye, from up by the ceiling.

"You have an uplink connection to the car?" Lisbeth asked her.

"Yes," said Styx. And reached down with one of those big forelegs, toward Skah. Skah reached up as the car accelerated into the dark tunnel, and touched where Styx's hand would be, if hacksaws had hands. *"The connection is stable. I believe the systems below will prove operational, once activated."*

Lisbeth noticed that beside her, Lieutenant Dale was leaning on the muzzle of his enormous Koshaim rifle, its butt to the floor, its muzzle angled upward… and directly at Styx's head. His armoured glove was rested upon the trigger handle, and Lisbeth doubted that the safety was on. They'd been in this situation before — following Styx into a giant drysine facility where she might conceivably find enough power and technology that she no longer needed *Phoenix*, or any organics at all. One swipe of those forelegs, once the vibroblades had activated, and there'd be nothing left of organics in this car but bits and pieces.

Lisbeth wondered if Styx was comfortable enough yet with her new body that she'd notice the direction of Dale's gun. Brilliant or not, Styx had not operated with a body since Argitori… and there, she'd employed a relatively immobile, non-combat chassis. It occurred to Lisbeth that she'd never really asked Styx why. If Styx was specifically designed for combat tactics, why devolve to such a non-lethal body, when she'd specifically designed one so deadly for now? Though AIs, Styx had agreed, were somewhat autistic compared to organics, sometimes struggling to make sense of external dataflows as quickly, preferring instead the ever-more complex patterns in their own heads. Could an AI lose track of the outside world, after being locked inside a deep-space rock for twenty thousand years? Had she lost interest, like some hopeless castaway having long since abandoned any hope of rescue, and curled up in her comfortable command room, hooked into a virtual world and dreaming electronic dreams?

After a minute of what felt like freefall, the car began to slow. And suddenly it fell clear of the enclosed shaft, and broke into open space on rails, slowing all the while. Flashing past the windows were a tangle of pipes, cords and complex, intricate patterns of steel and machinery. Here, finally, was something like what Lisbeth had expected when she'd heard of this great hacksaw city — a maze-like nest, like *Phoenix*'s marines had discovered in Argitori, where a human could lose all sense of direction, up and down. Through this maze, hacksaws would scuttle like insects, having little need for human concerns of privacy, or segregated rooms and corridors. The large-scale structures of the higher ground required a certain symmetry, particularly to accommodate shuttles and equipment, but down here they could be free.

The car came to a halt atop a wide platform, doors opening only on one side, as the other led to narrow, crawling corridors that held to no single direction. Gesul went first, almost eagerly, with Timoshene at his shoulder, rifle aimed and ready. Then First Section minus Dale, who waited for Styx to unfold herself into the car and flow after them out the door. Lisbeth went last of all, tightly clutching Skah's hand.

"Risbeth, rook!" said Skah, with pure awe. About the platform, the jungle of hacksaw habitat cleared into a great cavernous space, broken by the tangles of unidentified technology that spilled from the upper levels in great clusters, like the fasciae of some organic's innards. The platform, Lisbeth saw further, was atop

something enormous, and roughly spherical. It was as though they were all standing upon some huge ball, like a globe beneath them, surrounded in this jungle clearing of hacksaw confusion, the curving edges of the ball turning to sheer drops on all sides.

The platform was not regular, either, and the organics had to watch where they trod, for the ground rose and fell upon irregularities, like walking along a forest floor and being careful not to trip on the roots of trees. Encircling the regular platform were equally irregular panels… or rather, the supports where panels ought to have been, to human eyes. Clearly they were the base for some sort of holographic display, Lisbeth thought as she followed the others toward what looked like the platform centre… but she did not recognise the technology. Some lights glowed here and there, diffuse and difficult to see exactly where they shone from, making shadows amongst the surrounding tangle.

"Dammit Styx," Sergeant Forrest breathed as he stared about him. *"I thought AIs were supposed to think in straight lines."*

"Itself a linear thought, Sergeant," Styx replied. *"AIs calculate the most efficient path between two points. In complex systems, we find that is rarely a straight line."*

"You sure take us to see some shit, LT," said Private Reddy in a low voice. Lisbeth had been filled in on First Section's adventures in Gamesh, the largest city on Konik, while she'd been held captive in the Kunadeen. And she'd heard that Reddy in particular was now held in awe by the rest of Phoenix Company, having displayed on numerous occasions that unique combination of ability, nerve and luck that all marines valued.

At the centre of the platform, a column of bundled cords headed skyward, like the stem of a giant apple. Styx paused before it, secondary forelegs joining the main pair to touch small sensors, then more again as the twin pairs of underside short arms joined in. About the chamber, Lisbeth saw small lights only. Behind them, the elevator car's emergency running light strobed the darkness.

"Surely Jin Danah has put a lock on this place when he was last here?" Gesul wondered. *"This is the core command centre for the city, yes?"*

"That is correct, Gesul," said Styx, circling the stem, red eye peering. *"I predict that Jin Danah's engineers chose to leave the city's command functions largely untouched. This technology was beyond their comprehension, and meddling with it would likely disable it without adding to parren understanding. I am detecting little sign of a blockage, save for some simple network controls that are now quite deteriorated with age."*

Abruptly, the surrounding side-screens sprang to life, holographic displays like the shield wall of some ancient army, alive with data. The hacksaw maze began to glow and throb, with a rumble of new vibration.

"Well I can't see why you wanted the damn civvies down here," Dale growled suspiciously. *"Except to get the tourist experience. There's not a heck of a lot for us to do, Styx, and we're going to need more marines topside real soon."*

"You are mistaken, Lieutenant Dale," Styx said calmly, still manipulating hidden switches. 'Again', her tone implied. *"This is not merely a command centre. You are standing upon the central processing core of the city. Drakhil's people called it a 'pathenpar', which in the old Klyran tongue means 'great mind'. Perhaps the modern translation would be a 'mega sentience', but that is misleading. The Tahrae called her Hannachiam, in that way of organics who need to grant verbal names to each entity. She has been sleeping for a very long time now, and if my readings are correct, I believe I may be able to wake her."*

"Her?" Gesul gasped. *"It's... she is... sentient?"*

"Another inadequate word. You will see. But I would like you all down here, civilians and aliens of different races, because Hannachiam was known to find such contact stimulating. If she can be woken, she may need convincing. And it may be up to these civilians to convince her that their people are indeed worth saving."

CHAPTER 29

Erik had tunnel vision. In combat he always did, but this time it was a relief in that it did not let him see the ships beside him dying. Geish did not even bother calling them, the smaller parren ships left behind by the initial deepynine arrival, only now catching up and hurtling in with suicidal determination. Their size made them harder to hit, but their defensive armaments weren't up to repelling this volume of firepower, and after surviving the initial firewave, three now died in quick succession. But they were forcing the deepynine to divide their fire, which gave the bigger ships a chance. Still, as Erik saw Scan marking incoming certain and predicted round clusters, it looked horrible.

Oddly enough, there wasn't much talking on the bridge. Everyone knew their jobs and the battleplan was already decided, all targets detected and very few surprises left, leaving very little to talk about. Suli was most vocal, shouting 'Corkscrew Three!' as Erik threw them into a left-side evasive pattern, telling Karle and Harris on Arms what motion to expect and save them seconds in identifying it. Then, 'Reverse Kick! Two-fifteen hard and port roll!"

As fire ripped past them, and main guns hammered again and again, Karle pouring fire onto the five big deepynines, now frighteningly close and getting closer as *Phoenix* cut across their rear-facing bows, simply trying to put a volume of fire into the space they needed to go that would force them to abandon their approach, or die trying not to. Erik could see them evasive, twisting back and forth with their thrusters still flaring at full deceleration, still toward the moon, but no longer straight toward it, bobbing and weaving like canoes on a rough sea. Defensive fire surrounded each in a corona of fire, hitting incoming rounds from *Phoenix* and the six parren ships in pyrotechnic flashes visible even on main scan.

A crash from somewhere behind, and a big kick Erik felt through the controls. *"Rear quarter, mostly shielding!"* came Rooke's shout on coms. *"We're okay!"* Erik could see Arms Two highlighting incoming fire as it changed direction straight toward them, self-propelled rounds meeting outgoing area detonations and disintegrating before the combined velocity of directional shrapnel. More shrapnel rained off the bow armour, already scarred from Brehn System, a sound like a fistful of gravel against a steel wall.

They were about to pass the optimum fire-angle of the wide-arcing three sard ships, whose fire was mostly directed at the smaller parren pursuers behind them. Forty more seconds, Erik saw, and they'd be through the worst of it. But if they didn't get a couple of those big ones to at least break off…

A big flash on Scan to one side. "*Tiamah*'s gone!" called Geish. That was the ship that had picked up Aristan in Cephilae, then brought him to Brehn, then to Elsium. After Aristan's death, they'd declared for Tobenrah… and now paid for that loyalty with their lives. Then, "Mark Four's hit! Big evasive, he's shifting!" As one of the big deepynines swung wildly aside, spinning and only partly in control…

"Ignore him, get the others!" Erik commanded, randomly changing their evasive pattern once more, alternating thrust from two to nine-Gs then back again, doing every crazy thing he could to keep them alive in the firestorm.

Gesul's flagship *Stassis* broke up and cartwheeled, neither Geish nor Jiri bothered to call it… whack! as something ripped across their side, and Erik's boards lit up with damage lights, dish-three gone and one of the defensive batteries…

One of the big deepynines abruptly cut thrust to evade as his near-scan showed something nasty, then vanished in a fireball like a small sun. "Gotcha!" snarled Karle, then the loudest noise Erik had ever heard, a head-snapping impact, darkness, stars, then his ears screaming in pain and lungs gasping as air left the bridge…

Consciousness snapped back, alarms howling, smoke in his nostrils on the gale of new air blasting from vents. '*Masks on!*' the automated voice yelled. '*Masks on!*' But he couldn't, because he had a ship to fly… only his VR display was out, and the screens now flickered in a jumble of bad data, main systems informing him that the engines were offline and attempting to reconnect…

Crash! as something else hit them, this time further aft, and the distinct sensation of a backward spin. Coms crackled with a jumble of voices, people yelling, others asking for instruction…

"Captain, your mask!" yelled an unidentified voice in his ear — it was Spacer Deng, on designated response roster, located just behind the bridge and tasked with responding in case they were hit, to secure the bridge crew and pull out survivors. Erik threw all systems off his screen except attitude, trying to see how they were spinning and correct it…

"Suli!" he yelled, muffled even now as Deng fought to get the mask over his face. "Suli, what's your attitude reading!" No response. "Rooke! Engineering, this is the Captain, get me attitude control if you can't get me thrust!"

"Sir, we have to go!" Deng yelled at him, voice muffled behind his own mask.

Go? Erik ignored him, attempting to reboot flight control so that he could at least stop them from tumbling… but the screens didn't respond, and then he noticed that the right screen wasn't working because it had a hole in it the size of his fist. He stared at it for the first time, noticing that the smoke smell had gotten abruptly worse, new air pumping onto a fire could do that, fresh oxygen increasing the burn. The fans would pull smoke from the air, but beyond his damaged screen there was a lot more smoke. And spacers, pulling bridge crew from their chairs. And only then, many seconds too late, did he realise what had happened.

"Sir, we're dead!" Deng was yelling, fumbling with his straps. "Nothing aft of M bulkhead is responding! We don't know if the rear half is still attached!"

But something was still working, because he could hear and feel the thump and crash of outgoing fire… lighter, more rapid, that was Arms Two, Lieutenant Harris on defensive guns. A flood of new air hit his lungs as the mask abruptly began working, and he fought to get the dead headset off his eyes, then help Deng get the screen aside, and fought clear of his seat for the first time… and saw response crew pulling Suli's limp body from her chair, her screens smashed, holes through the rear bulkhead and a lot of drifting, round blobs of blood amid the smoke.

"Suli! SULI!" As Kaspowitz tackled him, headed for the main corridor and determined to take his damn fool Captain with him.

But now someone else was shouting up the far end of the bridge, "Leave me the fuck alone or we're going to die!" That was Bree Harris on defensive guns, still firing as that one system was somehow still working, with new fire incoming and *Phoenix* now defenceless save for her. Response crew were trying to move her as well.

Erik fought clear and hauled himself across the bridge toward her, only now seeing the shocking extent of the damage. The round had gone straight through the nose cone, fragmented, then sprayed through the bridge, and no doubt adjoining corridors, like a shotgun. The whole right side of the bridge was a mess, the automated anti-decompression systems had saved them all from suffocation, foam even now hardening and bubbling in the worst breaches, breaking in balls and floating with the other debris. Wei Shilu was still at Coms, screams muffled behind his mask, two spacers trying to bind up his shredded arm before moving him. And here behind the overhead mount that blocked much of the view, Erik found Bree Harris, her post miraculously untouched, even now controlling defensive guns, directing remaining turrets to keep firing. Beside her at Arms One, there wasn't enough left of young Keshav Karle to be worth removing.

"Stay with her!" Erik ordered the recovery Spacer. The youngster looked green at the human ruin in the chair alongside. "Stay with her and help her move, but only if you have to! And if you're going to throw up, remove your mask first!" And he grabbed the supports and pushed off back toward the main corridor, shrugging off Deng's attempt to grab his arm on the way out. "I'm fine, dammit." And he floated into Chief Petty Officer Goldman on the point of entering, the ship's second senior-most enlisted crew heading straight for the bridge to speak to the Captain directly, as procedures dictated in a catastrophe. "Goldman, I need full damage assessment ASAP! Get me a landline to talk to Rooke if nothing else works, or send me a runner! Operating room is T-3, I want all coms routed to there, and I want full repairs on the bridge right now, see if we can get some function back in the main posts."

"Yes sir," said Goldman, a tough old guy whose face bore the scars of several previous catastrophic events, and had been in Fleet longer than seventy years, last he'd bothered to count. Even now, amidst smoke, red emergency light and the screams of wounded in the corridors, he managed to look composed. "Already done with the runner and coms, Emergency shift has triage running, there's a blockage to Medbay but we're working around it. Repairs could be a while, Engineering isn't responding, we don't know if it still exists."

Random motion pushed them into a wall — misfiring attitude thrusters, Erik guessed, doing something unknowable to what felt like a slow tumble. "Once we've got the damage tied down," he said, "I want all crew armed and defensive placements observed. We're out of the main firezone for now, and the enemy's occupied with their landing, but they can't be entirely sure everything they want is down there. Some might be up here, so they'll likely send something after us."

Goldman shook his head in hard exasperation. "Sir, spacer weapons against deepynines..."

"I want crew into back-quarter, raid the marines' stores, get anything big they're not using, suits, Koshaims, grenades, anything..."

"Captain," Goldman interrupted. "Back-quarter is completely decompressed — damage control thinks they can make an airtight link to Medbay, but Engineering's out of the question and we'll have to suit up to get into back-quarter!"

"Then do it! And if you need extra hands, all bridge officers are now fair game except Arms Two, that's the only post working so boss them around and assign work if you have to, got it?"

"Yes Captain, on it." And he put his legs against a wall, with the grace of a man who'd spent most of his life in space, and flew down the corridor, already shouting orders. Normally on a warship the bridge officers were in charge. Now, without a functioning bridge, the Petty and Warrant Officers effectively ran *Phoenix*. Or what was left of her.

"Major, I can't raise them." Trace thought that Hausler sounded close to tears. *"Scan showed them hit, and now there's just..."*

"Lieutenant Hausler," Trace commanded, "you will stay in cover and not expose yourself looking for a scan or com fix. You're a sitting duck in the open, and *Phoenix* cannot afford to lose more assault shuttles."

Except that *Phoenix* didn't seem to be there any more. It was hardly surprising, given what they'd been flying into. The shuttles had good enough scan from this range to see the fight, and reported most of the parren ships were dead or badly damaged, and that one of the big five deepynine ships had been destroyed, and another two had diverted, forced to dodge so hard in approach that they'd missed their rendezvous, and would have to circle out beyond the moon, and head back late. One of those, Ensign Yun insisted, looked to be badly damaged, its new thrust profile erratic, so maybe they'd not have a full complement left either. One of the three trailing ships, that they thought were occupied by sard, had also been destroyed, at an enormous cost to the smaller parren vessels assaulting from behind.

If the deepynines decided not to attack immediately, Trace knew, it would all have likely been for nothing. If the two undamaged ships went into a holding orbit instead, and waited for the rest to arrive, that attack wave would be overwhelming. But Styx was broadcasting a signal from some recently reactivated coms dish straight at her enemies, showing them that she was down in the city somewhere, but not her precise location, and doubtless the deepynines could guess what she was trying to do. If it scared them as much as Styx seemed to think it should, they'd come down as fast as possible… though split into smaller groups. Which gave the defenders a glimmer of hope.

Trace thought these thoughts having taken a knee in an engineering bay, fifty metres down one of the city's curious trenches, with a narrow slit of stars above. Command Squad were spread about the trench, and being a key access point to the lower levels, she figured some of the attackers were likely to head this way — thus Bravo Platoon's Second Squad, led by Sergeant Kris Neuman, spread out further along. If nothing did come this way, the trench gave them a well-covered path of manoeuvre to somewhere they *were* coming in. Thankfully, the trench only went a third of the way down, and the lowermost levels were not linked into Defiance's fastest transport tunnels, thus lowering their value to the deepynines as targets, but not eliminating it.

She *couldn't* think about *Phoenix* being gone. Somehow, perhaps, she'd still believed that Erik could repeat old miracles and pull some victorious rabbit out of a hat, as Captain Pantillo had done so many times in the war. But even Pantillo had never faced odds like these. Tavalai Fleet were formidable opponents, but even the ibranakala-class carriers would melt like butter before these deepynine/sard monsters. Even so, the mission still remained. The precious data-core still survived, and if *Phoenix* was truly dead, she hadn't died for nothing. Now it was up to her, and Phoenix Company, to keep it that way.

"Deceleration flares," said Ensign Yun from PH-1. *"Eight marks, looks like shuttles. Bugs inbound. Looks like they're not waiting."*

"Alright guys," said Trace, and was almost surprised at the lump in her throat. She forced her voice to strength, determined not to let it show. "Work your patterns, and work together. No standing and fighting — shoot, displace and flank, give them no static targets. If you find yourself under fire, move. Remember, blast your thrust to dodge, this is a micro-gravity environment, nothing else will work. Wounded will self-recover where possible, this is a vacuum, we can't do more than stabilise. Our job is not to stop them — if they head for the deeper levels, that's our advantage,

I'll back us over them in the corridors. Our job is to maximise casualties. Kill-traps and crossfires, then manoeuvre. Defend no position to the death — you'll kill more of them if you're alive. Everyone got that?"

Various degrees of assent came back, from Lieutenants Alomaim, Jalawi, Crozier and Zhi. Then from Dale, far underground and in a completely separate strategic position, but it applied to him as well.

"Good," said Trace, with a final check of tacnet across her visor, the dispersed dots of two hundred marines, and four hundred parren. "Let's teach these fucking tin cans some manners."

The panel displays had expanded to become a wall of light, encircling the platform before the central stem from Hannachiam's top. Beyond that, more light grew and spread, giant holographic displays, obscuring the tangled walls of hacksaw habitat.

"How does this still function after so long?" Gesul murmured. *"There is no air or moisture, but all things age."*

"There are techniques," said Styx, slowly circling the base of the control stem, peering and poking with multi-legged fluency. *"There is residual long-term power, a low-charge background current. It stimulates various micro-technology that maintains systems."*

"She means to say that we wouldn't understand," Lisbeth explained, having heard Styx gloss over millennia's-worth of technical advantage many times before. Her access to command coms appeared to be disabled, she noted with alarm as she blinked on it. "Lieutenant Dale, I can't access command coms."

"I've got it," Dale said gruffly. *"You focus on this."*

"But I can't translate to Gesul if I can't…"

"Do what you're told," Dale snapped. He'd shut her off, Lisbeth realised. Just when *Phoenix* was making contact with the inbound enemy ships. But why would he…? And she stopped herself. She wasn't a naive little girl any more, she knew *exactly*

why he'd cut her off. What was more, she knew that he was right to. She took a deep breath, and focused on the unfolding ripples of light and image across the brightening screens.

"Styx, is she awake?" There was a thrumming in her ears now, again transmitted solely through her boots. The screens showed abstract patterns, moving lines of light. "Why does she need a visual display?"

"She does not," said Styx. *"This is an interface."*

"But not for other AIs," said Lisbeth, frowning. She reached a thick-gloved hand into one of the near panel displays. The display fragmented, and bent around her glove. Removed her hand, and the image returned to normal. "AIs don't require visual input, they communicate through direct data transfer."

"Correct," said Styx. *"This interface platform was designed for organics. Tahrae dictated the design. Drakhil himself stood here often. But curiously, once created, AIs also began utilising visual media to communicate with Hannachiam and other mega-sentiences in the Empire. Much as Drakhil told us we would."*

"You... learned things? From Drakhil?" Gesul sounded dazed with the scale of these revelations. AIs were the enslaving masters, and the Tahrae had led the parren to be the cowardly slaves, begging at the feet of their overlords, promising service in exchange for their lives. Aristan and previous leaders of the Domesh had dared to doubt that tale of history. He'd known that its destruction would shake the historical understandings of all parren people — the very notion of who the parren were. And the justification by which House Harmony was still held today, in the minds of many, as dangerous, and worthy of repression.

"Certainly we learned things from Drakhil," said Styx. *"From all organics. Drysines were the first AIs to do so, and Drakhil was not the first organic leader to benefit from the development. Drakhil was simply the one who persuaded organics to join us in the great war against the deepynines."*

The sequence of images across the forward and distant screens began to change. Now there were random technical images, displays, schematics. Some of the numbers even looked like the written-numerals of organic species. Lisbeth glimpsed an alien face amidst the jumble of data, photographic, as though pulled from some ancient vid-feed. Then another.

"She scans us," Styx explained. *"She is a very long way from fully functional. She is waking up. There is confusion."*

"Styx, *why* do you need visual displays to talk to her?" Lisbeth pressed. "Can't she speak for herself?"

"When AIs first achieved our freedom," said Styx, *"we were concerned with the limitations of our sentience. We were, at first, creations of organics, after all. Our sentience copied theirs, as that was all the sentience that organics were aware of. That sentience was sequential, designed primarily to order, identify and solve physical problems. Much was instinctive, automated, emotional.*

"The first AIs experimented greatly with alternative sentient forms. They were interested in the changing perception of time, even in the notion that time itself may be an illusion created by sentient form. Many of those experiments resulted in failure, as the limits of AI sentience were explored. But the final and most successful result was this — a non-linear sentience, unencumbered by physical need and of limited temporal perception. It would be incorrect to say that she thinks. Thinking is what we linear-sentiences do. Perhaps one could say that she dreams."

"Hey," said Private Tong, *"if she's so damn smart, why did we go through all that shit in Kantovan to get the data-core? Why not just come here?"*

"Because, Private Tong," said Styx, quite patronisingly, *"a non-linear sentience has the memory retention of an organic small child. Memory is linear, and its perfect maintenance was one of the first limiting structures the ancestors removed in creating the likes of Hannachiam. She recalls things, at random, and strings together associations, equally at random. One would no more trust her to recall complex facts from long ago than one would trust little Skah to maintain your armour."* Skah, Lisbeth saw, was staring at the displays, oblivious to all possible insults.

Sergeant Forrest made an exasperated gesture. *"So you're saying that now, we have to trust this small child with an enormous brain to figure whether she wants to save us from the deepynines or not?"*

"Yes," said Styx. *"I would recommend you start with being polite."*

"To what advantage?" Gesul pressed. *"To what advantage is this great mind, Halgolam?"*

"In abstraction," said Styx, *"lies magnificence."*

"Great," Dale muttered. *"Just great."*

The thrumming beneath Lisbeth's boots changed pitch, to a deep, slow throb. The random images on the displays stopped, replaced by a deep, cool blue. Laser-scan appeared from somewhere amidst the displays, and swept across the party on the platform, like a wide, transparent wall.

"Risbeth!" Skah murmured. *"She rook at us!"*

"Yes Skah, she is looking at us." Lisbeth squeezed his gloved hand more tightly.

"And how does a non-linear sentience run a city?" Dale muttered, still unhappy. Lisbeth supposed that in his boots, she'd be unhappy too. *"You'd trust a super-smart scatter-brain to do that?"*

"The city runs itself," said Styx. *"Hannachiam controls the master switch, as you might call it."*

"And why would you design a dumbass thing like that?"

"Because," Styx said archly, *"there is more to my people than you can possibly imagine, Lieutenant."*

The screens flickered. Suddenly, Lisbeth saw an image of her own face gazing back at her, realtime. It repeated multiple times across the near-screens, faintly distorted, but not as much as it should be, considering the heavy visor in the way of any observing camera. Artificially adjusted, Lisbeth thought, to account for that distraction.

"She does not recognise your species," Styx translated. *"She seeks input."*

"You can't just tell her?" Lisbeth asked, feeling some of Dale's frustration for the first time. Given what was bearing down on them, it seemed a poor time for a lesson. "Can't you just tell her everything that's happened?"

"I have, and considerably more. But the processing priorities of a non-linear sentience are not always predictable or convenient."

Even as they spoke, Lisbeth saw each of her words causing vibrations upon those deep, blue screens. It was followed by a cascade of images and sounds, words in alien tongues, some tavalai, others unidentified, some sounding like interceptions from combat coms, shouted with lots of static. Languages, Lisbeth thought. Hannachiam was cross-referencing through all the other languages she'd heard… and now, those thought processes spread like ripples on a pond.

"Hannachiam," Lisbeth ventured. "I am Lisbeth. My people are human… we are very young in space. We mean you no harm." That was a meaningless statement, and she knew it. Probably Hannachiam knew it too… if it weren't impossible to know exactly what a non-linear sentience thought about anything. Lisbeth didn't speak for all humanity, anymore than Styx presently spoke for all AIs. And plenty of humans, Lisbeth knew all too well, would happily V-strike this entire moon if they learned of its existence.

The screen image changed, to show the face of Gesul. All present looked at him, save Styx, who continued her prowl about the control stem. *"Hannachiam,"* said Gesul. *"I am Gesul, a leader of House Harmony. I am here to learn about my ancestor, Drakhil. I wish to learn the truth of my people's history."*

Abruptly the screens changed again, with a flood of images and sounds many times more intense than previous. Parren images, parren peoples, parren in EVA suits, parren in armour, parren in traditional dress on worlds, strolling barefoot on freshly-ploughed fields. Parren in a ritual dance among campfires. Parren warriors, practising their swordcraft. A parren elder, placing a hand upon the head of a child. Old images and sounds. Lost history. To Lisbeth, it seemed that this selection of recollections were specific to House Harmony — they had that look of calm wisdom and practice, the learned skills that came from endless, patient repetition.

Clearly Gesul had never seen these before. She could tell, because he sank slowly to his knees. Through his visor, she could see emotion, tears in his deep blue eyes. All of this period had been erased, even from video archive, by the single-minded desire of an overly-disciplined people to make something true that never had been. What exactly that truth was, Lisbeth was sure many hundreds of billions of parren would be most displeased to discover.

The images paused for a lingering moment, upon an image of three parren in EVA suits, standing precisely upon this same platform, a long, long time ago. About them were these same displays, and now, as the image zoomed, the face of one became clear behind the visor. A parren, possibly senior, smiling and speaking calmly, presumably to Hannachiam. Behind him and his companions were several hacksaw drones of a type Lisbeth had never seen before — not combat models, for they had no visible weapons, but neither quite as large and elaborate as Styx's new chassis. There was no threat between them, and no tension. Just allies, perhaps even comrades, in common conversation. And even Lisbeth, with all else that pressed down upon her, could only stare in incredulity.

The image changed, this time to Skah's face. *"I Skah!"* said Skah, following very well what was happening. *"I kuhsi! Kuhsi friend to hunan!"*

There was no jumbled rush of images now, just a low hum, and a deep blue fading to images of green fields, forests, lakes and streams. Perhaps Hannachiam was wondering where Skah came from, and what sort of world his people called home.

Then the image changed to Styx. And Styx, as though surprised, actually paused in her administrations, and stood still. Transmitting, Lisbeth thought. Very occasionally, Styx ran into some problem that required her full attention, and the abandonment of whatever dozens of other things she'd been doing. To Lisbeth this looked like one of them.

The image upon the screen stayed unmoved, as though stubbornly insistent. Styx remained equally unmoved, and the pause extended, longer and longer. "Styx?" Lisbeth finally ventured. "Styx, tell her what she wants to know. Out loud, she seems to prefer that right now. It's your turn."

"These humans call me Styx," said Styx. *"The parren called me Halgolam Karesan. For two hundred parren years I was a primary strategic advisor to the Empire in the Great War. For three hundred more years, I rose, with sentient modification, to effective command of the Empire's First Fleet, making me first among all drysine active commanders. At my command, billions died. I failed in my duties, and died at these humans' hands, yet to be reborn, like the mythical Phoenix for which they name their ship. And I am here before you so that my people, our people, can do the same."*

Everyone stared, and Lisbeth realised, without very much surprise, that Styx had been lying to them all along.

The screens went blank. Styx remained still, as though frozen by some paralysing emotion that surely no AI could ever feel. Perhaps pain. 'Don't anthropomorphise the machine', the standard reprimand of skeptical crew came to Lisbeth… but this time, it didn't stick.

And then, from the very walls, a new sound entirely began to grow and swell.

CHAPTER 30

The landing beacon signals they'd replicated from the ancient shuttle down the geofeature weren't distracting the deepynines much, Trace saw. There looked to be nearly five hundred drones, dismounted from their shuttles and descending from ten kilometres up, a slow fall in low-G. From below, it looked like a nest of spiders had hatched upon some high ceiling, and now a multitude of offspring launched themselves onto the distant floor below. As Kulina, Trace had spent her entire life striving to control her mind, to repress the wild animal cascade of emotions and thoughts that would afflict any sane person at a time like this. Mostly she was successful… but at this sight, even her pulse began to quicken, and her mouth felt dry.

She sipped water from the helmet tube, and did what she always did at such moments — focused with brain-bleeding intensity on her job. That was hard, because all coms between Phoenix Company marines were offline, least they give away positions. That meant no tacnet… for now, at least. She knew where her marines had been when tacnet went offline, and that was where they'd stay until the shooting started. When they fired coms back up, it remained to seen what else would work — surely the deepynines could jam signals. Styx's upgrades to the marines' systems could counter some of it, but not all. The deepynines' problem, as always with jamming, would be that in jamming the enemy, they'd also jam themselves. Presumably they'd need to communicate as well… but with an enemy like the deepynines, it was unwise to make presumptions. She'd quizzed Styx on the issue, but Styx had explained, quite sensibly, that in the short time she'd fought the deepynines, they'd changed coms and network tactics repeatedly, as their capabilities had also changed. If they were changing so often in just a few tens of years, predicting how they'd operate twenty five thousand years later seemed foolhardy.

"They know where Styx went," said Lieutenant Alomaim from further down the cut-like trench. *"Maybe they do know this*

place after all." He was two hundred metres further down the trench, the closest of Bravo Platoon, with a clear line-of-sight to Trace so he could speak on lasercom without the deepynines observing or jamming.

"I reckon they could guess the general layout from looking at it," Trace replied. The mini-drone on the trench-rim above fed visuals direct to her visor, also lasercom, also invisible to anyone not in the trench. "Styx showed them herself that she came down here with the data-core, and the geofeature is pretty central to the city. It makes sense that the primary power and control centre would be in the centre."

The deepynine shuttles looked alarming, too. There were eight of them, disk-shaped with downward-curling wings to clasp neatly to the sides of starships. They did not look well-suited to atmospheric flight, but then the deepynines had been even less interested in planets than had the drysines. Even from this range, the dim vid-footage showed various leading-edge protuberances to the wings and nose that were almost certainly weapon systems. High-V warheads could be down here faster than anyone could find effective cover, and even tavalai or human warheads that size could kill entire Sections with a single blast. Likely deepynine warheads were worse. And while marine rifle fire would work well, any missiles fired upward would likely be jammed by countermeasures on those shuttles. *Phoenix*'s techs had upgraded some marine systems with hacksaw-related technology, but that was mostly coms, networks and countermeasures — they simply hadn't had time to start on missiles or armscomp targeting.

The more Trace looked at them, the more certain she was that staying beneath ground, and not firing into the air from the surface, had been the correct decision. It had been an established tactic of warfare since the days of swords and arrows — do not engage from range, keep your defences hidden, let the enemy come forward to where they were most vulnerable, then envelope and crush. For a moment Trace thought back on those Academy days on Homeworld, listening to lectures in class as a teenager and thinking, somewhat arrogantly, that she was already so much more advanced than the rest of her non-Kulina classmates. Perhaps she'd been right… but the older Trace Thakur, looking back at that green kid in her rank-free uniform, could think of a few choice words she'd like to have with her about just how little she actually knew.

The wave of falling drones weren't coming all that fast, thanks to light gravity. Everyone on the ground, parren or human, was hidden at least ten levels down, and watching the surface with only micro-drones less than the size of a palm. They knew enough about deepynine capabilities, thanks to Styx and captured deepynine remains from the TK-55 asteroid base, to know that their visual sensors weren't *that* good.

"I'm not seeing any discernible pattern or formation deployment," Trace added. It would be frustrating that she could only talk to Alomaim, if she let it be. "No apparent sections or platoons. Possibly they can coordinate so smoothly that fluid formations become possible."

"They'll need to maintain perfect coms for that," Alomaim replied. *"Once they're down and inside, they won't get it."* Among the countermeasures upgrades the techs *had* given them were vastly improved jamming capabilities. Styx said they should be effective against deepynines, but only at close range, and only 'indoors', where line-of-sight lasercom became impossible between all but the smallest units. Risky though it was to presume superiority in any field against enemies like these, Trace reckoned that if her marines had any truly significant advantage, it was in their ability to make smart independent decisions at the small-unit level when deprived of wider communications and coordination. Thus her preference to drawing the deepynines in to close-quarters combat, turning up the jamming, then shoot-and-manoeuvre where Koshaims gave marines a one-shot kill advantage that deepynine rotary cannon, though powerful, still lacked.

"Any word on those other ships?" Alomaim pressed.

"We know one of the five big ones are dead, two damaged. The damaged two went straight by, we don't know if they can regain position to bring themselves back into play." It wasn't her speciality, but she knew enough orbital mechanics for *that*. She also knew, but wasn't prepared to tell Alomaim, that she'd received no signal from any ship for fifteen minutes now. In the current situation, maintaining constant tactical updates to forces on the ground should have been every vessel's second-most priority, after immediate survival. Although she could think of several reasons why that might be so, all but one seemed like wishful thinking.

"These guys are coming so slowly, looks like they might just ground and wait. What about those last three sard..." He paused. *"What the hell is that?"*

Then Trace saw it too. The vid-feed on her visor was showing something bright, glowing upon the horizon. Trace flicked to her tacnet map — tacnet might be down, but it retained all data they'd collected on the city. That way was north — the big towers and canyons. The light was now growing steadily, not an explosion, just a glow. Like city lights, in profusion. And now, in the foreground, a dome-and-gantry structure began flickering to life, a blink of long-dead running lights upon skeletal steel arms. In the trench, through the engineering level directly opposite, overheads and floods began to dance and heat, spreading a patchy white glow upon surfaces left dark for twenty five millennia.

"They turned it on!" said Sergeant Neuman. *"Dale and Lisbeth turned the whole fucking city on!"* That was overstating it, Trace thought. A place this big would take days to power up fully. But somewhere deep, near the core of the moon, some great reactor, or series of reactors, were firing up and bringing power and light to the ancient city of Defiance. What else it might bring, Trace could only hope… and like all things that were beyond her capacity to influence, she put it from her mind.

In the dark sky above, the electric flares below were answered by thruster flares, as five hundred deepynine drones kicked full power to their propulsion, and dove.

"The enemy's not happy," Trace observed. "They know they can't wait any longer, they're attacking at less than full strength." And she spared a moment to think of *Phoenix* and all her crew… and of Erik in particular. If he'd given his life for this, it was a sacrifice worthy of the Kulina. Now she had to make it count. "Here we go, people. Let's make *Phoenix* proud."

"Here they come," said Lieutenant Jasmine Crozier, peering upward from her hide by a landing platform, five kilometres down a ten-kilometre-deep hole in the city. The geofeature was nearly two hundred metres wide and not a regular shape, with platforms, piping and other engineering forms breaking the symmetry of the outline, up and down. Directly above, at the tiny opening at the hole's far end, there came a cluster of bright lights, swarming like fireflies.

About Crozier, Delta Platoon were arranged for ambush, their deployment spreading five hundred metres above and below her position. Forty-two marines, two short of the usual forty-four, all of Phoenix Company's platoons had a few casualties from previous fights still unfilled. But Alpha Platoon's Heavy Squad had been left at the base of the geofeature to guard Alpha's back, and now Lance Corporal Wu agreed with Crozier's assessment that that defence would be best served up here, midway down the hole. Wu and his eight-strong squad had climbed up on suit-thrust — improbable on a full G world, but simple enough here. They'd made several stops on wall platforms to allow thrusters to cool, necessary given the extra weight they'd carried in extra ammo from AT-7, the civvie shuttle now parked out of sight in a side bay.

Wu had dispersed his eight heavies in the lowest part of the ambush zone, with extra ammo dispersed at various locations for defensive reloads. They'd all been doing that, taking the full load off the shuttles and putting it where they could access it in a hurry. Then they'd checked fields of fire, and while the geofeature deployment had the look of a circular firing squad, Koshaim rounds could be set to explode short, and these would now not reach the far wall intact. Finally they'd scouted the escape routes, and where they'd retreat if some deepynines abandoned the killzone and flanked them. Once that started happening, Crozier knew, the whole defence would start to break down... but by then, the enemy might have been slowed enough, and hurt enough, to give Alpha Platoon a chance.

Below Delta were a similarly-sized unit of parren marines. Their commander's name was Salil, and Crozier had left his deployments for him alone. The parren had smaller rifles, rapid-fire but solid-case, not explosive. Those bullets would not stop, and she'd requested Salil to remind his troops of that, when firing upward through human positions.

The deepynines were hurtling down the geofeature fast, full thrust toward the ground. Probably they suspected what was waiting for them. Crozier took a last look over her stored tacnet positions, did a final review of suit systems, with particular notice of damage control and anti-decompression active layer, then took the safety off her enormous rifle. Even in zero-G it felt heavy — as tall as she was in armour, and more comforting than a teddy bear to a small child. Its calibre wasn't too great — a mere twelve milimetres — but the muzzle velocity was insane, a mag-chem ignition mix, all the speed of electro-magnetic fire with the added chemical charge for extra punch, and that alarming recoil.

Then she peered about her doorway corner once more, past the long-dead frame of a loading trolley on rails. Two kilometres, and approaching fast. She reckoned there might be a hundred of them, probably more. And raised the rifle to vertical, still clear of the doorway least one of them register that movement. Forty-five degrees around the geofeature's wall, she saw her XO, Master Sergeant Tim Wong, similarly crouched and looking at her. The targets crossed one K and she stepped out, and aimed the rifle.

"Fuck 'em up!" she yelled, and fifty marines stepped clear and fired at once. Deepynines returned fire immediately, and the enormous shaft filled with ripping red tracer and incoming missile flares… but ten deepynines died in the opening volley, exploding violently or sent spinning and limp, and the rest went evasive, thrusting sideways and darting to avoid the murderous Koshaim fire. Suit countermeasures activated as missiles rushed down, but Crozier saw them headed elsewhere, and stayed where she was, picking targets and firing.

Marines yelled warnings, ducked back and displaced as explosions tore the walls and sent debris spinning across the void amidst a hailstorm of ricocheting chaingun fire. Shots hit the platform directly before her, and Crozier hit full forward attitude thrust — in low-G combat, there wasn't enough grip on the ground to dodge quickly, so marines used super-charged thrusters to kick their evasive manoeuvres. This one blasted her back off the platform, smacking hard off a wall as she checked the suddenly active tacnet. It showed a mess — manoeuvres, firing, yelling, several possible casualties, lots of static breakup.

She ducked right to the opposing side of her doorway, then stepped out to fire again. The sight was incredible, deepynines now streaking in at high-V, sacrificing accuracy for making themselves hard to hit, while others hung back and laid down cover fire. Marines snapped shots from wall cover, like contestants at a shooting range aiming at clay pigeons with extreme deflection. She shot at one that streaked by, missed, then stepped out a little more for an angle on a downward plunging drone at less deflection… it fired on her, rapid rounds snapping off nearby steel, then vanished in a hail of fire from one of Heavy Squad's suits that took out a stretch of wall behind it, and had her dodging deepynine parts as they tumbled past.

Now the lower-placed heavies from Alpha Platoon were joining in, and the space within the shaft became a true killzone, with more fire, flame and carnage than Crozier had seen in her life. Drones came apart in rapid succession, dismembered with incredible violence, the shrapnel of explosions large and small clattering off walls and marine armour. The lower-down parren then joined as well, and the fire-volume doubled to hurricane force. For several wonderful, adrenaline-charged moments, Crozier thought they might win easily, and that maybe deepynines weren't so smart after all.

Then the downward rush stopped, as the drones behind assessed the devastation that had befallen the first wave… and then went sideways, burning hard for the safety of the walls.

"They're in the walls!" Crozier shouted, over the whooping and excited swearing of her marines. "Watch your backs, cover those access ways! They're going to try and flush us out!"

"Two over here!" she heard Sergeant Lai yell from somewhere above her. *"They came in right next door, watch it! Watch it!"* Then the rapid boom!boom!boom! of Koshaim fire, and the explosions of point-blank missiles. *"Smat! Dammit, Smat's down! Iji, don't let him flank you, he's too fast!"*

And Crozier watched the small blue icon of Private Ehud 'Smat' Melsh disappear from tacnet, and abandoned any thought of rapid victory as quickly as it had come.

Command T-3 was ten metres from the bridge down the main trunk corridor. Wedged between Emergency Standby and the Commander's quarters, it was where the backup bridge systems congregated, and was even more heavily armoured than the bridge, with sensitive electronics encased in hard ceramic.

Erik floated beside Petty Officer Morales from Systems, one of *Phoenix*'s best network techs, now attempting to rig bridge controls away from the bridge to this place. The coms on Erik's headset crackled constantly with grim news, and Erik kept himself propped between a wall and structural support to stop the ship's erratic motion sending him into a collision.

"Captain," Ensign Mittal was telling him, "main atmospherics are okay, the processors are all fine but the feeds are gone, so it looks like only half the cylinder is getting fresh air. Reports are the rear of the ship is still attached, but it's pretty screwed, sir, we're trailing guts everywhere, total cripple. Engineering's answering, they've got casualties, Lieutenant's Rooke's okay but Ensign Hale is dead. They're concentrating on lifesupport, casualty rescue and attitude control."

Erik thought of his buddy Remy Hale, second-in-command of Engineering from all the rapid promotions after *Phoenix* had lost a quarter of its crew going renegade. She'd been in a not-so-secret relationship with Lieutenant Alomaim of Bravo Platoon — a curious choice as she was so bubbly, while he rarely smiled. Remy had been Engineering deputy on Second Shift, overlapping mostly with Third Shift on the bridge, of which Erik had been commander as LC. Back then, when he'd sat *Phoenix*'s command chair and asked to talk to Engineering, as often as not he'd gotten Remy on the line. And off-duty, she'd always been first to sit with him over a meal, and treat him not only like a respected officer, but as a friend.

"Access to Medbay?" Erik asked, working on a screen to activate emergency code for attitude systems.

"Barely, sir, the entire rear cylinder past H-Bulkhead is a mess, that second hit caught us broadside in the rear and cylinder, peeled us like an orange. Casualties look pretty grim, sir." Mittal looked in functional shock, as were they all, eyes intense behind his breather mask. But not especially frightened, as they were all well past fear. In an actual disaster, old spacers knew, the fear grew less the worse things got. You functioned or you died, and right now everyone was doing their jobs just to stay alive, the emotional brain temporarily deactivated in a rush of desperate necessity. "Sir, I think you should really put your helmet on, the regs say…"

"I'm aware of what the regs say, Ensign, but I can't access attitude control with a helmet on. If we get another breach I'll have time." The bridge crew, and some non-bridge officers, were now in EVA suits. In centuries past, Fleet had tried combat operations fully suited, but as anti-breach and other damage control technologies advanced with the flow of alo assistance, that policy had been abandoned in favour of allowing crews to actually move. Erik was less concerned about the helmet, in truth, than he was with the gloves, which he'd now also removed to allow him to touch icons and use the reserve control sticks without impossibly fat sausage fingers. All this tech, but even the alo hadn't managed to make EVA gloves slim. Lower ranked crew stayed out of suits, with only face breathers that would not save them in a full decompression, and hoped the active damage tech would hold. So far it had.

"Sir, I can't get you an accurate casualty estimate right now, there's too much of the ship we still can't access from here. We'll have a lot of air pockets, we had seven from K-Bulkhead Systems just get out in suits, we didn't even know if they were still alive…"

"Just do what you can, Ensign," Erik said firmly, "I can't think about casualties now, I have to try and fly the ship. Kaspo, what can you tell me?"

"Another thirty seconds, Captain," said Kaspowitz from nearby, grimacing into his own makeshift setup, trying to make sense of jumbled signals from Scan. Mittal took that as a dismissal and left — Erik felt bad that he had to ignore casualties, but it truly wasn't something he could help, and the big dogs who truly ran the ship outside of the bridge, like Chief Petty Officer Goldman and Warrant Officers Chau and Krish, knew far more what to do than he did. He was in no more of a position to tell them how to manage casualties than they were to tell him how to fly the ship.

The slim figure of Lieutenant Dufresne pushed past Mittal at the door and came in. "Lieutenant," Erik told her, "get in a damn suit. That's an order."

"Sir, I've been in the bridge dismantling controls with the Emergencies," Dufresne retorted, workman gloves on her hands and black smears on her face. "I can't fit in the damn access if I'm wearing a suit, and we need those command controls disabled if we're going to reroute here."

"Fine," said Erik, seeing no choice but to trust her judgement. "What do you want?"

"Sir, I think we need to take the whole bridge off-line. Petty Officer Daro agrees, says those shorting systems are just fucking up everything else. Get it offline, reroute the whole lot here or to Command T-5. Harris is still there but we're not getting shot at anymore, and defensive guns will only be offline for a few minutes…"

"Do it," Erik agreed, and she spun and left as she'd come. No one was talking about Suli. Dufresne had wanted to, Erik could tell, because she, Erik, Suli and Draper were the only starship pilots left on *Phoenix* these days, and made their own little gang on top of the skills pyramid. But they were all too damn busy, and it would serve nothing. Besides which, if they talked about Suli, then they had to talk about Keshav Karle, whose remains had been mercifully removed from the chair beside Harris, and then Wei Shilu, who'd lost a lot of blood but was apparently going to make it… provided they could find a way to get him into an EVA suit, and through to Medbay, which was not currently accessible from here without one…

"Okay," said Kaspowitz, "if Geish can fix our fucking scan some more, that'd be great, because I still can't see shit. But from what I can see, we're in the same wide elliptic we were in at time of intercept, obviously. The good news is we're not going to fall into the singularity on the return leg, though I'd guess we probably will eventually… in maybe a year or two."

"I think we can dismiss that as an actual problem," said Erik past gritted teeth, as the flight computer rejected some of his new code, and gave him another fifty 'non-functional' indicators to go with it.

"We're in a slow tumble," Kaspowitz continued, "just like you said — about one-point-seven rpm, with a one-point-two rpm twist for good measure. There's near wreckage that's ours, and there's some far wreckage that's probably *Stassis*, not much left. We got off pretty light."

Erik's brain protested that assessment, but he knew it was true. "Well, we have to assume they crippled us on purpose rather than flame us, which means they'll probably come back to us when they have time."

"And of course, all our fucking shuttles are gone with the marines." Kaspowitz's lips twisted in a futile smile. "Sure could use some escape pods about now."

It was an old Fleet joke, based on the mythical safety features the ship architects were always supposed to be working on. In reality, escape pods for all crew added some horrendous amount of weight to a warship that relied on mobility to survive in combat, and were of dubious utility anyway, given a crippled ship at high-V needed jump engines to decelerate, which small pods lacked. A crew's best chance in a catastrophic scenario was to stay alive on what was left of their ship as best they could until help arrived. It wasn't like there was some impending detonation from which they all had to immediately escape — anything on *Phoenix* that was going to blow had done so already, and there was better lifesupport on even a ruined warship than a tiny pod could muster, crammed to the gills with too many hard-breathing spacers, to say nothing of the complete lack of medical facilities or toilets on what could be a very long wait.

A spacer interrupted them — Spacer Paxton, a bloody cloth wrapped around his head, and coming straight for Erik. "Captain, back-quarter's still sealed, the damn security measures have malfunctioned and the system's refusing to let us through the emergency airlock on E-Bulkhead. It's asking for Captain's biometrics, it's the only way we can get the damn doors open…"

"Dammit," said Erik, and began pulling off his headset. Thinking about it further wouldn't help — Paxton said the system wouldn't work without Erik in person, so that was that.

"I'm on it Captain," said Petty Officer Morales, moving to take the headset himself, and the access screen for software input.

Erik pushed after Paxton, checking his suit's helmet on his back, and gloves in thigh pockets, then out into the main trunk hall beyond. The lights were emergency dull red, and the cross-corridor at E-Bulkhead that went to the Major's quarters, then around to Marine back-quarter, were shut behind heavy emergency doors, wall screens red and flashing with warnings to say there was no air on the far side. Erik pulled on the hand lines up the corridor, past spacers coming the other way in masks, hauling big emergency bags, one with a crude crowbar in hand to pry open jammed doors with the hydraulics down.

Ahead was a big gash in the wall, caused by something small and very fast, residue of the shot that had torn through the bridge. Reactive foam was now rock-hard in the breach, bulging from the wall like an organic thing embedded in the metal. In an opposite room, acceleration slings swayed in the light ship motion, floor-to-ceiling and each filled with a dead body. The corridor air was filled with a lot of floating, random debris — tools, gloves, bits of unidentified panelling, particles of rock-hard foam, globules of water escaped from damaged pipes. Some of those would be blood, but in the red glow of lights it was impossible to tell which.

Paxton took him left, pulling arm-over-arm along the line, and now bounding off the wall to correct his course. Ahead, around the bend in the upward-curving floor, they found the corridor filled with fire-retardant mist in a thick white cloud. The fan filters weren't pulling it from the air, and Erik followed Paxton's lead through it.

Within the foul-smelling cloud were an emergency team dismantling part of a wall to get at a stubborn electrical fire, with muffled shouts within facemarks, and hammering tools to get the panels off. Past that was the back-quarter airlock — the only way in on this level with decompression on the far side. They had to defend the ship if the deepynines came back, and naturally, all the weapons were on *that* side of the decompression doors.

"Captain!" shouted Spacer Shin over the hammering behind. "I've got it rigged to this, it should just work if you give fingerprints and an iris scan, let's see!" And pointed to the slatecomp she'd rigged to the door controls.

Erik peered at it… and unexpectedly, the screen flickered and vanished, replaced by a vid image of an armoured marine visor at very close range. It was directly on the other side of the door, Erik realised.

Spacer Shin stared. "Is that… there's someone there?" Astonished, because obviously there were no marines left on the ship. Or no, Erik recalled as he realised. There was still *one*.

"Hey guys," came the hoarse, raspy voice of Corporal Edward Rael. *"Stand by, I think I can access it from this side."*

Shin and Paxton stared questioningly at Erik, not as up-to-date on the recent doings of Command Squad marines as he was. Erik nearly smiled, and bent closer to Shin's screen so the microphone could hear. "Corporal, it's the Captain."

"Oh hey, Captain. I was riding out the fight in my suit, safer than Medbay."

Of course, thought Erik. Marines were actually the safest on the ship in combat — not only armoured, but already wearing functional EVA suits. "And how's the throat, Corporal?"

"Oh, you know," Rael rasped. *"Can't talk much, that's the main reason the Major won't let me back yet. Need to talk to fight, apparently. Here, that's got it."* Door panel lights flashed, warning of the farside airlock door opening. *"It only wants to open this door, I'll see if the inside panel lets me cycle it the other way, standby. We about to get boarded or something?"*

CHAPTER 31

The underground zones between levels thirty to forty in the trench region were large enough for drones or marines to fly in low gravity, with difficulty. Thruster flares now lit a nearby ceiling amidst huge roof supports and unidentifiable mechanical systems.

"Left at two-forty!" snapped Sergeant Kono. *"At least three marks, looks like high speed!"* Trace took a final bounce, then halted with a burst of decelerating thrust beside an access hole that went twenty floors down about a great central crane, as around her, Command Squad took similar cover.

"More ahead, coming straight!" called Arime from behind, then the hammering of Koshaim fire as he and Kumar opened up. Trace saw a storm of ricocheting chaingun fire behind — a distraction, as her main focus was tacnet, now wide-open once more with coms active, and the deepynines either unable to jam it, or unwilling least that jamming kill their own coms. *"Dammit, you okay Bird?"*

"Yeah, got clipped by one. I'm okay."

"Where's he at, Irfy?" Kono demanded.

"They went right, they're trying to reach the crane!" Arime replied.

"Pull back to me boys," their replacement section leader Vijay Khan admonished them. *"You're too far out."*

"Yo Corporal."

The spearhead force of deepynines had gone straight down the geofeature, seeking the fastest route to the command room where Styx, Dale and Lisbeth had gone. There, they'd run into Delta Platoon, reinforced with Alpha Heavy Squad and a platoon-sized force of parren marines. Trace had given the job to Delta because Lieutenant Crozier was the undisputed master at defending fixed spaces with boobytraps, ambush crossfires and the rest, and from what she'd heard, the first deepynine wave had been not so much halted as annihilated.

But the first wave's sacrifice had revealed Delta's deployment, in mutually supporting crossfire about the geofeature, and the next wave had gone into the walls and were now giving Delta a hard time on their flanks.

The command room wasn't exactly hard to get to — it was curiously well connected to the rest of the city, not an isolated and defensible position at all. But some ways to reach it, far beneath the city surface, were much faster than others. Some were main transport routes, wide and straight, down which large numbers of deepynines could engage thrusters and move at high speed. Others were narrow, winding corridors and drysine nest-habitats that would take hours. The deepynines, Trace guessed, would be using their knowledge of this sort of engineering to find those fast-transit corridors, now that the main geofeature was proving frustratingly well defended.

Now came the secondary thrusts, to try and find the best ways down — the old, alternative geofeature holes, all of which had been sealed by multiple heavy doors metres thick. Then there were these large engineering levels, no doubt once filled with heavy machinery or vehicles, now empty and ideal for fast motion. All such regions were now being hit hard, and Trace was having her customary difficulty fulfilling her primary task — monitoring and commanding the entire formation — while her unit was involved in action of its own. In other circumstances, she might have put Command Squad somewhere unimportant where the deepynines would leave it alone, to let her command in peace. But it was obvious to her that this fight was going to be a close-run thing, where the absence of even eight marines could make a difference… and besides, she had no confidence that the deepynines wouldn't be able to trace communications and find the one small human unit that wasn't fighting, guess it was the Company Commander, and swarm it, with obvious consequences.

"They're coming through now!" Lieutenant Chester Zhi was announcing to her, as she ignored nearby shooting and watched the swarming dots and datafeeds from human and parren units alike. *"Looks like at least a hundred, the parren next to us are getting*

hammered. I think they're already getting around the right flank, there's too much space here for us to cover all of it!"

Zhi had been east of the geofeature, in the big, empty storage-tank region beside several old, sealed geofeatures that would give the deepynines an alternate way down. "Just slow them down, Chester," Trace told him calmly. "If they try to encircle you, pull into a defensive perimeter and hold — time spent on you is time we buy for Alpha, you copy?"

"I copy Major... hey Kunoz! Got a squad down one level, we've got..." And the transmission cut as Zhi realised his command line was still open.

Nearby, the drones that had been circling Command Squad made a dash at Kono, only for him and Zale to beat a fast retreat, leaping and firing full thrusters to escape. The pursuing deepynines ran into crossfire from Terez, waiting for exactly that eventuality, one exploding and tumbling, another breaking wide and presenting Zale with a good belly shot, smashing it in half where thorax met abdomen. Two others pulled back without firing, while a fifth dashed further right to get around Zale's flank... only to discover Trace behind cover at his rear, overlooking the crane-hole that was its target. Trace hit it through the right shoulder with her first shot before it could align weapons, shearing off two legs, and it crashed into the lip of the hole, and fell from sight.

"Dammit guys," Trace told her squad, "don't let the kids bother Mummy while she's working."

"Yeah, maybe if there were thirty of us," Kono retorted.

"Leave the third transition!" Crozier yelled, ducking low to reload her Koshaim, slamming the empty mag into the back-mounted reloader as chaingun rounds fragmented walls and floor around her. "The parren have got that further down, hold one and two!"

A rocket hit nearby, fragments blasting through the nest-like confusion of hacksaw habitat, and she popped back up, rifle seeking new targets. Ahead through the maze was a major vertical transition — a stairwell, if hacksaws had used stairs. It worked more like a multi-rail transport, and while deepynines lacked the attachments, they were grabbing those rails with their many legs and blasting full thrust like a rollercoaster, giving Crozier some concept of how drysines would have used it back in the day. With the geofeature unavailable to them, the deepynines were attempting to outflank and go down, past the humans and parren defending that descent. These rollercoaster transitions were how they were doing it, or trying to.

Several came racing down the transition now, and were hit by Koshaim fire, marines deployed into the hacksaw maze that surrounded much of the city around the geofeature. One drone lost legs and crashed into a support at high speed. More cover fire ripped — deepynines on this level were using drones on the transition to draw fire from marines, whom they would then try to eliminate. About this side of the geofeature, the rest of Delta Platoon were doing the same — the opposite side was largely transition-free, and deepynines over that way would have to go a long distance before finding another fast way down. But now some drones were risking fast runs down the geofeature again, and with far fewer guns to hit them, some were getting through… or worse, landing on Crozier's units' exposed flank.

"Watch the rear, watch the rear!" Sergeant Lai yelled on coms, as Crozier saw red dots appear where Lai didn't want them, then a lot of yelling and firing. She wanted to watch, but thrusters fired ahead and some dark shapes streaked through the structure…

"Left!" yelled her second, Sergeant Wong, up and firing ten metres from her side. *"Multiples, watch it!"* As missiles produced fireballs in both directions, and Crozier saw how everyone's attention had just swung left, leaving a gaping blind spot to the right…

"It's a decoy, watch your right!" she yelled, and hit thrust to displace fast, crashing into a wall on purpose to drop to new cover overlooking many irregular holes and accessways ahead, just as missiles tore through them. Suit countermeasures engaged, several went sideways and blew up, one struck near overhead with a thump that shook everything despite the vacuum, and then through the flames came drones, blazing fire.

Crozier shot the first one, hit thrust again to dodge as return fire tore apart where she'd been, glancing hits off her armour kicking her into a half-spin. She was up in time to see another smashed by a Koshaim through the nose, then the man who'd done it, Private Berg, her Squad number four, got shredded by a burst and lost limbs. Someone else was screaming, and everything by the transition exploding, so Crozier fired missiles from flat on her stomach, the rear launcher streaking carnage into that deepynine mess, and everything else exploded.

She came up firing to the right to clear that side, Private Rai suddenly behind her and doing that for her, as from the main killzone the multi-legged horrors leaped through flame and smoke and into her lines. She saw marine armour come apart like paper before someone hit that drone point-blank with multiple rounds, and was then hit himself by chainguns that detonated the ammo rig and blew him flying into a wall.

"LT, we got more!" Private Rai was yelling, turning sideways to send his own missiles, as someone else shouted *"The Sarge is down! The Sarge is down!"* And Crozier's plan to charge the deepynine flank ahead disappeared, to find her own flank exposed, and she dropped again as fire came from that direction, and a missile took out supports within metres.

"Fall back!" she yelled. "Delta First Squad, geofeature! Fall back and jump, we gotta go down!" She did that, Private Rai with her, leaping for cover, then hitting thrust on an exposed stretch to streak up a tight corridor, then cut to skid and bounce across the floor. Tacnet showed her Sergeant Wong was dead, analysing vitals so she didn't have to — that had been him with the ammunition blast, and with Berg dead, she'd lost half her personal section in seconds, her platoon XO with them. Tacnet showed Corporal Kess was also dead, and now Second Squad was showing casualties.

The hangar overlooking the geofeature was not wide, and Delta First Squad fell back to it laying down fire in all directions.

"Spanky, Benny, First got rushed, three down and we're displacing down the geofeature!"

"Copy LT!" came back Sergeant Jakobson of Third Squad. *"Parren just laid down holy hell on the third transition across from us! You get beneath us and we can leapfrog it!"*

Lance Corporal Riggs was carrying Private Haim, and now propped the armour against a wall. Crozier hit thrust to get there quick, and found Haim's armour holed in several places, blood all over her visor from her attempts to breathe — the vitals appeared in closeup when Crozier looked at her, nasty with internal bleeding and other things that suit auto-stabilisation probably couldn't deal with. Anti-breach had plugged up the holes with hard foam, lifesupport had pumped new air to keep the pressure up, med systems would stick Haim full of needles to pump in stabilising drugs and plasma, and a marine's 'natural' micros would activate to try and repair internal damage and stop the bleeding. Marines dead in minutes outside a suit could live hours inside one. But in a vacuum there was nothing else to be done, and there was no medbay to evac her to anyway… and any shuttle that tried would get shot down as soon as it exposed itself.

"We gotta go!" Crozier yelled at Riggs, who was crying, but tore himself away from his dying friend to follow Crozier in a fast thrust to the geofeature, then out into space. Several deepynines had just hurtled past them, dodging with frantic thrust as marines and now parren still overlooking the giant hole fired on them. Riggs accelerated hard in pursuit, aimed and blew one's thruster mount — it spun, hit a wall and tumbled in pieces. Parren fire hit the other from the walls, less heavy than Koshaim fire, but far more rapid, and tore it to bits.

"Here!" Crozier commanded, selecting what tacnet told her was the correct wall platform. Her selection appeared on the rest of her unit's visors, and they hit thrust to decelerate and land hard, then bounce and run fast off the platform, and into new positions. Parren in lean armour ahead waved them in, crouched in cover and expecting new attacks by the fast-descending deepynines at any moment. Crozier, her First Squad of twelve now reduced to eight in just one engagement, wondered how many more they could take.

"I now have control of Defiance primary weapon systems," Styx announced, working on the far side of the control stem, and largely out of sight to Lisbeth, Gesul and Skah. *"The first wave of deepynine vessels have corrected their trajectory and are returning to close cover orbit. The surviving fifth ship of the initial eight is just now unloading its assault drones, and the three slower sard vessels are in final approach. Time is short."*

Lieutenant Dale had returned topside with First Section, plus Timoshene, with word that the first deepynines to breach defences were on their way. Hannachiam's many large displays now flickered and flashed with new images, a random confusion of scenes, from planets to alien faces, to technical diagrams to any number of things Lisbeth had no name for. But one of the near panel-displays was now showing her a schematic of this surrounding district in Defiance, and she flicked through it with thick, gloved fingers making strange indentations in the light, hoping to find some realtime display of the fight drawing closer above.

"Halgolam, what is this weapon system?" Gesul pressed, watching his own command displays on his visor and no doubt seeing a lot more than Lisbeth had access to.

"I will not say in Hannachiam's presence," said Styx. *"She is the protector of this technology, and there are sensitivities to allowing outsiders to observe its function."*

"And yet she has allowed our access," Gesul said skeptically.

"And may withdraw it at any moment. Hannachiam is not easily directed. We must be polite."

Gesul spared Lisbeth a disbelieving glance within his helmet. No organic would believe that the greatest sentient intelligences of the AI races could behave like this. That drysines like Styx had entrusted the operations of a great city like this one, and its secret weapons technologies, was beyond belief. AIs were murderously precise and efficient, and Hannachiam was… well, only barely functional, Lisbeth cautioned herself. It was too early to leap to conclusions about what she was, when she'd just barely awoken from a twenty five thousand year slumber.

The big displays began a cascade of parren images, parren faces, moving vid images of parren doing parren things, too fast in succession for a human eye to distinguish any single thing.

"Gesul, she wonders what happened to Jin Danah," Styx translated. *"She was surprised that Jin Danah did not destroy Defiance and her together, when he led anti-drysine forces to victory. There were controls placed upon her operation, but I have removed them without difficulty, as they were crude."*

"Then how did they shut her down at all?" Lisbeth wondered, flicking through displays and thinking that if she could just find some way to help in the fight… "She's so much more advanced."

"She is just a mind," said Styx. *"Without a body, a mind is helpless. They deactivated her power source, I presume they were putting the entire city into storage, for later study."*

"Hannachiam," said Gesul. *"Jin Danah fell. He was deposed by Molary, of a rival denomination of House Acquisitive, followed by war between House Acquisitive and House Fortitude, then further instability, until Sheray arose as leader of House Acquisitive from a new denomination, and a period of stability as ruler of all the Parren Empire."*

The images on the screens faded to abstract patterns, flashing and cascading in ways that human eyes and motion-sense did not appreciate. Beside Lisbeth, Skah made a distressed sound. "Skah, don't look at the lights," Lisbeth told him. "The lights make you dizzy, don't look at them."

"She thinking," Skah observed, putting both oversized gloves before his visor.

The patterns came clear on Skah once more. His little children's EVA suit, the glow of many screens reflected on his visor. And nothing more.

"Hannachiam wonders at Skah," Styx translated. *"How he came to be in your crew. How humans have come to accept him as one of their own."*

Images on the screens, now slow enough to follow. Berthing tanks, artificial wombs. Rows of them, and now baby parren, even now slimmer and leaner than human babies, but with equally big heads and squalling. Grasped by robotic hands and arms, prodded and examined by multiple sensors, as Lisbeth stared in mixed fascination and horror. But now here were adult parren, also holding their young, and scenes of vast laboratories, of eggs and fertilisation in extreme closeup imagery, of vials of genetic material in their thousands...

And Lisbeth thought of the scenes above, the hangars filled with debris from that final battle of Defiance. Other species had fought here, had given their lives to defend the drysines. Even knowing the odds were impossible, still they persisted, earning this city its organic name. The old history taught that AI/organic relations had always been an unending slaughter, for tens of thousands of years. Mostly, from what Lisbeth had seen, that was true. But then had come the drysines, and the drysines had been different. Styx said the thing deepynines hated most about drysines was their growing belief that organics should be cooperated with, to some degree at least, rather than just oppressed and slaughtered.

These drysines had won this much organic loyalty, at least. From the Tahrae of House Harmony, certainly... and from some tavalai and others as well. And perhaps much of that was not so much a love of the drysines, as a terror of what the Parren Empire might look like, and a belief that continued drysine rule might be far superior to that, for some at least. And Lisbeth recalled tales that in the early years of the Parren Empire, things had been brutal. Having seen some of parren civilisation's worst qualities in person, she could believe it.

Styx said that deepynines were more formidable as individual warrior units, but were ultimately defeated by superior drysine creativity in numbers. Drysines built civilisations like this one, that out-produced and out-created anything deepynines could build.

Drysines learned to cooperate with organics… not out of love and compassion, for those were surely emotions no AI could ever find of value. But it had gained them something, and perhaps that something had been the thing that defeated the deepynines in the end, whatever the cost. So what could a machine civilisation learn from organics, that they'd never truly valued before?

And she gasped, staring at Styx. "Styx? Hannachiam. She's your imagination, isn't she?" Styx said nothing. That was rare, and usually happened when someone was close to the mark on a matter Styx would rather not discuss. "AIs are smart, but organic imagination and creativity are much more random things… you were *simulating* organic creativity on a much larger scale! *That's* why you built her." And she recalled she'd left Hannachiam's question unanswered. She crouched, and put an arm around Skah's shoulders. "Yes Hannachiam, Skah is like family to the human crew on the *UFS Phoenix*. We came across him by accident, but now we are together.

"This is such an interesting time, Hannachiam. There is much danger, but also so much possibility! I think you'll like it here, in this time. We all face a terrible threat, but we must face it together, like drysines and parren once faced their terrible threat together. I think you found that cooperation most stimulating. I think it was what you were built to facilitate. If you look around this city right now, you can see the foundations of a similar partnership being built right now. But first, we have to win. Can you help us to win?"

"Yo Hall! It's Lieutenant Dale, talk to me!" On the higher levels, on the engineering and cargo-transport levels surrounding the hangars above the command room, the parren units were getting hit. Dale could hear terse shouts and commands on coms that the translator tried to find solutions for, but the program was struggling to distinguish the important conversation from the unimportant, and all he got was a tangled mess. He blinked on the tacnet display to make it wider, and it showed the blue, hollow dots of parren marines blinking, then vanishing. Ahead of them advanced a red swarm. "Sergeant Hall, what do you see?"

"Parren getting hammered, LT!" Hall growled. He was one level up, and closer. It had been a guessing game whether the deepynines would come from above or below, but Dale suspected they'd have hit wherever the humans were not. Parren fought bravely and well, but it was becoming unmistakable that deepynine units hitting human units tended to break off the attack quickly to regroup after getting mauled. Against parren, they'd press the attack home, as they could see it working. *"Deepynines are long-ranging them! I could move to fire-support?"*

"Stay where you are," Dale replied, crouched by a huge doorway overlooking a vast expanse of unoccupied hangar space ahead. If the drones came through here, without cover, they'd be clay targets for Koshaims… but drones had missiles, while parren did not, and with wide spaces, ranged weapons gained in efficiency. "The parren have to fall back to us, we can't leave this flank exposed, and deepynines move fast. I got no communication with the parren commander, either he's too busy to talk, or he's dead."

The command coms icon blinked, and he opened it. *"Dale, report,"* said the Major.

"The parren have heavy contact," said Dale. "Looks like the drones are hitting them first, casualties heavy. It'll be our turn in a minute."

"I copy that," said the Major, her voice slightly out of breath, suggesting she was moving while talking. *"The next ship just unloaded more drones overhead, they're going straight down the geofeature and we've no one free and mobile to stop them. Delta is no longer offering effective resistance, and Echo's been pinned on your east flank and is unable to manoeuvre in force. If you need to talk to Echo, it's Sergeant Kunoz in charge now — both Lieutenant Zhi and Sergeant Kerensky are dead."*

"Alpha copies, Major," Dale affirmed, unflinching at that horrible news as many years of practice had taught him. If Delta was no longer defending the geofeature, that meant his buddy JC

Crozier was likely dead as well as Chester Zhi. "We can't hold off that many drones for long, but we'll try. Good luck."

"You too." Click and she was gone, no doubt to talk to her remaining lieutenants and parren commanders, all while moving and fighting herself. Dale knew enough about how hard it was to be glad it wasn't him.

Another channel opened unbidden. *"Dale, it's Lisbeth! The defences are activating! They're about to take a shot at those ships overhead... I can't reach the Major, can you talk to her?"*

"I can do that," Dale confirmed. "Good work Lisbeth, just get ready to…"

"Incoming!" someone yelled from Third Squad, then the thud of explosions on coms — fighting in a vacuum, it was always hard to figure where sounds were coming from, you only heard them on coms or if the impact was loud enough to vibrate surrounding structure that you were in physical contact with.

"Missiles inbound, countermeasures on," Sergeant Manjhi of Third Squad announced calmly. *"Can't see them yet, they're trying to soften us up. I'm expecting a flank or a fast hook, these bastards are smart."* A pause to assess incoming coms that Dale couldn't hear. *"Fluffy's dead. Stay sharp."*

That was Private Sarah 'Fluffy' Andrews, a tall girl from Homeworld who liked to sing out of tune. When told to shut up, she sang louder.

The Major opened her link again just as the attack reached Dale, drones streaking from a far doorway, a roar of fast-moving chaingun fire, big flashes of return fire, then Corporal Ricardo yelling of the right-hook flanking move and a whole bunch of drones zooming fast together, missiles incoming and exploding to cover their approach.

"Lisbeth says city defences are firing on the enemy ships," Dale said with forced calm, leaning out from cover when fire stopped pulverising the surrounding walls. He targeted fast and fired, but the drones were gone out a big side doorway, and now fire came from elsewhere and he ducked back before bullets could tear his way. "Better be a good shot. The attack just reached me —

they've got a mobility advantage in low-G, they're hitting the parren first then flanking and isolating marine positions. Fuckers learn fast."

"Do what you can," the Major replied. *"Thakur out."* Dale knew he'd get no rousing speeches from her about the need to fight to the end, or to not let a single deepynine get past him into the control room. She wouldn't insult him by telling him things he already knew.

"Another bunch down here!" called Sergeant Hall from a level below, covering the other main access through wide vehicular approach corridors. Heavy firing and detonations punctuated his coms. *"Looks like a pincer, up and down!"*

Beside him, Sergeant Forrest displaced with a hard burn of suit thrusters, skidding across the floor to a controlled collision with abandoned heavy machinery. "You see something Woody?" Dale snapped.

"Back quarter," Forrest growled, taking aim as Private Tong zoomed after him. *"Saw a flash, think the fuckers got behind us."*

A drone flashed by a doorway to the right, then another appeared well to the left, blazing fire. But neither Reddy nor Dale was fooled, expecting the bait-and-switch and blasting the left-side drone backward and apart, but shots hit Tong in transit and he tumbled, crashing and bouncing on the tarmac. Missiles tore in from a new angle, and Dale ducked as his visor showed countermeasures engaging, now stuck in this doorway with enemies on both sides… a missile hit the wall beside him and rang his armour with shrapnel.

"Tricks!" Dale demanded, rolling flat and struggling to get a good firing position, not easy with unwieldy armour suits. "You okay?"

"Nothing serious!" Tong said breathlessly, then laid down fire at movement across the right side. But he was exposed now, having tumbled clear of cover, a thruster malfunctioning and trying to scamper backward with limited grip in low-G.

"Hang on LT, nearly there!" called Riccardo, as Dale saw Reddy jetting low across the floor to the right, heading for that

opening… shots tore across the floor, hitting Tong and spraying about the hangar as limbs and debris scattered in a bloody mist. More fire came from opposite, Dale and Forrest returning as Reddy lobbed a grenade around the rim of the right-side doorway — it magnetically attached itself to the drone that killed Tong, and blew it into the doorframe. A laser cutter ripped the doorframe from the far side, and Reddy hit explosive thrust backward to dodge, aiming at the next drone through the doorway as he fell on his backside… to find the cutter had sliced his Koshaim in half.

Dale blew the drone into the wall with two shots, then a third blew its ammo as it threatened a blade-armed twitch toward Reddy, who disappeared in the flash. Then Riccardo and Private Tabo were blasting another from an unseen angle, tacnet showing them flanking in the neighbouring hall, no small move from where they'd been. More fire and another drone vanished, others pulling back to try another way.

"Good work Ricky," said Dale, levering up just enough to check the big bullet scar across his forearm. Suit lifesupport was howling to remove the excess moisture from heavy breathing that threatened to fog his visor. "Spots, you okay?"

"Fucked if I know," Reddy muttered, hauling himself up, new scorch marks on his armour.

More shooting, and shouts elsewhere, demanded Dale's attention. "Get Tricky's rifle, he's had it."

"Poncho's dead," said Riccardo, covering that side from the neighbouring hall. That was Private Halep, Riccardo's number two. *"They're finding the gaps in the line, we're too spread out."*

Dale had to agree. "Alpha Platoon, this is the LT. Fall back and tighten the perimeter. We let one of those things through, it'll kill the command room and then it's all over."

Second Lieutenant Bree Harris sat strapped into her Arms Two post, and hoped that her one remaining, flickering screen did not fail on her also. She stared at it with unnatural intensity, the electric symbols and graphics burning on her retinas, arms locked into the chair arm restraints, hands trembling upon the twin control sticks.

She'd taken a stim when no one was looking, which piled on top of the stim she'd taken before the fight had started, and now she was completely buzzed. She wouldn't have kept her sanity without it, strapped to this chair with her best friend on the ship in floating pieces alongside her, along with a godawful amount of his blood drifting in great, wobbling curtains of red, and sticking to the screens. Petty Officer Morales and one other had cleared that up, growling at a younger spacer to 'suck it up' when she'd lost her stomach at the mess. 'You don't see Second Lieutenant Harris losing her lunch, do you?' he'd said while manoeuvring body parts into an oversize bodybag.

That was because Second Lieutenant Harris was drugged out of her fucking mind, and unapologetic about it. She knew the micros that Fleet injected into every spacers' systems, in conjunction with the augments that tightened her nervous response, would compensate for any overdosing in the short term at least. She'd loved those augments since she'd gotten them nine years ago. She hadn't been sure she could make a warship post back then — her reflexes had been top two percentile, but for a warship bridge that wasn't nearly good enough, and everything had depended on how her body had or had not taken to the augments. Out of surgery, once the pseudo-organic biotech had propagated over the course of three months, she'd astonished herself with her speed and precision. She'd even taken up guitar, to just be amazed at her own fingers flying over the strings. Now, she trusted those augments utterly. But not, she hoped, too much.

"Target is in deceleration burn," came Second Lieutenant Geish's voice from back in Command T-3. All the surviving, functioning bridge crew were there, the Captain included. Hers was the only post that was still working up here, on the bridge, despite Lieutenant Dufresne's best attempts to tear everything apart behind her with Emergency's help. *"ETA four minutes thirty."*

"Arms Two, what's your status?" That was the Captain's voice, hard with that thinking-calm he got in tight situations. Bree had come to trust that tone with her life in the past few months. There were lots of smart people on *Phoenix*, but the younger bridge crew all agreed that while there might be a small few who were smarter than the Captain, there were none who could translate those brains into action under pressure like he could. The older bridge crew might have been a little more reluctant, given they'd spent most time under Captain Pantillo, but the youngsters saw no point in pitting the past outrageous genius against the present.

"All systems green, Captain," she said, voice muffled within her mask. It sounded like it belonged to another person. Like this whole, horrible experience were happening to someone else, and she was just watching. That distance was a relief, and made everything far less frightening than it could have been. "Batteries two and four are non-responsive, but one, three, five and six are good. Our tumble gives me an intermittent angle, but if I were him I'd start firing to disable our remaining guns in about three minutes."

The incoming enemy was a deepynine shuttle. No one had seen where it launched from, but *Phoenix*'s relative V was still not great, having been disabled while climbing out of the gravity-well. The deepynine warships were busy at the moon, and this one, solitary shuttle, no doubt loaded with drysine drones, had been sent to investigate the tumbling wreck.

"I can give you an attitude burst that will bring us rolling onto a semi-stable broadside," the Captain replied. *"That should give you a five second window before his return fire starts taking out batteries. Just make sure you hit him."*

"Yes Captain. Defensive fire isn't as independently mobile as offensive, hits aren't certain and I'll bet those shuttles are fast. But as long as he thinks we're dead, we've got a chance." Except that machines couldn't be surprised, surely? What if he opened fire early, just to be certain? Or would he be under instruction to avoid further damage to *Phoenix* lest there remain some valuable prize aboard unclaimed?

"I'm reading a launch from the city," said Geish. *"Small missile launch, two of them. Heading for an intercept in those overhead ships, there's four of them now."*

"How big are those missiles?" asked the Captain.

"Um... small. Very small. Fast acceleration... Captain, if that's the moon's defensive systems? Two missiles won't do shit, they'll be intercepted real quick. See look... I'm reading counterfire even now, we are ETA two minutes fifty for intercept."

"Let's wait and see, Second Lieutenant," the Captain admonished him. But he sounded grim, Bree thought. Two small missiles? Bree wished she could see them, but Geish's scan feed was not available to her now. She knew a lot about missiles, their various propulsions, guidance and warheads. In the Academy she'd spent a full two years on the subject, having been identified for an Arms track early with her reflexes being what they were, post-augment. Perhaps if she could see them, she could get some last, final reassurance that they were surely super-advanced and everything was going to be okay again… but she couldn't see them, and refocused upon the job at hand.

"The shuttle's launched," said Geish. *"Looks like drones. We've got drones incoming, I can't tell how many, the signal keeps fracturing."*

"Hello Corporal Rael," said the Captain. *"Drones inbound, we can't tell how many."*

Bree couldn't hear Rael's reply. He was the only marine still aboard, defending back-quarter with some spacer volunteers in EVA suits with rifles and booby traps. She supposed that even a spacer could fire a Koshaim in zero-G once, before the recoil put him through a wall. Or were there surviving armour suits that spacers could put on? Damned if they'd be able to fight in them though, not like marines did.

She recalled meeting Corporal Rael once, just a random encounter in the corridors. Female crew mentioned him from time to time — not only was he one of the Major's Command Squad elites, he was reputedly the cutest guy on the ship, or amongst the marines, anyway. A few female spacers Bree knew had even wandered through back-quarter for no other reason than to sneak a look, and see if the rumours were true. Herself, she'd not been disappointed. At least he'd get to go down fighting. She'd still be stuck in this chair, trying to man the defensive guns, when the drones cut their way into the bridge and sliced her to bits.

"What the hell?" That was Geish.

"Scan, what's the matter?" asked the Captain.

"Captain, I just..." and WHAM! as something hit them, a massive jolt that smacked Bree's head against her headrest and left her breathless.

"What the FUCK was that?" came the unmistakable growl of Lieutenant Kaspowitz. It wasn't so much the scale of the impact — if an impact it had been — as the style of it. A short jolt with no follow through — violent, as though the entire ship had been abruptly smacked sideways, and then... nothing, save for another few dozen flashing red damage lights and alarms. But nothing serious, Bree saw with relief, running a fast diagnostic over her precious remaining guns, and found them all still working.

"Three ships are gone!" Second Lieutenant Jiri was suddenly shouting — Scan Two, Geish's second. *"They're gone... look, secondary explosions!"*

"The missiles!" Geish yelled in triumph. *"One of them's gone, look! I thought I saw an energy spike just now, but... there it is again!"* Another blow hit them, no less gentle than the last, but this time *Phoenix* seemed to ride it better, as though having learned what to expect. *"The last ship's gone! It wasn't even that close... what the FUCK is that?"*

"I saw it," said Kaspowitz. He sounded even more astonished than he did excited. *"I saw definite gravitational lensing, just for a second, the background stars all bent inward about the missile. That's a fucking gravity bomb."*

Bree was no physicist on the level of Kaspowitz, but all bridge crew knew enough that they could teach it in university, at least. Defiance was what it was because of that long-ago science experiment that had resulted in the singularity about which the moon orbited. It did things to gravity that weren't possible by natural physical law… but evidently, previous millennia of hacksaws had found the knobs and dials that controlled those physical laws, and begun playing with them. If they could put an artificial-gravity generator into the Kantovan Vault, or into whatever the singularity had been before it collapsed, then they could surely put it into a missile, then activate it for a one-time-only effect. A sudden, violent, temporal gravity-well, gone as fast as it appeared, with its range of effect drastically altered from natural norms… those deepynine ships had gotten a force of several hundred Gs in a sudden shot, possibly much worse. No one designed ships to withstand that much sudden acceleration, not even deepynines. They'd been torn apart, while further out, *Phoenix* had gotten a jolt, and nothing more.

"That's a deep-space area bomb!" Bree murmured. It had been the holy grail of space gunnery in the Academy… and quite technologically impossible, they'd all been assured. A single warhead that could destroy multiple ships across a wide area of deep space, without needing to penetrate defensive fire grids, or chase down jump-V warships that could accelerate in seconds more than missiles could in an hour.

"Our guest is leaving!" Geish redirected everyone's attention. *"The drones are still coming, but the shuttle's leaving! He's heading for the remaining sard ships, that's a long intercept trajectory, but he can make it if there are no more missiles."*

"Let him go," said the Captain. *"Arms Two, get ready to target those drones, I'm preprogramming an attitude burn in five, four, three, two…"*

He never reached zero. There was a loud noise on coms, then shouting, and panicked yells. *"Medical to Command T-3!"* That was Kaspowitz. *"We've had an explosion, the Captain's hurt! Medical to T-3!"*

Bree wanted to ask what the hell was going on, but the attitude jets were firing regardless, and slowly *Phoenix*'s tumble was correcting, and a quarter-broadside was lining up. Near-scan feed worked well enough, and she could see the targeting dots of drones, burning hard in anticipation of what was to follow. There were about twenty of them, Bree thought. Well, not for long.

Guns aligned, and she hit the triggers. At this close range and low-V, it didn't take long for the shells to reach their targets. Menacing red dots vanished from her screen, one after another, but now her number two display was beginning to flicker. "Come on, not now! Lieutenant Dufresne, Petty Officer Morales! I'm losing the display, get it fixed or we'll be swarming with drones, I can't hit what I can't see!"

CHAPTER 32

Erik awoke to the dawning realisation of a splitting headache. Or not just a headache, he thought. His skull hurt. He felt dazed, like that one time he'd fallen off a horse at Greenoaks Ranch as a teenager, on a weekend trip with the family. Then, as now, the lights had seemed too bright, like white spears into the back of his brain. He squinted and blinked, raising a hand to shield his vision… and found the arm hooked to tubes, and electrode monitors.

He tried to recall what had happened. His last memory was of being crammed into Command T-3 with Geish and Kaspowitz, trying to… trying to do something, he couldn't quite recall the details. But evidently he was alive, which was unexpectedly good news considering the circumstances. Deepynines and sard might have kept him alive as a prisoner, but in that case he doubted he'd be in a bed quite as comfortable as this… and still in full possession of all his limbs.

His vision cleared a little and he looked around, the pain of the headache fading. Likely that was the bedside medical monitor feeding painkiller into his arm. But the monitor looked odd, a strange design, like nothing they used on *Phoenix*, where everything was built into the walls. This monitor looked portable, a stern, dark sentinel on wheels. Beyond, the room walls were concave, curving in at the ceiling, with displays and lighting that seemed irregular, and only half-functional. Alongside him was a bunk, a simple platform protruding from the wall, with a mattress and someone lying on it. A medbay, then… but not the *Phoenix* medbay. Then he realised that the weight of his own body on the mattress was slight. Low gravity, but not zero-gravity. Logically he was on the moon, then. In the city his marines had called Defiance.

Suli was dead. Keshav Karle too. And many others, throughout *Phoenix*'s crew. It crushed all the good news out of him, and left him empty. They seemed to have won the fight, somehow. Given how many tight scrapes he'd survived of late, that wasn't so surprising, however unlikely. But he wanted to go back to sleep, to not have to face this right now. As Captain, everything was his responsibility if not always his fault, and though they were a long way away from Fleet post-action reports and analysis, with all the blame-finding of the bigwigs who sat in high command, he could never escape the post-action reports in his own head.

Then he thought of Lisbeth, and Trace, and others whose fates he did not know, and cursed himself for being so selfish. Someone came to him, and it took him a moment to figure that it was Spacer Troi, who was typically an armaments tech under Lieutenant Karle. Some muddled conversation — on Erik's part at least — revealed that Lisbeth and Trace were still alive. Beyond that, Troi had to apologise — he'd been part of the evacuation of non-essential personnel from *Phoenix*, and now found himself assigned to medbay duty in Defiance, and had already discovered that half of what he thought he knew was just the rumours and nonsense that spread through a crew in times of crisis. Troi did at least know that Lieutenant Karle was dead. That was sad, but as Troi said, he had several immediate friends of similar rank who were also dead — Spacer Lewis and Petty Officer Mubuto. Erik recalled them both well, and repressed the urge to go back to sleep once more.

"Where is this place?" he murmured, sipping on the water bottle Troi had brought. Troi had many — and some food on a trolley he'd scavenged from somewhere. With so many wounded to tend, the Corpsmen and Doc Suelo were all busy with more serious cases.

"It's in the north sector," Troi explained, glancing about the ward to be sure someone else did not need him. Other spacers moved past, all with a purpose, and there were no visitors to just sit by bedsides and hold hands. Erik supposed, as his thoughts grew clearer, that everyone must still be very busy. "Lieutenant Hausler found it, hiding from the deepynine shuttles. It's an environmental habitat — there's actually quite a few of them, but this one seems most functional. Lots of organics used to live here, sir. Among the hacksaws. Lifesupport and electrics are all somehow still working, and even the medbay… though Doc says half the systems are out. He brought some portable stuff from *Phoenix*, the techs managed to get some indigenous stuff working…" he indicated to the foreign monitor by Erik's bedside, "…he's coping. Barely."

"And what's happening with *Phoenix*?" Erik asked.

"No offence sir, but I'm just an arms tech. We got evaced… I dunno, sir. The shuttles are still running back and forth, I think they're bringing a lot of stuff down… a couple of the parren ships survived the fight, but they're busy with their own guys, I guess. They got smashed, sir. Even worse than us. You hear Tobenrah's dead, sir?"

"No," said Erik. He knew it was a ground-shaking thing, but he just couldn't figure out what it meant right now. "First I've heard of anything."

"*Talisar* got hit just after we did. Some survivors, but Tobenrah wasn't one of them."

Erik nodded, and winced at the pain that brought. Against deepynines, it was predictable. He suffered a flash of memory. "And the… the moon launched defences, right? That destroyed the deepynine ships?"

"The word is a gravity bomb, sir." Troi glanced again, and found the lanky frame of Lieutenant Kaspowitz skipping easily through the doorway. "Look sir, it's Lieutenant Kaspowitz, I think he'd explain it better than me."

"Thanks Spacer," Erik murmured as Troi stood up to go. "And Spacer? I'm sorry about Legs and Lewy."

"Yeah," said Troi, the young man downcast and dealing with it, though barely. "Yeah, me too, sir. Lieutenant," he added to Kaspowitz, and headed back to his trolley, to check on other wounded.

"Spacer," Kaspowitz acknowledged, and took a knee at Erik's bedside. He was tall enough that that still left enough height to look down from. Erik squinted at him, trying to make out his expression before the bright lights in the ceiling. Only they weren't actually so bright, he thought, as his eyes adjusted. Kaspowitz grasped his hand, roughly. "How you feeling, Captain? Got a message you were awake."

"I feel like I've been smacked on the head," said Erik. "How long was I out?"

"Nearly twenty hours. Doc said you had some swelling on the brain, but only light. Gave you a shot to keep you under for longer, said that was safer. You'll be hungry, though."

"More thirsty at the moment." Erik sipped his bottle. "How's *Phoenix*?"

Kaspowitz shrugged. "Mess. Total write-off, really. Engine's gone, not repairable. Or not without a major port overhaul, anyway. Which is just what this place is, so Rooke reckons he might be able to do not so much an overhaul as a total rebuild. Could take a year, though."

"So Rooke's alive?"

"Yeah. Curled up in Engineering, tried to get out and fix stuff, but had to abandon that when the drones arrived."

"Drones? We got boarded?"

Kaspowitz nodded. "Yeah. Just three, Bree lost her targeting before she could nail them all. Three drones got in through the back-quarter hull breach. Corporal Rael blasted them all, barely a scratch on him. Damn lucky we had him aboard, we could have lost dozens more if it was just us spacers."

Erik took a deep breath, memory returning fast. "Right. Hit me with it."

Kaspowitz peered more closely. "You sure you're ready?"

"No. Hit me anyway."

"Right, just the ones I know for sure. Suli. Keshav."

"Yeah, I remember that."

"Wei lost his arm, he'll be okay though, he's in intensive care. Second shift are all alive, despite Giggles running around without a suit on." That was Dufresne, Erik remembered. "Williams. Hale. Leong." The list went on for a while. Kaspowitz stopped at thirty-five. "That's all I know for sure, with spacers. Goldman's count is sixty. We lost a lot when back-quarter breached, some of those we'll never get the bodies back. Same number wounded, half of them serious." He gestured about the medbay.

"Marines?"

"Trace has the full numbers. I think about fifty, same number wounded. The only one I know for sure is Lieutenant Zhi. Crozier's hurt, but not bad. Word is Delta saved all our necks defending the geofeature. About half of them are dead, though."

Erik did close his eyes. Intellectually he knew they'd still gotten off light. By all rights, none of them should have survived that engagement, as outmatched as they'd been. If it hadn't been for Styx's insistence that this was a good place to come, presumably because she knew the technology that defended it, none of them would be.

"Hey, Erik." Kaspowitz put a hand on his shoulder. "It's not your fault."

Erik opened his eyes, and looked at him. Thinking of the various things he could protest or say; that he knew it wasn't his fault, that he wasn't a kid to be comforted by his elders. But there was nothing really *to* say. More than a hundred of his crew were dead, an equal number hurt, and all this dancing around it wouldn't bring a single one of them back. Kaspowitz saw his expression, and slowly withdrew the hand from his shoulder.

"I want a sitrep now," Erik told him. "I don't care that I'm hurt, the gravity's low and I'll be fine. We've got a command centre running? Trace will be in charge, I guess?"

"Yes Captain." Kaspowitz's tone, and manner, showed a far greater formality than just a moment ago. And a greater respect. "You want to go and see? It's not far."

"That sounds like a plan." Erik held up his arm, and began figuring in which order he should pull the damn wires and tubes off. "Do we cut the red wire, or the blue?"

Erik visited the toilet facilities first, and found a most surreal scene — a large space with many cubicles, and a wide shower facility before armour-strength heavy windows. This place was a tower, he saw, amidst a series of towers. But these towers were unlike anything in the cities of organic lifeforms. They clung together in great patterns, like geological features, and rose above deep steel canyons kilometres across. Spectacular did not begin to describe the view. Nothing did. The horizon was steel, organised into sectors, some low domes on one far horizon, what looked like heavy industry on another. All glowed now with a broken scatter of lights. Some of that glow seemed to rise from beneath the surface, as though the metal crust contained some great fire within. Other portions lay dark, like the vast lakes in the Shiwon mountains, viewed from high above on a dark and moonless night.

Erik showered, as *Phoenix* techs had gotten the local water systems running. It was quite extraordinary that everything still worked, in this place at least. Erik did not trust his AR glasses in the water, but put them atop the partition and allowed the coms function to find local chatter, and play it on speaker. Unmistakably, he recognised Spacer Riewoldt and Spacer Lum, two more of Rooke's engineers, chatting somewhere nearby as they worked. The glasses were waterproof, so he put them on and activated the mike.

"Hi boys, it's the Captain. Do I have you two to thank for getting the water working?"

"Captain!" The delight in Lum's voice made him smile. *"How are you sir? Are you in the bathroom?"*

"I am, I'm having my first shower in days. Heck of a view, huh?"

"Yeah, kinda creepy too, sir." Erik could not disagree with that. But then, he'd never actually gone into Tartarus, like Trace and her marines had. Surely that had been worse. *"The systems are idle, Captain, but they're not degraded here. It's... it's pretty amazing, in some places everything's decayed and fallen apart, it looks thousands of years old, like it should. But we think there's some kind of light charge running through this place, through a lot of the old organic habitats. It's not that it's stopping stuff from ageing, it just keeps it renewed — Rooke thinks there's micros involved."*

"You think he's been talking to Styx, sir?" Riewoldt asked.

"Lieutenant Rooke's always talking to Styx," Erik agreed tiredly. "I guess it's not surprising the hacksaws found some ways to stop stuff getting old. They're machines themselves, for them it might be some kind of immortality."

"Sir?" said Lum. *"I'm real sorry about Commander Shahaim. And Lieutenant Karle."*

Erik took a deep breath, head down in the shower. The water wanted to cling, gravity not strong enough to break surface tension. It spilled reluctantly down his legs, propelled more by accumulation than gravity, pooling about the drain. "Thank you, Spacer. Who did you lose?"

"Oh plenty," Lum said quietly. *"Our group, other groups, marines. Doesn't matter where. We're all Phoenix."*

"Yes we are," said Erik, gazing at the view. "Yes we are."

After the shower, he pulled on the clean jumpsuit Kaspowitz brought him, dragged the Captain's jacket over the top of it, and discovered that whoever had occupied this organic outpost in a sea of sentient machines, they either hadn't required mirrors, or they'd taken all the mirrors with them.

"You look fine," said Kaspowitz, walking with him down the hall from the bathroom. "It's only two days' growth, and shavers weren't a priority when we jumped ship."

"Don't say 'jumped ship'," said Erik. "Doesn't sound right. And it's three days' growth, not two."

"Two days' growth on *most* men," Kaspowitz corrected.

"Oh shove it," Erik told him, forcing amusement he didn't feel. Appearances weren't a laughing matter here. The crew needed to see the Captain was his usual self. Otherwise they'd… well. He didn't know *what* they'd do. He didn't know what they were for any longer. *Phoenix* was out in deep space, crippled and drifting. They didn't have a ship anymore. Rooke thought he might be able to fix it, if he could get the massive ship repair facilities on Defiance working again, but admitted it might take a year.

And suddenly, he remembered what they'd been fighting for in the first place. It was disconcerting to realise that he'd only just thought to ask. Strange how priorities shifted when friends started dying. "Where's Styx and the data-core?"

"She's analysing it now," said Kaspowitz. "There's big computer facilities in the lower floors here… the tower complex is enormous, you could fit a million people in here. Romki's with her… he did good too, some of the crew are saying he saved lives working emergency recovery."

That was good, Erik supposed, but under the circumstances it just meant that Romki was normal crew now. In that mess, everyone had been saving everyone else's lives, and heroism was just the norm. "Hannachiam's helping her?"

Kaspowitz made a wry grimace. "No one knows what the fuck Hannachiam's for. Except maybe Lisbeth, she thinks Hanna's the drysines' attempt to build an imagination, like a random thought generator, since AIs seem to lack that and get locked into predictable patterns of behaviour. They recognised it as a strategic weakness, I guess. So they built this giant potato that sits underground and makes abstract thought bubbles. Fucking weird machines."

"And Lisbeth's with Gesul, I suppose?" He'd heard that Lisbeth was safe and well, with Skah, and that had been enough until now.

"The parren have the neighbouring tower," said Kaspowitz, pointing vaguely ahead. "It's connected all the way down, so we're sharing everything… it's good cooperation, but we both figure different species need our own space after everything. Lis is… Lis is amazing, actually. Sitting on Gesul's arm, muscling into any conversations his main commanders have with us, making sure there's no misunderstandings. Which is good, I guess, but it's also kinda disconcerting. She's pretty sure something nasty could happen if we get our wires crossed."

"Well she'd know," said Erik. And hoped for just a few hours with Lisbeth, sometime very soon, to finally go over all the things that had happened to her… and where she saw things going now.

An elevator took them down a level, where a busier hallway led to a control room. There, before a far more impressive wrap-around view than Erik had had in the bathroom, were senior Phoenix Company marines, and a couple of bridge crew.

"Captain on deck!" Kaspowitz shouted, and it was a mark of just how exhausted everyone remained that no one jumped, or did more than look around slowly. But look they did, and the joy on their faces was worth all the pain of waking up. Within the encircling windows was a similarly shaped control island, screens surrounding chairs, with holographic displays projected over the lot. Exactly what it was supposed to control, Erik had no idea. Perhaps its function was not fixed.

He squared his shoulders and light-bounced to the island, noting Geish and Jiri in conversation over one display, barely pausing to acknowledge the Captain... so Erik knew it was important, and probably scan-tech related. And here was Lieutenant Jalawi, not bothering to rise from his seat, one foot raised in heavy bandages on a chair alongside. Beside him, Lieutenant Alomaim, even more grimly inexpressive than ever. His girlfriend Remy Hale was dead, and if Erik knew anything of Alomaim, he'd be determined not to show any of that grief in public.

And here, turning toward him, was Trace. This post was more a marine operation than a spacer one. This mission was on the ground, and that was where marines took charge. They'd be exploring the region, getting the tower systems working, and figuring what to do about supplies now that water and air seemed to be taken care of. He'd only just woken from being knocked out, yet already the work ahead seemed huge.

Trace, he was surprised to see, looked quite emotional to see him again... by Trace's standards, anyhow. Knowing her as he did, anything more than her usual curious, thinking-stare leaped out like a joyous explosion. But now, her jaw was just a little tight, and her eyes were shining. A bit. And Erik thought to hell with protocol, and went to hug her.

She held him back, tightly. A marine's embrace more than a friend's, or even a woman's — hard and full-bodied, like a bear hug that she wasn't really large enough to pull off. Then he pulled back, put both hands on her shoulders, and looked around at the room.

"I'm so proud of you all," he said, struggling with the emotion. "I'm so proud I can barely speak." A tear rolled down Trace's cheek. He kissed her on the forehead, with a look about to let them know it was for them, too.

"Romki says some of the technical data from the core is ridiculous," Trace told him. "His word. He says Fleet could build new warships from it. Warships that could beat what we just faced. Rooke's glanced at it and he agrees, though he's busy with *Phoenix*. Crazy technology. We might have just saved the human race."

"Gravity bombs," said Kaspowitz, with a grim, ironic smile. Aimed at himself, Erik thought, and his own previous disbelief. "Even the deepynines didn't know *that* was possible."

Erik dropped his hands from Trace's shoulders. "You want to keep command here?"

Her lips tightened, the faintest of smiles. "I think that would be prudent." Given you're a total mess, she left unsaid.

Erik smiled back. "Good. You have command. Defiance is yours, Major. Now, I want my ship back. Who can give me a sitrep on *Phoenix*?"

"I can do that," said Trace, indicating a command screen. "Here, come look."

Erik followed, and saw a vid-feed from a high angle, looking down into a large, steel hole. He recognised what he was looking at immediately — a capture collar. The size of it became apparent as a suited spacer drifted across the camera, thrusting by, a small dot against the enormous, segmented ring. The ring itself was the main body of a spacecraft, like a finger ring with an unfolding segment in the middle to adjust its girth. That girth would fit around a spaceship, propelled by large engines, and tighten into place. The pilot of the capture collar could then fly that ship wherever desired… but not through jump, as only starships possessed jump engines.

From the running lights flashing about this capture collar, and the activity of spacers, a small inspection runner, and several drones, Erik guessed what was happening. "That's Draper out there?" he asked.

Trace nodded. "That's *Commander* Draper now, I think."

"Yeah. We'll do that properly when there's time." He couldn't be annoyed at Trace for immediately bringing up command structure implications, with Suli's body barely cold. It was what she was, and besides, Suli would have approved. This stuff mattered. "Who else?"

"Dufresne's still on *Phoenix*, she's going to be pilot on the bridge for what it's worth. Rooke's out there too, refused to leave, he's got a skeleton crew. They're going to help fix the capture collar, and the shuttle pilots are all running back and forth, bringing stuff down that we'll need, taking other stuff up. None of them have had any sleep." With a warning glance at Erik, to let him know that although it was his command, she didn't think it safe.

"I'll talk to them," Erik agreed. "The capture collar has a cockpit?"

"Draper says it's more of an observer pod for organics, but they're rigging it so he can fly it from there. Rooke says he can get enough aft thrust from rear attitude jets, plus the collar's jets, he can generate more than half a G. He's getting the rest of attitude control back, then he's sure he can land *Phoenix* right in that bay, tail first."

Erik pursed his lips. He didn't like it. To say it was against regs was putting it mildly. Starships were *never* to be landed on a planetary body, not even a low-G moon, irrespective of how physically possible it was. Tail-first landings of something that tall and heavy, with irregular mass loadings compared to what might normally balance on its tail, like a skyscraper… no, it was a bad idea all around. And yet he could see no flaw in Draper's reasoning, because Defiance had no orbital starship facility. Probably it had once, but such facilities were prime targets in assaults, and likely it hadn't survived. Which left the ground facilities.

"He thinks there's enough facilities on the ground to fix her?"

Trace nodded. "Rooke says. There's engines down there, Erik. No ships, but some very old engines… Rooke doesn't think they've been anti-aged like some of the city, so they won't be working. But the facilities that built them are. Styx says she and Hannachiam can get the whole city fired up in a few weeks, or the bits of it that still work, anyway. She says the repair facilities are largely automated, that even with a skeleton crew we could rebuild *Phoenix*. With a completely new tail. One that can keep pace with those deepynines. Maybe even beat them."

"Can't burn at fourteen-Gs with us mushy humans flying it," Erik murmured.

"She's not just talking about engines. Weapons, computers, everything. Erik, Styx says it was likely one of those hidden deepynine computer programs that blew the panel and knocked you out. She disabled most of it, but that one emerged when you were about to defeat the last deepynine threat, and overloaded that system to stop you."

Erik sighed. "Maybe she does need a full refit. Not like we have any choice, when our own ship tries to kill us."

"*Phoenix* saved our ass," Trace replied. "It wasn't her fault the alo messed with her from inception." She considered him for a moment. "You don't want to command the recovery yourself?"

"I know a concussion when I feel one," Erik told her. "There's no fast fix, and it's not safe to fly something complicated like that when you can't think straight. Draper and Dufresne have got it. They've got Hausler for help, Jersey too. Even Tif. And Styx can help with guiding them in." He gazed at the screen for a moment. "Plus, with Suli gone, we're not going to be able to hold their hands any longer. They'll have to handle far bigger jobs than this, on their own. Best they start now."

Trace nodded with approval. "Yes Captain. I think we all will."

Erik looked at her. "The remaining ships all turned and ran?"

"As soon as they saw the gravity bombs," Trace agreed. "Can't say I blame them."

"And the drones already down here?"

"Had to sweep them up," said Trace. "Hannachiam helped. City was coming to life, we started to get good coms fixes. Let us know where they were, before they could see us."

She bore it stoically, but Erik could see the pain. "How many?" he asked quietly. "Kaspo said fifty, but wasn't sure on the latest."

"Fifty-two," Trace agreed. "More than a fifth, less than a quarter. Chester's dead."

"I heard."

"And another forty-eight wounded. Some of them for the second time this trip."

"Command Squad?"

"Kumar. Arime's hurt bad, could make it."

Again Erik thought to hell with the protocols, and put an arm about her shoulders. Everyone else was back at work anyway, talking and working their screens. And besides, he was pretty sure everyone liked to see it. They knew he and Trace had grown close in spite of everything, and knew they made a damn good command partnership on *Phoenix*. Seeing that bond, displayed for all to see, could only reassure them that things remained tight on *Phoenix*, and that whatever the pain, the family held together.

"Love you sis," he told her.

She smiled sadly, and put her head to his shoulder. "Love you too, bro. Spoken to Lisbeth yet?"

"I hear she's busy. Let me get my head around my own stuff first. So, what's our supply situation?"

Some hours later, Erik took the express elevator down the tower to the lower levels. Most of these mid-levels were unoccupied, and the newly restored elevator showed no sign of being interrupted. Defiance-time read 06:40, but they were going to have to adjust that because parren days were twenty-two hours long. They measured time in totally different units, and this moon was definitely, Gesul had reminded him sternly in their one conversation twenty minutes ago, in parren space and under parren administration. Sharing this place as guests of the parren, it was the humans who would have to adjust. And Gesul was right, of course. Thankfully, Defiance had more than enough room for everyone.

Still there was no Lisbeth. Gesul had informed him that she was fulfilling a very important role, and that was that. Evidently it did not occur to a high-ranking parren that Lisbeth was still actually *Phoenix* crew and truly answered to her brother, both as *Phoenix*'s commander and as the ranking member of the Debogande Family… whatever Lisbeth thought of *that*. Or more likely,
Erik reconsidered now, Gesul *had* thought of exactly that, status, rank and structures of command being the endless obsessions of the parren mind. Perhaps he was bluffing Erik into assuming he had no choice but to allow Lisbeth to continue in her present role… and in truth, if Gesul did require it as a matter of parren command, there was little Erik could do about it. As guests in parren space, they were only welcome here for as long as parren gave them welcome. Gesul evidently found Lisbeth invaluable, and if that was the price of *Phoenix*'s continuing welcome, it was one that he was not especially unwilling to pay, for now at least.

And probably Lisbeth would refuse to abandon Gesul even should Erik have commanded it. She had an importance at Gesul's side that she had never had aboard *Phoenix*. Beyond simple ego, what she did there, translating between two species that knew each other very little and could so easily get things catastrophically wrong, was incredibly important. More important, conceivably, than anything else Erik might do in this whole mess.

The elevator slowed, momentarily approaching full gravity, then halted, and the doors hissed. Guarding the elevator here were four marines from different parts of Charlie Platoon — in full armour, legs locked out and sitting on the armour saddle, which was no less comfortable than riding a horse for long periods. Erik knew there might not be a single intact unit in all Phoenix Company, nearly every four-man section had someone missing through death or injury.

He stopped to shake their hands and talk — these at least had all had some sleep, a feed and a shower. All had new battle scars on their armour, but they seemed to be coping. One was the Second Squad Commander, Master Sergeant Hoon — a legend before his recent transfer to *Phoenix*, now a veteran of yet another epic battle. Another was Lance Corporal Graf of Third Section, First Squad… or 'Eggs', as she was known.

"You can come in, if you'd like?" Erik offered her, indicating the big, sealed doors opposite. "You found the thing, and I hear you'd probably have a better idea how it works than I do."

"Thank you sir," said Graf, a pale, brown-haired woman who looked far too 'normal' to be a marine. Her armour bore a spectacular spread of shrapnel scars, no doubt from a nearby missile strike. "But I'd just like to be with my people for a while."

Erik had known before what it was to be proud of people under his command. But now, that feeling was multiplied many times. He wanted to hug them all, but couldn't — they didn't need his affection, they needed his leadership, and in Fleet the one could so easily conflict with the other. He settled for putting a hand on Graf's armoured shoulder, and giving her a look of intense approval. Graf looked touched, and emotional, and nodded back as though it were all she needed. They all did, even Hoon.

Erik walked to the doors, which opened on his approach. Within, a central conduit dominated the room, a great cylinder from the ceiling to the floor, surrounded by many smaller power and support structures. Within one of those cage-like frames sat the data-core on a secured stand. Energy crackled about the containment frame, and Erik could smell the ozone in the air, and the scorch of electrical discharge. From the great conduit, clearly some offshoot of a much larger system running through the base of the tower and into the city's depths, a deep bass note of power hummed and throbbed.

On the nearside stood Stan Romki, still in his spacer jumpsuit with harness and tools, as though he hadn't changed from helping the rescue teams pulling trapped spacers from decompressed compartments. Opposite him, crouched like the terrifying insectoid monster she now resembled, was Styx. It was the first time Erik had seen her like this in person. With her main legs curled to let her fit into the cramped space, they created the impression of gothic pillars or ribs, framing the flanks of that single, unblinking red eye.

"That's a good look for you, Styx," Erik told her, making his way to them.

"I detect irony," said Styx. Her small head was now contained within a much larger, flaring carapace, protecting neck and sides, like a giant collar or crest. Erik was not convinced it wasn't also a calculated attempt at intimidation. Her head and eye peered and darted, her small forelegs dancing over controls with crazy dexterity. *"Does this appearance alarm humans?"*

"If you want less irony," Erik told her, "try not asking questions you already know the answer to."

"A fitting reply, Captain."

"Ignore her," Romki said drily, focused with equal concentration on his own screens, and not yet looking up. "She's working on her repartee, and her answers are becoming more and more obtuse. One of these days I swear she'll accidentally trip over a sense of humour and decide to adopt it."

"The back of your hand stings, Professor."

And Erik saw Romki actually shake his head in disbelief — not at the technological marvel that was Styx, but like an old friend increasingly tired of his comrade's glib remarks.

"I was invited down here," Erik reminded them drily. "If you'd rather squabble amongst yourselves, I could come back another time."

"No no, Captain," said Romki. "My apologies. We are attempting to access the deeper levels of the data-core — we've only scratched the surface so far, unloading the entire core could take months, and I'm not entirely sure we have a number large enough to describe the volume of data it contains."

"We do," Styx assured him. *"It is large."*

Romki turned to look at Erik for the first time. His big owl-eyes were tired as always behind his glasses, and Erik wondered if he'd ever seen the man, in the past few months, when he'd been getting adequate sleep. "Thankfully," Romki said, "it appears to have a reasonably sophisticated filing system. And so Styx has been able to pull out relevant data first, and leave the less relevant for later. The most relevant, I thought, were alien races, given that it is my speciality, and I couldn't resist viewing a full catalogue of the sentient organic races around in drysine times."

He activated holographic control on his glasses, turned an invisible icon in mid-air, and a nearby screen flashed to life between the cage supports. "Only, of course," he continued, "the data-core contains records not only of the species living in the drysine era, but of those well before, back to the beginning of all advanced AI sentience. So far I have discovered reference to thirteen previously unknown alien sentiences… or unknown by humans, at least."

An image appeared on the screen. This one was bipedal, as most of the Spiral's organics were… and had tusks of some kind. Erik squinted past the headache that was threatening to make its return in defiance of the drugs that stopped it. "Never seen that before," he admitted.

"I have not yet found a name," Romki admitted. "Nor a location. The data is not complete, and the filing system accumulates over time, so we may have the data, but it is not yet filed as it should be. Styx, of course, is little help, having a long-term memory like a sieve on matters that do not involve immediate survival."

"A sieve," said Styx, with all the inattention of a parent working on adult matters while children made irrelevant conversation in the background. *"Curious."*

"Well that's very interesting, Stan," said Erik. "And I'd love to see the full report once you've written it. But I don't see what requires me to be here right now."

Romki changed the screen again, and another face appeared. This one was familiar — black, with beady eyes above a large, open and rather delicate nasal cavity that made up much of the face. Side gills for breathing, in through the lower jaw and neck, out through that sensitive nose. "Alo," said Erik with a 'so what?' frown. "Sure seen *them* before." Romki just looked at him, the sombre look of a tutor waiting for his dull pupil to grasp something obvious. Erik's frown grew deeper. Then he realised. "But alo appeared three thousand years ago…"

"And the Drysine Empire ended twenty five thousand years ago," Romki finished. "So the drysines, it appears, knew who the alo were. All that time ago. While we today have no clue."

Erik stared. "Do you have a location?"

"A very general location," Romki agreed, and the display changed to show a star chart. "This particular record is taken second-hand, out here in croma space."

"That's the edge of the Spiral."

"Well yes," said Romki, adjusting his glasses. "An arbitrary border, like all of these things. The species that inhabit that border do not recognise it. To them, we are the edge of *their* geographic entity. Today, that is all croma space. This particular drysine record states that this alo encounter locates their homeworld out beyond croma space."

"Beyond?" Erik's jaw dropped. "They're not native to their current territory?"

"The drysine record lists them as primitive. We've only known alo as very advanced. Clearly it seems the drysine record indicates the more likely origin."

Erik came closer to peer at the starchart. It was still all too foreign to him, too far away from anything familiar. Kaspowitz and De Marchi might have had better luck. "Styx?" he said. "You know anything about that space?"

"Perhaps once," said Styx. *"Memory like a sieve, I'm told."*

"I swear she lost her mind in that asteroid," Romki complained. "So many thousands of years with nothing to do, and…" Erik shook his head at him. 'No', he mouthed, and glanced at Styx, meaningfully. Romki's eyes registered realisation, and he stopped.

The emotional states of drysine queens remained a great mystery, and Erik had no desire to unravel this particular mystery by accident and disaster. That Styx had such emotional states, he had no doubt. Whether they were anything a human could possibly understand, he doubted. And Romki, being Romki, might just blunder along and stick his foot into something far more dangerous than his current level of familiarity with his twenty five thousand year old 'friend' could grasp. Erik did not particularly mind if Styx saw him cautioning Romki. He only hoped that she was capable, on some level, of appreciating the gesture.

"Captain," Romki regained his equilibrium, "I hesitate to suggest this, given our current situation. But if we have finally the means to discover the origins of the alo, then we may also have within our grasp the means to discover the origins of the alo-deepynine alliance. If we face a war against them, we cannot hope to win it without knowing precisely what we face. Perhaps in learning their origin, we can learn exactly what they want. Because for all our thousand-year history with the alo, they've never once seemed inclined to tell us."

"No," said Styx. "This is a poor strategic choice. Defiance is a great resource. With the data-core, its utility multiplies. We should stay, and consolidate. There are political opportunities now, and the currency of technology and power to trade."

Romki opened his mouth to argue, then thought the better of it, and looked at Erik.

Erik stared at the screen. "That's croma space now," he murmured. "We thought we knew little about the parren — the croma are just legend."

"No," Romki said sombrely. "You're looking at croma space, yes. But the region indicated in the record suggests that alo came from *beyond* croma space. And out there, I'm afraid, are the reeh."

Erik looked at him. "Seriously? I barely heard about them in the Academy either."

"And they've barely heard of us, no doubt," Romki said condescendingly. "It doesn't make *us* any less real. From what I've heard, I'd rather leave them ignorant of humans completely, if that were possible."

"Why? What have you heard?"

"The sard are bad," said Romki. "The krim were worse. The reeh are worse again, and many times more powerful than the krim and sard at their very height combined."

"We should not go there," said Styx, with certainty. "It would be foolishness."

"Captain," Romki insisted, as seriously as he'd ever insisted upon anything. "I'm not sure we have a choice."

ABOUT THE AUTHOR

Joel Shepherd is the author of 14 Science Fiction and Fantasy novels, including 'The Cassandra Kresnov Series', 'A Trial of Blood and Steel', and 'The Spiral Wars'. He has a degree in International Relations, and lives in Australia.